Bratva Treasure

Sabine Barclay

All rights reserved.

No part of this publication may be sold, copied, distributed, reproduced or transmitted in any form or by any means, mechanical or digital, including photocopying and recording or by any information storage and retrieval system without the prior written permission of both the publisher, Oliver Heber Books and the author, Sabine Barclay, except in the case of brief quotations embodied in critical articles and reviews.

PUBLISHER'S NOTE: This is a work of fiction. Names, characters, places, and incidents either are the product of the author's imagination or are used fictitiously. Any resemblance to actual persons, living or dead, business establishments, events, or locales is entirely coincidental.

Copyright © 2022 by Sabine Barclay.

0 9 8 7 6 5 4 3 2 1

Published by Oliver Heber Books

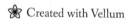 Created with Vellum

Thank you to everyone who has encouraged me along the way to branch out and be even more daring with my writing. It's been so freeing to write these Mafia characters who still value family above all else, just like my Scottish Highlanders when I write as Celeste Barclay.

Subscribe to Sabine's Newsletter

Subscribe to Sabine's bimonthly newsletter to receive exclusive insider perks.

Have you read *The Syndicate Wars*? This FREE origin story novella is available to all new subscribers to Sabine's monthly newsletter. Subscribe on her website.
www.sabinebarclay.com/joinnewsletter

The Ivankov Brotherhood

The Bratva Darling

The Bratva Sweetheat

The Bratva Treasure

The Bratva Beauty (Coming 11.1.22)

The Bratva Angel (Coming 12.13.22)

The Bratva Jewel (Coming 1.24.23)

Do you also enjoy steamy Historical Romance? Discover Sabine's books written as Celeste Barclay.

Chapter One

Niko

I hear a woman speaking Russian as I make my way to my brother and sister-in-law's shared office in their Queens home. I don't recognize the voice, since I know it's not my mother's or Laura's. Before I can knock, the sound of one, then two infant cries fill the air. I knock, but don't wait for anyone to answer before I open the door. I take in everything in the room, a habit drilled into me more than a decade ago.

A young blonde woman with piercing, luminescent green-gray eyes stares at me. My sister-in-law, Laura, is holding my infant niece and trying to scoop my infant nephew out of the bassinet beside the desk. I step in and lift Konstantin into my arms while Laura tries to soothe Mila. Konstantin bats at me with the arm that escaped his swaddling. I let his tiny hand latch onto my index finger as I make a funny face at him. I waggle my eyebrows and scrunch my nose as I bounce him. He's soon blowing bubbles while Mila continues to cry.

"He only started because his sister did. Can you watch Konstantin while I nurse Mila?"

Laura recovered quickly from delivering the twins a month ago, but I can see the exhaustion in her eyes. I nod before my gaze shifts to the mystery woman who's still watching me. I can tell she doesn't know what to make of me. I'm nearly six and a half feet tall and look like I could have been an American football player. I was in high school. I also share the same features all of my brothers have. If she's met my oldest brother, Maksim, then she knows I must be a younger brother, since we all have dark brown hair and blue eyes. Icy-blue, as more than one person has told me.

"Of course. Konstantin and I have much to discuss."

And I have much to observe. Who is this woman? Why is she sitting at Laura's desk? Why does she have stacks of contracts in front of her?

I sit in the chair across from the desk as Laura settles into the rocking chair Maks bought so Laura could feed the twins while they work. Speaking of Maks, where is my brother?

"Hello. I'm Nikolai."

I offer to shake the young woman's hand, which she's quick to take. But her gaze turns suspicious. She glances back at Laura, who's settled Mila under a blanket to nurse. I look down at Konstantin and make faces at him again. He tries to kick his legs free while blowing more bubbles.

"Should I find somewhere else to work, Laura?"

"No need. Niko, Maks isn't here right now. He went to the flex site."

"Oh, okay. I just stopped by to see how you're doing. I'm headed to Deuces Wild tonight, but I had some time to kill. I thought I might give you a break."

"I think you came to see if there're any of your mom's *pelmeni* left."

"Are there?" I grin at Laura, but my gaze shifts to the young woman. "My mom makes the best Russian dumplings."

"Where does she get the minced lamb?"

I stare at her for a moment before I remember how to talk. "There's a butcher in Brighton Beach that she prefers. How do you know what goes into *pelmeni*?"

"Because I've been making them since I was five."

I know Laura is watching us because I see her shit-eating-grin as she rocks a now silent Mila.

"I didn't catch your name. I'm Nikolai, but as Laura said, people call me Niko."

"I'm Anastasia Antonov."

"Russian?"

"*Da*. At least, half. My father is Russian, and my mother is American."

Interesting. That explains why she speaks the language, unlike Laura, who learned in college. Now I need to know why she's in Maks and Laura's house and why she's got business contracts in front of her.

"Niko, Anastasia is my new legal assistant. Maks convinced me I need help now that the twins are here."

I know my face doesn't show a single reaction, but in my head, my eyebrows shoot up to my hair. Laura was a corporate lawyer who worked for a fancy New York City firm. She represented a company that my brothers' and my company, Kutsenko Partners, merged with. She negotiated a killer deal for her client. A couple months later, she and my oldest brother married, and now she's our business attorney. She only handles our legal ventures, but I know she's also privy to most of our less than legal ventures. She's counseled us more than once in the past year that she's been with Maks.

"Welcome to Kutsenko Partners."

What else can I say? If her father is Russian, is she bratva? Does she know we're Russian mafia?

"Thank you. Today is my first day."

I figured since I've never seen her before. I didn't even know Laura was looking for help. As the questions bombard my brain, Konstantin chooses that moment to explode his diaper. I look down to see the mustard-yellow ooze seeping into my suit coat and button-down shirt.

"Niko! I'm so sorry."

Laura looks anything but remorseful. Her grin has only gotten bigger.

"It's fine. I'll get him cleaned up, then I'll raid Maks's closet. I'll be sure to leave this in his dry-cleaning hamper."

I walk to the changing table attached to Konstantin's bassinet. I clean him up as I make faces at him again.

"What did you do, you little stinker? I shall remind you of this when you're older and asking if you can ride my motorcycle."

"I can do this if you want to get changed."

I knew Anastasia was beside me. No one moves in a room, and definitely no one approaches me, without me knowing. But I'm surprised by my reaction to her nearness. I get a whiff of her perfume that makes my cock twitch. She's taller than I expected, so her breath tickles my neck as she whispers. Mila's asleep now as Laura places her in her bassinet. I hide it, but a shiver runs through me.

"You don't have to. It's good practice for Niko."

Laura's as observant as anyone raised in a mafia family, even though she wasn't. It comes to her naturally, and she reads people better than most. She knows my brother better than anyone, so it often feels like she knows me better than anyone. We're all four peas in a pod. It's disconcerting that I'm sure she's figured out what I'm thinking.

This woman is beyond desirable. She's gorgeous in a rather nonconventional way. Now that I know she's half Russian, I can see the Eastern European features. She's only six inches shorter than me, which must put her at five feet eleven. She's willowy, even verging on too thin. But there's something about her expression. She's an enigma that's drawing me, making me want to discover what lies within her mind.

"Thank you. If you don't mind. He made a bigger mess than I realized."

I can feel it soaking into my skin. I'm going to need a shower if I wait much longer. I step aside and let Anastasia take my place. But I can't bring myself to leave the office yet. I watch how natural she is with my nephew.

"Have you been around a lot of babies?"

She glances at me, surprised that I'm still here.

"Yes. I used to babysit a lot when I was younger. I nannied a few summers during college."

"Did you go to school around here?"

I'm suddenly far more curious than I am uncomfortable. But I see her look down at the enormous stain across my middle. I'm sure she's wondering why I'm lingering.

"Barnard."

"I went to NYU."

Why did I just blurt that out? Half the people I tell that to don't believe me. Despite the designer tailormade suits, most people assume I'm some type of pro-athlete or a trust fund baby. My build and wealth confuse them.

"I considered it, but I like Barnard better."

I offer her what I hope is a sexy smile before I whisper to her.

"We'll have to compare notes sometime." I don't wait for her answer before I turn to the door. When I get there, I look at my sister-in-law. "Laura, I'm going to use the guest bathroom.

I'll be back in fifteen. I'll take Mila and Konstantin for a walk if you want."

"Thanks."

Laura calls after me as I walk out. I hurry up the stairs, taking them two and three at a time. I'd like to make a better impression on Anastasia than a shit-stained suit. But I also can't just lurk when I said I came to see the twins. And I did. I love being an uncle. I think it's far more enjoyable than being a dad. Maks looks like a haggard old man every time I see him, and he's not even the one who birthed the babies.

I grab clothes from Maks's closest and hurry to take a shower. All four of us, Maksim, Aleksei, Bogdan, and I, are the same size. We're worse than teenage sisters with trading clothes. My hair is still wet, and I'm running my fingers through it when I return to the office. Laura already has the babies in the stroller and is shoving the diaper bag in the basket beneath the tandem. They're in the car seats and facing me. Konstantin looks groggy, and Mila is practically snoring.

"I fed Konstantin while you were upstairs. He should fall asleep any minute. Have fun."

I know Laura doesn't trust anyone outside the family with the infants, but it makes me proud that she's so comfortable letting me take care of my niece and nephew without reservation.

"Laura, I'm done with the annotations. Is there anything else before I take off?"

"No. You've been so much help. You've done more in five hours than I'm able to do in a week these days. Thank you."

"If I'm headed back toward Barnard, I can catch the R train and transfer at Times Square to the one local, right?"

"Yeah, forty-second street."

I chime in before Laura can answer. I look at Laura, who's standing behind Anastasia when she turns to me. She's shaking her head. She must know I'm about to ask why Anastasia isn't using one of our town cars. The warning look tells me all I need to know. Anastasia doesn't know about us being bratva. She doesn't know that she works for the *pakhan's* wife. Maksim leads our branch. I serve in the Elite Group as one of his senior advisors. Aleks and Bogdan make up the other two members.

"I'm headed in that direction. I can walk you to the station."

Laura's still giving me a warning look, but now I think she's warning me away from hitting on her new assistant. Anastasia hesitates before she nods. How much harm does she think she'll come to with a man pushing a double stroller?

Anastasia grabs her purse before looking at the desk one last time. She puts a pen back in the desk organizer before she smiles at Laura.

"I'll see you tomorrow."

"Thanks again for all your help."

As we step outside, I realize what Laura must have. I'm going to have at least two armed guards just for the twins, plus my own personal bodyguard. I wonder what Laura said to explain the practically paramilitary security that roams the property. I watch Anastasia as she takes it all in before she looks up at me. I see the uncertainty in her eyes.

"Is this all really necessary?"

She keeps her voice low. I can tell she hadn't considered the intense security since she arrived. It wouldn't surprise me if Laura asked the men to be less conspicuous when Anastasia got there. But they're on patrol now, clad in all black with bulletproof vests, rifles, and extra ammunition.

"We're very wealthy, Anastasia."

She nods at my blunt response. I watch her eyes as she scans our surroundings before we reach the gate. A guard opens it, and we walk through. The moment we're on the sidewalk, she spins around, noticing the three men who followed us. Her eyes are like saucers. These men are plain-clothed, wearing suits, but their demeanor screams *do not approach.*

"Are they following us?"

"Me and the twins. You because you're with us."

"It that necessary?"

I understand now why Laura didn't approve of my offer. Questions come that I don't want to answer. But then again, they're inevitable if Anastasia is going to work for Laura. It frustrates me that my sister-in-law didn't give Anastasia any heads up.

"We've had threats before. Maks and Laura take precautions now that the babies are here."

"They need three bodyguards?"

"The man on the right is mine. The twins have one each."

"You have one?"

"Yes. I'm as wealthy as Maksim and Laura. All four of us are. We're equal partners in our business."

"Four?"

"Maksim, Aleksei, Bogdan, and me."

"Oh. I forgot. Laura mentioned their names, but she said little about you or your brothers."

"You'll meet them, eventually."

"Are you close? I mean, I know you do business together. But outside of business? Are you and Maksim the closest?"

If I didn't know better, I would avoid all of her questions. But if Laura hired her, Anastasia's had a background check that surpasses anything the FBI or Department of Justice can do.

"We're all extremely close. We see each other every day and not just because we work together. Do you have siblings?"

"No. I'm an only child. I suppose that's why I'm always interested in big families. It's so different from what I'm used to."

"Are you close to your parents?"

"Yes. But they live in Maryland, so I don't see them that often anymore."

"You moved to New York for college?"

"Yeah. I graduated a couple months ago."

"Congratulations."

That makes her probably six years younger than me.

"Thanks. Do twins run in your family?"

"Not that I know of."

"You and Maksim could be twins. You must be close in age."

"We're all mirror images. Maksim's the oldest, then Aleksei, then me, and finally Bogdan. We're all a year apart."

"Wow. Your poor parents."

"We were a handful."

"Who was the worst?"

She smiles, and I'm certain a choir of angels is blowing their trumpets. Her entire face radiates an easygoingness that I'm not used to. It's probably her youth. Bogdan's wife is close to our age. Christina worked for the city planner's office for nearly five years before she met Bogdan. Now she heads our construction division. Laura was an attorney for four years in private practice before marrying Maks and becoming our corporate lawyer.

"Maks was the ringleader, and not just because he was the oldest. He could find trouble like it was his sixth sense. Aleks is the most reserved of all of us. Bogdan and I just wanted to keep up with Maks and Aleks. Most would say Bogdan's the most easygoing of all of us."

"You don't sound as though you agree."

"Don't I?" I laugh. "I think I am, especially now that Bogdan is married. He's still fun, but he's a bit more serious than he once was."

I see her glance at my left hand, which is on the stroller handle. She looks back up at me and finds me smiling.

"I'm not married, and neither is Aleks."

"Oh."

We're almost to the subway station, and I find I don't want to reach it. We're just sharing small talk, but I'm so curious about her.

"You grew up in Maryland and came here for college. Do you plan to stay?"

"For now, yes. I'm thinking about law school."

"Have you applied?"

"No. I want to work for a year and save up before starting a new round of student loans."

I nod and hope my look is sympathetic. Bogdan and I went to NYU on academic scholarships. We weren't wealthy when we started. Our cousins, Anton and Sergei, went to college in Philly on athletic scholarships. Neither Maks nor Aleks had the luxury of college. They were already too entrenched in our bratva.

"Are you thinking about law schools here in the city?"

Why do I want her to say yes so much?

"Yeah. But I'm also thinking about Baltimore and DC. Those are closer to my parents."

"Do you want to practice in Maryland or DC?"

"Maybe. I like it here in the city, but my parents are my only family, so it's tempting to go back. I'll have to see where I get in and how work goes."

She flashes a smile as she realizes that she's talking to her boss's brother-in-law.

"I didn't know Laura was looking for an assistant."

"I don't think she was. She was at the park with the twins, and I was there with the kids I was nannying. We got to talking while we sat on a bench. I found out she was a lawyer and mentioned my plans. One of the little girls came up and burst into tears because it was my last day. The family is moving. Laura asked what I was going to do next. I said find an office job or move home if I don't. One thing led to another, and she asked if I would consider being her legal assistant. I've worked for law firms before. I only nannied as a summer job."

"Sounds like kismet."

"Maybe. I know whatever it was made me very lucky."

This time, her smile is timider and her cheeks flush. I change the subject to make her more comfortable.

"Where is your father from in Russia?"

"Moscow. I think that's where Laura said your family is from."

"We are. But we've been here since I was twelve."

"You must have been here for longer than you were there."

We're always cautious and make sure people know we've been in America for more than a decade. We're all citizens now, and we have no business ties to Russia. We do still have family there.

"We have been. You don't have an accent. Were you raised here?"

"Yes. My dad's family came over here just before I was born. Do you still remember much about Moscow?"

I force myself not to grimace.

"Yes."

"Maybe you know where my dad grew up. Serpukhovsky."

My heart is racing even if I don't show any emotion.

"I know where that is."

It's close to where I lived, and it's a neighborhood run by the Podolskaya bratva. The very people we fled. Laura and Maks must know this. For whatever reason, Anastasia passed the background check. I keep telling myself this.

"Is it close to where you grew up?"

"Not far. Have you been to Moscow?"

"Yes. But only a few times and really only to be a tourist, since none of my dad's family is still there."

Sure. Are they not there? Or does her dad not want her to meet them? Or does he not want to go back to his old neighborhood? Even if he was never bratva, there's no way he's ignorant of them.

"A Russian dad and American mom aren't that common. How'd your parents meet?"

"My mom worked for the U.N."

I didn't expect that answer.

"That must have been interesting back then."

"She wasn't there that long. My parents say just long enough to fall in love."

Long enough for her dad to get married and qualify to immigrate with an American sponsor.

"People often joke that they got married so fast so my dad could get a Green Card."

Is she a mind reader?

"They didn't, of course. My dad actually studied here in America. Technically, they met in college, but his visa was only good for when he was a student. When my mom got an assignment to Russia, they reconnected. Well, here I am. Thanks for walking with me, Mr. Kutsenko."

"Niko. If you call any of us Mr. Kutsenko, you'll get all four of us."

She blushes and nods. I watch her head down to the subway platform before I turn back toward the house. I have so many more questions. And I intend to get all the answers.

Chapter Two

Stasia

Holy fuck. Nikolai Kutsenko is the hottest man I have ever seen. He has a brooding aura, but when he smiles... Shit. My panties must be soaked. And how he is with his nephew. Swoon. I nearly fell out of my seat when I saw him, and I might have fallen in love when he picked up Konstantin. He took the gastro-pyrotechnics in stride. He rides a motorcycle? That's even hotter.

Thank my lucky stars that he came at the end of the day. I wouldn't have gotten a damn thing done if he'd arrived in the morning. I can't stop thinking about him. When I shook his hand, I felt a charge zing all the way up to my shoulder, then all the way down to my pussy. I have experienced nothing like it. I'm sure he barely noticed me, but I sure as hell noticed him. Then again, he walked me to the subway.

I cannot be his type. He probably dates models. That's so cliché. But I'm sure he dates them, not some girl from the outskirts of Baltimore who's a secretary. Legal assistant. Sure. I sort papers, answer emails, and maybe type some letters or contracts. It's more that he was so suave in his suit—both of them. I feel dowdy in my sensible trousers, blouse, and ballet flats. I walk to and from the subway in summer in New York City. He probably has a driver. I saw Maksim get in a chauffeured car. He's gotta be a millionaire, like Maksim. Regular people do not live in houses like Maksim and Laura if they aren't. I'm a practically broke recent college grad. We revolve on different planets.

I can't believe how lucky I am. If Laura hadn't sat down next to me last week, I would be packing my apartment and heading back to Maryland if I didn't find a job soon. As is, I barely convinced my landlord to extend my lease. He wanted to double my rent at first. I mentioned it to Laura this morning. By lunchtime, my landlord texted me and is actually giving me a discount for extending. I think Maksim had something to do with that. While Niko is the hottest guy I've ever met, Maksim Kutsenko is by far the most intimidating. Maybe people think that about Niko too. But he seems way easier going than his oldest brother.

I'm meeting friends, so hopefully that will distract me. I enter the bar to an oppressive heat. There are way too many people packed in here for happy hour. I can see a ribbon tied to an AC vent waving, so it's on, but you can't tell. I see Beth and the others waving. I squeeze between people to get to them. There aren't many times when I appreciate being so skinny, but crowds are one. I bet crowds part like the fucking Red Sea when Niko walks in. He's one of those "girls want to date him, guys want to be him" kinda men.

Beth is the first one to greet me.

"How was your first day? I got you a cider."

"Thanks, Beth. It was good. I think Laura is going to be a

great boss. I can already tell she's not a micromanager, which I appreciate."

"How do you know?"

"She gave me a stack of depositions to annotate and summarize. She explained what she wanted, then she sat at her desk and worked until her twins needed feeding."

"Twins? Holy fuck."

"That's what I thought when I met her in the park. They're a month old. She said she'd needed to get out of the house before the walls closed in. It was her first time out and alone with the babies since they were born. She was only there long enough to chat and offer me a job."

"You lucky bitch." Gracie stirs her drink with a straw.

I roll my eyes.

"Thanks, Gracie."

"Haven't you heard of the Kutsenkos? They're fucking rich as fuck. And I've heard they're all smoking hot."

"They are both."

"You met some of them?"

"Gracie, I work in Maksim's house and for his wife. Yes, I met him. And I met another brother. Nikolai."

And he's the hottest man on Earth. I sip on my cider, hoping Gracie changes the topic. Blessedly, she does. We all just graduated, so everyone is talking about new jobs and travel plans. I'm fortunate that I met Laura when I did. Maryland is fine, and I like Baltimore as much as anyone can. But I love New York. I have since the moment I arrived. Admittedly, it smells kinda funny half the time, and I can guess why. But the vibe is what I love. There's always something to do at any hour of the day or any day of the week. People could live in one borough their entire lives, never leave it, and still have a completely full life. To have five to choose from, to have tons to do in all of them, is what I like best. And not for nothing, I went to a great university.

"Hey, Earth to Ana."

"Huh?"

I don't know what Beth was just talking about. I know Laura calls me Anastasia, but she's my boss. I'm used to my friends calling me Ana. I still wasn't paying attention.

"Dreaming about the Kutsenkos?"

Actually, no.

"I was thinking about how I would have had to move back to my parents if I hadn't met Laura."

"How'd they take the fact that you changed your mind?"

"Well. I felt badly backing out of the job at the mayor's office in Baltimore. It was a great opportunity, but I just like New York so much better."

"Is the pay just as good?"

"Are you kidding? Working for a rich lawyer in private practice, rather than barely being more than an intern for a public servant. This is way better pay. They even offered me benefits. I have health insurance and a 401K."

"For being an admin assistant?"

"Yes. But Laura made it clear in the park and this morning that she intends to train me to be her paralegal. She said in a couple months, she has a major deal coming up and will need a paralegal's help. She wants me to be that person. I'm just getting my feet wet right now."

"That's really cool. I didn't know it was that big a deal."

"Yeah, Beth. She was crazy generous with the compensation packet. I guess she wants to be sure I'm willing to stick around in a house with two babies who cry during the day. I can only imagine what it's like at night. Her husband looked exhausted this morning."

"Twins. I think that would be cool."

Gracie might, but I don't. I can't imagine having twice the diapers, twice the laundry, twice the feeding, twice the everything. Laura made it look easy today, but there were a few moments here and there where I caught how tired she was. I think she wishes she could have taken a real maternity leave. I heard Maksim say something about that before he left the house. He's hoping I work out, so Laura can do less. I hope I do too. And not just because of the money. I really like Laura.

"What do you want to do this weekend?"

"It's Monday, Beth. I don't even know what I want to eat tonight."

"I enjoy having things to look forward to. You know that."

"I do, too. But I haven't thought that far ahead."

I can barely think about anything right now. Images of meeting Niko keep flashing in my head. I'm trying to focus, but I'm failing.

"The Dubliner has live music, and we always love it there. How about that on Friday?"

I'm glad Beth suggested that. I love that Irish pub, and it's always a good time.

"Sounds good to me. Peter can come."

Gracie and Peter have been together since freshman year. He proposed the day after graduation. They've been on cloud nine since then. I'm actually surprised Gracie is here without him. He's a little too possessive for my taste. I worry about his temper sometimes.

"Speaking of men, have you heard from that douchebag you were dating, Ana?"

"He called and texted, but I've blocked his number. I do not want to talk about him."

Talking about that asshole will only ruin my night. I don't even want to think his name. What a wasted few months.

The evening progresses, and it's a great way to celebrate my first day. My friends bought my dinner and drinks, which was super nice. But we did the same thing when Beth landed her job at the hospital. I swear she must have the best bedside manner of any nurse. She's one of the kindest people I've ever met. She's practically a genius with all things science, and she's compassionate. I suppose that's exactly what a nurse should be. Gracie is taking a year off before grad school like me. She knew Peter was going to propose sometime this summer, so she wants a year to plan the wedding. What the hell kind of shindig is she planning that she can't work and plan? I suspect it's Peter pressuring her not to work. He's the type to want a trophy wife. I'm not sure Gracie's cut out for that. But whatever she decides and whatever the future holds, I'm there for her.

"Good morning."

I look up to find Niko standing in the office for a second day in a row. Is he a fucking ghost? I didn't hear him at all. The door to the office was even closed. Fuck me to hell and back. He makes wearing a suit better than a naked man in porn. Suit porn. That's what he is. He's in a charcoal gray one that must have been custom tailored for him. The steel gray shirt is the perfect compliment. He's not wearing a tie, and the top two buttons are undone. He has to know how gorgeous he is.

"Good morning, Mr. Kutsenko."

"Niko. We all go by our first name, otherwise, it's too confusing."

I nod because I can't think of anything else to say that won't come across as prying. What are you doing today? Why are you here? Do you have a girlfriend? Do you want to fuck? Yeah, no. I can't ask any of those.

"Maksim and Laura are upstairs with the twins."

"Sure."

What does that grin mean? I glance past him and can see the stairs. Maksim and Laura are on the landing, and the kiss they're sharing is definitely meant to be private. I can feel myself blushing, and it must be obvious, because Niko twists to see where I'm looking. When he turns back to me, he cocks an eyebrow.

"Come on, *starik*." Old man. "I don't have all day."

Niko's looking at me, but he's talking to Maksim. Niko said they're each a year apart, and Maksim definitely does not look like an old man. He's practically a twin to Niko.

"Good things come to those who wait, *bratishka*. You'll see one day." Little brother.

Laura and Maksim exchange a quick kiss, but I can see him squeeze her ass. Oh, Lord, she does the same thing back to him. I look down at the contract in front of me. Laura left instructions on how I'm supposed to type it up. I shift my focus to the laptop in front of me, but I'm aware of Niko.

"Good morning, Anastasia."

"Hi, Laura. I've started on the contract that you left out. I think it'll take me about ten minutes."

"At the rate I'm doing things these days, it would have taken me a week. Thank you. When you're done, I want to go over how to review a brief. I have a stack of case law that I need to familiarize myself with before an upcoming meeting. It's boring as all get out, but I really need the help."

"I'm happy to."

I smile as Laura walks past, and I can feel Niko watching me. I'm trying to ignore him or else my face is going to be scarlet. The brothers say their goodbyes and leave. I have no idea what they do during the day, but I know they own several businesses.

"Hey. You know it's lunchtime, right?"

"You are way too silent."

I smile up at Niko, who has two bags in his hands. It looks like he just came from a deli. I blurt out what comes to mind, but I feel way more comfortable around him than I did at the beginning of the week. I see him every day, and he makes a point of saying hello. We've even chatted. He's asked me more about college, why I chose New York and stayed after graduation, about my family, like what my parents do and where I grew up. He's shared some of that, too. I know he went to NYU on an academic scholarship, and his younger brother, Bogdan, did the same. He seems a little more mortal than the god I thought of when we first met. But he's still so far out of my league, we're not even playing the same sport.

"I stopped at Schwartz's Deli around the corner and grabbed food for you and Laura. Maks says she's not eating enough."

"I see her eat all the time, but she's nursing twins. If I drank as much water as she does, I would float away."

"I brought sandwiches. I have roast beef for her. I noticed you had pastrami the other day, so I hope you don't mind that's what I got for you."

"Thank you. You didn't need—"

"My mom would kill me if I brought food for one person and not for everyone else. Besides, I don't know how to order anything that isn't enough for a small army."

I've seen some photos in passing of Niko's family. The men are all like him. Huge. And in the bodybuilder sense, not the NFL linebacker sense. Lean. That would be the right word. Muscular and lean. Bulging muscles and sex on stilts. Well, at least Niko is. My crush is only getting worse by the day. He keeps being chivalrous and outgoing with me. I can't believe he remembered I had a pastrami sandwich the other day. I can tell it's his nature, but it makes me feel special. A little crush now and again isn't so bad. My last relationship was a disaster. This won't be anything more than acquaintances, but I can enjoy it for now.

Chapter Three

Niko

I can't stay away. I have no reason to go to Maks's place every day. But I keep finding excuses. I'm so intrigued, and I keep making it worse by feeding my curiosity. Part of me is genuinely interested in getting to know Stasia, but the other part of me is suspicious as hell. I trust next to no one who isn't family or bratva. My sisters-in-law are the rare exceptions, and I wasn't sure at first. I was impressed and respected Laura from the get-go. She wrapped us around her little finger to the tune of forty billion when she out negotiated us for a merger with a company she represented.

Christina was an inspector for the city planner, and she showed up at one of our building sites for a rather untraditional and unforgettable meeting. Poor Bogdan. I will never forget the look on his face when he recognized her. He clearly wasn't over how they parted the first time they met a few days earlier. But she was incredibly helpful and sorted out more than one mess for us. She's so good that we made her the head of our construction branch.

But Stasia. I don't know yet what to make of her. I want to fuck her into next week. That much I know. She's beyond pretty. She's not stop-you-in-your-tracks beautiful until she smiles. Actually, I take that back. I think she's beautiful and hot as fuck, but I know a lot of men wouldn't see her that way. That's more than fine by me. She's almost too thin, but more in a leggy supermodel kind of way. Eastern Europe produces some of the most gorgeous women in the world. Her half-Russian side is strong.

But I still find it hard to trust her. She's in my brother and sister-in-law's house every day and around my niece and nephew. I know she passed a background check, but anyone new makes me uneasy.

"How do you like the job so far?"

I know that's an unfair question, but I ask it anyway. I want to see her eyes, her gut reaction, not hear her profess she loves it.

"It's great. I love working for Laura."

Sincerity. Either she's telling the truth, or she's a sociopath with no compunction about lying. I think it's the former.

"Better than what you did before?"

"I'm still changing a diaper here and there, but only because I offer. So, yes, I prefer this. I like kids, but I enjoy doing things that are closer to what I went to college for."

She majored in pol-sci and government, with a minor in urban studies. I looked at Sergei's background check. I know plenty of technical details about her. Only child. Middle-class upbringing. Graduated from Barnard with honors. One speeding ticket when she was sixteen, but other than that, a spotless record. That only tells me what anyone else can know.

Bratva Treasure

I want to know who she really is. If it's because I have a tiny crush, so be it.

"Has Laura started teaching you paralegal stuff?"

She laughs.

"Yes. Plenty of paralegal stuff."

Half the time we speak Russian, and I don't even notice. We have been today. It's enough to lull me into thinking that she might be fully Russian and would understand our life. But she'll stumble over a word or have to think about one for a moment. It all comes crashing back down that she isn't. She's only half. But all of her was raised in America. Then my suspicions start all over again. What happens if she finds out? What were Maks and Laura thinking bringing a stranger into their home?

Not just because we're bratva, but because the twins are here. She doesn't seem like the type, but I've seen "The Hand That Rocks the Cradle." I remember that Soul Asylum song I used to hear sometimes on the Classic Rock station. "Runaway Train." That was one with the music video with the woman who grabs the baby out of the stroller. I watched it once, and it's stuck with me ever since.

I have an overactive imagination. That's what my dad would tell me when I was really little. It was usually when I made Bogdan pretend to be my dog. My parents wouldn't get one. Our apartment in Moscow was barely big enough for the six of us. I would make Bogdan crawl around with me. I was five, and he was four. What was the point of having a little brother back then if I couldn't get him to do things for me?

"Big plans for the weekend?"

"No. I'm just going to help my friend Beth move and then hang out at my place. My friend Gracie and her fiancé are going out of town."

"I don't miss the days of helping people move. I spent a

summer working for one of those college guys moving companies. Good money, but never again."

I pretend to shiver.

"Monday nights are actually our night to go out. There's a place near campus that has great happy hour specials."

Tucking that little nugget away.

"Hey, Niko. When did you get here?"

I lean over and kiss Laura's cheek and hold up the bags.

"A few minutes ago. I brought lunch for you both."

"Are you staying?"

"No. I have to go back to work."

"No rest for the wicked, huh?"

Laura grins at me.

"Don't I know it."

Stasia's watching me, and I wonder what she's thinking. Her expression is speculative. Is she wondering just how wicked I can be? I'd show her if she gave me a chance. Fuck, yes. Relationship, no.

Liar. You'd break that rule in a heartbeat if she agreed. You want her in a way you have no other woman. Why else can't you stop thinking about her? Why else are you so suspicious? You don't want your worries to be right. You want to go out with her and not have it blow up in your face.

All of that is true.

The warehouse is not where I want to spend my weekend, but here I am. It's a location we control. There are no city cameras anywhere nearby. It isn't on any city records or deeds. It's where we take care of people who are a complication or threat. It doesn't take that long to get here since it's in Queens. It's next to the Flushing River, which makes disposal easy.

Why can't the Irish get the message? We've taken out the last two leaders. Donovan went after Laura, and Declan went after Christina. Now Dillan's fucking causing trouble. What's up with the D names? Donovan, Declan, Dillan. Original. Probably the best any O'Rourke can think of. It's about as far into the alphabet as any of them know.

It's Monday night, and I've been here since Friday afternoon. I left the sandwiches and was about to head into Jersey to check on the casinos we own. Aleks called, and my driver had to turn around.

"You've been here for three days. You think you're a badass because you haven't cracked. Fine. Take your secrets to the grave. We'll only draw out the agony. You know you aren't leaving here. Why make it so hard on yourself?"

"Fuck you."

"Why would I need to when I can fuck your wife? It's not like you're doing it anymore. But I hear Danny Byrne is. Maybe he'll take a break long enough for me to slip it in."

"Fu—"

I slam my fist into his junk. He sags forward, but we stretched his arms above his head, and his feet barely touch the ground.

"You're repeating yourself. Tell me when the next coke shipment comes in."

"No."

I grab a piece of wire and wrap it around his throat. I cross over the ends and stretch my arms out to my sides. I tighten it, and I know he's panicking. He pisses himself. He knows he's about to die. We give people like him just enough water to keep them alive and keep them talking coherently until we're done. There isn't much to come out, but it does. I step to the side to avoid it, and it allows me to tighten the noose.

"A'wite."

I immediately release the tension. There's a deep groove in his neck, and the wire broke the skin. He lost all of his toes, and we've slashed his belly and back. The cuts are deep enough that they bled, but they aren't enough to kill him. He's actually held out a lot longer than I expected. But nearly choking him to death finally broke him. His voice rasps, and his words are halting after choking him and the beating he's taken for three days.

"Dillan made a deal with Enrique. Since you took over control of the docks and now Salvatore pays you for access and protection, Dillan paired up with the Cartel. He has the same arrangement as he did with Salvatore but the reverse. Instead of getting paid, he pays Enrique to let his ships dock and to keep the feds away."

"That tells me nothing about the coke."

"I'm getting to it. Enrique wants to double the price. Dillan refuses to pay, but he knows he has to. He bought the coke from Enrique's rival down there. Those Colombians are trying to outdo Enrique, so they're undercutting the price to build their clientele. Dillan got a deal on the price. He's going to sell it to the Triad. He'll get the money he needs to pay Enrique, and he'll set up an arrangement with the Wo Shing Wo."

That's the last thing we need. The Triad are the major Hong Kong-based Chinese organized crime syndicates, and they generally leave most of us alone. They don't get involved in our business. But some shit went down over a Triad girl years ago that's still causing bad blood between some of the Irish and the Cartel. Enrique has kept it under control by not acknowledging it. But if Dillan is going to the Triad, this will blow up like a powder keg. We wouldn't care if they annihilated each other, but we're going to get stuck in the middle. Laura grew up next door to Enrique's nephews and was practically like a niece. She had clients who were Triad. That's going to put us in the middle, and clearly, there's still bad blood between us and the Irish.

"When?"

"Next month."

"Beginning, middle, or end of the month?"

"End, but I'm not sure. I never heard a date."

"How much?"

One kilo can be worth upwards of sixty-grand.

"A hundred and forty."

Shit. That's over three hundred pounds. That's eight point four million dollars. That's a shit ton in one shipment. Dillan's got some balls. I'll give him that.

"Is it coming in through Jamaica?"

"Yeah."

That's all I'll get from him. He's not high enough on the food chain to know more. But that confirms what we thought. The Coast Guard only gets about a quarter of the drugs smuggled in by sea. The chances are in our favor this will get through. We will be waiting. We won't bring the product anywhere near the U.S. shores. It'll go straight to Belgium or the Netherlands. Maybe split between the two.

"You've been helpful after all. Good choice. This'll be quick."

I pull the gun from the holster at my lower back and put one between his eyes. Maks and Aleks come out of the office where they were watching.

"You have the magic touch."

"Thanks, Aleks. What I have is little patience."

"Eager to get to Maks's house to see Anastasia?"

I scowl at both of my brothers. I have said nothing about my interest in her, but clearly, I've been obvious. I'm less suspicious than I was, but I'm still not convinced. Maks already had her followed all of last week, just to be sure we aren't wrong. He called off the detail this morning. I think I'm going to pick up where they left off once I'm clean.

Fuck me. Are they spending the entire night in this fucking bar? I'm exhausted and starving. I've been outside this place since six o'clock, and it's now after midnight. They're going to shut the place down, and I can barely keep my eyes open. I paid the bouncer not to hassle me while I hang out around the corner. Every thirty minutes or so, I poke my nose in to see what Stasia's doing. She's at a table with two other women and a guy. The guy has his arm draped around a brunette. Even from a distance, I can see it's not a lazy hold, or even an affectionate one. He's keeping her pinned to his side. But the girl doesn't seem to mind. She's leaning against him, and she has had little to drink.

Stasia's had a few, which makes me wonder if she's drunk. She's so petite that it surprises me she can still stand when she goes to the bar. She has a tolerance, I'll give her that. But then again, if she's really that Russian, she can drink vodka like water. I've noticed she's in shape, so I think she's either an athlete or works out a lot. The muscle would also help keep her sober longer.

"Last call!"

Fina-fucking-ly. I'm going to keep my distance and follow her home. I know she's taking the subway, which pisses me off. I shouldn't care as much as I do, but it's needlessly dangerous. She could take a cab from Manhattan to her place in Queens, but I saw her get on the subway when she left Maks and Laura's. She was getting off the one local near Barnard when I spotted her again. I asked some roundabout questions last week to find out how she usually gets around. Apparently, she has a car, but she doesn't drive it into Manhattan if she can help it. I don't blame her.

I duck back around the corner as I watch her and her friends come out twenty minutes later. I glance at my watch. It's nearly one o'clock. This bar shuts down early. Thank God.

"Ana, you sure you can make it home? Why don't you take a cab?"

"And waste the money? No thanks, Beth."

"It's one o'clock. You really ought to take a cab or crash at my place, Ana."

Her friends are right. She should. I'm going to ask her flat out tomorrow how she gets around. I'm going to hammer home why she needs to take a cab if she's going to stay out this late and go home alone. I watch her hug the two women and smile at the guy. I follow her to the first train and spot her getting her subway card out well before she enters the station. She has her keys in her other hand. She must know to use them as a weapon since she's not anywhere near her front door. I hop on the car behind hers. I follow her when she makes the transfer.

I'm being a total creeper. I know. If she finds me following her, she'll freak out, and rightly so. A stalker or an attacker is exactly what she needs protecting against. She doesn't know I'm not either of those.

I watch her move toward the door as we approach her stop. There's next to no one on the trains right now, so I'm lucky she never looked toward my car. She would have seen me through the doors' windows. I wait until the last minute to get off, but I keep an eye on her as she heads toward the street level. I hang back as she goes up the steps and emerges on the street. Then I hurry to follow her. I give her a two-block head start. She lives like half a mile from the station. That's way too far to be walking alone at night. I'm definitely having a talk with her about that. Fuck, I'll even give away that I followed her just to prove my point.

Who the fuck is that? I creep closer as a guy steps out of the shadows toward her. She's not screaming or bolting. Her body language says she knows him, but she's tense. I know she still has her keys in her hand. She needs to get around him —

What the fuck?

The moment he makes a move toward her, I'm running. I'm in great shape, and I run often. But this is more like a long sprint. I'm two blocks behind her, and she has a block left to get to her place. Thank God for streetlights or else I wouldn't be able to see any of this. The guy's chasing her. She's got her key in the door as I make it to the end of her block. She's inside, but the guy slams through the door. Whoever he is, I'm going to fucking kill him. He tried to touch my *malyshka*.

Chapter Four

Stasia

I have never seen a more gorgeous man in my life. I can't stop thinking about him. It's on a loop in my head. Gorgeous, gorgeous, gorgeous. I've seen my boss's husband plenty of times over the past week, and I didn't exaggerate that they look like twins. But there is something about Niko that makes my panties wet. The way he smiles. He's fucking sin incarnate. My cheeks must look like apples every time I see him. I feel myself blush, and my skin is way too fair to hide it. He must have thought I was a simpering idiot the first time he met me. But he's been really nice since then. I still feel nervous, but I think I can at least hide that. I like how much we've gotten to know each other in the past week. I realized we've talked a lot about our lives and our past.

"Ana!"

Fuck me.

I met friends for dinner and drinks again near campus, but now I'm almost back to the ground floor studio I rent in

Queens. It's actually not that far from where I work. Just a couple subway stops. But I wish I'd accepted Beth's offer to crash at her place.

"What do you want, Antonio?"

"You've been ignoring me."

"Because we broke up. I told you to leave me alone."

"I told you we can fix things."

"No, we can't."

"Ana, I promise I'll never do that again. I don't know what possessed me to hit you."

"I do, and I'm not interested in getting back together. Go home."

I try to step around him, but he blocks me. Antonio Caruso is not a man who accepts no. He basically bullied me into our first date. But then he was such a gentleman after that. He wined and dined me and swept me off my feet. We dated for a few months, but we broke up three weeks ago after he shoved me into a wall and slapped me.

"To your place. That's where my home is."

"Never. We were never even remotely close to moving in together, and there isn't a chance in hell we ever will. Move."

When he lunges for me, I sidestep and dart into the street. I'm in ballet flats as usual, so I'm able to run. He's fast since his legs are longer than mine, but not as fast as me. I ran track and field and cross country in high school. I continued in college and ran sprints. I'm not that far from my apartment, only a block. I just have to make it there.

"Ana!"

I ignore Antonio bellowing at me. The streets are quiet because it's past midnight. But he's going to draw way too much attention. I hope he keeps yelling. Maybe someone will stop him. Who am I kidding? This is New York. No one's going to notice, and if they do, they won't get involved. I make it to the steps of my apartment and push my key into the lock. I always carry them in my hand from whenever I leave a place until I lock my front door. I push it open and spin around to slam it shut, except Antonio is already there. He rams his shoulder into it and barges in. I fall backwards and crash into the entryway table, where I leave my keys and purse. That's going to leave a mark.

"I don't think you get how this works, Ana. You don't get to decide."

"I'll decide to get a restraining order."

Antonio laughs. Like laughs really hard.

"No cop is coming near me."

"You aren't above the law."

"Yeah, I am. I have connections."

Connections? The look on his face is so self-assured.

"Are you—"

"Yeah. Took you long enough to figure it out."

"Mafia?"

"*Cosa Nostra*, bitch."

He reaches for my throat. When he steps closer, I send my knee into his junk. He bends over immediately. I turn toward the bathroom, hoping I can lock myself in. But I don't make it two steps before his hand knots in my hair, and he yanks me backward. I can't help but scream. Then there's a roar and the sound of something hitting the wall. Suddenly, I'm free. I whirl around and don't know what to make of the scene in front of me. Niko has Antonio on the floor, pinned with Niko's knee on Antonio's throat.

"Who're you?"

I barely understand Antonio.

"The new boyfriend."

I'm unsure how to take Niko's declaration. He lands one punch after another until Antonio's nose, jaw, and cheekbones must be broken. I hear the bone crunching. He's...dead? No. His face isn't even purple. But there is blood dripping onto the carpet. My landlord is going to *plotz*.

"Stasia, are you all right?"

"Niko?"

He wipes his hands on his suit coat, smearing blood on it. He stands, waiting to see if I run. I can't make my feet move until he takes a step forward. Then I'm rushing into his embrace. I can feel myself trembling as he wraps his arms around me. He presses my head against his chest as he holds me. I just watched him beat the shit out of my ex-boyfriend, and I have never felt safer than while he's hugging me.

"Stasia, did he hurt you? Was I too late?"

"No. He pushed me into the table, but that's it."

I feel Niko stiffen, and his body twists to look back at Antonio. When I look up, I can tell he's considering whether to do more damage.

"Are you injured?"

He loosens his hold, but that only makes me tighten mine. I'm suddenly petrified he's going to let go. I shake my head, and he pulls me closer.

"*Malyshka*, would you tell me if you were?"

Baby girl? No one has ever called me that, but I recognize the endearment.

"Yes."

I realize that's the truth. I feel like I would tell Niko all my secrets if he kept me feeling this protected. But my brow furrows as my own question pops into my head.

"What're you doing here?"

I lean back and look up at him. If the man showed any emotions, I think his eyes might appear guilty.

"Why are you here, Nikolai?"

"Niko."

"Why?"

"I followed you."

That should make me flee. Am I replacing one stalker for another?

"Why?"

"That's complicated."

"You followed me. Not that you were waiting around. How did you know where I would be? Did you follow me from Laura's?"

"Yes. You mentioned to Laura what your plans were for tonight."

"Did she tell you to follow me?"

"Of course not. She's going to be livid when she finds out I did. She'll be relieved for a moment because you're okay, then she will lose her shit."

"Then why? And do not tell me it's complicated. You've seen me every day for the past week."

"I am not a trusting person with anyone outside my immediate family."

"You don't trust me. Is it to work for Laura or to be around your niece and nephew?"

"It was both."

"Was? What's changed, Niko? You rescue me and suddenly, you don't have to worry that I'm a threat?"

Now I'm irritated, and his embrace feels oppressive. I push away, and he releases me immediately. I look at Antonio and inhale deeply before the sigh comes from my soul. What the fuck am I going to do now?

"Who is Antonio Caruso to you?"

"How do you know who he is?"

"He's a low-level *Cosa Nostra* member. I've known him since I was a kid. I didn't give him much chance to recognize me."

"He was my boyfriend for a few months. I ended it three weeks ago when he pushed me and slapped me."

I watch Niko's gaze harden. Nothing else about him shifts. If I hadn't been staring so intently, I wouldn't see it. Okay. Maksim might not be the most intimidating Kutsenko.

"Niko, what are you going to do?"

"Get him out of your apartment so you don't have to deal with him when he wakes up."

"Where are you going to take him?"

"I'm not taking him anywhere."

He pulls out his phone and makes a call. He greets someone named Sergei in Russian, but when he looks at me, he switches to English. I suppose it doesn't matter which language since I understand both. There's nothing private about the call.

"I need you and Anton to meet me in Queens. Laura's new assistant was attacked. It was Antonio Caruso...Yeah...That's what I want...Now."

He hangs up and looks around before he points to the kitchen sink. I follow him as he washes his hands.

"You didn't give Sergei my address."

"Your info is in your employee file."

"Why does this guy have access to that? Who is he?"

"Sergei and Anton are my cousins. Sergei handles background checks on everyone who comes to work for us."

"Laura ran a background check on me?"

"Plenty of employers do."

"I know. I just didn't think about it. Niko, you still haven't told me why you were following me."

"I told you, I'm not that trusting. We haven't had any new employees in a while. You work in my brother and sister-in-law's home and are around my niece and nephew."

"You don't trust your cousin to have been thorough?"

"I do. I saw your file. You haven't had so much as a speeding ticket since you were sixteen."

"And you still think I'm a threat? You let me change Konstantin, and you let me walk with you and the babies to the subway. You've seen me hold both babies. We've talked every day."

"No, I don't think you're a threat. I don't have a good answer, Stasia. Something just told me I should. I listen to my intuition. It's sounder than half the decisions I make after thinking things through."

We stand staring at each other until I suddenly feel exhausted. I move to the sofa and sit down. I watch him pat down Antonio. He pulls a knife from each pocket. He rolls Antonio over and pulls a gun from a holster on his belt. What the ever-loving fuck?

"Why does he have that? Was he going to kill me?"

"I don't know. But I know him, and I know it's not unusual for him to carry it."

"He never...I don't think he ever carried one with me."

The look Niko shoots me makes me feel like an idiot. It tells me that Antonio probably did. But I never saw it.

"Niko!"

"Yeah. Come in."

I look up to find two equally large men standing just inside my doorway. One is blond with blue eyes, and the other is dark-haired with brown eyes. They don't look like each other, but they both look just like Niko. How is that possible? How did they get here so fast?

"Anastasia, these are my cousins. Sergei and Anton, this is Anastasia."

"Hello."

They speak at the same time, but that's all they say to me.

"Here. This was handy."

The blond hands Niko a duffle bag while the other guy takes the weapons Niko pulled off Antonio.

"Can I use your bathroom to change?"

"Mhmm."

I nod as I watch Niko's cousins hoist Antonio onto his feet. Where are they taking him?

"Are you letting him go? Shouldn't we call the police?"

"No, Stasia."

Niko answers from within the bathroom. Sergei and Anton shake their heads as they drag my still-unconscious ex-boyfriend out of my studio. The blond one pulls the door shut, but it doesn't fit properly. I go to fix it, but Niko steps out of the bathroom. He's in jeans and a tight-fitting t-shirt. Holy fuck. Every muscle is on display as though he weren't wearing a shirt. He grins and winks at me, and I realize that I'm practically drooling.

The dark-haired cousin comes back in and takes the duffle bag.

"I'll check in with you tomorrow."

Niko nods to his cousin before the man leaves. Niko adjusts the door and pushes his shoulder against it until it closes properly.

"Do you have carpet cleaner? You need to get this stain out soon."

"Why didn't we call the police?"

"Stasia, I'll explain everything, but we really have to get this stain out. It can't wait."

"I don't have any."

"Distilled vinegar?"

"No."

I see Niko grit his teeth. He pulls out his phone and makes a call again.

"Anton, I need carpet cleaner...Yeah, well, I don't have much choice, do I?...Thanks."

"What don't you have a choice about? Niko, what the hell is going on?"

He walks over to me and squats in front of me while I sit on the sofa. He tucks hair behind each of my ears before taking my hands. His are warm, and I can feel callouses at the base of his fingers.

"Stasia, I know I said I don't trust easily. But I need you to trust me now. I will take care of this. Then I will tell you what I can. Can you do that?"

"Do I have a choice?"

"Yes. But there's only one good one."

"Fine."

I look up as the dark-haired cousin comes back in. I guess he's Anton. Niko takes the bottle from him and rags. I watch as he kneels and scrubs the carpet. I've never seen carpet cleaner work that well. It must be industrial strength because the blood stain comes out almost immediately. He hands everything back to Anton.

"Goodnight, Ms. Antonov, Niko."

Anton just dragged a body out of my studio and brought back supplies to hide that anything happened, and he's addressing me formally. What the fuck is going on? I watch Niko wash his hands again. I notice that he's extremely thorough just like last time and could be a surgeon scrubbing before an operation. He comes back and squats in front of me again.

"I think you have a lot to tell me. You may as well sit."

"Stasia—"

"Why do you call me that?"

"Call you what?"

"Stasia. No one else does. I go by Ana if I'm not using my full name."

"Do you not like it? I didn't mean to offend. I didn't really realize I do that."

"No, I—I—like it. I'm just not used to it."

"Can I call you that?"

That and anything you fucking want if you keep looking at me like that.

"Yes."

My voice is barely a whisper. He sits beside me, takes my hand, and rests it on his thigh. It's like a wood plank. It must be solid muscle.

"Do you know what *Cosa Nostra* is?"

"The mafia."

"Yes. The Italian mafia. Antonio and his family belong to the Mancinelli family branch."

"Mancinelli? Is that like the Gambino John Gotti kind of mafia?"

"Yes. The Mancinellis are the top of their food chain. The Carusos serve them. Stasia, did you meet any of Antonio's family or any of his friends?"

I shake my head. My heart is racing, and I can feel I'm trembling again. My eyes are watering as fear consumes me. I'm not prepared for Niko to lift me onto his lap and cradle me. Why am I not trying to get off?

"*Malyshka*, shh. I'm not trying to scare you." He kisses the top of my head. "I just need you to understand what's happening. I followed you to the bar and waited outside once I knew you were there. When you left with your friends, I got on the subway car behind yours. I didn't get to you sooner because I was trailing two blocks behind you. I could see you, but I couldn't hear what Antonio said. I didn't recognize him from a distance. When you took off running, I did too."

"You must be fast. It felt like time slowed, but it couldn't have been more than a minute or two before you got here."

"I've never run so fast in my life."

I look up at him from under damp eyelashes. I didn't notice the tears falling.

"Thank you for coming to me. It should freak me out that you followed me, but I'm too grateful that you did. And I suppose, with the security around Laura's house, it shouldn't surprise me that you don't trust newcomers."

"I'm glad I did. But I regret being suspicious of you. I'm sorry."

"Have you always been this untrusting?"

He doesn't answer for a moment, and I think he won't. I'm waiting for him to change the subject.

"No. But I dated a girl once who I thought I was helping get out of a dangerous situation. She played me and nearly hurt my family."

"That sounds horrible. Why did your cousins bring you clothes? And how did Anton get the carpet cleaner so fast?"

"Sergei asked if I needed them, and I said yes. And we like to keep our cars spotless."

"Those are about the most evasive answers I've ever heard."

Niko sighs.

"When I told Sergei someone attacked you, he knew how I reacted without me saying anything. He knew I would need fresh clothes."

"Are you always violent? Is that what you mean?"

"No, I'm not violent by nature. But I've been in a lot of fights over the years. I may live in a nice place now, but we came to America with nothing. I didn't grow up in the kind of neighborhood where Maks and Laura live. That's how I know Antonio. This isn't the first time I've knocked him out."

"Do Sergei and Anton know Antonio?"

"Yes. That's why they knew how I would react. Maks, Aleks, Bogdan and I all grew up with Sergei, his brother

Misha, Anton, and his brother Pasha. It's always been the eight of us."

"It must be nice to have so many cousins. I don't have any on my dad's side, and my mom's family is in California."

"It is. It's noisy and full of testosterone, but it's great."

"Okay, so that explains the clothes. Why the carpet cleaner?"

"I told you. That's not the first fight I've been in. We didn't call the police because of who Antonio is affiliated with. You don't need the police knowing you dated a member of *Cosa Nostra*, and you don't need any evidence left behind that can implicate you."

"Why do you know so much about this? Like how to deal with—" I wave my hand toward the drying carpet. "—crime scenes."

"Because no one benefits from the police getting involved with the Mancinellis."

"Niko, why didn't you leave with your cousins?"

"Because I'm spending the night."

Chapter Five

Niko

"No, you're not."

Stasia's shaking her head, but she's not the one who's going to decide. I wish she would stop because she's wriggling in my lap. She's going to feel how hard she's making me in a moment. I need to put her back on the sofa.

"Yes, I am. I don't know who Antonio might have told that he was coming over here. I don't know if anyone else followed you or him. I don't trust your door to withstand a strong wind. And I don't want you to be alone."

"But—"

"I will sleep on the couch, Stasia. Or I can pull your armchair toward the door and sleep with my back toward you."

"You're not sleeping in a chair, Niko."

"But I am sleeping here. Stasia, please don't fight me on this. I'm not leaving."

She's staring at me, and I think she can tell she won't

dissuade me. She nods and stands up. I watch her head to the bathroom and close the door. I hear the water run and an electric toothbrush turn on. There are a couple minutes of silence before she steps out in pajama shorts and a tank top. Holy fuck. If I could go to bed and wake up every morning with her, I would die a happy man. If I can get my dick to calm the fuck down, I won't freak her out.

I watch her as she moves to a chest at the foot of her bed. She lifts the lid and pulls out fresh bedding. I move out of her way as she pulls the sofa cushions off, and I realize there's a sofa bed beneath them. I take her place and pull it out. She watches me as I make the bed before she spreads a blanket over it and puts pillowcases on two pillows.

"Do you snore?"

It's the first glimmer of humor I've seen. I shake my head.

"Do you?"

"I don't know."

"I will wake you if it gets too unbearable."

She smiles and nods her head before she looks around.

"If you were outside the bar all night, did you skip dinner? Do you want something to eat?"

I'm starving, but I'm already intruding by insisting that I stay.

"I'm all right."

"Did you eat, Niko?"

I don't want to lie when I don't have to. There are plenty of things that none of us will ever be able to tell Stasia. I don't want to deceive her about the most basic things.

"No."

"I'm making you something."

"You don't have to, Stasia. It's all right."

She steps in front of me.

"Call it my Russian babushka coming out, but I feel like I

need to feed you after all of—" She waves her hand toward the wet carpet again. "—this."

"Do you have any borscht?"

I'm teasing, so I don't expect her answer.

"No, but I have a batch of *solyanka* I made yesterday."

"That's my favorite."

"Hang on."

She walks to the kitchen, and I almost come when she leans forward to get something out of the fridge. Her shorts are hardly indecent, but they show an ample amount of her thighs, and they show an ass I could hold on to for hours. I don't even realize I'm joining her in the kitchen until I take the container from her. She smiles and reaches for a bowl. She's tall, so it's not a stretch. But her tank top pulls tight, and I can see the side of her breast. I'm usually into bigger tits, but I bet hers are spectacular. From how thin she is, I didn't expect her to look so athletic. Everything about her is tone. It's lean muscle, like she's a distance runner.

"You shouldn't have told me you have this. I might not leave any for you. It looks amazing."

"We'll see what you say once I heat it up."

"If it's as good as it looks, I'll eat it cold."

She hands me a spoon while she picks up a ladle with the other. I dip the spoon into the carrots, cabbage, potato, and onion soup. I snag a piece of ham with the spoonful.

"Hey!"

"Never tell my mother this, but this is better than hers."

I might marry this woman tonight.

"Wait."

She playfully smacks my hand away. She fills a bowl for me and pops it into the microwave. I watch her go back to the fridge. Fuck me. I should look somewhere else, but I can't. Her ass and legs looked great from a distance. Up close...Fuck me.

47

"Pickles and lemon?"

"Of course."

I'm answering, but I'm not even sure what I agree to. I watch her dice a pickle and slice off two pieces of lemon. She's done when the timer beeps. I pull the bowl out and set it on the counter. Holy hell, that's hot.

"I didn't have time to warn you. My plates and stuff heat really fast. I would have given you oven mitts or gotten it. I'm sorry."

"My mom would say that'll teach me not to be impatient."

"How old are you? I don't think you're going to learn that if you haven't already."

"I'm twenty-eight. And probably not. How old are you?"

"I turn twenty-three in three weeks."

She adds the pickles and lemon to the soup and grabs a set of oven mitts. She carries the bowl to the table before coming back to the kitchen. I watch her, trying to stay out of her way. She opens the freezer and pulls out a bottle.

"One or two fingers?"

"You really are Russian."

"You can see it's mostly full. It's here for when my parents visit. I drink a little now and then, but my dad is the vodka drinker."

"It's our water."

"That's what he says."

She laughs, and she looks so much more relaxed than thirty minutes ago. She pours me a drink, and I take the glass from her. Our fingers touch again, and this time it feels like a burst of electricity shoots through my arm and down my spine. When I held her hand before, I felt calmer. Now I just want to drag her to her bed and fuck her until the sun comes up. We're staring at each other, neither knowing what to do. I think she felt it too.

I slide my arm around her waist. She lets go of the glass,

and her hands slide up my chest to my shoulders. She's tall enough that I don't have to bend over as my lips hover next to hers.

"Stasia."

My voice sounds breathy to me, but she must like it because she lifts her chin. Then our lips are fusing together. I reach behind me until I can find the counter. I place the glass on it before I wrap my other arm around her. I back her against the side of the fridge. I'm ready to maul her. My tongue slides into her mouth as she tunnels her fingers into my hair with one hand and clings to my t-shirt with the other. I rock my hips forward, letting her know what she does to me. Her moan is my encouragement. I press against her and lift her leg to hook over my thigh. She tilts her hips toward me, and I tug on her lip.

"*Malyshka*, tell me to stop if this isn't what you want."

"I want you to keep calling me that."

Her admission surprises her. I can see it from how she sucks in a breath.

"Tell me when to stop."

"Dawn?"

"*Malyshka*, if we do this, I know I want more than one night. Is that what you want too?"

"I don't know, Niko. I can't think straight. Are you—you saying we'll hook up again?"

"I'm saying than I want more than just to fuck you. Will you let me take you out? Would you consider dating me?"

I can't stop the words from tumbling out of my mouth. I don't date. I don't even hook up that often. I mean, I'm not a monk, and I don't have to pay for sex. I go out sometimes, but I'm not Bogdan. He's the only one who used to have a girlfriend all the time. When he met Christina, it had been three years since his last serious relationship. Our lives are not conducive to them.

"Your sister-in-law is my boss. You're practically my boss. I work for your company."

I let go of her leg, but she doesn't move it.

"What do you want, baby girl?"

"This. You. Tonight. Niko, I don't know beyond that."

"Fair enough. But I know what I want, and I won't change my mind, Stasia."

"What about your soup?"

She laughs before I snare her mouth in another kiss. She arches away from the fridge. I lift her, and her legs come around my waist before I carry her to her bed.

"I know what I'm going to eat instead."

"Niko!"

She's shocked but laughs again. It's like that angel choir is back, and this time they're singing. I lower her feet to the floor before pulling up her tank top. Her tits are better than I imagined. I'm sucking on one before she even gets her shirt over her head. My hands slide beneath her shorts and cup her ass. She pushes them down until they fall to the floor. She wasn't wearing any panties. I think I'm leaking. I pick her up again, and she encircles my waist with her legs as I climb onto the bed. I'm careful not to trap her hair as I lay her back against the pillow. I'm still sucking on her tits. I might never let her go.

"Niko, touch me, please."

I hear the neediness, and it only fuels my desire to be inside her. But I am hungry, and it has nothing to do with my favorite soup. I slide down the bed before hooking her legs over my shoulders. I spread her pussy open and blow cool air. I watch her get wetter.

"What do you want, *malyshka*?"

"Anything. Everything. Niko, please."

I lick her and watch as her stomach tenses. I do it again, pressing my tongue inside her before latching onto her clit. I flick it with my tongue then suck. She fists the sheets. She's so responsive, and I know she's not faking it. Her cheeks are already flushed.

"Do you want me to make you come with my tongue?"

"Yes."

"You're delicious, *malyshka*. You might be my new favorite."

She gasps as I go back to licking and sucking her clit. I slide a finger into her, and she tries to lift her hips off the bed, but my free hand presses her belly down. She tries again, but my hand grasps her hip and holds her in place. A second finger slides in, and her increased breathing tells me she likes it. I press a third in and start working her.

"Niko, more. God, I want you."

"I'm going to taste you while you come. Then I'm going to fuck you, *malyshka*."

"Hard. Really hard."

Part of me wants to take my time, drive her wild with need. But the other part of me needs to be inside her. My thumb works her clit as I flick my tongue in and out. I feel the moment she comes. Her heels press into my back as her thighs tighten around my head.

"Condom. Bedside table."

I shift and reach past her. I pull the drawer open and snatch one. I notice there's a variety.

"I didn't buy all of those. And no, guys didn't leave them here. My friends thought it would be funny for Christmas. I'd said all I wanted was a good lay. They made sure I'm prepared."

"Did Santa bring you what you wanted?"

Why the fuck am I asking that? I don't want to know. It's bad enough that I already know she was fucking Antonio.

"No."

I climb off the bed and strip. She watches every move I make until she's staring at my cock.

"Holy shit."

I'm not sure she realizes she said that out loud. I stroke myself as I watch her. I think to tease her, but her expression changes.

"Stasia?"

She looks up at me for a heartbeat before looking back at my cock.

"I want to do that."

"Stroke me?"

"Yes."

"With just your hand?"

"No. With my pussy. Niko, I want you."

I rip the condom wrapper and push it down my dick. I climb back onto the bed and settle between her thighs. She guides me to her pussy, and I thrust. Fuck! She's so tight, I'm scared I'm going to hurt her. She tenses for a moment, then sighs.

"That feels so good, Niko."

"You're so damn tight, Stasia. I don't want to hurt you."

"You're not. I told you, I want it rough."

"Your wish is my command, *malyshka*."

"I don't want to command you."

I freeze for a moment as I look down at her. She looks vulnerable as she gazes up at me. But there's trust there too.

"Good."

I take her hands and pin them over her head with one of mine. I move, driving into her hard.

"Yes... Niko...Yes."

She tries to raise her hips to match my thrusts, but my free hand grips her hip and holds her in place.

"I'm fucking you, *malyshka*."

I feel her relax. Her hands go lax. It's not like she's given up. She's handed over control.

"Do you understand what that means?"

"No."

"You come when I say you can. If you come without my permission, I'll fuck you again, but I'll make your wait for hours before I let you get off. I decide how fast or slow we go. You follow my instructions, *malyshka*, and I will make you come all night. Do you agree?"

"Yes."

There's a wildness in her expression, as though I've set something free. It's eager and excited. I pound into her harder, and I can feel her core tightening.

"I need to come. Please."

"Please what?"

"Please, may I?"

"Please may I what?"

"Please may I come, Da—"

She freezes. Her eyes are wide with shock for a moment before she's mortified. I can guess what she was about to say. I let go of her hip and cup her jaw. I kiss the other side until I work way down her neck. I come back up until I reach her lips.

"Let me hear you say it, *malyshka*. I've never called a woman that, and no woman has ever called me that. I want to hear it."

"I've called no one that. Not in English, at least. And never a man I'm—"

"Say it, baby girl."

I kiss her jawline again. I feel her relax under me as I hold still.

"Please may I come, Daddy?"

Why the fuck does that make me want to come? It's the fucking hottest thing I've ever heard a woman say to me. I enjoy being in control. I even like it when women sometimes call me sir. But hearing Stasia call me Daddy is the most erotic thing I've ever heard. Part of me wants to think it's perverted, but I won't listen to that.

I thrust again. I use the hand that was cupping her jaw to press her bent leg back toward her. She does the same thing with the other.

"You are so fucking tight, Stasia. Are you sure I'm not hurting you?"

"You're not hurting me, Daddy. I would tell you. I promise."

Something dawns on me.

"Are you a virgin?"

She blinks a few times before she shakes her head.

"No. I've been with two other guys, but it's been a while."

I want to beat my chest and scream "mine." From the rooftops. Why does it feel even hotter that I know she hasn't been with that many guys? I'm certainly not a virgin. But neither am I the most promiscuous of the four of us brothers. Bogdan and I had a few wild nights out together in college, but I've calmed down a lot since then.

"A while?"

That finally registers with me.

"Yeah. Since before Christmas."

That was nearly seven months ago. That means not with Antonio. I stare down at her, but she looks away. I nudge her chin until she's looking at me.

"What's the matter? Why won't you look at me?"

I've stopped moving again.

"I'm probably not as experienced as most of the women you sleep with."

"I don't care if you are or aren't. You feel better than anything else I've ever done."

I didn't mean to say that out loud, but it's true. She feels amazing, and it's not just because she's practically squeezing the cum out of me. Everything about being with her, being inside her, feels as emotionally right as it does physically. That should freak me the fuck out, but it doesn't. Realizing it is actually calming.

"I don't have a lot of experience actually having sex, but I have enough experience with guys to know that no one has ever felt like you. Not while going down on me or having sex with me. Daddy, I need you to fuck me. My pussy aches so much it hurts. I—Please."

"Shh, *malyshka*. Let me make it good for you."

"You are, Daddy."

She seems less shocked every time she calls me that, and I love it more each time she does. I don't hold back. I slam into her, over and over. I feel when she comes. The moment her body relaxes, I pull out, flip her onto her belly and land three stinging slaps to her ass, before I flip her back over, and thrust into her.

But the moment I'm back where I belong, I freeze. My ears are ringing, and my heart is racing. But it's not from physical exertion.

"Oh my God, Anastasia. I'm sorry. Are you okay? I didn't ask. I'm so sorry."

"That you spanked me?"

"Yes. I didn't ask if you were okay with that. After what happened earlier. I—"

"Daddy, let go of my hands, please."

I do immediately. I'm ready to pull out, but she locks her ankles just beneath my ass. She cups my jaw with both hands.

"Nikolai, you didn't hurt me. I didn't ask if I could come. You told me you would punish me, and I liked the idea. I didn't come on purpose. I tried to hold off, but I couldn't. I like the spanking. You didn't hit me or slap me out of anger. It's not the same."

"I should have gotten your consent."

"Am I pushing you away? Daddy, I liked it. If you need to hear me give my consent, then all right. I want you to spank me. I want—"

"What, baby girl? What do you want?"

I still feel horrible.

"Are you—"

I watch her swallow.

"What, *malyshka*?"

"Are you a dom?"

"No. Have you been a sub?"

She shakes her head.

"I'm curious about some of that, but I don't want to be a sub."

"I don't want to be a dom, definitely not your dom. I don't want you as a sub either, Stasia. I told you, I want to go out with you."

This is not a conversation I've ever had during sex. My dick is still hard as a fucking pole despite holding myself still. It might actually be harder than before.

"I enjoyed being spanked. I think I'd like other things too, but I don't know."

I lower myself onto my forearms and kiss her cheek. I rock into her again. I'm not hammering her pussy like I was a couple minutes ago. This is different. This is…I don't even know. But we're watching each other. Her fingers are gliding along my back, and we're equals now. Both kinds of sex are better than anything I've ever had. I'd fall asleep inside her once we both come.

"Daddy, may I come?"

Thank God. I don't think I can last any longer.

"Yes, *malyshka.*"

She arches beneath me, and our mouths meet. I pour all these feelings swirling around in me into this kiss. I don't know half of what I'm feeling, but I'm having the best orgasm of my life with a woman I met a week ago. A woman I want to stay buried in until my last breath.

Chapter Six

Stasia

I haven't slept this well in years. Probably since before I pulled my first all-nighter in high school. I could stretch and purr like a kitten. Niko is grazing his fingers up and down my spine while his other hand rests at the top of my thigh, which is bent and resting on top of his. My head's on his chest with my arm slung around his waist. I'm so utterly content...until I remember what happened last night. All of last night.

"*Malyshka.*"

Just that one word, and I can feel my body relax. Niko rolls us, so he's now hovering over me on his forearms. He kisses me with such tenderness that I can't help but wrap my arms around him and open my legs for him to rest between.

"How do you feel this morning, *malyshka*?"

"Like I haven't slept that well in years. I can't believe after what happened last night that I slept at all."

His grin is pure temptation and sin. He snares my mouth in

another kiss, and this one is demanding and unrelenting. His left hand squeezes my breast, and I arch into him. He pulls away from my mouth and bends to suck my nipple. When his teeth tug on it, I can't help how my fingertips dig into his back. As he keeps sucking, his hand trails down to my pussy. I'm watching him. The muscles in his shoulder and arm bulge as he supports his weight on one forearm. The palm of his free hand is pressing against my clit as he dips two fingers into me.

"Were you dreaming about us?"

He shifts and settles his shoulders between my thighs before his tongue laps my pussy. I was. I must be drenched down there if he guessed.

"Yes."

"I hope it was as good as reality."

No dream could ever be as good as reality. Fuck. He's going to make me come.

"Niko, I—"

My body tenses. I'm right there. But he pulls away. His gaze darkens as his eyes meet mine. Oh. We're not done with the roleplay from last night. That makes my clit ache even more.

"*Papochka*..."

"Tell *papochka* what you need, baby girl. I'll give you whatever you want."

"I need to come, Daddy."

"Not yet, but soon."

Why is calling him Daddy so fucking hot? Why doesn't it feel as awkward as I thought it would this morning? Both languages feel natural.

I watch as he keeps eating me out. I'm fisting the sheets to keep from pressing my hips up and my pussy into his mouth. I don't want to think about how he got so talented, but thank God for whoever he practiced on. I'm getting close again.

"Daddy, I need to come."

He pushes up and hovers over my body again. When he looks at the drawer with the condoms, I nod. He grabs one and rips the wrapper open, but I take it from him. I want to touch him, even if it's only for a moment before he fucks me. I roll it down his cock, and even though it's the largest brand I have, it's still tight. He could be a porn star with this dick. I let go after I guide him to my pussy.

"Fuck, Stasia. You're so tight. I'm the one who's going to come right away."

"I want to make you come."

He thrusts into me and rocks his hips. I press my heels into the mattress and meet each thrust. Holy fuck. Now he's thrusting, rocking, and circling his hips. He keeps repeating the pattern, and I'm barely hanging on.

"I know you're still close. *Printsessa*, if you come now, I won't last. Can you keep going?"

"No, *papochka*. I'm—"

I don't get to finish my sentence as my orgasm crashes over me. I barely register the new endearment. I press my head back into the pillow as my neck arches. I'm holding his chiseled ass, and I can feel every muscle flex as he pounds into me.

"I didn't tell you, you could come, *malyshka*. Now I'm going to make you keep coming until you can't take anymore. Death by orgasm, baby girl."

His endurance seems to have rushed back into full force. This is the roughness I craved last night, and what I find I need this morning. My bed is banging against the wall as it rocks in time with our bodies. He snags my left arm and brings it over my head.

"Give me your other hand."

It's not a request. It's a command, and I'm quick to obey. He pins them over my head as his mouth devours mine. I need to come again, but I can't ask while he's kissing me. My moan is the only sound I can make to warn him I'm about have another orgasm. He growls. Growls! As he nips at my neck before whispering in my ear.

"You shouldn't have done that, baby girl. Your orgasms are mine to give when *I* want."

"You did give me an orgasm, Daddy."

I can't help the smirk. But I shouldn't have. He pulls out, and just like last night, flips me onto my belly. He spanked me more than once last night. I glance at the clock and realize that I only slept for two hours. How am I that well rested? We fucked for nearly three hours, and I'm still horny as hell.

"You have a habit of not following directions, *malyshka*. I think you love having my hand against your ass, don't you?"

"Yes, *papachka*."

He rains down five swats that make my skin burn. Then he grabs my hips and pulls me onto my hands and knees. He hasn't fucked me doggy style yet, but I'm ready when his cock enters me. I push backwards to meet each thrust. He gathers my hair into one hand and tugs. He doesn't do it hard enough to hurt, but it's enough to lift my head. His free hand goes around my throat. There's no pressure, but it feels heavy. He's in control, and I feel my entire body relax. I can't keep my eyes open. All I can think about is how good it feels to have this man in control.

"I'm too fucking close again. I want to see you when I come."

He pulls out again, and I can't help the sound of annoyance that comes out. Once he's lying on his back, he lifts me to straddle him. Not like he guides me. He lifts me off my hands and knees and brings me over him. I know I'm skinny enough to be scrawny, but he makes it look like he's lifting a feather, not a person.

I slide down his cock, and his hand returns to my throat. Beyond a few spankings, we have done nothing kinky. I lean into his hand, and it tightens.

"Do you want breath play, Stasia? You have to tell me yes or no."

"Yes."

I can't believe I'm agreeing. The idea has intrigued me, but I've never done it. I'm trusting a man I've known barely a week to strangle me but not kill me. Shit. I've never hooked up with a guy this fast. But Niko is so damn different. Maybe it's because he saved me last night. Maybe that's why I feel like I can trust him to do anything and still keep me safe. Which is dumb as fuck, considering he was here to save me because he stalked me.

But I get why he did it. After the way his cousins swooped in last night, I can tell they're a super close-knit family. His cousins dragged out my ex-boyfriend without question because that's what Niko needed. They're also all rich as sin. I can see why they're protective of each other. Even if they ran a thorough background check, which I'm sure they did, and found nothing, which I know is the case, I'm still a stranger entering his family's lives and home.

"Snap if it's too much, Stasia. Don't do more than you can."

I try to nod, but I can't move my head. I ride his cock as he tightens his grip. I can feel it getting harder to breathe until I'm holding my breath. I'm feeling lightheaded. It's happening faster than I expected. I need to snap, but my arms don't want to cooperate. Then I feel it. Holy shit. I'm coming. This is the most intense orgasm I've ever had. Niko releases my throat the moment my body tenses. I flop forward, and he wraps his arms around me as he continues to thrust into me.

"I'm still coming, Daddy."

"I know, *printsessa*. I'm coming too."

His hands grip my hips and hold them in place, pressing down onto him as his hips keep rocking. I'm spent by the time he stops moving. He strokes my head as we catch our breath. He smatters soft kisses on my forehead.

"That was the first time you've done that, wasn't it?"

"How'd you know?"

I feel a moment of panic. I'm nowhere near as experienced as Niko is. Did I do it wrong?

"I saw the surprise on your face when you started to come. You put a lot of trust in me, *malyshka*. I don't take that lightly."

I can only nod my head. I don't know what to say. But I squeak when he sits up and swings his legs over the side of the bed. I cling to him as he stands. I live in a studio. There aren't too many places he can take me. He carries me to the bathroom while I'm wrapped around him like a koala. He finally puts me on my feet after he turns on the shower. I point to the trash can where he drops the condom. The water is warm almost immediately, so we step in.

I've never showered with a guy before. It's the most erotic thing I've ever imagined. We keep kissing as he lathers shampoo into my hair. I feel lightheaded again, but it's from feeling so relaxed and trying to keep my legs from folding underneath me.

"I could fall asleep right now."

I don't realize what I'm muttering until after I say it as he guides me under the showerhead to rinse my hair.

"I would spend all day in bed with you, *malyshka*, but we both have to go to work."

That's like a bucket of icy water over my head, despite how warm the shower is. Holy fuck. I have to face my boss today knowing I slept with her brother-in-law. My other boss, her husband, is the brother of the man I've been fucking for nearly the last five hours straight. What was I thinking?

I was thinking he's the hottest man I've ever seen. He wants to have sex with me. *Me.* And everything about it felt right last night. And if I'm going to be honest with myself, it felt hella right just now. But remembering my job is taking the edge off of the enjoyment.

"I need to hurry, too. I wasn't thinking about work when I noticed the clock."

"What time does Laura expect you?"

Shit, shit, shit. I thought that would be enough for him to take a cue and hurry, too. I have plenty of time.

"Eight. But I'm still getting used to taking the subway in Queens. I'm used to riding into Manhattan. I know it's a shorter ride, but I'm not sure how much shorter. I need to pack my lunch and everything."

"Would you let me take you out to lunch? And I can drive you there."

"I thought you took the subway last night. Do you live near here?"

"No. I live in Manhattan, but I can have a driver take us."

I just stand and blink. The last time I rode in anything with a driver was a limo to prom five years ago.

"Niko, I don't think it's a good idea for me to show up to work with you. It's only my second week."

"Do you want me to drop you at the end of the block?"

His grin is irrepressible and makes me want to smile too. But this is serious.

"That might be a good idea."

Now he's scowling. He doesn't agree.

"Or I could say I saw you walking from the subway and offered to drive you the last few minutes."

"I—I don't know, Niko."

"Do you regret this?"

"No."

I blurt that answer. It's the easiest thought I have. I don't regret it, but it'll embarrass me when Laura and Maksim find out.

"Let me drive you, *malyshka*. I'll answer to Laura and Maks if I need to."

"Fine."

"Do you drink coffee?"

"Yes."

That's not what I expected him to say next.

"How do you take it?"

"Three creams, three sugars."

"All right. Let's finish and then get dressed."

The rest of the shower is quick. I offer him a fresh toothbrush that I have because I bought a twin pack the day before yesterday. I know he's watching me as I pick out my clothes. He puts the jeans and t-shirt back on. He looks so good, even when he's casual. I feel frumpy in my trousers and short-sleeved blouse. I slip on my usual flat shoes since I'll be walking to and from the subway on the way home.

"The car is here, *malyshka*."

"It is?"

I look toward the kitchen. I haven't made lunch. Neither of us has made coffee. I don't want to keep Niko and his driver waiting. Sigh. I guess I'll be looking for a deli or something near work for lunch. I grab my purse and follow Niko out the door.

"My landlord is going to have a fit when he sees the door."

"It'll get fixed within an hour."

"What? How?"

"Anton texted me and said one of our guys will be over once we leave. I told him we were on the way out ten minutes ago."

"When did you text him?"

I didn't see him touch a phone. But then again, his driver knew to be here.

"While you folded up the sofa bed."

I nod as I look at the man standing beside the open backdoor. The town car is the most polished vehicle I've ever seen in New York. I guess what he said last night about liking to keep their cars clean is true. I slide in and immediately smell coffee. There's a to-go cup in the cup holder. I inch around the armrest and sit.

"That one's yours."

"How do you know?"

"Because I would never get in the car before you."

"How does your driver know that?"

"He's Russian."

I furrow my brow. What does being Russian have to do with anything?

"*Malyshka*, ladies first was ingrained in all of us since we were children."

There's something else that he's not saying. But I don't know what. I just sense it. I don't have time to ask because he opens a paper bag that I hadn't noticed. There're four different pastries in it. I snag a chocolate filled croissant.

"These are my favorite."

"Mine, too."

"I'll split it. I didn't realize."

"I also like the Danish. Eat your *petit pain au chocolat*."

I watch him as he pulls out a lemon Danish. He doesn't take a bite. I realize he's waiting for me. How old-fashioned is he? The moment I take the first bite, he takes one too. We eat in silence. He convinces me to have a second one. I snag a cruller.

"I've liked the spiral donuts since I was a kid. I always wondered how they were made until I went home with a friend to Minnesota over Thanksgiving my sophomore year of college.

Her grandma made them. The novelty wore off once I realized they weren't that difficult. But I don't love them any less."

I feel my nervousness creeping up my spine as we arrive at the gate to Laura and Maksim's house. The driver opens the door on my side, and Niko opens his own.

"Thank you."

When we get to the front door, Niko punches in a code and opens it for me. I'm certain my face is on fire. Every guy patrolling the driveway and front of the house saw me get out of the car with Niko at seven-forty-five in the morning. I hear voices, but I don't know my way around, so I'm not sure where Laura and Maksim are. Niko leads me into the kitchen, where I spot the couple having breakfast.

"Oh, my goodness!"

Laura practically jumps out of her chair and rushes to me.

"Are you all right?"

"Yes."

I'm uncertain why she's asking. Is it because I arrived with Niko? Am I being paranoid?

"Good morning, Ms. Antonov. Niko, I'll meet you in an hour."

Maksim nods to me as he greets me, then he comes to stand beside Laura. The kiss they share is practically rated R. I don't know where to look, especially when he pats her on the backside.

"Maks."

Laura hisses, and I can tell she's mortified. He whispers something in her ear that makes her grin. I feel like an intruder.

"I'm going to grab one of your suits."

Niko turns to head out of the kitchen with Maksim.

"You already took one of mine yesterday, little brother."

"And you took mine three days ago. I expect that dry-cleaned, old man."

I watch the brothers banter. There's neither anything little about Niko, nor is there anything old about Maksim. But it's funny, and I wish I had siblings to joke with like that.

"You didn't tell me if you're all right, Anastasia."

I look back at Laura, and I see the concern.

"Uh, Niko and I were headed in the same direction, so—"

"I know he stayed with you last night. If he hadn't volunteered, I would have insisted."

"You know?"

"Of course. Sometimes it's a pain in the ass that everyone knows everyone's business in this family. But it's almost always for the best. Anton and Sergei called Maks, and he put them on speakerphone."

They really do know each other's business. For an only child, this feels like a lot.

"They really—helped."

She looks like she wants to say more, but we hear Niko coming back into the kitchen. The man dresses faster than anyone I know.

"Do you have those papers Maks was leaving for me?"

"Yes. They're over here."

Laura grabs a manila folder from the table and hands it to Niko. He doesn't open it, but he looks at Laura, then me. I suddenly have a burning question that I should have asked last night.

"What did Anton and Sergei do with Antonio?"

"Made sure he understands he can't bother you anymore."

Niko is too quick to answer. His tone is too absolute.

"He said he's *Cosa Nostra*, and you agreed. That's the Italian mafia. Won't they do something to you once they see how you beat him up? Are you in danger now?"

Each word that comes out of my mouth makes me feel more panicked. I look at Laura, and she's as cool as a cucumber. How is that possible? Her brother-in-law beat the shit out of a mafia guy. Niko only shrugs before answering.

"No."

"That's it? No? He's mafia."

"There aren't any cement shoes in my future, Stasia."

"What about me? He's my ex-boyfriend who you beat up over me. What about when he heals and is even more pissed?"

"He will not come near you."

"How can you be so sure?"

"Because I am. I asked you to trust me last night. I'm asking you again. It's been taken care of."

Taken care of? What the fuck does that mean?

"He isn't the type to forgive and forget, Niko. I live alone."

"And you'll have someone watch your house around the clock. I'm assigning you a bodyguard. But I don't think you'll need any of it. It's just a precaution."

"Assigning me? No." I turn to Laura. "Tell Niko that's unnecessary. This is ridiculous."

"Anastasia, he accosted you in the street and broke into your place. Niko's right. It's guards or stay with friends."

"No."

Niko's tone is emphatic. This is not how I imagined my second day of my second week at work. This doesn't even feel like work. It feels like I'm a child, and my parents are setting the rules.

"Why not?"

And I sound like a petulant child.

"Because being with friends might complicate things, but it won't stop someone who's determined. But I'm telling you, Stasia, this is only a precaution. I'm certain this is over with. Neither Antonio nor anyone else will do anything."

"Being rich doesn't mean you can stop the mafia."

Everything about Niko's expression and how he now has

his arms crossed says he can stop them. The only people I can think of who could stop the mafia is the mafia. No! No! No! No!

"Are you...?"

I spin around to Laura, and her expression is grim. I look back at Niko, and I know he understood what I couldn't say. Is this whole family mobsters? Did I fucking sleep with a mobster?

"Anastasia, please trust that Niko is telling the truth. You're safe, but *I* would feel better knowing that you have a guard. I'm the one who suggested it."

"When? Niko, how many texts did you answer in the two minutes it took me to fold up the sofa bed?"

"Laura may have suggested it to Maks, but I decided last night."

"Last night? I—"

I'm tempted to say I quit. But if I hadn't met Niko through work, he wouldn't have followed me. Antonio still would have showed up, but there wouldn't have been anyone there to stop him. Niko reaches out his hand. I stare at it.

"Let's go talk, Stasia."

I hesitate, but then I take his hand. What the hell is there to talk about now?

Chapter Seven

Niko

She's ready to bolt. She's going to quit, and then what am I supposed to do? How the hell do I explain any of this while telling her nothing?

I lead her out of the kitchen to the back patio. There are men patrolling the backyard, but they can't hear us from a distance. I lace my fingers with hers and tug her forward until I can wrap my arm around her waist. Her gaze darts around, nervous that the men will see us. They know she works for Laura. If they didn't, she wouldn't have been allowed onto the property last week when she arrived. It looks questionable that I'm holding her against me, but none of them would know how and why she got hired.

"Stasia, whatever you think you know, is a guess. This is a lot for your second week of work, and after only knowing me for that long. Way more has happened than anyone could call normal. I get that. But if I hadn't been there, he would have hurt you. I'm not trying to scare you or control you with a safety detail. I truly don't think anyone will come near you, but I would feel better knowing someone is there if I can't be."

"If you can't be? Niko, what happened, happened. You make this sound as though you're my boyfriend. I know you said that to Antonio, but it was just to intimidate him."

"Can you not see yourself with me? I can see us together clear as day. I don't think you're the type for one-night stands or fucking a guy the night you meet, Stasia. I'm past those days and have been since college."

"I don't do one-night stands or sleep with guys I just met. Until last night, I hadn't—"

She snaps her mouth shut. She closes her eyes and turns her head away. She hesitates when I lead her back inside, but this time it's into a sunroom with the shades drawn. I back her against a wall and pin the hand I'm holding above her head, then do the same with the second. My other hand cups her jaw.

"Until last night, what, Stasia?"

"Nothing."

"Don't lie to me again. You lied last night, didn't you?"

"I was too embarrassed to tell you the truth."

"Why would you be embarrassed to tell me you were a virgin? I was way too rough with you. I shouldn't have taken advantage of you. That is not how your first time should have been."

"You were not too rough. It was what I wanted. You did not take advantage of me. I knew exactly what was happening, and I wanted it. As for how my first time should or shouldn't have been, that was my decision."

"Why last night? Why me?"

"I don't know. Not putting out made Antonio mad the first time."

I still. My heart was pounding from our nearness, but now it's racing.

"Did he try to force you?"

"No, but he was angry when I kept turning him down. He said I was a cock tease not to have sex with him after three months together. He knew from the beginning that I was a virgin. When he pressured me, I broke up with him."

"You said he'd slapped you and pushed you. Did he do anything else, Stasia? Tell me the truth."

"He didn't. I'm telling you the truth. We were outside his place, and someone saw him. The woman threatened to call the police, and I got away. He's texted and called, but I didn't answer, then I blocked him."

"I saw the bruise this morning. You fell hard against the table last night."

"Yeah. I saw it in the mirror."

"*Malyshka*, what made you decide to go through it last night? Why me?"

"Because it's the only time it's ever felt that right."

She whispers her answer.

"What do you mean?"

I need to know. I'm certain about how I felt last night and this morning. There's something about Stasia that's already under my skin. Never have I been so drawn to a woman.

"I don't have a sound reason. I know that. But it felt right. It wasn't adrenaline. I didn't feel indebted. I didn't feel pressured. Everything about the way I felt when you held me made me want to finally have sex without any doubts. It's not like I was a nun. I've done everything but have sex, but something always held me back. I've had boyfriends, but I never felt the same need as I did last night. It's not like I expected the heavens to open up and angels to appear when I met the right guy. I wanted my first time to be special, to be with someone who I was so into, I couldn't bear turning him away. That it was you is a surprise, but I don't regret any of it."

I press a kiss to her lips, and she opens for me. I try to be gentle. Every time I am, it feels like such a contradiction. I'm not gentle during most things. I'm not gentle during sex. I'm not gentle with the men I deal with. But Stasia is so—I don't know. She's not frail or weak despite how thin she is. But she's precious, like a treasure I want to make sure I don't break or spoil.

I reach over and push the door closed. If there were a lock, I'd turn it. But next to no one uses this room. It's why I brought her here. I continue to kiss her as I unbutton her pants and slide my hand beneath her panties. Her hips tilt forward, meeting my fingers and inviting me in. I press two into her pussy and find she's as wet as I am hard. She yanks her hands, and I release them. She's unbuttoning my trousers and sliding down the zipper. I'm wearing boxers, and my dick is practically shoving its way through the opening. As I work her pussy, she strokes me. I'm going to fucking come and have yet another of Maks's suit that needs cleaning. How the fuck am I supposed to see Laura with cum all over me? I seize her wrist and pull away from our kiss.

"I want to enjoy making you come, *malyshka*. No distractions."

"And if I want to make you come, *papachka*?"

"Maybe later."

"But—"

"Who decides?"

"You, *papachka*."

"Good girl. Now let me finger fuck you until you're struggling not to scream."

That's exactly what I do. I thrust my fingers into her pussy over and over while my thumb works her clit. She's kissing my cheek, then my neck, before she latches onto my earlobe and sucks. Holy fucking shit. I'm going to come, anyway. I fight against the desire to pull her pants down and fuck her.

"Daddy, I need more. I want you to fuck me again."

We're pushing our luck, but I don't want to deny her. I reach back to my wallet and pull it out. I have a condom in there that I pray isn't expired. I don't even remember when I put it in there. I shove my wallet back in my pocket before I rip the wrapper and shove that into my pocket, too. I pull down my boxers, then roll down the condom.

"Turn around, *malyshka*. I want to see that fine ass of yours while I fuck you."

"It's too bony."

I spin her around and land three hard spanks.

"Do not insult yourself. I said I want to see your fine ass. Believe me, it's perfect."

I pull her hips back and thrust into her. I'm back to not being gentle. Her hands rest against the wall. I'm careful not to slam her into it.

"Stasia, tell me if it's too much after last night and this morning. I'll be upset if you let me hurt you."

"It feels amazing. I told you, I want it rough."

"We'll see how you feel in a few hours."

"Are you going to fuck me again then?"

I growl next to her ear.

"I'm going to fuck you until you can't see straight, *malyshka*. Your pussy and orgasms are mine."

"Good, *papachka*."

That only makes me ram my dick into her harder. Her fingers bend as she fights not coming.

"Ask."

"Please may I come, *papachka*?"

"Yes, *malyshka*."

Fuck. Her cunt is fucking squeezing the cum out of me. I

can't hold back. I press my hips into her and feel my cock shooting my load into the condom. Fuck. How does coming inside her keep getting better?"

"Thank you, Daddy."

"Thank you, baby girl."

I pull out and only now think about what I'm going to do with a spent condom. I'm not throwing it away in my brother's house. I shouldn't have been fucking anyone here. I knot it and put it in my pocket. Gross, but it'll have to do. Once we have our clothes back in place, Stasia turns back to face me. She looks at me, and I try to guess what she's thinking. I know the moment her post-orgasm calm ends.

"Niko, I need the truth from you. What have I gotten into working for your family and spending the night with you? Are you mafia too? Do you work for the Italians?"

I chuckle, but it's not humorous. So much for cuddling. Right back to business.

"I definitely do not work for the Italians. What do you know about the neighborhood your dad grew up in?"

"Not much. He had little as a kid, but most people didn't during communism. It was a rough neighborhood with crime. He was in the military before he went to college and met my mom."

"He was in the army?"

That surprises me. That's not what usually happens with men from that neighborhood.

"I think so. I know he worked for the government for several years. He's ten years older than my mom."

"Do you know what his job was in the army?"

"No. He won't talk about it."

"Does he have any tattoos?"

"Yes. One of them is a lot like yours."

My stomach knots. All of my tattoos are bratva. They signify ranks and initiations.

"The star you have. He has the same eight-point one."

"Is it on his chest, too?"

"Yeah. What does it mean?"

"Strength, leadership."

That's only sort of the explanation. It means someone with a high rank. I got mine when I became a member of the Elite Group. I suspect Stasia's father wasn't in the army.

"Did he go into the army right after he finished secondary school?"

"Yes. Some type of academy."

KGB. Just like my father was.

"Why are you asking me all of this? What does it mean?"

"I just wondered since a lot of men from your dad's neighborhood get them. He grew up near where I was born. My neighborhood was like his."

"What aren't you telling me, Niko? You want me to tell the truth, but you're being evasive now. Why did you ask about where he grew up in the first place?"

"Like you said, it was a rough neighborhood. I just wondered if we had more than that in common."

"You said you don't work for the Italians, but you know Antonio. You're certain none of the *Cosa Nostra* will bother me. You don't seem worried about anyone coming after you once they find out what you did. Who isn't afraid of the mafia? The only people I can think of are cops and other mafia members. I know you're not a cop. Niko, is there a Russian mafia?"

I don't want to lie. I don't want to tell the truth. She already asked once. Obviously, I'm not answering fast enough because she's pushing against my chest. I step back. I don't want to crowd her if she doesn't want me close. It hurts to feel the rejection. But what can I expect?

"Your silence tells me everything. You may as well have screamed it."

She steps away from the wall and looks around until she realizes how close we are to the door. She hurries to it, then down the hall until she gets to the kitchen. My sister-in-law is holding the twins while she sits at the table. Stasia dropped her purse onto a chair before she followed me outside. She grabs it and looks at Laura.

"Thank you for this opportunity, but I can't work for you. I—This isn't the right job for me."

She turns back and slams into my chest. I catch her, but she jerks away.

"Don't."

Her response is a hiss as she bats away my arm since my hands went to her waist to steady her.

"Anastasia, wait. Niko, what did you say to Anastasia?"

"Not enough and entirely too much. I know what your family is, and I want no part of it. I don't want to ruin my chances of getting into law school by doing stuff that's illegal. How can you, Laura? You could get disbarred."

"Nothing I handle—which means nothing you would handle—is illegal. Kutsenko Partners own many businesses, including bars, nightclubs, casinos, construction companies, and pharmaceutical companies. They are all legitimate and require an attorney. I do nothing that could get me disbarred."

"Are you serious? Your husband is—is—"

She huffs, and I can tell she doesn't want to say it out loud. I know that makes it too real for her.

"I wouldn't hire anyone if I thought I was endangering them or their career, Anastasia."

"Being in your house—I'm sorry, but I can't."

"Stasia, now that you know—"

"Are you going to kill me?"

I glance at Laura, who is trying not to laugh. I find nothing amusing about this. I hate that stereotype, even if there's plenty of truth. I take Stasia's hand and practically drag her back to the sunroom.

"I get why you asked me that. But that you actually did, hurts. I protected you last night, and I want men with you who can protect you."

"Yeah, but not because of Antonio. It's about me working for your company and about me fucking you. You don't want me to tell anyone."

"I trust you."

"And I don't trust you. Not anymore."

"What have I done to make you think I would hurt you? I told you I'm not trying to control you with a safety detail. I want to make sure no one like Antonio can ever come near you again."

"Which is way more likely to happen if I'm working for the mafia's rival. You're like him."

"Anastasia—"

"Don't do that."

Her brow furrows, and she whispers now when she was speaking in a normal tone a moment ago.

"Don't do what?"

"Don't call me that."

"It's your name."

"And it sounds like you're scolding me. It sounds distant. I..."

"Don't like it. I'm not scolding you, *malyshka*. I just want you to know I'm serious."

She swallows, and I can tell she's willing herself not to cry.

"Don't call me baby girl, either. I'm not."

"We both know you are. I have never told a single soul what my family and I are. I have never let anyone figure it out. Some have hinted. But I have never let anyone know for sure."

"Why me?"

"Because something makes me trust you in a way that I don't trust anyone else. It all changed last night, and you know there's something here. Why else would you have slept with me last night? You've waited all these years, and you picked me."

"That was before I knew."

"Was it really? I think you had your suspicions before you even made me a bowl of soup."

"No, I didn't. At least not mafia."

"Bratva."

"What?"

"The Russians are bratva. The Italians are *Cosa Nostra*. The Colombians are Cartel. And the Irish—well—they're the mob. They're not so original."

"Niko, can't you get why this is too much?"

"Of course, I can. That's why we don't exactly proclaim it to everyone."

"I assumed that was so you don't get arrested."

"Exactly. I trust you, *malyshka*. You know a secret that could destroy my entire family, not just me."

"And I'm supposed to keep it."

"You know Antonio was *Cosa Nostra*."

Her eyes widen, and her nose flares.

"Was?"

Shit.

"Is. I just meant that you found that out yesterday."

Technically, it's still "is."

"And I didn't sleep with him. I didn't know until after."

"You dated for three months. Didn't you hang out with any of his friends? Meet any of his family?"

"No. He said he wanted to focus all of his attention on me when we were together."

"You didn't think that was at all odd?"

"I thought it was flattering."

She sounds so defeated, and it breaks my heart. I cup her jaw, and she lets me. She doesn't pull away when I kiss her forehead.

"Niko, I still can't. I will always keep your secret. You've only been kind to me. But I'm sorry. I just can't."

She kisses my cheek, then walks to the door. She looks at me before leaving the sunroom. I follow her, but neither of us speaks. I glance at Laura before I watch her walk out the door. I haven't felt this kind of loss since I was eleven, and my dad died. It's like my heart is withering. I barely know her, and yet I feel like my entire future is evaporating.

"Niko?"

"She isn't coming back."

"I'm sorry. I never imagined she would find out so soon. I hoped she never would, or at least not before she knew she could trust all of us."

"I need to talk to Sergei. Her father was KGB."

"What? Did she say so?"

"No. But I'm sure of it."

"Did you tell her?"

"No. And I'm certain he was Podolskaya bratva, too."

"How do you know?"

"The neighborhood he grew up in. It was like ours. He couldn't have escaped it. She said he has a star like all of us. He had a high rank. How did Sergei not find all of this?"

I pull out my phone and dial my cousin. He's the head of our intelligence gathering and is an expert hacker. It shocks me he didn't know this. If he did, I would know. We would all know. This type of information isn't a secret for anyone to keep.

Who knows what would happen if—no, what *will* happen *when* she tells her dad that she worked for us for a week?

"*Privet*."

Sergei answers me in Russian, and I continue in it. Laura's been fluent since before she met our family. She sounds like a native despite not learning the language until college.

"Did Anastasia's background check show that her father was KGB and Podolskaya?"

"No. How do you know?"

"She thinks her dad was in the Russian army. She thinks he joined right after high school. But he has our star tattoo. He's bratva. Maybe he was army, but I doubt it."

"You know it's almost impossible to find out who was KGB. They still have those records locked away. I hacked the FBI and the DOJ to do her background check, since she's half Russian. There wasn't even a hint. Antonov is a common last name, too. I hacked her parents' employment records."

"You need to find out. She just quit. If she tells her father about us..."

I don't need to finish my thought. We all know that a shitstorm is brewing if he finds out. This is why we don't bring anyone in from the outside. Either you're bratva or you're not. Laura and Christina are the only exception. There's nothing left to be said, so I hang up with Sergei.

"I'm headed to the warehouse. Antonio still needs dealing with."

Laura nods and sighs. She doesn't know where the warehouse is, but she knows what it is. When I get there, I slip surgical booties over my shoes before taking off my watch and belt. I'll leave them in the office with my cell phone that I turned off in the car. Maks and Bogdan are already here. This will not go over well.

"She knows we're bratva."

"What?"

Maks spins around from the two-way mirrored window. We can see out, but our guests can't see in. They strung Antonio up like a side of beef. It looks like they have done nothing to him but strip him. I mangled his face last night.

"She figured it out. She got suspicious and nervous when I told her she's safe from *Cosa Nostra*. She wanted to know why. I tried to be evasive, but she's as intelligent as Laura and Christina."

"It's both a joy and a pain in the ass that our wives are so smart."

Bogdan grins at Maks. Aleks and I are perpetually single. But Bogdan and Maks fell in love with their wives almost instantly. I enjoy having sisters-in-law. They're both awesome, and they make my brothers happy. Last night, I thought maybe Stasia was going to be my *the one*. I should have known it was ridiculous. All it's done is blow up in my face.

"It gets worse. I'm almost certain her father was KGB and Podolskaya. He grew up in Serpukhovsky."

"Sergei mentioned that in his report, but there was nothing to show he was bratva."

"Maks, how could he not be? There are like ten men in that neighborhood who probably aren't. Besides, she said he has the same star on his chest that we do. She quit."

"Where is she now?"

"Anton said she headed home on the subway. He followed her, and Stefan met him there."

"Do you think she'll tell the police?"

Bogdan's humor from a moment ago has completely evaporated. Maksim was never smiling.

"No. I'm positive she won't. But I think she's going to tell her dad. Why wouldn't she? She's going to have questions."

"If she is going to call, she probably already has if she's

home. Give her a few hours, then go see her."

"And force my way in like Antonio did, Maks?"

"Of course not. Check on her and tell her as much. I saw how you looked at her this morning."

"What's that supposed to mean?"

"That I know you did more than just keep her company last night, and that she's more than just a quick lay. No one outside our family can read us like we can each other. Laura sees more with me, and Christina more with Bogdan. But we can't hide from each other what we do the rest of the world. Don't deny what I already know, Niko."

"There is something about her. But I don't know that it's like you and Laura or you and Christina."

I look at each of my brothers. I thought I would never meet a couple more in tune with one another than Maks and Laura, but Bogdan and Christina are the same. It reminds me of my parents before my dad died.

"I've known her for a week."

"So? Not so different from Tina and me."

"Or Laura and me."

"True. Fine. Let's deal with this shitbag, then I'll go see her."

I go out to the main area and pick up the iron pipe laying on a table. I swing it like the baseball bat I used to swing while on my high school team. It cracks against Antonio's right ribs, and he howls as he comes around.

"What made you think you could touch Anastasia like that?"

"Fuck you."

"No, but I did fuck her."

He isn't leaving this warehouse alive, so I'm not worried about him telling anyone else. I have a pang of guilt for talking about her like that. It was more than just a fuck.

"No, you didn't. Her pussy's locked up like Fort Knox."

"And there's a key to every lock. My dick was it. What made you think you could touch her?"

"I decide when I'm done with a woman."

"You aren't deciding anything ever again. Now it's my turn. I'm going to decide how to torture you, then I'll decide how to kill you."

"And while you're here, who's watching the bitch? Salvatore knows where I went last night."

"Does he know you intended to rape her? He's old school. He'll kill you himself. But I get to have that fun."

Salvatore Mancinelli is the don in New York City. He's as brutal as any of us, but he draws the limit at hurting women. They're to be respected and protected in his book. He would kill Antonio if he knew what he tried to do. What he did do.

"You really want to start a war over that skinny, tight-assed bitch?"

"A war implies both sides fight. I'm going to give you misery unlike anything you can imagine. Then I will toss you in that vat of acid alive."

The next two hours pass in a blur. I follow through on all my threats. Antonio is unrecognizable by the time I'm done. Even his own mother wouldn't know it's him. I'm in the office, stripping down, when Sergei arrives. I look over my shoulder as I get into the shower. We never leave the warehouse until we've scrubbed every part of us, and we always wear fresh clothes. We will incinerate the suit I wore before I leave the property. The ash will dissolve in the river.

"Niko, she's on ninety-five headed south."

"What? She's going home. Fuck."

I thought she'd call. I never imagined she'd go see her parents. I'm so screwed.

Chapter Eight

Stasia

I need to see my dad. There's more than what Niko told me. When I told him where my dad grew up, something changed. Nothing about his expression gave it away, but it's like there was a pulsing high voltage in the air. My dad doesn't talk much about his life in Russia. I get why. Other than when he was in university in America, it was rough. He grew up poor, and I can't imagine anything about the Russian military is enjoyable. I used to ask him to tell me stories when I was little, but he would only tell the same ones about meeting my mom.

I can't imagine having this conversation over the phone or via text. I want to look him in the eye and know if what I've thought all my life was a lie. Was he not in the military? Niko didn't say it, but I feel like there is way more to my dad's past than what I've been told. I'm feeling more anxious with every mile. I'm dreading hearing my dad's answer, but I need it. It's going to frustrate me because it'll be lies, or it'll devastate me because he'll be what I'm sure Niko is.

Maybe the movies exaggerate what the mafia does to people. But every stereotype has at least an ounce of truth at the beginning. Everything I know about Russia makes me think that how the Kutsenkos handle things is violent and final. I don't want to imagine Niko hurting people any worse than what I saw him do to Antonio last night. I know he only stopped because I was there.

Damn. I need to get gas already. I'm barely in Delaware. I need to stop now, and I suppose I could grab a snack, too. I got home, threw some clothes in a bag, and took off. I didn't think about lunch.

"Ms. Antonov."

I spin around as I lock the pump into place. It's the dark-haired man from last night. Which cousin was he?

"Why are you here?"

"I followed you."

When I back up toward my door, the man puts his hands in the air.

"I won't come any closer, Ms. Antonov. Niko will kill me if I scare you any more than I already am. The only reason I came over rather than keeping my distance is because your rear right tire is getting low. I'll fill it, then I'll leave you alone."

"Leave me alone? Does that mean you stop following me?"

The look he gives me is answer enough.

"I didn't agree to a security detail, and I definitely didn't agree to being followed."

"I know."

"But here you are."

"Ms. Antonov, I think the same thing Niko does. I don't think you're in danger from anyone Antonio knows. But I do think it's worth the precaution in case we're wrong."

"I think Niko doesn't trust me not to tell."

The man's brow furrows before understanding dawns. He didn't know I'm aware of who—or rather what—they're family is.

"I believe Niko trusts you a great deal. For his sake, I hope it isn't misplaced."

"Or what? You whack me?"

I keep my voice low for the second question as I look around. I want to be sure no one hears me, but I also want to know if there's anyone to stop this guy.

"None of us harm women. And I definitely wouldn't hurt someone important to Niko."

How the hell am I important to a guy I met last week unless it's to keep me silent?

"Which cousin are you?"

"I'm Anton."

"Popular name."

"My first name and your last name are quite common. I think it's rather funny that they're so similar. It's odd to say it."

This man could charm the panties off most women, even when he's not smiling. But right now, when he is—holy hell. He's just as hot as Niko, but there's no appeal. I can appreciate his good looks, but I feel none of the excitement, as I do with Niko. It's not that I fear him. I'm surprisingly at ease, which makes me feel like a fool. But I don't get the same sensation, like I'm a magnet being pulled toward another. Fitting analogy since my life and Niko's couldn't be more opposite.

"Will you let me fill your tire?"

My pump just clicked off. I look at it, then at Anton before I nod. I put the nozzle back on the pump and get in my car. I pull around to the air station and keep my doors locked. I hear Anton moving around before he comes back to stand a few feet from my window. I only open it a quarter of the way.

"You can stop following me."

I know it's futile. He only shakes his head. I wind my window back up and pull out of the gas station. I still have a couple hours ahead of me, but I'm banking on him not knowing his way around. I get off interstate ninety-five and hop onto six-ninety-five. It's not that congested, but I drive like I'm from Maryland. I weave and speed. I usually use my turn signals, but I don't want to give Anton any hints. I watch my rearview mirror and see him falling farther behind with every lane change. When I get to my exit, I can't see a black town car anywhere.

I pull into my parents' driveway and park in the same spot as I did in college. My little compact car sits off to the left. I haven't been home since Christmas, and I didn't tell them I'm coming. I know they're both at work right now, so I let myself into the house. Huge sigh. This doesn't exactly feel like home anymore, but it's still comforting. Since I didn't grab a snack at the rest stop, I raid the fridge. I'm ready to sit down with my salad and sandwich when the doorbell rings.

Please no. No. No. No. Fuck me. It is.

"Niko, you shouldn't have come."

"And you shouldn't have bolted."

"You shouldn't have your cousin following me."

"And you shouldn't have bolted."

"You're repeating yourself."

"It bears saying twice. Do you want to have this conversation on your front stoop?"

"I don't want to let you in."

He looks genuinely hurt before he masks his emotions. It makes me reconsider. My shoulders droop, and I step back. When he walks in, I sense he's taking in every single detail at once. I bet if I blindfolded him right this minute, he could describe the entire foyer and living room. He pushes the door closed behind him and watches me. I think he wants to touch me, hug me, but he's uncertain.

"Why did you follow me if Anton already was?"

"Because Anton isn't the one who scared you. He isn't the one who—Stasia?"

"I told you I can't do this."

"And you ran to your parents as soon as you could. You went home, grabbed your stuff, and took off."

"How do you know?"

He only arches a brow and crosses his arms.

"Anton followed me home. How did he get a car so fast?"

"He did. It was easy for him to have one of our drivers bring one."

"Why him?"

"Because I couldn't get to you fast enough. I had to leave a meeting before my other cousin could tell me. I took off from there."

I lean to see out of the window and notice a Porsche parked behind the black town car. So much for losing Anton. He must have my address. Why wouldn't he? They're the fucking mafia.

"Niko, there's nothing to talk about. I—"

He crosses the living room and picks up a photograph. His face goes ash white. He carries it with him as he opens the front door and waves to Anton. His cousin rushes to the door. He doesn't say a word as he hands the framed photograph to his cousin. Anton has the same reaction.

"Is this your father?"

"Yes. Why?"

"Do you know who these men are? Do you know why he has this photo out?"

"They were army buddies of his. He said they were his best friends. They're the only thing from Russia he misses. Why?"

I watch Niko swallow. I swear there are tears in his eyes. He points to a man in the middle, next to my dad.

"This was Kirill Kutsenko, my dad. This is Anton's dad, Grigori. This is Sergei's dad, Radomir. This had to have been taken a couple months before my dad died. It's in—"

He can't finish. He's still white as a sheet, and his hand is trembling. Anton is staring at Niko, who's still staring at the photo.

"Niko?"

My voice is barely a whisper.

"I'm sorry. I haven't seen a photo of my father that doesn't belong to our family since I was twelve. I wasn't ready for it."

Anton says something in Russian that I can't make out and takes the frame from Niko. I never imagined he could appear so rattled. He'd stood up from beating the shit out of Antonio and didn't have a hair out of place. He barely showed any emotion this morning, except for a couple quick flashes in his eyes before the mask fell back into place. The way Anton is watching him, I can tell this is not normal for Niko.

"Niko, why don't you sit down? Do either of you want something to drink?"

Niko only nods. Anton does nothing. I go into the kitchen and think about getting him a glass of water, but I decide to open the freezer. I pull out the vodka and grab two glasses. When I get back to the living room, I pour one for Niko and one for Anton. They both down the full glasses as though they're shots. Neither seems to find it any stronger than water. I would be ready to hurl.

"When does your dad get home, Stasia?"

"Not until five."

"I think you better call him and ask him to come home sooner."

Niko is staring at the picture that's now sitting on the coffee table.

"What's going on?"

"Your dad wasn't in the army. They took that photo in Chechnya during the Second Chechen War."

"Of course he was in the army. Look at his clothes, and he's carrying a rifle."

"Stasia, my father was never in the army. Neither were either of my uncles. You need to call your dad right now."

"I can't disrupt—"

"*Malyshka*, please."

I glance at Anton, but he doesn't seem to notice the endearment. He's staring at the photo, too. I look closer and realize that Niko's dad and Anton's are practically twins. But the third man looks exactly like Sergei. I can see similarities to Niko.

"Your family genetics are remarkable."

I pull out my phone and call my dad. He answers in English, but I switch to Russian. No one at his work will understand him.

"*Papa, mne nuzhno, chtoby ty vernulsya domoy. Ya doma. Ya v poryadke, no eto ochen' vazhno. Ya ne mogu ob"yasnit' po telefonu.*" Papa, I need you to come home. I'm at the house. I'm all right, but it's really important. I can't explain over the phone.

"*Chto ne tak? Ty pravda v poryadke? Pochemu ty doma?*" What's wrong? Are you really all right? Why are you at the house?

"*Vernis' domoy, pozhaluysta.*" I just need you to come home, please.

"*Chto sluchilos?*" What's happened?

"*Nikolay i Anton Kutsenko sidyat na divane. Papa, ya v bezopasnosti. Oni ne prichinat mne vreda.*" Nikolai and Anton Kutsenko are sitting on our sofa. Papa, I'm safe. They aren't here to hurt me.

"*Ya idu.*" I'm coming.

I hang up and sit next to Niko. He's poured himself another drink, but he can't stop staring at the photo. His elbows are resting on his thighs as he leans forward. I don't know what to do. I slide my arm around his and rest my hand on his bicep. He turns and kisses my forehead, but he still says nothing. I lean my head against his shoulder, and I finally feel him relax. Not completely, but he doesn't feel like a spring about to pop.

"Do you want me to make you something to eat? I'm guessing neither of you had lunch. I already have some salad made, and I can make more sandwiches."

"You eat, *malyshka*. I didn't mean to interrupt your meal."

He speaks as though he's in a trance. I lift my head and look over him at Anton, who shakes his head. I don't know if he means no to the food or that he doesn't know what to make of Niko's reaction. We sit in silence for the half an hour it takes my dad to get home. He comes in through the garage, but he freezes when he sees Niko and Anton. They both stand when they hear the door open and reach behind them. But when they see my dad, they freeze too. I can see Niko's hand is on a gun. What the fuck?

"Anton, Nikolai, I never expected to see you in my house or with my daughter."

"And I never knew the man my parents named me for was still alive."

"What?"

I can't help but blurt out my question as I look at Anton. I nearly cry when Niko speaks.

"My father saved your father's life and died in the process."

Chapter Nine

Niko

Antonov is a common last name. Never would I have guessed that Stasia could be one of *these* Antonovs. I'm still reeling. I can't gather my thoughts, but I know that the moment she wrapped her arm around mine, I felt better. But now I'm back to being sucked into a black hole. I cannot believe Yuri Antonov is standing in front of me after all these years.

"Niko, you still look as much like your dad and your uncles as you did when you were a boy. Anton, you could be your father."

"You're not as scary as you were when I was twelve, and you showed up to tell us my papa was dead."

"You've met? Why didn't either of you say so when you recognized my dad?"

"Because neither of us is feeling very chatty looking at a picture that was taken a couple months before our worlds fell apart."

There's venom in Anton's voice that surprises Stasia, but when I look at him, it doesn't seem directed at her dad. The target is something invisible.

"Stasia, probably within a week of this being taken, Sergei's dad, my uncle Radomir, was injured and sent home. He, Aunt Svetlana, Sergei, and his brother Misha escaped and moved to America."

"Escaped? You said he went home."

"Our fathers weren't Russian soldiers, Stasia. They were Podolskaya bratva. It was the same as being drafted, but they were still Russian mafia."

Yuri lunges forward, but she steps between us. I'm sure she's thinking that the last thing we need is Anton and me shooting her dad.

"Papa, I already know Niko and his family are bratva. I found out this morning. It's why I came home. I had—have—questions." I look back at Niko. "That's why you asked if my dad has tattoos."

"Yes. I guessed before you told me about the star. There was no way he grew up in that neighborhood without being pulled in. Anton's dad got my mom, my brothers, and me to St. Petersburg and onto a plane to America after my dad died. He barely made it home to my Aunt Alina, Anton, and his brother Pasha. They went into hiding before they could leave Moscow too and come to New York."

"Is that how you all became bratva? Because your dads were?"

"No."

I'm not reaching for my gun anymore, but I'm glaring at Yuri, who's watching every breath I take.

"Then how?"

"Ana, my guess would be four sons without a father were

easy targets for the Ivankov bratva. What Kirill tried to avoid is what happened anyway, just in America."

Anton and I nod.

"I'm sorry."

Yuri looks down at the photo on the table, and he looks so much older than a moment ago.

"I haven't told your daughter what you did before the bratva. You should."

"Papa?"

Yuri takes a long time to answer, but eventually, he nods.

"I met Niko's dad and uncles while we were all in KGB training. We were barely more than kids. We went to different schools growing up, but we were all the same age. We were all KGB for nearly five years before the Soviet Union fell. They gave none of us a choice when we went home. It was join the bratva or watch them slaughter our families. Niko's mother and aunts are three of the most beautiful women I've ever seen. Niko's mom and Sergei and Misha's mom are sisters. They grew up with Anton's mom. All of them were in danger, but Niko's mom—she's—she's—she was a target because of her looks. Galina and Kirill had their four boys, one after another, to protect Galina. It saved her when all of us went to Chechnya. Trouble was already brewing, so it wasn't a surprise when they sent us."

"Where was Mom in all of this?"

"Still in America for parts of it. Ana, I didn't come to America for college. I was in the KGB then."

"What? But the photos I've seen."

"They sent me here."

Stasia doesn't look like she can take all of this in. She looks up at me, and I'm already watching her. I wrap my arm around her back and draw her against me. She inhales my expensive cologne, and I'm certain she can feel the heat radiating from me. She sags against me, but she watches her father. I glance over and see the surprise, but there's no disapproval. It's more like acceptance.

"None of us knew you left Russia."

Anton speaks up while I look back down at Stasia. She whispers to me.

"I'm all right."

"It was best for everyone. There's a big Russian community here, but no bratva."

"Does Mom know all of this?"

"Of course."

"If you didn't meet in college, how did you meet?"

Yuri clams up as he looks at Anton and me.

"Do you really think we're going to endanger your wife with whatever you tell us?" That annoys me. "You let your half-Russian, Russian-speaking daughter move to New York—to *Queens*—and you didn't warn her. And you're worried that we might tell the wrong person how you met your wife? Stasia knows who we are. We could already be at Rikers if she told anyone. I think we're already showing a lot more trust than we ought to."

"How do you know *Ana*?"

"I met Niko's sister-in-law in the park the last day of my nannying job. She mentioned she needed a legal assistant because she has newborn twins. She's Kutsenko Partners' corporate lawyer."

"You went to work for the bratva?"

"She didn't know. My sister-in-law only handles our legitimate business deals. Anastasia wouldn't have been any the wiser, but there was an incident last night with her ex-boyfriend. You probably should have warned her about the Mancinellis too. I think she was a target."

"What?"

I'm no longer looking at her. She shifts her focus back to Yuri, understanding written across his face.

"No one knows about my past. Neither my wife nor I have uttered a word about it in nearly twenty-five years. If your sister-in-law hired Ana, then no one knew about her ties either. They wouldn't know. She wasn't a target."

"Stasia, did you tell Antonio about your dad being in the Russian army?"

"Yeah. I mean, we talked about our families a little."

I arch an eyebrow, but Yuri shakes his head.

"There are plenty of Russians in New York who are not bratva. She's from Maryland."

"Maybe they didn't. But you can't deny that they could have."

"Niko, you think Antonio dated me because he thinks my dad was bratva?"

"Is. There is never any 'was' unless you're dead. It doesn't matter if your dad hasn't spoken to a person in Russia in a hundred years or never met a bratva member in America, he's still marked. You don't just walk away because you want to."

Stasia's still overwhelmed. Who wouldn't be? She sinks back onto the sofa, and I sit next to her. I wrap my arm around her shoulders, and she leans against me and closes her eyes. This is all too much.

"Wait, you never said how you met Mom."

"When the KGB sent me here, there was a leak. The Americans found out who I was and started watching my parents. They said they could bring my parents over and give them asylum for my cooperation. When I got back to Russia, my cooperation was feeding them information. Your mom was my liaison."

"Mom was a spy?"

"Sort of. As far as anyone knew, she worked for the U.N.,

but she was American intelligence."

Stasia's trembling, and I can feel her growing more anxious. I feel like I can't breathe. All of this information, all these revelations, are suffocating me. I can't imagine how she's feeling. She gets up and heads into the kitchen. Yuri reaches for her, but she shakes her head and walks around him. I know she senses me following her to the backdoor. She waits for me on the patio.

"Nothing I believed about my family is true."

"*Malyshka*, I'm sorry. This is my fault."

"No, it isn't. Even if last night hadn't happened, I would still work for your company. I would still be ignorant of the truth. And who knows who else might have guessed what you did. Who knows if Antonio did, or someone he told did?"

"I never imagined this is how you would find out. I suspected your dad was KGB and bratva, but I never imagined he was my dad's best friend."

"What did you mean your dad saved my dad and died for it?"

I sigh, and she looks like she regrets asking.

"My dad saw a landmine tripwire that your dad was about to step on. He pushed your dad out of the way, and in the process, triggered it."

She pulls back and covers her mouth. My guess is she's picturing the gruesome scene. It had to have been horrifying. It is whenever I imagine it.

"Did you know that when you found out?"

"Yes. Uncle Grigori and your dad came to tell us together. My mother sent us all to our rooms after we found out. Maksim and Aleks shared a room, and Bogdan and I shared a room. Bogdan went with Maksim and Aleks, but I said I wanted to be alone. I sneaked back out and heard your dad tell my mom what happened. I burst into Maks and Aleks' room and told them. Maks was thirteen and almost as tall as he is now, even though he was much skinnier. He ran downstairs and hit your father before anyone knew what was happening. Your dad hugged him while he sobbed. Uncle Grigori hugged Aleks, and Bogdan and I clung to our mom. Everyone was sobbing. That was the only time I ever saw your dad."

"Niko, I'm so sorry."

"It was a long time ago."

"Don't do that. Don't pretend like it doesn't still hurt. I saw your face whiten when you spotted the photo."

"I haven't had to think about that day or how my dad died in a long time, Stasia. I still think about my dad all the time, but not about that. It all came flooding back."

She cups my face and brings it to her before she kisses me. She slides her arms around my neck as I return the kiss. This isn't passionate or sexual. It's about her offering what comfort she can, about connecting with me in a way words can't.

"*Malyshka*, please don't run from me again. I'll only keep following you."

The change of subject surprises her, but she nods.

"Niko, I don't understand what's happening between us."

"Neither do I, *malyshka*. But I know that this isn't the end of whatever is brewing, and I'd much rather deal with this with you by my side."

"*Papachka*, I'm not going anywhere."

She whispers her response before she kisses me again. She wraps her arms around my waist before she rests her head on my shoulder. I kiss her temple, and we stand together for a long time. I feel myself calming for the first time since I arrived. I finally feel like I'm where I belong. It's been sixteen years. Not since my dad died.

"I don't want to, but we should go back inside, *printsessa*."

"I know. We abandoned Anton, but I don't want to face

any of that. I don't want to face the lies I've been told. The pain seeing my father causes you. The confusion about what it means that my dad is bratva, and so are you. I keep thinking I should be angry—furious—at my parents for keeping this from me, but I get it. Especially after you just described how dangerous it was for your family. But it just all feels so heavy."

"I know, *malyshka*. I'm here to help carry that weight. But I need to know whether you understand I can never walk away like your father did. His tattoo means he was high ranking, but he left it behind in Russia. I can never leave it behind anywhere I go in America, and I sure as shit am not going back to Russia. I can never leave my family behind."

"I wouldn't imagine asking that of you. I just feel so uninformed about what I'm getting myself into. But I thought about you the entire drive, how sad I was that I couldn't be with you."

"Couldn't or can't, Stasia?"

"I thought I couldn't. Now, I need time to figure out how this will work. I don't want you or your family to fear I'll tell anyone if we don't work out. Obviously, my family is up to their eyeballs. If I said anything about you, I would give away my family, too."

"I will give you whatever you need. If it's time, then we have all of it in the world. If it's space, it might kill me, but I'll do it. But the one thing I will not back down on is a safety detail. You don't have to see me if you don't want to, but one of my brothers or cousins will be with you at all times. Even if it's the night watch in a car."

"Maks can't. He has babies at home. Bogdan's a newlywed, isn't he? That leaves Aleks and you. You mentioned a Misha and a Pasha. I don't want your family to babysit me."

"It's not babysitting, and I don't want you to think it ever is. Your safety is paramount to me. There are only seven other people in this world who I trust implicitly with your life and their ability to protect it. My three brothers and my four cousins. No one else is good enough."

"When we walked to the subway, none of the men who came with us were your family."

"Yes, they were. They had sunglasses on, so you must not have realized it. The twins' guards are Misha and Pasha. The man who was there for me was Stefan. He was my driver this morning."

"I thought I recognized him, but he had sunglasses on that day, too."

"I can take care of myself, but I have a guard as extra help. But Maks doesn't trust his children with anyone other than our brothers and our cousins. Sergei is usually Laura's guard if she has to go somewhere, and Anton is Christina's. If we don't need Misha and Pasha to guard the twins, then they'll be with you."

"I'd rather it was you, Daddy."

"You don't want space?"

"Time, yes. Space, no. I want us to get to know each other to see if this will work. Space won't let us do that."

"Stasia, I won't share you."

"Good, because I definitely won't share you. Either we're a monogamous couple or we're not anything, Niko. Nothing about any of this is normal."

"But it is us. *Malyshka*, I will go as slowly or as fast as you want, but I've never been so certain of anything in my entire life as I am about how right being with you feels."

"I know. I had to flip a coin to decide between my top choice colleges. It took me years to know what I wanted to study in college. I'm still not sure about law school. But you—you're as easy as A-B-C, one-two-three."

She grins before we kiss again. I hear the backdoor open, and she looks over my shoulder. From Stasia's expression, her mom must be there, and she doesn't look pleased. She lets go and takes my hand. I turn to see a woman who is so similar to Stasia that there's no doubt they're mother and daughter.

"Mom, this is Nikolai."

"Kutsenko. I know. I recognize you, Nikolai, from Yuri's photo. You and Anton look like your fathers."

"Hello, Mrs. Antonov."

I step forward to shake her hand, and she looks at it as if it's a snake that might bite. She takes it, and her grip is firm. There's a warning in her gaze that a blind man couldn't miss. This woman was definitely not a secretary working for someone in the U.N. She's shrewd. She looks at Stasia and releases my hand. Stasia steps into her mom's embrace, and Mrs. Antonov squeezes Stasia until she pulls away.

"Mom, there's a lot we need to talk about."

"I gathered as much when your father called on the way home and told me who came home with you."

Stasia shoots me a warning glance, and I have no intention of telling her mother that Anton and I followed Stasia without Stasia agreeing. Mrs. Antonov leads the way back into the living room. Yuri now has his own glass, and he and Anton are sipping vodka. They both stand when the women enter. Old habits die hard.

"Allison, I've told them we met in America, but that I wasn't in college. They know you were my liaison."

Shock and disapproval are written across Allison's face. It only deepens when she looks at how Stasia is holding my right hand over her stomach, and she presses her back against my chest. I feel like Stasia's almost protecting me, and it makes my lips want to twitch, but years of being drilled into not expressing my emotions are stronger. Allison studies me, and the longer she looks, the less I think she likes what she sees.

"No."

"Mom?"

"No. You are not getting involved with the bratva."

"I'm already involved, and you never told me."

"Your father left that behind when he left Russia for a reason."

I clamp my teeth together to keep from speaking. It isn't my place, and it feels like Anton and I are intruding. I let go of Stasia's hand, but her nails dig into the back of my hand.

"Stasia, this is something you should talk about with your parents. Anton and I will go."

"No."

Now it's Stasia's turn to be emphatic about her refusal. She doesn't ease her grip on my hand.

"Mom, Niko stays, which means Anton does too. I won't expect Niko to keep secrets from any of his family. And there have been enough secrets for the past twenty-two years. Niko was right when he asked Papa how you could send me to New York and not let me know the truth."

"Because all anyone needs to know is that your dad was a Russian immigrant, just like thousands of other people after the Cold War. Papa wanted away from that life, not to have his daughter sucked into it."

"Better the bratva than *Cosa Nostra*."

I watch both Yuri's and Allison's shock. Yuri recovers faster.

"What do you mean?"

"I didn't know until last night that Antonio, that guy I dated for a few months, was Italian mafia. If Niko hadn't been with me last night, things would have been really bad."

Yuri looks at me, and I shake my head. His chin dips just enough for me to notice. He understands, and he won't ask questions. Apparently, Allison doesn't get it.

"What happened to him?"

She's looking right at me.

"He won't bother Stasia ever again."

"My daughter's name is Anastasia. She goes by Ana."

"Mom, I prefer Niko to call me Stasia."

"Since when?"

"Since I met him."

"Which was when, *Ana*?"

"Recently. The point is, if I'd known my family's history, I probably would have known what to look for and avoided Antonio. As is, I'm worried that somehow someone in the *Cosa Nostra* knows about us. What if they targeted me for a reason?"

"There wasn't a reason to. I never thought your type was a thug."

"*Mom.*"

"Stasia, stop. She's scared. Your father left Russia for the same reason my family did. But my mom was a widow with four kids. We went where we had family. My uncles did what they could to keep us out, but even they couldn't keep my cousins away from it. Everyone has done the best they can."

"Don't make excuses, Niko. Mom, don't talk to my boyfriend like that."

Everyone goes still. Yuri doesn't look surprised. Anton is silently watching everything like a ghost no one notices. Allison looks ready to go apeshit, and I don't know what to think beyond being relieved that Stasia sees us as a couple already.

"You couldn't have known each other long. You said you broke up with Antonio three weeks ago. You are not the type to bounce from one guy to another, Ana."

"I'm also almost twenty-three and haven't lived at home in four years. You don't know everything about what I do, Mom. Niko and I started dating recently, but I'm serious about him. He didn't tell me he was bratva until I told him I was sure he was. He didn't tell me anything about Papa or what he suspected. He could have, but he wanted you guys to explain."

"If you want us to still pay—"

"Allison, enough."

"No, say it, Mom. Tell me I have to break up with Niko, so you'll keep helping me pay my rent. You knew Papa was KGB when you met, so you sure as hell knew when he became bratva. Don't be a hypocrite."

"And I know how many times I waited to find out your father was dead. He told me what happened to Kirill. That could have been your dad."

I want to bolt. I want out of here, but I won't leave Stasia behind.

"Mom! How can you say that? Niko and Anton are standing right here. Niko was eleven when *his* dad died saving *my* dad. Stop."

Allison looks like she just realized what she said. She looks embarrassed as our gazes meet.

"Wait. If Niko was eleven, that means I was five. How?"

Her parents look at each other before they look at their daughter. It's her father who speaks first.

"We got married while I was in America, but no one on either side could know. I'd been in the KGB for only a few months. Your mom got pregnant while she was in Russia. They sent her home, but I had to stay there. I missed most of the first five years of your life, Ana. You were too young to remember that I came and went every few months."

Stasia's trembling, and I tighten my hold around her. I feel her tears drip onto my hand. I turn her toward me, and she burrows against my chest. I can only imagine the level of betrayal she feels right now. I'm surprised she's still standing.

"Mr. and Mrs. Antonov, none of this is what any of us would have wanted. Anastasia didn't know what the bratva was until this morning. She knew nothing about this life. I didn't want to be the one to tell your family's secrets. But I will stand by her, and I will protect her if she wishes to be with me. She knows there's danger, and she knows that being with me means accepting a safety detail. She's smart enough to understand why without anyone spelling it out. There are parts of my life that I can never share with her, and I will have to explain that soon. But you both know what that means. Mr. Antonov, I'm certain I am everything you assume. But I'm also Kirill and Galina's son. You know what that means. You know how I will treat Anastasia."

"I do, Niko. Ana, I want to talk to you alone."

Chapter Ten

Stasia

I'm not sure I can leave my mom with Niko and Anton. I don't know what she's going to say. She's acting completely out of character, but I get it. She's freaked out. We're all freaked out. I don't know how I'm going to convince her to accept Niko. Can I live with her refusing?

"Ana, sit down."

I take a seat at the back patio table with my dad. He looks out at the backyard, and he could be a million miles away.

"Kirill, Grigori, and Radomir were best friends when I met them. Kirill was less than a year younger than Grigori. Radomir grew up with them and married Niko's aunt a month before Niko's parents got married. They accepted me into their circle like I was a fourth brother. We all saved each other more times than I can count, both in the KGB and the bratva. You and your mother were here when Kirill died. He gave up a life with his family. He made his sons give up having a father. He did it without a second thought because he saw I was in danger. He got me out of the way just as someone screamed that there was a mine. It startled us both, and he took a step sideways. I still have nightmares. Niko didn't have to tell me he's Kirill's son. I can see it in everything he does. It's not just because he looks like his father. He stands like him. He talks like him. He carries himself like him. He was a child when his dad died. These are not things that he could have learned back then. It's nature and nurture. They are the product of how Kirill and Galina raised their boys. He will die before he does anything his father would disapprove of or anything that would disgrace his father's legacy."

"You know all that from just an hour? Not even?"

"I know it about Niko and Anton. If I met any of the other brothers and cousins, I'm certain I would see the same thing. Do not think I don't know how dangerous the Kutsenkos are. But I also know how honorable they are. I can try to explain this to your mom, but she's never met them. And she's understandably scared for you."

"I know. But I'm nervous about even leaving them alone in there."

"Niko and Anton get it, Ana. But I want to talk to you about what life will be like if you decide to be with Niko. I've never hidden it from your mom that I'm still in touch with Grigori and Radomir every year on the anniversary of Kirill's death. I know what they went through when they moved here. I know what type of man ruled the bratva back then. That man is dead now, and Niko's brother Maksim is in charge. Did you know that?"

"No. I didn't know that the bratva existed until this morning. Niko hasn't told me any specifics yet."

"Maksim is now the *pakhan*, or boss. He runs all the bratva in New York. I know that Niko and his other brothers are part of the Elite Group. They're the *pakhan's* senior-most advisors.

Anton and Sergei are right below them. Sergei is in charge of intelligence, and Anton is in charge of security. Have you met Sergei?"

"Last night. Briefly."

"Do not be fooled by any of their appearances. They are all large men, but they aren't the meatheads most people probably assume. Maksim and Aleksei didn't go to college because they were both too entrenched to have that luxury. But Niko, Bogdan, and their cousins did. They're all well-educated and highly intelligent. They aren't millionaires and billionaires by accident. They've earned much of that legally."

"Millionaires and billionaires?"

"Your boyfriend is extremely rich, Ana. With that alone come threats. Add on being part of a syndicate means you cannot take anything lightly. If Niko or his relatives tell you something is dangerous, you listen. Do not argue with him about it until he says it's safe."

"What am I getting myself into?"

"A lot. The man who was in charge before Maksim was soulless. He was a sociopath. He had no conscience at all. He never did. I met him when I first joined the KGB. He was almost done with his time. He was a torturer because he liked it. Grigori and Radomir have never told me the details, but they know I've guessed. But it probably pales compared to the truth. Niko and his brothers would have had it the worst without a father to protect them. Anton, Pasha, Sergei, and Misha had their dads living with them. Niko and his brothers were easy targets for this man. Ana, I don't doubt Niko was tortured, probably for years."

"What?"

I look back toward the house. I saw scars last night, and I didn't ask about them, but I never imagined they came from torture. I don't know what I assumed caused them. I was pretty distracted.

"The old *pakhan* likely used tactics that made grown men crack. That all eight of those boys grew into men and are functioning members of society is a miracle. But not only were they tortured, they were trained. They were probably boys when they learned to do the things that I learned as a man. Nothing about Niko makes me think he would ever physically hurt you. Just the opposite. I don't doubt he would kill anyone who threatened you."

"Oh, my God. Antonio pushed his way into my apartment last night. Niko stopped him. Anton and Sergei came and took Antonio. Do you think he's dead?"

I watch my dad. He doesn't say a word, but I can hear everything he's thinking.

"Did Niko do it?"

"Probably, Ana. But I wouldn't know without asking, and I won't. You shouldn't either. If Antonio was *Cosa Nostra*, then it was for the best. You don't need them around you, especially if they learn you're Russian. Even if you didn't know the Kutsenkos, there are people among the Italians that would gladly hold a Russian girl hostage knowing the Kutsenkos wouldn't ignore you."

"Do you think Niko's killed a lot of people?"

"Men. Never women and never children. I know his parents. I don't want to answer that, Ana, so I think you know what that means."

"Am I with a murderer?"

"It's not that simple, sweetheart. I told you, they trained him to do the same things I was. I was bratva before I left for the war."

"Are you a murderer?"

My ears are ringing. I'm trying not to panic.

"Ana, it sounds barbaric, but it's kill or be killed in this world. If I hadn't done what I had to, someone else would have done it, then come after me. I had to defend myself. But it was only me. If Niko didn't do what that man wanted, the old *pakhan* had seven other boys and two men to punish. I don't know any specifics, so please don't think I'm keeping them from you. But I know how the bratva operates. There is somewhere, probably a warehouse or factory or something like that, that is abandoned. That will be a place they can control. It will be a place where they take care of the things no one can know about. He will *never* tell you where it is, and he will *never* tell you what happens. Do *not* push him about it and do *not* try to find it. He will hate every secret he keeps from you, but he will do it to keep you and the people he loves alive."

"Are you saying that's where they kill people?"

"I'm saying that's where things happen. When he goes there, he will not have a way to communicate with you. If he disappears for a few days, that's why. I suspect someone in his family will let you know, but if they can't, you need to know that something serious happened. If he ever tells you to stay away, it's not because he doesn't want you. It's because he doesn't want you to see him that way. Something will have happened that wasn't in a controlled environment. I know how I was. I never would have wanted your mother to see me as that man, that monster that I had to become."

"You're scaring the bejeezus out of me, Papa."

"I know, sweetheart. But you have to understand these things. I don't doubt he would tell you, but I don't want you to underestimate their importance or think he's exaggerating. I knew Kirill, and I know what he did to protect Galina. Things that I bet Niko and his brothers don't know. But I can tell Niko is the same man as his father. He will not hesitate to do whatever he thinks is necessary to keep you safe. He brings you into a world of danger, but no one will try harder than him to keep you safe. Your mother can't understand because she's never been a true bratva wife. She was never a true KGB wife. I don't have the same fears your mother does because I know this life, and I know the Kutsenkos."

"You think I should be with him?"

"If he makes you happy. If you want out and you feel you can't get out, you come to me. If anything happens and you can't get to Niko or his family, you come to me. I hate saying it, but not your mother and me. Just me. Your mother has a history too. She is not just the intel analyst you think. She was essentially a spy. She can protect you better than you'd imagine, but she doesn't know the bratva like I do. She doesn't know syndicates like I do. You come to me, Ana. Understand?"

"Yes, Papa."

"Do you have questions?"

"Like a thousand. But some of them are best left for Niko to answer. But I have one for you. Do you think I'm cut out to be a bratva wife?"

"Yes. Ana, my guess is you've only known Niko for a few days since you told us you broke up with Antonio three weeks ago. If he's brought you this far into his world, it's because he wants you to stay. I mean permanently. He'd never force you, but I want you to understand that he isn't a man who will toy with you. If he is as much like his father as I believe, he will love the woman he's with, with every bit of him. He will be loyal until his last breath. I believe he sees you as that woman. He wouldn't be here, he wouldn't have let you know what he is, who he is, if he didn't."

"Thanks, Papa. I don't know what it is about Niko. I can't name why I feel like I do. Papa, we met a week ago, but I knew I was drawn to him in a way I've never been with anyone. But I feel like he's been part of me my entire life. It's so strange to explain. It's like—I don't know—it's just as natural to be with him as it is to be with myself."

My dad takes my hand and helps me out of my seat. He kisses my forehead as he hugs me.

"I get that. It's how I knew I needed to make a life with your mom. I didn't realize it within a week, but I know that feeling. Trust Niko, sweetheart."

"I do. Thank you for explaining all of this. I love you."

"I love you, peanut."

He hasn't called me that since I learned how to ride a two-wheel bike. It feels good. I sigh. I know I have to go back inside. I want to be near Niko. But I'm dreading my mom. Why can't my dad bring her outside for a talk like this?

"Ana, I'll talk to your mom tonight. I'll explain the same way I did to you."

"Good. I—"

"Stasia, we have to go."

I look at Niko as he bursts out of the backdoor.

"You're leaving?"

"We're leaving. We have to get back to the city."

"But—"

"Stasia, now."

"Go, Ana. Remember what I told you. Trust Niko. If he says you have to, then do it."

I see the unguarded surprise on Niko's face, then the gratitude. He reaches for my hand as he looks at my dad as he speaks.

"*Vypolnyayte obeshchaniya, dannyye drugim voram.*"

Make good on promises given to other thieves. What the hell does that mean?

"Stasia, say bye to your parents. I'll explain in the car."

"In the car? We drove separately."

"We're riding together. I have men on the way to drive our

cars back."

"What? Why?"

"I will explain, I promise. But we really have to go. Please."

I can't begin to guess what's going on. I don't understand why this is so urgent, but my dad told me to trust Niko, and I do. If my dad trusts Niko without knowing him, then I doubly trust Niko. It's not like my car is the Porsche, but I let no one drive mine. My parents drilled it into me in high school.

"Who's driving my car back? Why can't I?"

"Because I don't feel that you driving between Anton and me is enough. I thought about it, but I'm not comfortable with it."

"What is going on? You are not taking my daughter back into whatever disaster you're part of. You are not risking her life."

My mom is waiting for us at the door, and she's even angrier than before I came outside with my dad.

"Antonio was having you watched, Stasia. He didn't just plan to force you that night. He was going to take you. When you talked about your family with Antonio, he must have relayed all the information back to Salvatore. They had their suspicions, like I did. They haven't found your parents yet, but they will if you stay here. Anton checked your car when he filled your tire. There was a tracker on it that wasn't well hidden. He crushed it and threw it away. I think they planned to ransom you, either to my family or to the Podolskaya."

"Aren't they in Russia?"

"Yes. No one just walks away from the bratva."

Niko shoots a meaningful look at my dad, and I realize he must have fled like Niko's family. Are the Podolskaya holding a grudge more than twenty years later?

"Who were you to them, Papa?"

"By the time I left, I was the *Obshchak*. I was equivalent to

Anton."

"I don't understand."

I look at my parents, then at Niko and Anton.

"I promise I will explain everything, Stasia. But we can't wait around. If they get here, they will take you. I can guarantee they are coming with more men than your father, Anton, and I can defend you against. Your parents need to use their contacts and get away from here."

"Why can't I go with them?"

Niko lets go of my hand, and I feel the loss keenly.

"Is that what you want?"

"I don't know what I want. I don't understand any of this."

"You should stay with us. We can keep you safer than going back to New York with a man who's the reason they're even after you."

My mom just wants to blame Niko. It's easier, and I get that. But it was dating Antonio that did this. It was my ignorance about organized crime and my family's history that did this. I don't know that I would have recognized Antonio as mafia, but I would understand why what's happening is so urgent.

"Stop blaming Niko, Mom. It was my mistake dating Antonio. If it weren't for Niko, Antonio would have raped me and taken me. If they're after me to get to you, then the last thing I should do is be close to you."

"We can protect you, Ana. I work for the government in intelligence. I have connections that can get us far away from here."

I stare at my mom as she talks. Two weeks ago, I wouldn't have hesitated to listen to her. But my intuition is screaming that I need to go with Niko. I look at my dad, and he nudges his chin toward Niko. He believes I should go with him.

"Papa, what will happen if they find you?"

"That depends on what their deal is with the Podolskaya. If that bratva paid for you, then it's revenge against me or to force Niko's family to rescue a Russian woman in danger of being sex trafficked. You will go to Russia. If the Italians plan to sell you to the Podolskaya, they will bribe Niko to keep them from sending you to Russia. Either way, the Podolskaya will try to find me and force me to return. They will use you as leverage."

"This is all because I told Antonio that you were in the Russian army?"

"Did you tell him where I grew up?"

"No. He never asked."

"Did you tell him about my tattoo?"

"Yes. I mentioned it when I asked him about one of his."

"A Russian girl with a father who has an eight-point star is connected to the bratva."

"Stasia, whatever you choose, it has to be now."

Niko's voice is growing more strained each time he talks. I look past this shoulder and see a black town car pull up, and three men rush from it.

"Niko!"

I point behind him. He pulls his gun as he turns. Anton does the same. My dad yanks open the coat closet he's standing next to and reaches to the top shelf. He pulls out a rifle I have never seen before. I didn't even know there was a gun in the house. This isn't a hunting rifle. This is some type of semi-automatic thing.

"They're ours. They're here for the cars and to escort us back. Stasia?"

Niko and Anton holster their weapons, and my dad puts the rifle back.

"Dad, why do you have that?"

"Because no one just walks away from the bratva."

I feel so utterly betrayed. My parents blithely sent me off to school for four years in New York City, the capital of gangland in America. I never knew what to watch for. I never knew I could be in danger.

"We did what we thought was best, *lapochka*."

My dad has called me sweetheart all my life. It's always made me feel better until today. I reach for Niko's hand again, but I'm looking at my dad.

"I'll remember what you said. I'm going with Niko."

"Ana, no!"

My mom takes a step forward with her hand raised like she wants to grab hold of my arm, but I step closer to Niko. He wraps his arm around my shoulder.

"Mom, I'm going with Niko. I love you, but Niko has a team of men to protect me."

I step away from Niko and hug my mom, then my dad. They both look distraught, and I can't blame them. I feel that way too. But the government won't get involved between the mafia and some illegal group in Russia.

"Bye."

I hope this isn't the last time I speak to my parents. I'm scared to leave them behind. I want to ask Niko to bring them with us.

"Stasia, trust your parents to take care of themselves. You're the target."

"Wouldn't they want my dad instead?"

"No. You're worth more to the Italians and the Podolskaya. You're young and beautiful."

I follow Niko outside and hand my keys to one of his men. Niko gives another guy his. Anton and the new driver get in the front seats while Niko and I climb in the back. I notice the privacy screen is already up. I watch the house I grew up in fade in the distance. Niko lifts me into his lap and holds me close. I feel safe with him. But how long will that last?

Chapter Eleven

Niko

Stasia is curled into my lap like a kitten, and all I can do is hold her while I gather my thoughts. I trust Sergei did as thorough a background check as he could. I believe Stasia and her parents have no public or private records with the FBI and the DOJ. Between that and hacking their employment records, he wouldn't have dug any deeper than that because none of us suspected a half-Russian girl from outside Baltimore would have any type of bratva affiliation. It just isn't a *thing* in that area like it is in other large cities.

"Stasia, when you're ready, I'll explain what I can. Ask what you want, but if I can't answer, it's to protect you, your parents, or my people. I don't want to be purposely evasive."

"I know. My dad and I had a good talk. I know there are things about your past and your present that you can never tell me. My dad warned me not to press you on it, and he said that if you tell me to do something, I need to trust that you're telling me the right thing because of your experience."

"He's right. I haven't brought anyone into my world because of things like this. I can't reveal to people that I'm bratva, and I don't want to risk people guessing. Some friends have, but I keep most people at arm's length."

"Would you have brought me into your life if my dad wasn't who he is?"

"Yes."

I don't hesitate with that answer. It's like it's deep into my marrow that Stasia should be part of my life.

"You'd bring me into this danger because you want me."

"Stasia, most of the time, my life is pretty normal. I go to work, and I come home. I spend time with my family, go out to eat, go to the movies. That sort of thing. When I was younger, I went to parties and nightclubs. I'm cautious, and I take a bodyguard. But there's always risk. There's also a lot of my life that I can't share, even if I wanted to. It isn't safe for anyone involved. I've always hated it, but now that I've met you, I doubly hate it. It's who I am."

"Will you keep a lot of secrets? My dad said there's probably a place you go where you handle things. He said I'm not to ask about it or try to find it. That you could be gone for a while. He said that if you say you don't want to see me, it's really because you don't want me to see you like that."

"*Malyshka*, I will always tell you what I can. There are a lot of secrets. Some you'll learn, and some you can't even imagine."

"Who was the man who was *pakhan* before Maksim?"

What the fuck did her father tell her? This is jumping onto ground I have no desire to tread. Those days haunt me because they made me who I am. My parents raised the good part of me, but that man made the monster in me.

"Vladislav Lushak."

"My dad said he knew him in the KGB, that he was a psychopath."

"He was. He was a brutal man who did brutal things to anyone he wanted. He had no limits. He was violent for his own pleasure. When my brothers and I arrived in America, my family tried to keep us shielded from the Ivankov bratva. But it didn't take long for people to hear my uncles and dad were Podolskaya. The moment Vlad found out, he came knocking. Uncle Grigori and Uncle Radomir kept my cousins out for a few more years than my mother could. They tried to intervene, but they were powerless against Vlad and his men. It would have been a death sentence for us all if they'd fought against it harder. There were years when I wish they had."

"Niko, did your scars come from being tortured?"

Her voice is barely more than a whisper. I'm torn between being enraged that her father told her so much and partly grateful that he forewarned her.

"Yes."

"I don't want to make you relive old memories. I shouldn't have asked that. I'm sorry."

She sits up to look at me, and I press a soft kiss to her lips.

"*Malyshka*, ask your questions. Vlad used us to force each other to follow his orders. If he told one of us to do something, and we didn't do it well or fast enough or we tried to refuse, he would pick a different brother and torture him until whoever it was gave in. He went after Bogdan most often because he was the youngest and the smallest. He was only eleven when Vlad sucked us in. He beat it into us to show no kind of emotion, no reaction at all. I've been far more unguarded with you in the past week than I have been with anyone outside of my family since I was twelve. I've let you know what I'm thinking and feeling. If I didn't want you to know, you wouldn't."

"Did he teach you how to torture and kill?"

I don't want to answer that. She already knows, which means she already knows that part of me is no better than Vlad.

I take no enjoyment in what I do. None of us feel compelled or seek a thrill. Sometimes retribution is satisfactory, but none of it makes us feel good about ourselves. We do what we have to protect the people who rely on us, and that's more than just our family.

"You didn't call the police last night, and I understand better now. But what happens if you get hurt or arrested? You'll end up in prison and likely on death row."

"We have a doctor on staff, and we avoid going to the hospital at all costs. Our doctor can heal most things. Hospitals ask too many questions. As for the police, most are smart enough to leave us alone. Many are funding their retirement with what we pay them to leave us alone. But if anything ever happens when we're together, you get to one of my brothers or cousins immediately. If we're apart, one of them will protect you."

"My dad said not to question you if you say something's urgent or dangerous. That I should trust you and that you'll explain if you can."

"I will."

"What did you mean when you said, *vypolnyayte obeshchaniya, dannyye drugim voram?*" Make good on promises given to other thieves.

"There is an oath we all swear. *Vory v Zakone*. It's known as the thieves code. That is the last line of it. Your father made the same pledge as I did, as my brothers and cousins did, and as my father and uncles did. I promised your father that I will protect you. I will always make good on that promise, *malyshka*. Always.

"Niko, I'm really scared."

"I know, *malyshka*. I am too."

"You are?"

"Yes. Anything that puts you in danger terrifies to me. We just found each other. I don't want to lose you."

"How can you be so certain?"

"Because you're mine."

Heat flares in her eyes, and I can see she likes my possessiveness. I pull her in for another kiss. She runs her hands over my neck and into my hair, but I capture them.

"There's still something we need to discuss. You ran from me, *malyshka*."

"I freaked out."

"I know, and I get that. But we could have done this together. We could have come to your parents and asked together instead of me having to chase you. You can't run just because you're scared. What if Anton hadn't followed you? What if he hadn't spotted the tracker?"

My expression is stern, and she looks repentant.

"I fucked up."

"You put your life at risk, and that's not acceptable to me. The entire way here, I kept thinking about how itchy my palm is."

"Itchy?"

"Yeah, and the only way to scratch it is to lay it across your perfect little ass."

"You want to punish me and spank me?"

"Thoroughly tempted, even right now."

"Really, Daddy?"

Fuck. My cock hurts from how badly I want to be inside her. Is she giving me permission?

"Would you let me?"

She bites her lip before she nods.

"You have to say it, Stasia?"

"Yes, Daddy."

I unfasten her pants and pull them and her thong off. I guide her over my lap, and I can see her pussy glistening.

"Have you been wet for me all along, *malyshka*?"

"Yes, *papachka*. Since you arrived. My mind was on our conversation, but my body was on you fucking me."

"Do naughty girls deserve a good fucking?"

She looks back at me with serious doubt in her eyes. She really thinks I'm going to forego the chance to fuck her after spanking her.

"I don't know."

Her voice is little more than a whisper.

"If you take your spanking well, then all is forgiven. This was serious though, Stasia. I need you to understand that."

"I do, Niko. I am sorry."

"Ten spanks to each side. Do not get your hands in the way. If I hurt you by accident, I won't be pleased."

"I've never been spanked, except for the ones last night."

"I haven't spanked a woman before. Hold my ankle if you don't think you can keep your hands out of the way."

I'm careful with each slap. She's so thin that there isn't much to absorb my strength except for bone and muscle. It's still the most perfect ass I've ever seen. She must be a runner. After every couple on each side, I rub away some of the burn. When there are only two left for each side, I lean and can see her pussy is dripping. Her thighs are wet, and her clit is swollen. I slide my finger into her, and she jerks on my lap.

"You like it when Daddy spanks you, don't you, *malyshka*?"

"Yes, Daddy. So much. It hurts like hell, but I like it."

"I can tell. Don't you dare come yet. If you do, there won't be any point in fucking."

"There's always a point to fucking, *papachka*."

I can't help but laugh at how earnest my nearly virgin *malyshka* is.

I rain down the last four across her horizontal cracks. I know they burn, and I can feel her tense after each one. Her ass is bright pink and so tempting. Today isn't the day to claim it. That might be awhile, but just like her cunt, her ass is mine. All of her is mine.

I sit her up, careful not to graze her sore skin against my pants, so her ass rests between my thighs. I fist her hair and hold her head in place as I control the kiss. She's happy to follow my lead. As the kiss deepens, she moves to straddle me. I guide her hips against my cock, which has been hard since the moment she sat on my lap. I unbutton her blouse and kiss my way down to her bra. She arches her back and pulls her bra down. I unclasp it and pull it and her blouse off. She's pushing back my suit jacket. I let go, and she helps me take it off, tossing it on the seat beside us. Then off comes my button-down. Her clothes are on the floor. I cup her tits and make a meal of them.

"Daddy."

Fuck. I love hearing that word. I never in a million years thought it could be such a turn on, but I want to fuck her more than I want to take my next breath. I twist, so she's lying on the seat, and I'm kneeling. Thank heavens for privacy glass. Maybe Stefan and Anton have guessed what's happening. It means they won't open that glass without warning.

I can see the promised land. I hook her legs over my shoulders before leaning forward to kiss her mouth. It was clear last night that she had experience, even if she was a virgin. That's something I need to give more thought, but not right now. When her nails graze along my scalp, I pull back. My tongue laves her pussy, and I inhale. I want to get her off before I fuck her.

"Daddy, that feels amazing."

I slide one, then two fingers into her. How did I fit last night? I work her inside with my fingers while my tongue flicks and sucks her clit. Her hips try to rise to meet my mouth, but my free hand holds her down.

"Who decides, *malyshka*?"

"You, *papachka*."

I graze my teeth over her clit, eliciting a moan that makes my cock twitch. She's watching me and knows I enjoy hearing her. I keep working her until I see a flush rising from her chest and up her neck.

"Daddy, I'm close. May I come?"

"Yes, baby girl. Let me taste you."

She grips the headrest and edge of the seat as her body stiffens. I unfasten my pants, but I stop. Fuck.

"Are you on the pill or anything?"

"Yes. It was never a matter of if I would have sex. Just when."

"I haven't been with anyone in a long time, Stasia. But I got tested the last time, and I'm clean. I don't have any condoms."

She nods and reaches for me. I push my pants and boxers down before lining my cock up with her cunt. I'm slow as I enter her. I want to thrust into her and fuck her, but my need to protect her includes from me.

"*Papachka*, I won't break."

"I don't want to hurt you."

"I was a virgin last night, Niko. But I have toys. I have one that's—big. Almost like you."

I push deeper until my balls hit her ass. Holy fucking shit. I could come right now. I circle my hips, and her fingers dig into my shoulders.

"Put your hands behind your head, *malyshka*."

"Can I ever touch you while we have sex?"

"Of course. Tell me if that's what you want."

"Not right now. I was just wondering."

She follows my instructions and puts her hands beneath

her head. I'm taking her to my place. I will use one of my ties and bind her to my bed. I might keep her there for days. I withdraw halfway and lick her nipple. I thrust back in, and her back arches. Each time I pull back, I suck her tits. Then I surge again. Her hips rise and fall with my rhythm. When she holds her breath, I remember how she enjoyed my hand around her throat when I squeezed. I haven't gotten in breath play before, but I've read about it. It's intrigued me, and it excited Stasia last night.

Rather than squeeze, this time I put pressure on her trachea. Her eyes widen, and she sucks in a breath. I release her immediately.

"You didn't hurt or scare me. I just didn't realize I would like you just pushing on my throat. Will you do it again? Please, Daddy?"

"Snap if it's too much. If you don't feel right, you let me know immediately, Stasia. I'm new to this, too. I'll give you whatever you want, but it doesn't mean I'm not afraid of hurting you."

The trust in her eyes eases my fears, so I put my hand back over her throat, the space between my thumb and forefinger pressing against her trachea again. She sucks in a deep breath before I increase the pressure. If I didn't already know as much as I did about choking and suffocating, I would never dare try this. But I know what to look for. I watch Stasia like a hawk as I thrust into her, picking up my steady rhythm once more. Rather than panic, she relaxes. I feel the tension ease from her body, but the moment I feel her body tighten, I release her throat. She's held her breath long enough.

"*Papachka*, may I come?"

"No."

Her eyes widen in surprise. I'm using every ounce of control not to come already. I want this to last. We fucked four times last night and twice this morning. Each time gets better than the last. This is sublime. I'm in no hurry for it to be over, but the moment her pussy squeezes my dick, I'm going to explode.

"If I can't come, will you let me touch you?"

I can see this will soon turn from pleasure to frustration, and not the kind that leads to more pleasure. We may have had a lot of sex last night, and she might have a dildo or vibrator, but that doesn't mean she's prepared for the emotions that go along with the first few times you have sex. Hell, I've had plenty, and I'm not prepared to handle how I feel right now. I can see this is important to her.

"Yes, *malyshka*."

Her fingers follow the muscle grooves along my shoulders and down my chest before her palms sweep over my abs. Her hands wrap around and grasp my ass, and I feel her shudder. She likes my body as much as I like hers. Her hands settle on the divots on the outside of my hips. She found the hollows last night and kept her hands there through two rounds of sex.

I'm holding myself up on my hands, and my arms feel like they're going to shake. I also can't enjoy touching her as much as I want. I swoop her up and sit, so she straddles me again. She dives in for a kiss that has me fisting her hair and keeping her head in place. I tweak her nipple, and I feel the beginnings of her orgasm.

"*Papachka*, please. I can't hold back when you do that."

"Come, *malyshka*."

I'm fighting against my orgasm. I steady my breathing as I watch her throw her head back. I slide my teeth along her neck as she holds onto my biceps.

"*Papachka*."

I grip her hips and move her as I thrust into her.

"Yes... Rough... More."

I give her what she wants. She watches me and brings her hands to rest against her lower back. I feel her grasp her wrists.

"You're such a good baby girl. I'm not even close to done fucking you."

And I'm not. I suddenly find I can keep going. Her submissive pose and watching her come makes me want to keep going for forever. I don't want this over.

"Daddy, I want to make you come like you made me. Don't I feel good enough? What do I do?"

That knocks the wind right out of my sails. I stop and cup her face.

"*Malyshka*, you feel so fucking good. I don't want this to end. I'd walk around with my dick buried in you night and day if I could. Please never doubt that you are good enough or that you are doing something right. It was taking me everything not to come a moment ago. Then, the way you positioned your arms, that makes me want to keep going for hours."

"We have about two and a half until we get back into the city."

"Cheeky, *malyshka*. We'll work up to that. As much as I want to fuck you every minute of the day, I don't want to hurt your either."

I kiss her as I move again. My hands are still cupping her jaw until I feel my orgasm coming. I keep her on my cock until the very last second before I lift her off and come all over my stomach. She watches as I erupt. She rocks against me, her clit rubbing my dick.

"I can come again."

"Good."

I support her upper back as she arches and moans. I could listen to that sound like some people listen to the symphony. She collapses against me and rests her head on my shoulder as we pant together. I want to finish in her so much, but that's irresponsible. Nothing is foolproof short of not having sex, and I'm not giving this up. I won't trap her, and I will never give up a child. I want Stasia to be mine because she chooses it.

"Daddy, I'm glad it was you."

I understand what she means. It shocked me when she admitted it, even if I suspected it. I haven't been with a virgin since I was one. The girl was a senior in high school like me, and it was the blind leading the blind. It lasted about half a second with lots of fumbling, me embarrassed, and her dissatisfied. Not one of my finer moments.

That Stasia picked me is something I don't take lightly. I want to be worthy of that privilege. And not just during sex. She's placing her life in my hands. I've never wanted a woman to trust me, and I've never felt so driven to protect one who isn't my mother. I'd lay down my life for my two sisters-in-law without reservation, but it's not the same. I might not be in love —yet—but I get Maks and Bogdan now.

"Here."

Stasia hands me some tissues from a box in the door. I wipe myself off and crumple them into a ball. I reach for my pant pocket and shove them in. While my cousin and driver wouldn't disturb us on pains of death, we can't remain naked the whole time. Disappointing as that is. Stasia realizes that too as she puts her bra back on. She reaches for her thong, but I snag it first. I sniff and smile wickedly.

"Mine now."

"Just this once."

She winks and presses a hard kiss to my cheek before she pulls on her blouse. Once we're dressed, she sits beside me and leans against my shoulder. I wrap my arm around her, and her left hand comes to rest on my chest over my heart. I cover her hand with mine.

"What happens now, Niko?"

"I'm taking you to my penthouse. We're going to stay there until Sergei has more information. If I have to leave, I'm taking you to Laura. She'll know what to do, which is keep you occupied and distracted. She'll want the same from you. If I'm gone, that means my brothers will be too. Anton and Sergei will stay in the house with you, and Maks and Laura have a full security detail there."

"Are you going to—"

I feel her stiffen and her face flinch.

"*Malyshka*, I don't know."

"Is it always necessary to go that far? Antonio's dead, isn't he?"

"Don't ask questions you'll regret the answer to, Stasia."

"You said I could ask."

"You can, but that doesn't mean you'll always like the answer."

"So you killed Antonio."

She pulls away, and I'm not sure if she's upset at my evasiveness or my actions. Maybe both.

"Stasia, that's something I can't tell you whether I did or didn't. Now you know the type of man I am. If I tell you if that sort of thing happens, you become an accomplice at the worst, or you're aiding and abetting. They will make you to testify against me. Even if I was certain you would reveal nothing, I don't want to put you in that situation."

"If you were certain? You think I'd narc? What the hell, Niko?"

"I didn't mean you'd do it intentionally. You aren't part of this world. You don't know what little detail could endanger all of us."

"If I'm such a risk, then why did you bring me into this?"

"Because you're mine."

"I am not. I'm not a possession, Niko. I'm my own person.

My parents treated me like a child until today. They didn't think I needed to know any of this. They didn't trust me to keep this family secret. Look where it got me. Almost raped and kidnapped. You're no better than them."

She doesn't like my possessiveness after all. Maybe only in sex.

"They did what they did because they love you more than their own lives. They're your parents. Maybe they were wrong, but they kept it a secret for the right reasons."

"That's how you're going to justify all the secrets you keep from me. How will I know if some secrets you keep are things I could actually know? Should know? It sounds like you have all the control, and I have none."

"While you're learning about this world, yes. I have the control."

"No. You want to be controlling when we fuck, fine. I'll play along. But I decide what I'm doing with my life."

"You won't get to decide a damn thing if the *Cosa Nostra* gets ahold of you. I know I'm asking for an inordinate amount of trust, Stasia, but if you're with me, then you have to give it."

"You're demanding it."

I sigh. I am. I know she's scared and overwhelmed. This is way more than anyone should have to process in one day. Last week, she had a brand-new job and lived a practically carefree life. Today, she learns the man she slept with is in the Russian mafia. She learns her father was, too. She learns another syndicate wants to sell her overseas to be sex trafficked. At best, just ransomed. I need to be more patient, but I'm new to letting someone into my life. This is exactly why we don't.

"I know, *malyshka*. I'm figuring this out as I go along. Maks and Bogdan went through the same thing. I learned some stuff from them, but I wasn't privy to conversations they had when they were dating their wives. I don't know how to do this, but I'm doing my best."

She watches me before she nods. But she pulls away and looks out the window.

"Stasia?"

"I need to think, Niko. You want me to trust you, but you don't trust me."

"But I do. If I didn't, I never would have let you know what I am. You could turn me over to the police. You could turn me over to *Cosa Nostra*. You could sign my death warrant and those of every member of my family. Don't tell me I don't trust you enough. I think it's the other way around."

"You're the one who knows how to defend himself and what to do. I don't have a fucking clue. I'm supposed to place all my faith in you. One person against at least two mafias. Do you not see how terrifying that is?"

"Of course, I do, *malyshka*. I was twelve when I learned about this."

That makes her go quiet. I didn't say it to be spiteful. I meant it as empathy. I need to give her space. We drive north for a half an hour before she says anything. We're both looking out our windows. She doesn't turn to me when she speaks.

"What happens if I want out?"

"Do you?"

"Don't answer me with a question. Am I in for life?"

"It's not a prison sentence."

"It feels like it. Life without the possibility of parole."

I grit my teeth as her comment pieces my heart. I don't know if it's today's events or if she would react this way, even if I tried to ease her into it, but I can't fault her. Fuck. I wanted to run away from home the first time we met Vlad. There were years when I wished I was dead. For me, it *is* life without parole. I don't want her to feel like that's how a relationship with me will go.

"I will ensure you still have a safety detail until I'm certain the threat isn't there. If you decide to stay in New York, I recommend you get your own bodyguard if you don't want one of my men. I offer mine for as long as you want. If you aren't with me and don't want my protection, the best thing to do would be to leave New York."

She looks at me, slack jawed.

"Anastasia, people know who your father is. Even if you never see me again, you're still his daughter, and people know. You're safer with me, even if we don't have a relationship, than you are on your own. If you want to work for Laura or not, we're still the best people to protect you. Once this threat is over, if you want me to take you back to your parents, I will. Your dad is the only other person you can trust to know what to do."

"That's what he said."

"He's right."

"I'm always going to be looking over my shoulder, won't I?"

"Not necessarily. I don't know yet. Sergei hacked into some networks that let us know who's involved. But there wasn't a lot of information available. You know what I know. When I find out more, I will tell you everything I can."

"Basically, I don't have a choice about having a bodyguard. I need one, and I get that. But I don't want you, Niko."

Forget Vlad "the Impaler" Lushak. He was a fucking fairy godmother compared to the pain that one sentence causes me. I rest my head back and close my eyes. I haven't cried since I was twelve and Vlad held a knife to Bogdan's throat and broke all his fingers because Maks flinched. It's been sixteen years, and I'm ready to sob.

Chapter Twelve

Stasia

Why did I say that? Or at least, why did I say it like that? He's resting his head with his eyes closed. His face looks at peace, and I didn't see any reaction when I said it. But he warned me he won't share his emotions unless he wants me to know them. Despite not seeing any proof, I hurt him. It was careless and vindictive. I lashed out. And he doesn't deserve that. He's doing his best, and I know that. I at least understand that much.

I'm so fucking torn right now that I don't know what the fuck to do. My intuition is telling me to trust him implicitly, so I will. My heart is yelling that I'm a fucking crazy bitch who just ruined her entire life. But my mind is telling me to run as far and as fast as I can from Niko and everything to do with the bratva. But I can't. Even if I leave Niko's protection, then what? If the Podolskaya knows where my dad is, will they have to move? Do I go with them?

I'm lost in my thoughts for the next hour. I don't realize we reached Manhattan until the car stops. I look past Niko to a high rise, then I look at him. Can't I just hide in the car?

"Anastasia—"

"Stop calling me that. You did it earlier, and I don't like it. It doesn't feel right. I'm sick of being treated like a child. I don't need that from you. I don't need to feel like you're scolding me."

"And you dumped me. I didn't think I had the privilege of calling you anything else."

My shoulders slump. Why the fuck does it matter to me that he isn't calling me Stasia? Until yesterday, it wasn't a name ever used for me. I like that only Niko uses it. It feels special. I feel special. Anastasia feels closed off, remote, uncaring, disinterested. It's all the things I'm being to him that I don't want him to be to me. I'm a fucking hypocrite.

The driver opens Niko's door since he's by the sidewalk. He steps out and offers me his hand. I stare at it before I take it. He helps me out, then drops it as I look around. We're in a part of Manhattan I've only passed by. I can't afford a cup of coffee in this area, let alone anything more. Anton steps beside me, and the driver closes the door and follows behind us. I'm shielded. I notice Niko and Anton each have a hand in their pocket. I bet, if I look, the driver is doing the same thing. What do they have in them? Knives? Do they expect someone to jump out and attack?

I enter the building with the three men, and Niko greets the doorman and the concierge in Russian. I'm almost positive both men are armed. Niko's place doesn't make up this entire building. Who else lives here that they need this kind of security? Or are those men placed here just for Niko's sake? I have so many fucking questions.

I step into the elevator with Niko and Anton. The driver doesn't join us. I watch the floors tick by until we reach the penthouse. Niko uses biometrics to get us to the top floor. I don't know what to expect when the doors open, but I should have guessed there would be an armed guard stationed there. The man doesn't look at me. It's as though I don't exist. I want to say it's a courtesy, but who the fuck knows? We walk down a short hallway. There's only one door on this floor, so we're at Niko's place. There's another armed guard stationed here. He nods to me, but he goes still. I look up at Niko and see his glare. I guess no one may be polite to me either.

"Motherfucker, you're home."

I'm not prepared for that greeting when Niko opens the door.

"I missed you too, Sammy."

There's a medium sized gray parrot in a cage by the floor-to-ceiling window.

"About time, motherfucker."

"Sammy, enough."

The bird draws his head back, and if birds can glare, this one is spitting daggers at its owner.

"Hi, pretty lady."

How the hell does he know that? How many pretty ladies does Niko bring here? Why do I fucking care?

"Bogdan thought it was hilarious to teach Sammy to swear. The only good thing he did was teach him to be polite when my mom arrives. That's basically the only nice thing he knows how to say. My mom is blonde too, so that's why he probably knew what to say to you."

I nod.

"Stasia, I don't bring women home."

"Okay."

"It's written all over your face. You thought he says that to all the women who walk in my door, and you thought there must be plenty of them."

"Fine."

He sighs before he takes a deep inhale. He motions toward a door, and I follow him. He opens it and steps aside. It's clearly a guest bedroom. It looks like no one has stepped in it except to dust. The bed is freshly made, but there are no decorations in here. There's nothing on either bedside table. I can see into the bathroom, and there are no towels on any of the racks.

"If you want me to, I will send someone to get your clothes from your place. I can order you anything you need, and it can be here in an hour. I'll make dinner, or I'll order you something. I know you didn't get to eat your lunch. I saw it on the kitchen table."

"You'll order me dinner? Not us? Just me?"

"I'm not hungry."

"Niko—"

"What, Stasia? I know you don't want to be here. I'm sorry, but I don't know what else the fuck to do. Your prison is three thousand square feet. I will stay out of your way. There's a treadmill and weights in this room." He points to a door across from mine. "My room is on the opposite side. Feel free to get whatever you want from the fridge. There's a TV in here or in the living room. I'll give you space."

"You'll abandon me."

"What do you want from me, Stasia? You told me point blank that you don't want to be with me. For tonight, this is the best place I can bring you. Tomorrow, I will take you to Maks and Laura. You'll be a house guest, not Laura's employee, unless that's what you want. I'll have a security detail worked out. It will be my cousins or Aleks."

"Not you?"

"No."

I feel tears welling in my eyes, and I don't know where to look. Niko's body language says he won't come anywhere near me. I can't tell what he's thinking from his expression. His tone tells me I'm pissing him off. And I feel utterly unable to handle any of this. I nod and turn away, but not before the first tear falls. Niko snags my arm and pulls me against him.

"*Malyshka*, I am so sorry this is happening to you." He kisses the top of my head. "I'm trying to do what's best for you and what you want."

I cry against his chest, and my heart and intuition are yelling at me to stay right where I am, that it's right where I belong. But my head is louder. It's telling me I'm a stupid girl with a death wish to stay with him.

My tears are soaking his shirt by the time I pull away. I feel better for the cry, and I needed Niko's comfort. But I haven't changed my mind. I don't want to be with a man like him. It's too much.

"Thank you. I'm sorry I'm being such a colossal bitch. I know you're doing your best, and I appreciate it, even if you can't tell."

"If you need anything, let me know. Do you want me to make dinner?"

"Can I make myself a sandwich or something?"

He nods, and I can tell he thinks I'm rejecting him. That I won't even accept food from him.

"I'm sure you have stuff to do, Niko. You might even be tired. Neither of us got more than two hours of sleep. I just don't want to make you do more than you already are. Thank you for your offer."

"I'll do anything for you, *malyshka*."

He walks to the kitchen and waits for me. He points to the bread bin, then opens the fridge. I can see it's fully stocked. The fruits and vegetable drawers are practically overflowing. There are different deli meats and cheeses. There's food in containers that must be leftovers. I spot creamy peanut butter and grape jam. Suddenly, a PB and J sounds better than anything else in the world.

"Do you want a peanut butter and jelly sandwich?"

"Sure. Thanks, Stasia. I need to make some calls. The door at the end of the hallway is my bedroom. The one to the left is my office. I'll be in there for a few minutes. Anton went back to his place, but I know you saw the security. You're safe here. No one comes up unannounced and nothing arrives without being x-rayed."

That is not as reassuring as he wants it to be. Just how many threats does he get that he needs all of that?

"Okay."

I watch him walk to his office before I pull out the bread and stuff from the fridge. He didn't point to where he keeps his plates or silverware, so I open a couple cabinets and drawers until I find what I need. I wonder if he's like me and prefers jam to jelly because it's easier to spread. I make myself one sandwich and him two. It doesn't look nearly substantial enough for a guy Niko's size. I pull out what I need to make a salad. I'm finishing cutting the cucumbers when he comes back out.

"I thought two sandwiches might not be enough. I hope it's okay that I pulled this stuff out, too."

"That looks great. Thanks. You can use whatever you want. It's there to be eaten."

He grabs salad dressing from the fridge, and I grab forks and the two plates and carry them to the dining room table before I realize he might not want to sit with me. I look up and find him watching me.

"Do you need to get back to your work? I wasn't thinking. You probably need to work."

"I'd like to have dinner with you."

He doesn't seem to know what to do. Gone is the confident

man who insisted I leave my parents' house to come with him. Gone is the man who pinned me against the sunroom wall this morning. Gone is the man who fucked me senseless in the car a couple hours ago and all night in my bed last night. Gone is the man who didn't hesitate to defend me and probably killed for me. In his place is a guy who doesn't know what to do in his own home. He's trying so hard.

"I'd like that."

I wait to say anything more until he brings over the salad and serves me some before serving himself. Once he's sitting, I try to get my jumbled thoughts in order.

"I shouldn't have said what I did, how I did. I'm sorry. It was hurtful and on purpose. You didn't deserve it. I don't want you to be walking on eggshells in your own home, Niko. I won't bite your head off. You're being kind, and I appreciate it."

"I've fucked up your world, and I can't change it back to what it was before yesterday. But you are welcome here."

"You didn't do that. Antonio did. I did. You're trying to hold everything together. I think we're better suited as friends."

You fucking liar!

Even my head has chimed in, and it's for Team Niko. He nods before looking at his plate. We eat the entire meal in silence before we wash the dishes together in silence. It would be a scene of domestic tranquility if there wasn't so much charged anxiety hanging in the air like a wet blanket trying to suffocate us. I retreat to the guest bedroom, and he retreats to his office. There's a door next to the bathroom that doesn't look like a clothes closet. I discover linens and towels. I pull out what I need and decide on a shower. Everything feels better when your hair is clean. I don't know why that's the case, but I've felt like that since I was a teen. I turn on the shower and strip, but just before I'm about to step into the shower, I hear a knock.

"Niko?"

"Yeah. I realized you have nothing to sleep in. I don't know if you put on pajamas because of me last night or what you prefer, but I brought you a t-shirt and pair of boxers. If the bathroom door is closed, I'll leave them on the bed."

He's seen me naked twice. He's eaten me out and fucked me, and he's still trying to respect my privacy. Why the hell does he have to be a mobster?

"Thanks. The bed is good."

"If you look in the middle drawer, there should be toothpaste and mouthwash. I don't have any spare toothbrushes, but I'll have one for you by morning."

I open the door and step out with a towel wrapped around me. I look at the clothes on the bed. He's eyeing me, and I can see he's hard. Fuck, my pussy has a short memory. It doesn't remember any of the turmoil or danger from today. All it remembers is how fucking good Niko feels inside me.

"You didn't tell me what you want, Stasia? Do you want your clothes from your place, or should I order stuff for you?"

"Can I go to my place tomorrow and get what I need?"

He hesitates before he nods.

"All right. I'll see you in the morning, Niko."

"Goodnight."

He leaves, and I jump in the shower. It feels great to have the hot water run over me. I stay in way longer than I usually do. I'm not one to dawdle or soak, but it feels good tonight. It soothes my tense muscles and is just relaxing. I'm also horny as fucking hell. I rest a forearm against the wall in front of me as my other hand works my clit. Memories of being with Niko at my place, the sunroom, and then in the car flood back to me. I'm swallowing every moan as I get myself off. When I'm done, I use the mouthwash and run my fingers through my hair. I slip on the clothes, and it feels like Niko hugging me. Everything is oversized on me, but it's comfy. I brought my purse in with me, so I reach for my phone.

Shit.

I hurry down the hall toward Niko's side of the penthouse.

"Niko!"

He pulls open his bedroom door, and he's standing in boxer briefs. It's almost enough to make me forget what made me panic. Forget Armani models or Calvin Kline. He's fucking Adonis in the skin. What's the male equivalent of a Victoria's Secret model for men? He's it in those boxer briefs. Holy. Fuck.

"Do you think there's a tracker or anything on my phone?"

"I don't know. Let me look. Can you unlock it?"

He takes it. I see him sliding and tapping things on the screen.

"I don't see anything. Sergei can look tomorrow. He's the best to know, but I think it's all right. Goodnight."

He hands back the phone and closes the door. He doesn't exactly slam it in my face, but that's how it feels. The walk back to my room is maybe a hundred feet, but it feels like a hundred miles. I sit on the bed and open my texts.

Laura: Are you all right? Maks said something happened, and Niko went down to Baltimore after you. He said Niko will bring you here tomorrow. Come whenever you want and for however long as you want. You're welcome as our guest.

I see one from a friend who was at the bar with me last night. It's hard to believe everything that's happened has only been in the space of one day.

Beth: I tried calling a few times. Did you want to join us tonight? We're doing late night specials at The Dubliner. You should come out.

If only I could. The place will be packed, even on a Tuesday night. I could lose myself in the crowd.

Mom: Let us know when you get back into NY. Call us.

That's the only one I can't ignore. I gear myself up before I hit Mom in my contacts. It doesn't even ring.

"Ana?"

"Hi, Mom."

"Where are you? We expected to hear from you over an hour ago. What happened?"

"I'm at Niko's. I'm sorry I didn't call right away. We ate, then I took a shower. I'm about to go to bed."

"It's seven o'clock, Ana."

"And I'm exhausted, Mom."

"What's he doing?"

"I don't know. Probably going to sleep too. We have our bedroom doors shut."

"Doors?"

"Mom!"

I can't believe my mom. Who is she today?

"As you pointed out, you're an adult with a boyfriend."

"Yeah, well, I'm only an adult right now."

"You broke up?"

"Try not to sound so excited, Mom."

"Come back home then. Not for good, but for a little while. We'll go on vacation until everything blows over."

"Where's Papa?"

"I'm here. You're on speaker."

"Hi, Papa."

"You broke up with Niko?"

"Yeah. We had an argument in the car on the way home. I told him this isn't what I want. I still feel safest with him, but I don't want to be in his world."

"Good."

"Allison, don't."

"What? I'm not supposed to be happy that my daughter isn't dating a mobster?"

"You married one, Allison. You knew when you met me. That's how we met."

"You were KGB then."

"Same difference. But you knew about the bratva too."

"Yeah, and you left Russia to leave all that behind, Yuri."

"Ana?"

"Yeah, Papa?"

"If you're done romantically, then be done. He won't let you know if he's hurt unless he wants you to know. But don't confuse his lack of emotion for lack of feelings. He's human too."

And that's exactly what I did in the car. I didn't make it any better when he was showing me this room. I don't know what I want from him.

"I'll remember that. Thanks, Papa."

"When are you coming home, Ana?"

"Mom, I don't think I can leave New York. And if people are watching me, I will not lead them to you. I hope you're not still at the house."

"We aren't. We're somewhere safe. But you could meet us somewhere, or we could come to you."

"Mom, you cannot come here. That's the whole point of us staying apart. You come here and you may as well knock on the don's door. Do they call them that in real life?"

"Yes. Get to the U.N., and we can meet you there. Ask for Robert Monahan. He was my boss for years. He'll help until we can get there."

"No, Mom. Stay wherever you are if it's safe. I'm safe with Niko. He's going to take me to his brother's place tomorrow."

"Which one?"

"The *pakhan*, Papa. He and his wife have around the clock security that patrols their property. It's like Fort Knox. I'm going to stay with them."

"Ana—"

"Allison, she's safer with Niko than roaming the city to get to the U.N. Ana, that's a last recourse. Understand?"

"Yeah. My battery's low, and I don't have a charger. I need to go. I love you both."

"We love you."

My parents answer at the same time.

"Bye."

"Bye."

My mom gets the last word, as usual. I know I'm terrified of all this. I can't imagine how my parents feel. I'm trying to be patient with my mom. I know how much she loves me. But it feels like another weight added on top of everything else.

I put the phone on the bedside table and crawl under the covers. I'm asleep before I know it.

I hear music. I rub my eyes as I try to focus in the dark. It's a piano, but I don't remember seeing one. It doesn't sound like it's playing on a device. It sounds live. I creep out of bed and open the door a sliver. Someone is definitely playing. It has to be Niko. I could only describe the tune as a lament. It's probably Russian.

I tiptoe down the hallway until I can see inside his office. I never would have guessed, but there's an upright piano against the right wall. Niko's back is to me.

"You should be asleep, *malyshka*."

I freeze. How the fuck did he know I was here?

"The shampoo scent carries. There was a draught when you opened your bedroom door. I have a sixth sense for when someone is creeping up behind me. It's how I've lived to the ripe old age of twenty-eight. Couldn't sleep?"

"No, I woke up to the music."

"Please don't stop the music, music, music."

"Your bird knows Rihanna?"

"He's very cultured."

"Who's a pretty boy? Who's a pretty boy? Sammy."

I look over at the parrot, who's bobbing his head as though Niko were still playing. At least someone is lightening the mood.

"Play it again, Sam."

"What doesn't your bird know?"

"When to be quiet."

Niko grumbles, but he's smiling when he turns around on the bench.

"About time, motherfucker."

I can't help but laugh. The bird is hilarious, and I need some comedic relief after the day it's been. I walk over to the cage.

"Polly, want a cracker, pretty lady?"

"I thought your name is Sammy."

The parrot nods his head and lifts a claw. It almost looks like he wants to shake, but I don't trust him with any of my fingers.

"Who's a pretty boy? Sammy. Sammy."

The bird flaps his wings, and I laugh again.

"Did you teach him most of this?"

"Everything but the profanity and the pretty lady compliment. Those were Bogdan."

"Shithead."

"Sammy, be polite. Or I will cover your cage."

"Go ahead. Make my day."

I laugh so hard I almost snort. This is beyond hilarious to me. Maybe I'm overly tired, but hearing a parrot tell a mobster to make his day like he's Clint Eastwood is feeling pee-your-pants funny right now.

"Good night, Sammy."

"Night, jackass."

"How long did it take Bogdan to teach him all that?"

"Unfortunately, not long at all. African gray parrots are supposedly the most intelligent of the mimicking birds. I swear he isn't mimicking at all. I swear he thinks everything he says is the God's honest truth. How else does he know the right thing to say?"

Niko grabs a cover that fits over the cage. Sammy flaps his wings in disapproval, but the moment it goes dark in his cage, he settles and goes quiet.

"How long have you had him?"

"Fourteen years."

"Fourteen!"

"Yeah. He was a gift from my brothers when I turned fourteen. At thirteen, Bogdan thought he was hilarious teaching Sammy bad words. My mom threatened to wash Bogdan's and the bird's mouths out with soap."

"Why a parrot?"

"Back then, I thought I could grow to be an ornithologist."

I furrow my brow.

"Someone who studies birds. They fascinate me. How they navigate and know how to fly in formation. How intelligent crows are. Scientists suspect crows might even be sentient."

"And you didn't?"

I regret the question as soon as it's out of my mouth.

"Vlad gave me a very different type of gift that year. I gained a skill they didn't teach freshman year of high school."

"Niko, I'm sorry. That was thoughtless."

"It's a normal question normal people could answer."

"You're normal."

He just stares at me. I'm digging myself deeper. If I thought there was anything normal about him and his life, I wouldn't have told him what I did when we were in the car.

"What did you study in college?"

"Finance."

"That's it? No minor or anything? I knew I was interested in law school, so I studied poli-sci and government with a minor in urban affairs."

"Music theory. That was my minor."

I can't help but stare. Niko is a Renaissance man. I suppose it's not a surprise now to learn he plays the piano. It seems antithetical from the life he leads now, but maybe it's his reprieve.

"Bogdan minored in Medieval Literature and Art. Be sure to point that out when you meet him. He loves to talk about it."

From his grin, I know Niko is joking. Perhaps it's payback in perpetuity for a bird that cusses.

"I'm sorry I woke you, Stasia. I know you must be tired."

"Aren't you?"

"Yeah. But playing helps my mind settle. I was just about to go back to bed. Goodnight."

"Goodnight."

I thought we made a moment's headway in becoming friends, but Niko just slammed the door shut on that. How the fuck long is this going to go on?

Chapter Thirteen

Stasia

"Niko?"

"Yeah."

I'm poking my head out of the bedroom door, and I can hear Niko in the kitchen. Yesterday and last night have left me feeling adrift. As much as I want space from Niko, all I want is for him to hold me. I need comfort from him because of him. I'm trying not to panic after everything I learned about my parents, but it keeps rushing back in, despite how I try to push it from my mind.

Why did I call out to him? He clearly wants me to leave him alone. What do I want from him? I wish I had said nothing. Fuck. Now he's coming over here.

"Stasia, do you need something?"

I swallow and want to shake my head, but I burst into tears instead. He runs down the hallway toward me. When I step back, he eases the door open. His gaze sweeps the room before he looks at me again. He opens his arms, and I fall against him.

I was about to get in the shower when I suddenly felt like I needed to see him. I have a towel wrapped around me like I did last night when he lent me some of his clothes.

"What happened, *malyshka*?"

I shake my head and burrow closer. He tightens his arms around me and kisses the top of my head. I'm so tall that I barely fit beneath his chin, but I'm just short enough that he can offer me that comfort.

"It's all too much, isn't it?"

I nod. He runs his hand up and down my back. I press closer to him and can feel he's hard. It's probably the worst idea I've had in ages, but I need him even more than two nights ago. I reach between us and tug my towel loose and let it drop. I press my naked chest and belly against him. I feel his inhale, and he gets even harder.

"*Malyshka*, this isn't what you want."

"It's exactly what I want, *papachka*."

"You made what you want very clear. And I made it clear the other night that I don't want to just fuck."

My dad warned me not to toy with Niko, that if we're over, then we're over. But I don't know what I want anymore.

"Niko, I'm confused and scared shitless. Everything feels so fucking out of control in my life right now. I only feel safe when I'm with you, which I know is completely contradicting what I said in the car. I don't know up from down anymore. Watching TV or scrolling social media will make none of this go away. I need you."

He doesn't move for what feels like forever. Then his forefinger tilts my chin up. He looks into my eyes, and I feel everything slipping away.

"What do you need Daddy to do, baby girl?"

"Whatever you want, Daddy."

He chuckles.

"Whatever I want involves tying you to my bed, fucking you senseless all day, then making you dinner and snuggling with you all night."

"Sounds good."

He stares at me as though he's trying to decipher a code.

"You want this just for today? No more, no less, right?"

"I think. Niko, I'm not trying to string you along. I'm drowning, and you're the only life vest I trust."

"Do you want me to take control for today, *malyshka*?"

"Yes, *papachka*. I don't want to think about any of this shit. I just want to follow your instructions and not have to worry about what's going to happen next."

"I spanked you in the car yesterday for running away. That was for putting yourself in danger. We talked yesterday. You had the chance to ask me questions. You could have told me you needed time to see and talk to your dad. I could have ensured you got there safely, even if you wanted me nowhere near you. It felt deceitful. I was going to give you space, then check on you after my meeting."

"I know, *papachka*. I freaked out and didn't trust you."

"Stasia, have I done anything that makes you not trust me?"

"No."

I drag my teeth over my lower lip. He swoops in and kisses me, tugging on my lip. He nips, and it almost hurts. I love it. He fists my hair, and I feel my pussy getting wetter. I wrap my arms around his neck. His hands cover my ass and squeeze mercilessly.

"If you want this, then you accept that it's my way, Stasia. You need to tell me a safe word. Something that you only say if you really can't take anything more."

I think for a moment. I've never needed a safe word before. He told me to snap if the breath play got to be too much.

"Capt'n Crunch. It's disgusting."

"All right. What are your limits?"

"I don't know. You're the only man I've had sex with."

"I know, *malyshka*. But you said you've done almost everything else. Is there anything you don't want?"

As I look at him and feel him pressed against me, I realize that I'll say yes to just about anything he wants. I know a lot of that is my fraught nerves and overstimulated emotions, but part of me believes I would feel that way, regardless.

"Can I say no if we start something I don't like?"

"Of course. I will never force you, *malyshka*. I want to bring you pleasure and make you happy."

The way he's looking at me suggests he's talking about way more than the sex we're about to have. I nod.

"Get on the bed, face down, and wait here, *printsessa*."

Niko leaves my room, and I'm tempted to peek to know where he's going. But I said I didn't want to be in control. That means curbing my curiosity. I climb onto the bed and lie on my belly. He's only gone a couple minutes.

"Close your eyes, *malyshka*."

I follow his instructions as he approaches the bed. He slides a blindfold over me, and it makes me relax when I thought I would tense. I hear the cap of a bottle flip open and the sound of Niko lathering something on his hands. He climbs on the bed and straddles my thighs. His hands are warm when he slides them up my back. He kneads the knots out of my shoulders and mid-back. His hands are strong, but he's not inflicting any kind of pain. He spends so long on my back that I'm nearly asleep. My right leg twitches.

"Are you awake, baby girl?"

"Yes, Daddy. I don't think I've ever been this relaxed before."

"Good." He shifts, and his body moves away from mine. "Roll over."

There's a note of command, and I love it. I hear him pour more oil onto his hands. Then it dribbles over each nipple and down my belly to my pussy. He spreads my pussy open and a drop lands on my clit. One hand massages my right breast as the other rubs my clit. He pinches my nipple hard and pulls. I feel him lean forward toward my ear.

"Your body is mine, *malyshka*. I will make you come all fucking day as long as you ask. If you come, and I don't give you permission, I will edge you until you cry because you need me so badly you can't think straight. Do you understand?"

"Yes, *papochka*."

"You fell asleep before I did the other night. I didn't imagine you would run from me or tell me you didn't want me. I did some shopping, and those things arrived. They are for just us, Stasia. We're in this room because it's only for you. You aren't sharing any of this with my memories or any ghosts from my past. This is only about us."

Holy fuck. That's almost enough to make me come. I'm sure I would have wondered if he was recycling whatever he's about to use. And I would have wondered how many other women shared his bed. I would have gotten over the latter, but I'm not sure if I could get past the former. Gross on multiple levels. It sounds like he's forgiven me, at least a little. It sounds like he might be willing to have more than today. God, I hope so.

He pinches and twists the other nipple hard enough for me to yelp. He sucks on it, taking some of the sting away until he bites. The pain shoots straight to my pussy where he's still rubbing my clit.

"Daddy."

"I know. You're close already. Don't you dare come yet, *malyshka*."

"*Papochka*, please. Just once. Let me get it out of the way, then I'll calm down."

He laughs.

"I know I never make you come just once."

He leans forward again and kisses along my neck until he reaches the spot just behind my ear. It tickles in the sexiest fucking way.

"*Malyshka*, all of you is mine. Your mouth, your pussy, and your ass."

"Yes, *papochka*."

I've thought about anal before, and I've thought about it several times with Niko. How the fuck would he fit?

"Roll over again, *malyshka*. I'm going to put a plug in your ass. If it's more than just strange or uncomfortable, you tell me immediately. If you take any of this and let me cause you any harm, I will be pissed beyond what you can imagine. This is about pleasure for both of us. I find no pleasure in truly hurting you."

"Yes, *papochka*."

After what I know happened to Antonio because he hurt me, I know he isn't kidding. He takes my wellbeing and safety to an extreme in some ways, but his intentions are good. It's why I've given him control. He kneads my ass for a moment before I feel him reach for something. Packaging rips, then I hear the bottle open again. Then there's something cool pressing against my ass.

"Relax, *moye sokrovishche*. We'll go slowly."

He treats me as though I'm his treasure, gentle and careful. He draws my hips up as he eases the plug into me. It's an unusual sensation, but the plug is way smaller than I expected.

"*Papochka?*"

"Yes, *malyshka*."

"Can we start with something bigger? I—I—it doesn't feel like enough."

"Yes."

He pulls the plug from me, and I wait as he prepares the next one. This one is probably twice the size of the last one. I definitely feel fuller, and it's a really odd sensation. But I've had his dick in me. I know that it's still way narrower than what he's going to fuck me with. I'm not prepared when his hand rains down four hard slaps across my ass.

"You knew the type of man I am, Stasia, from the beginning. Even before we fucked, you had to know. I told you I wanted more than one night, and I told you I was in control. You agreed to at least the second part, if not the first. I do not need to control you out of bed, but I warned you about your safety. I don't think there's any way you could have misconstrued that I was in command of that, too. You defied me."

"I know, Daddy. But I thought you punished me for that already."

"That was for running away instead of talking to me about our problems. This is to make sure you understand where we stand. Whether we date, whether we fuck, no longer matters. As long as there is a threat to you, I decide, Stasia. You are new to all of this. I need your trust, not just when I fuck you. I will not demand it. You have to give it freely. But you will understand that I mean what I say."

"Yes, Daddy. Um—harder?"

"Stasia, you're not used to having a plug in. I told you, I don't want to hurt you."

"I know. And I promise I'll tell you if I can't take it."

What I really want is for his hand to keep pressing my clit into the mattress. Without his fingers or his cock in me, he won't know if I get off. The next three slaps land one right after another. Fuck it feels so good. My ass is full, I like the pain, and my clit is pulsing. I'm so close.

"I know what you're doing, *malyshka*. You play a dangerous game continuing to defy me. I told you not to come, or I would edge you. You think you can, and I won't notice."

Fuck.

He rolls me onto my back and takes my hands. He snaps a handcuff around my right wrist, then I feel it loop around something before it clicks closed around my left wrist. He presses a hard kiss to my lips before he moves away. I'm not prepared when he practically sucks my clit right off me. My back arches, and I try to twist closer to his mouth. He pulls my right leg back and lands the palm of his hand against my pussy. He presses three fingers in, then withdraws. He slaps my clit again before pressing three fingers in. He does it three more times. I whimper and try to reach for him when I feel him back away from the bed. Of course, I can do nothing with my hands restrained.

"*Malyshka*, this is a spreader. If I stretch your legs apart too far, tell me."

"I know, *papochka*. I will."

Cuffs fasten around each ankle before a rod expands and pulls them apart. I'm wholly on display to him. It's unnerving. He pulls my blindfold off, and I find him naked. When did he have time to strip? He's stroking his cock. I watch him before I meet his gaze. He's observing me intently, and he knows he's making me jealous. I want to do that. I want to pleasure him, but I have no control over that. I open my mouth and turn my head toward him.

"You want to suck me off?"

"Yes, Daddy."

He climbs back onto the bed and straddles my waist. I drop my chin and open my mouth again. I'm eager to taste him. Just when I think I'm about to feel him against my tongue, he presses my tits together. They're not anywhere near big enough to properly titty fuck him, but I can see him breathing faster. His abs ripple every time he rocks forward.

"Who decides, Stasia?"

"You do. But don't you want that?"

"Very much. You shouldn't have assumed."

So he's denying himself too just to keep control. Why is that even sexier to me? In its own warped way, this is all about me. He'll deny himself what he wants, so that his focus remains on me. The guys I've been with have either flat out said they expect blow jobs in return for going down on me or hinted at it. Is Niko like this because he knows he'll eventually have sex with me?

"Stasia, I don't expect you to suck me off in exchange for me getting you off. In the future, if you want to give me a blow job, tell me. If you want me to eat you out, tell me. One doesn't have to be done to get the other."

Fucking mind reader.

"And if I want to give you a blow job to say I'm sorry and make amends? Or what if I want to do it to say thank you?"

"You don't have to pleasure me to do either of those things, *malyshka*."

"But what if I want to?"

Why am I asking? It makes it sound like we have a future. I only want today. Don't I? That's all I can handle right now.

"Then ask."

"*Papochka*, may I suck you off?"

"Yes, *malyshka*."

"Right now?"

"Is that what you want?"

"Yes."

I do. I've never minded blow jobs that much. When you

rule penetration off the table, it makes the other options more—necessary? Yeah, I guess that's it. This is the first time I'm giving one purely because I want to please my partner. And not just sexually. I mean, I want to get him off, but I also want to make him happy because I want to do it for *him*.

He slides the head of his cock across my lips, and I open for him. He shifts his weight and leans against the headboard. I take as much in as I can. I realize I can't stroke the rest of him because he restrained my hands. I relax my throat, opening it as wide as I can. He slides in farther. Sweet Baby J. He's even bigger than I realized now that he's sliding past where my tonsils used to be.

"Do you not have a gag reflex?"

He pulls out, so I can talk.

"I do. But I want this, Daddy. I'm ready. I've—it's never been this easy before."

Which is true. I've gagged plenty of times or enforced my own limits. But as he presses back into my mouth, I wrap my lips around him and bob my head. My eyes drift closed as I concentrate.

"Fuck, *malyshka*. You're going to make me come way too soon. Everything about being with you is incredible. Fuck."

I love hearing those words. But more than that, I enjoy hearing the lust in his voice. He's rocking his hips and thrusting into my mouth, but he's not like some guys who seemed to want to choke me. I taste the first drop of precum, so I redouble my efforts.

"Enough."

I don't listen. I open my eyes and look into his. I suck so hard I practically swallow him. I see his determination. He thrusts harder and faster, making tears come to my eyes. But I don't cave. I keep working him until I see his abs tense.

"Stasia!"

His head tips back as he roars my name. His cum shoots down my throat. I don't expect him to pull out so fast. He hops off the bed, picks me up, and flips me back onto my belly. This spanking is hard. I try to kick my feet, but the spreader doesn't allow me to. My wrists are crossed, and the handcuffs keep me in place.

"While that was hands down the best blow job I've ever gotten, you disobeyed on purpose. So now I will punish you on purpose."

I watch him turn on a vibrator that almost rivals mine. It's big. Like really big. The one I have is only slightly narrower than Niko's cock, but shorter. This one is just as long, but not as broad as his cock. He knows I'm soaking wet, so when he presses it in, it's like the thing is moving along a slip and slide. Next, I hear something else turn on. I shift and see a wand massager with a foam head. He holds that in one hand while he grabs a paddle with the other. Fuck me. Like really, really please fuck me. I know he won't let me come. I already think I might expire from unsated lust.

"Daddy?"

"Yes, baby girl."

"I'm sorry."

"No, you're not. But you will be."

The wand hits my clit as the paddle hits my ass.

"Argh!"

"Yup."

I clench my fists as I fight not to come. I don't know what I'm going to do if it happens. This is almost too much. I don't know that I can withstand more than this, which is exactly what I'll get if I come without permission. I feel sweat dripping along my temples.

"Daddy, please, may I come?"

The moment I ask, I wish I hadn't. The vibrator gets

yanked out, and he doesn't touch me. My pussy aches so much it might be on fire. The need to come is making me tremble. I can't cross my legs to ease any of it. I force myself to breathe. The moment I get myself under control, I feel the vibrator slip back in, the wand hit my pussy, and the paddle land across my ass. Is he a fucking octopus? How does he manage three things with two hands?

The next time I feel an orgasm coming, I breathe through it, trying to hide how close I am. But he knows. How the fuck he does, I haven't a clue. He pulls everything away again. He does this four more times until I'm ready to scream Capt'n Crunch. He watches me the entire time. He's careful where the paddle lands, but he keeps his eyes on my face. He's reading me, knowing what I can and can't take. He turns off the vibrator and wand as he drops the paddle into the box beside the bed. He's more careful as he puts the wand and vibrator on top of the wand's box. I glance into the bigger box and see all sorts of things. I'm pretty sure there's a riding crop, a flogger, nipple clamps, a ball gag, and several more anal plugs. There's a *huge* dildo. It looks almost ridiculously large until I look back at Niko, who's hard again. They're the same size. God, all I want is his dick in me.

He brushes the hair back from my sweaty brow and presses the softest kiss to my lips. He unfastens my ankles from the spreader and moves my legs around to get the circulation back. It loosens my stiff hips too. Maybe it's so I can wrap my legs around him.

"*Malyshka*, you did that so well. I wasn't sure you could handle all of it. I'm so proud of you, *printsessa*. You don't have to ask to come this time."

"Thank you, *papochka*."

He pulls a condom out of the box and puts it on. My hands are still restrained as he pulls me onto my forearms and knees as he climbs onto the bed behind me. I feel his cock against my pussy. He pulls my hips back as he pushes in.

"Holy fucking, Daddy."

"Do you like it, baby girl?"

"Yes."

I whimper my answer. I pull against my cuffs.

"What's wrong, Stasia?"

He freezes.

"Don't pull out. Please, Daddy. Don't pull out."

I'm growing desperate.

Chapter Fourteen

Niko

Stasia endured a lot more than I imagined she could. I kept pushing her, but I watched. I didn't want to take it too far. I stopped edging her because I couldn't wait much longer to be inside her. But I think I overestimated what she could do. She's pulling against the cuffs, and she's begging me not to pull out. I have no intention of it. As much as I want to fuck her ass, I don't want to leave her pussy.

"Shh, *malyshka*. I'm not. Do you need me to unfasten your hands? Do you need your safe word?"

"I don't want to say it."

"That's not what I asked, Stasia. Do you need to say it?"

"No. I just want to touch you. *Please*."

I wrap my arm around her waist to support her as I lean forward and grab the key. I unfasten her hands and let the handcuffs drop onto the pillow. She twists and cups my jaw. Her eyes study me, and I nod. She presses her lips against mine, flicking her tongue against my lips until I open to her.

Her tongue presses between my teeth and strokes mine before she withdraws. When I slide mine into her mouth, she sucks. Holy fucking shit. I grip her hips and thrust into her. She sucks harder, and I thrust harder. It escalates until we're both trembling. I press Stasia forward. She releases my neck, thinking she needs to brace herself. I lace our fingers together as her belly meets the mattress. I rock against her.

"Come, *malyshka*. Make me come, too. Your cunt is so fucking tight... Fuck, Stasia...Yes."

"*Papochka*, I'm coming."

"I feel it, baby girl. God, you're going to squeeze me dry. Fuck."

I can't stop. I come, and I'm convinced every drop of cum that was in me is now in this condom. She's panting beneath me, and I feel like I could fall asleep buried in her.

"Niko?"

"Yes, *moye sokrovishche*."

"Will you hold me?"

"Stasia, I'm not letting you go."

Does she understand I don't mean just today? I roll to the side and pull her against me as we spoon. I'm drape my arm over her waist. She settles within my embrace.

"*Papochka*, can we take a nap?"

"Whatever you need."

"Can we do it again after we wake up?"

"Whatever you want, *malyshka*."

"Stasia?"

"Daddy?"

"How do you feel?"

I feel horrible. We fell asleep with the plug still in Stasia's ass.

"Horny?"

I chuckle. I guess she's all right. She shifts her hips, and I realize that not only did we fall asleep with the plug in her ass, but I was still inside her when we drifted off. I was getting soft, and now I'm looking down and seeing the condom is still on me. I pull it off and knot it. I reach over her and drop it next to the toys that need cleaning.

"Daddy, I'm serious. Can we?"

"Can we what?"

She shakes her ass against me.

"Can we put something better in there?"

"This plug isn't nearly big enough to get you ready, Stasia."

"Can we try? I swear I'll tell you if I can't."

I'm not convinced this is a good idea, but she's looking over her shoulder at me. There's something different in her expression than before. There's curiosity, but it's as though she thinks this is her only chance to try this. She's retreating from me. What did she dream about? What did she wake up thinking?

The possessiveness in me wants to fuck her in the ass, so I know that if I can't be the only man to be with her, then at least I'm the first for two things. I shift until I can reach the lube. She moves onto her hands and knees, but that's not what I want.

"On your back, *malyshka*."

I see her confusion. If she's going to withdraw from me, pushing me away again, then she's going to look me in the eye. I ease the plug from her and drop it with the other things to be cleaned. Part of me wants to throw it all away if she's going to reject me. The other part of me refuses to accept that and will hold on to them, practically like a shrine. I pour the lube onto my dick and stroke myself as she watches.

"Pull your legs up, Stasia."

She hears that command back in my tone. She draws her knees back to her chest as I press my cock against her ass. I'm careful as I inch past the initial resistance. She's watching me, and I can tell she's trying to relax. She's trusting me for this, something so incredibly intimate. But she won't trust me beyond that.

I slide further into her, stopping when I think she needs a moment. I reach forward and lace our fingers again as I rest on my forearms. Our eyes lock as I move within her. I kiss along her jaw to behind her ear.

"Is this what you want, *malyshka*? I've claimed all of you today. Tell me it doesn't matter, Stasia. Tell me you can walk away."

"Don't do this, Niko. Please. Just let me have this with you. I don't want to think that far ahead. I just need you right now, Daddy."

I can't push her. I have to accept where she's at, even if she's breaking my heart. Our gazes meet again, and we move together until I'm close. I release one hand and reach between us. I rub her clit until I see the flush move up her chest, into her neck, and finally across her cheeks as she comes. She's so fucking beautiful. It makes my chest ache. I feel my dick swell until it pulses within her.

"Fuck, Stasia."

I grasp her chin. My grip is firm, but my kiss is as tender as I can make it. Our foreheads rest together until I pull out. I climb off the bed. I get the distinct impression she wants her space. But I want to be sure.

"Do you want me to go, Stasia? Or do I stay and hold you like before?"

She sucks in her lips, and her eyes water. She whispers her answer.

"I don't know."

That's as good as a no to me. I nod, but I can't talk. The lump in my throat is choking me. What did I really think would happen? That two rounds of amazing, kinky sex would solve everything? That two rounds of amazing, kinky sex would make her feel about me what I feel about her? Clearly, that's not what happened. I pull my pants on and drop my shirt into the box of toys I ordered for the woman I thought was my soulmate but who doesn't want me.

"If you figure it out, Stasia, you know where I am."

I'll be pining in my room like a lovesick little boy instead of a man who's done unconscionable things.

It's been four days since my round trip to Baltimore and all the shit that went along with it. I didn't sleep the night I brought Stasia to my penthouse. I abandoned my piano since I woke her and just laid in bed until the sun came up. The next day was the most incredible intimacy I've ever shared, and it failed miserably. I assumed she would sleep late the second morning, and I was right. Anton and Sergei came over, and we were out for a run before six. They sensed I didn't want to talk, so they kept a conversation going. It distracted me, which I needed. How they still have so much to talk about after so many years is beyond me. But that makes me wonder if I would still have this much to talk about if I were with Stasia in ten years. I think I would.

They'd brought their clothes with them, so all three of us were cleaned up and ready to go when Stasia emerged from her room. She wasn't prepared for three huge guys moving around the kitchen while sipping fruit smoothies. She tried not to laugh, but then Sammy started cracking jokes, and it was downhill from there. But at least she was smiling when she left my penthouse. She was quiet all the way to Queens, so I didn't push her. She was warm to Laura and cordial to Maks, but she barely looked at me when I left.

I stopped by yesterday and the day before, but she kept to herself. Laura said she was sociable—just not when I'm around. I haven't gone over there today. I'm busy with my regular nine-to-five jobs. I have all of our casinos in New Jersey to visit. Bogdan's wife, Christina, now heads our construction division, so all of us have more time for our other businesses. We used to split the development projects, but Christina has a master's in construction management and worked for the city planner for five years.

My phone rings, interrupting my thoughts.

"*Privet.*"

"Niko, Bogdan and Aleks are with me. Can you come back to the house?"

"I'm on my way to the casinos, Maks. It's payroll."

"I know, but it's important."

There are three of them. Can't they handle whatever it is? I don't want to run into Stasia. I'm licking my wounds. I barely slept the last two nights because I've been worrying about how she's doing and when the next threat is going to pop up.

"Can it wait until this afternoon? We have a thousand people on our payrolls among the ten casinos. I can't not show up."

"You can't avoid her."

Bogdan calls me on it. Not that I want to hear it.

"I'm not, Bogdan. I'm working. Believe it or not, I have things to do besides babysit a woman who doesn't want me."

"Don't worry about babysitting me, Niko. You've dumped it on plenty of people."

Fuck my life. They might have mentioned she could hear the conversation.

"What's going on?"

I'm an ass to ignore her, but what's there to say? I'm being a little bitch because she hurt my feelings. That I was being a dick to my brothers, but I don't mean it. Both are true, but she's going to assume I'm making excuses.

"Salvatore sent us a message."

"Fine. I'm on my way."

I hang up. I don't know what they've told Stasia, but I sure as shit don't want her to hear about it if she hasn't. I'm not surprised when my phone pings like half a second later, and it's Aleks.

Aleks: Don't be an asshole.

Me: You could have told me she was there. You know what I meant but she doesn't. I was being pissy at my brothers.

Aleks: Sure.

Me: Don't you be the pissy one now. What's going on?

Aleks: Salvatore's decided any truce that came from what happened with Laura and Christina is over now that he thinks he can get Anastasia.

Me: What have you told her?

Aleks: Nothing beyond Salvatore sent a message.

Me: Then why was she there when you called?

Aleks: She wasn't. She walked in with Laura who didn't know we'd just called you.

Me: Great. So she knows I'm an asshole too.

Aleks: Yeah. Christina does too. She's here.

Me: Fucking wonderful.

Aleks: How far out are you?

Me: I just crossed over to Jersey. It's gonna take me a while.

Aleks: Fine. See you in a few.

Me: See ya.

I tell my driver to turn around. What the hell has Salvatore done now? How deep into this is he? What do we tell Stasia? I do not want her there while I learn all of this from my brothers. I need to know all of it before she knows any of it. That's going to land like a lead balloon. I close my eyes and let myself nap until the car stops outside Maks's place.

I let myself in and go straight to the office Maks and Laura now share. They have like twenty rooms, and they have to share this one. Fortunately, only my brothers are in there.

"Outside."

I don't want any of our voices carrying. I don't wait for their agreement. I head out through the sunroom. I look at the spot where I'd pinned Stasia's arms over her head, then fucked her. It was also the spot where everything turned to shit, where I realized what her father is. I couldn't bring myself to tell my brothers what I learned about our father and Stasia's. I chickened out and let Anton explain. I couldn't. I stood there while he spoke and nodded along, but my throat was too clogged to speak. It's hard to imagine eight men, all nearly six and a half feet tall, embracing. It was like a football team huddle.

"What was Salvatore's message?"

We're halfway down the garden, past the pool. We're far enough from the house that no one there can hear us, and our guards know better than to come within earshot. Maks pulls out his phone and holds up a picture. My ears ring, and my stomach knots. Salvatore's nephew Luca, who's his heir, is standing outside Yuri and Allison's house, waving at the camera.

"Were they there?"

"No."

Maks scrolls up until I can see what's written.

Salvatore: There's always a next time.

"Do you have any idea where they went? All I know is that Stasia's mom is in intelligence. I assume she works in DC or near there, even though they live near Baltimore."

"Yeah. Sergei discovered she works for the State Department when he ran Anastasia's background. It showed she's an analyst, but nothing said she'd ever done fieldwork. He didn't know she'd been a collector."

A collector. Such a benign name for someone who collects vital info to gain intelligence. There are plenty of times when that means the collector is in the thick of it in a foreign country. That was Allison when she was in Russia. That's what Yuri was when he came here. Basically, spooks. Spies. Not exactly, but close.

"Maks, what do you want to do?"

He's the final say in everything, even when he gets our opinion. I don't envy him that responsibility.

"She's your woman. What do you want to do?"

There is plenty I want to do, and there's plenty I want to say to my brother. But none of it is prudent, so I bite my tongue until I won't blurt out what I'm thinking. *Go fuck yourself. She's not mine, and you know it.* That won't get us anywhere.

"Make sure her parents are safe. Then find out what Stasia wants. If she wants a detail, then we give her one. If she wants help to hire her own, we give her recommendations. If she wants to go to her parents, a driver takes her."

"That's B.S."

"Not all of us got what we wanted from a one-night stand, Bogdan."

"Don't be a dick."

"What? It's true. I thought I would get as lucky as you with Christina. But I wasn't."

Aleks's eyes narrow. "So you're just going to give up because she's scared and confused. You're going to leave her to fend for herself. Or are you going to make us do it?"

"I never said I was giving up, Aleks. I'm trying to take into consideration what she wants as well as keeping her safe. What the fuck else am I supposed to do with a woman who told me point-blank that she doesn't want me?"

"She does."

"Last I checked, Maks, you weren't in the backseat of that car with us."

"And you haven't been here for most of the past three days."

"What does that mean?"

"She's been asking questions about you. She wondered if we're a musical family. I wonder why. She asked me what made me get into Medieval Literature."

"You outed my minor to Christina, so I did the same to you, Bogdan."

"And if she didn't care, she wouldn't have asked about either."

"Or she's bored, Bogdan."

This isn't doing anything to make me less annoyed. *What the fuck do people want from me?*

"You need to talk to her."

"She's your houseguest, Maks. You seem to talk to her plenty already. Do what you feel is best. I'll follow your decision. If you need me at the warehouse, I'll be there. Otherwise, I'm going back to work."

I turn around, but Aleks grabs my arm. I nearly hit him as I spin back. I have never hit one of my brothers outside a boxing ring or when Vlad made me. I uncurl my fist and step back. I shake my head and pull my arm out of Aleks's grasp.

"What the fuck am I supposed to do?"

I turn around, and this time, no one stops me. I don't go through the house but around the side to get to my car. I barely take the time to tell my driver to take me to Deuces Wild. It's our premier casino, and the one that takes the longest to run payroll. I close my eyes again, but there's no way I'm going to doze off now. I need to talk to Sergei and find out straight from him what he knows about Stasia's parents' whereabouts.

"*Privet.*"

It's easier to speak Russian when my cousin answers the phone in it.

"Where are Stasia's parents?"

"A State Department safe house of sorts outside of DC toward Fairfax."

"Good. But it's not like them being in Virginia is going to slow Salvatore down. They're still barely an hour from their home. How'd you figure it out?"

"The State Department's networks might be secure, but Yuri and Allyson's home one isn't. It was easy to get into. I found them transferring money from a savings account to checking. They filled up at a gas station near their house. Then I pinged Yuri's cell phone in Virginia."

"Who'd he call?"

"My dad."

"What?"

"Yeah. Needless to say, I called my dad right away."

"What did Uncle Radomir say?"

"Yuri asked him to keep an eye on Anastasia. They talked to her the night she got to your place. She said you had an argument and things weren't good. He wanted to be sure that she still had the protection she needs."

"He really thought I would abandon her because she doesn't want to date me?"

"No. Yuri told my dad that she might not cooperate if she thinks she's a burden to you. My dad thinks she might not because she's terrified. I saw her yesterday, Niko. She was in the kitchen trying to drink a cup of coffee. Her hand was shaking so badly, she spilled some and had to put it down. When she saw me, she pretended to be fine. I know what I saw. She's scared."

"I know. I still can't believe Yuri doubts me after everything he told her, after the way he encouraged her to come with me."

"He doesn't doubt you. But he knows his daughter. It truly isn't you. It's her, Niko. And you can't blame her."

"Did your dad say anything else?"

"No. Their conversation was only a couple minutes long."

"What about Salvatore?"

"He had some guys go to her place the first night she stayed with you, but no one tried to go in. They just peeked through windows. From what I can see, he had one of his guys hack her social media to track her location that way, but she must have them off. I couldn't find anything linking Salvatore to the Podolskaya yet. But it could have been phone calls on a burner. He has nothing digital or any money transfers lately."

"Thanks, Sergei."

"Maks already texted me. He said you almost hit Aleks."

"Fuck. Nothing stays private in this family."

"So?"

"I'm fucking frustrated with all of this shit, and I'm hurt that she doesn't want me. Everyone keeps asking what I'm going to do, and no answer is right. My brothers think I should keep chasing her. She wants space. I want to keep her safe. And no one thinks what I'm doing is enough. She's pushing and pulling, and the others think I've lost my balls and given up too easily. All I keep thinking is what the fuck do people want from me."

"For what it's worth, I think you're doing the right thing. From what Anton told me, she wants to have a choice. She feels stuck with everyone deciding for her, especially since her parents kept a monumental secret. You're trying to offer her a choice while still doing what we know will keep her safe. She needs time, which there isn't an abundance of. But unlike Bogdan and Maks, you aren't with a woman who can be pushed. Laura and Christina were in danger, but at least Bogdan and Maks both got more than one night with their women before the shitstorms started. You didn't."

"Thanks, Sergei."

"Relationships are hard."

Coming from him, that's the understatement of the millennia. At least, I don't have to hide my relationship, if ever I have one with Stasia.

"But you make it look easy."

"Bullshit, cousin. We just work at it and live with the fact that we can only control so much. Our world may never approve, but our family does. That's all that matters to Anton and me."

"You give better advice than any of my brothers."

"I know. I'll keep you posted, Niko. If the wind changes, you'll know first."

"No. It has to be Maks."

"No. It has to be you. He's going to defer to you, and you know that. He did for Bogdan. You need to have an answer ready."

"Thanks, Sergei."

"Bye."

"Bye."

Nothing connects Salvatore to the bratva in Moscow yet.

He must still be plotting. At least, from how it looks, the Podolskaya isn't after Yuri or Stasia. That's more reassuring than I expected. Salvatore is a pain in the fucking ass and is not to be ignored or overlooked. But the Podolskaya are the makers of nightmares. The one thing I can't reconcile is why Salvatore is targeting Stasia. I get there could be a fat payday for Salvatore, especially if he gets a cut from whatever price they would sell Stasia for. But he's steadfastly against using women in syndicate feuds. He's never pedaled flesh before. He might say things to get a rise out of his opponents, but he doesn't believe in involving women in men's business. Why is he willing to go against that? It can't be money. He has plenty of it and can get plenty more elsewhere.

When I looked at Maks's phone, it was a blocked the number. We know how to contact Salvatore. His phone number isn't a secret, so why did the photo come from a blocked number? Why was Luca in that photo? That's the type of bitch errand he sends Carmine on. He would either assume Yuri wasn't there, so he wouldn't need Luca to represent him. Or he wouldn't care if Yuri was there and beat the shit out of—or even killed—Carmine. Between Salvatore's two nephews, Carmine isn't the one he cares about.

The guy's a douche, but he's the baby of their family. Unlike Bogdan, no one's ever taken Carmine seriously. He doesn't man up because no one expects him to, and since no one expects him to, he never has the opportunity. It's a self-defeating cycle. He's not stupid. I know he isn't because I've known him since we were kids. But he's been the whipping boy his whole life. Given the chance, I think he's actually the one we should all worry about the most. And that day will probably come sooner than any of us expect.

But Luca. Why was Luca there?

Fuck.

I lower the privacy glass.

"Take me back to Maks's again."

"Maks!"

"Shh. I just got the twins to sleep. Who screams in a house with infants other than the infants?"

"Sorry, Laura. Where's Maks?"

"He and the others are still outside."

"Thanks."

I hurry back out to the garden. It surprises me they're still out there. They must still be talking about things they don't want Stasia to hear, even if it isn't about her.

"It's not Salvatore. It's Luca."

"What?"

Three practically identical faces turn toward me. It's like being in a house of mirrors since it's like looking at myself. It's not uncommon for people to mistake us for one another, even people who have known us for years.

"That wasn't Salvatore's number that the photo came from. It was blocked. When has Salvatore not been arrogant enough to show his number? Why is it Luca in the photo? This is the type of job he'd send Carmine on. He wouldn't risk Luca for something like this, and I doubt he thinks there's much information to get from Yuri if he's already discovered the connection. This isn't him. This is Luca, and this isn't sanctioned."

"*Pakhan!*"

One of our plainclothes bodyguards is running toward us from the side of the house. He spots me and goes white as a sheet. He stops and looks like he doesn't want to come any closer. I glance at the house.

"Where is she?"

There's only one reason he's looking at me and not my brother after calling out to Maks.

"She gave us the slip at the subway station."

I stalk forward.

"Why the fuck was she at a subway station? And who is us?"

"David and me."

"Who the fuck assigned you to her?" I spin back to my brothers. "I trusted you. You knew I didn't want her with anyone but you or our cousins."

"Niko, she said you gave her permission to go for a walk. She said you'd already talked to *pakhan*. You were already gone, but I saw you talking earlier. She walked at a normal speed until we got to the subway station. She bolted down the stairs and got on a train while David and I were halfway down the stairs. The doors almost trapped her."

"And why were you that far behind?"

"We weren't any farther behind than normal. But she's a lot smaller and more able to push through a crowd than we are."

"Which one did she get on?"

I'm telling myself not to panic, not to lose my shit, and not to strangle Stasia when I find her. And I will find her. When I do, her sweet little ass is going to be apple red by the time I'm done.

"The F toward Coney Island."

"The F?"

Bogdan's as puzzled as I am until I realize where she's connecting.

"She's getting off at Bryant Park. She's going to take a bus from 42nd and 6th to 42nd and 1st. She's going to the U.N. She knows if she goes that way, she won't have to walk like she would with the E."

"The U.N.?"

I look at Aleks, and my heart sinks.

"Her mom supposedly worked for them. Allison must have told her to go there if she needed to get away. They must have a contact there. It's the opposite direction from her place or campus."

I'm running toward the house as I strip off my suit coat and my tie. I don't know which brother catches them, but someone does.

"Maks, I'm taking your bike."

Our mother was adamantly against us learning to ride motorcycles, but since Vlad often had us steal them, we had to learn. She hates that we ride them for fun now, but I can go a shit ton faster on a bike than I can in a town car, my Porsche, or the subway. I can't lane split with any of those.

She didn't know I was here, or she would have known I would come after her. I want to believe that more than believing she knew, and that's why she took off. Either way, that sweet little ass will be red.

Chapter Fifteen

Stasia

My mom's text was brief, but I suppose she wanted to make sure no one knew where I was going.

Mom: Ana, it's Mom. I have a burner. Meet Dad and me where I used to work.

Niko just came back, and I don't want to see him. I need to get out of the house without him knowing. There's no way he would take me, and there's absolutely no chance in hell he'd let me go alone. I know he only wants his family to guard me. He made that plenty clear.

"Hi. I asked Niko, who asked Maksim, if I can go for a walk. They both said yes as long as I have two guards."

I'm lying to the guards standing in the driveway. I'm sure Niko will go berserk when he finds out what I'm about to do. I honestly feel bad for what might happen to them. I don't think Niko will go as far as taking them to whatever place they use, but he's going to be pissed. I figure if I say that Niko and Maksim want me to have two guards, that's more plausible, since I'm sure they've made it clear to all the guards that only they or their brothers and cousins can guard me.

"I should check, Ms. Antonov."

"Maksim and his brothers just went into a meeting. They don't want to be disturbed. It doesn't have to be a long walk. I'm just bored, and it's such a nice day."

It's fucking humid as hell, and the hair is already sticking to my neck. But I need out. The men look at each other, and two step forward. Once we're on the sidewalk, they keep a discreet distance, but they're only a few steps behind. I try not to rush, but I want to get to the subway station now. It only takes a few more minutes. I can't look back to see how close they are, so I'm assuming I can make it. I have my subway card in hand. When I get even with the steps down to the platforms, I veer right, and bolt down them.

"'Scuse me.'Scuse me."

I'm lucky I'm so fucking thin. Usually, I hate it. I love to run, but I can't keep any weight on. I feel like a 'tween standing next to most of my friends. But right now, it's saving my ass. I can squeeze between people. As I turn sideways to get around a heavy-set man, I can see my guards barreling down the stairs. They're large enough to make people want to move. But there's not enough room for them to pass easily. I blow through the turnstile as I pass my subway card over the reader. When I get to the platform, the announcer is warning the doors are about to close. I glance up and see it's the F train. It's the one I want. I'd be fucked if it were the E. I barely make it onto the car before the doors trap me. I stumble a step before catching myself. It's New York. No one notices or cares. I grab hold of the pole and watch the men shrink as they wave at me from the platform.

It's going to take me nearly an hour to get to the United Nations Headquarters. I can take this train most of the way, but I'm going to have to transfer to a bus. It's better than the other train. I would have like a fifteen-minute walk from the closest stop to the U.N. I pull out my phone to look like I'm reading or scrolling social media, but I'm watching everyone who gets on and off. No one looks in my direction.

I squeeze out of the car when we get to Bryant Park. I get my bearings and head up the correct stairs to the street. I look around and spot the bus stop. There are some people already waiting. They're a couple with a stroller, so they seem harmless. As I wait, a few more people join us. A guy who looks a little older than me, probably closer to Niko's age, stands next to me. He smiles, and I can tell he thinks he's God's gift to a tired world. He's hot, for sure. But he's not Niko-level hot. No one is. Not even Niko's brothers.

Niko. He has to know by now. He's going to lose his fucking shit.

"Thank God for AC. It's gross out today."

I glance at the guy, and I catch the touch of an accent. I can't tell what it is. I nod. It's July in New York City. Every day is gross out. The bus comes, and I concentrate on getting on. The guy who talked to me offers to help the couple get their stroller on before he steps back and gestures for me to go ahead. Chivalrous, I'll give him that.

Once I'm on, I notice there are only two seats left, and they're next to each other. I really don't want to chat with this guy. I just want to get to the U.N. and to my parents. Please don't let him be talkative. Please let him get the hint.

"Looks like we got lucky."

Here we go. The only people who get on after us are younger guys. There's no one for Prince Charming to give his seat to.

"Yup."

I look out the window, hoping he'll get the hint.

"I take this bus every day, but I've never seen you. You don't look like a tourist, though."

"I'm not."

That's not creepy at all.

"You don't sound like a New Yorker either."

"I'm not."

"Not chatty either."

"Nope."

He seems to get the hint and sits back. I look out the window and count the blocks. It's like a five-minute bus ride, but we're catching every red light. Fina-fucking-ly.

"Excuse me. This is my stop."

"Mine too."

The guy gets up as the bus approaches the stop. A car cuts in front, and the driver slams on the brakes. I pitch forward, but the guy grabs me around the waist. I feel something sharp poking in my waist. It's a fucking knife.

"Make a sound between here and the car we're getting in, and I will gut you and run."

I try to look back at him, but he nudges me forward. I try to move slowly, hoping someone might notice that I'm going against my will.

"Get the fuck off the bus, *puttana*. I know you're fucking Niko."

Puttana. That's Italian. Antonio called me that the night we broke up. I used Google translate to find out it means bitch.

"You're a Mancinelli."

The moment the words are out of my mouth, I regret it. The woman sitting facing the center aisle looks up at me. Her eyes are wide, and she's terrified. The driver heard me too. He's shifting in his seat. Clearly, they know the family.

"Shut up, or I gut you."

"I'm not worth anything to anyone if I'm dead. And I'm just as worthless if I have scars."

I step off the bus and try to break free, but his arm is too strong.

"Stasia! Stasia!"

"Niko!"

I look around. He has a motorcycle helmet on, and he's trying to push past two guys holding him back. The Mancinelli guy is pushing me toward the car that cut the bus off. I'm dragging my heels, but I weigh too little to do anything. I watch Niko headbutt one man. Blood shoots from the man's nose as the helmet hits his face. Free of one man, the heel of Niko's palm slams upwards into the other man's nose. He's free and running toward me.

"Niko!"

I'm looking at him, so I don't notice Prince Not-So-Charming's fist coming at my temple. I crumple but shake it off. It wasn't as hard as I expected. But it allows him to shove me in the car and climb in after me.

"Stasia!"

I open my mouth, but the knife that was at my waist is now at my throat.

"You're mine, *malyshka*. Mine. *Ya sozhgu vse dotla, prezhde chem poteryayu tebya.*" I'll burn it all to the ground before I lose you.

I don't doubt Niko for a moment. God help whoever this guy is and whoever the Mancinellis are. The rage I just saw on Niko's face is enough to make the Devil piss his pants. I know this guy with the knife at my throat saw it. His hand trembled for a moment. Niko intended him to see his anger, otherwise, it never would have shown.

"You're Italian, right? You better pray to the Trinity and Mary. You're so fucked."

"Shut up. No one asked you."

"I'm meeting someone. They'll know something happened too."

"You mean your mom at the U.N.? You are so fucking gullible. First with Antonio and how you loved his tattoos. You told him all we needed to know. Now with the text. Your phone isn't as secure as you thought. Niko didn't look too pleased when you got off that bus. Where were your bodyguards? That's right. You ditched them. And they weren't even your real guards, were they?"

I don't answer.

"You keep making this easier and easier. The moment my guy saw you walk out that gate with men who aren't Niko's family, you gave us a fucking Christmas gift with a huge bow. Then you ditched them. It's like Christmas and my fucking birthday all rolled into one. My guess is Niko told you not to do something so stupid, and you did it anyway. Selfish bitch. If you'd fucked Antonio, he'd still be alive, and we'd already have our money."

So he is dead. How does this guy know?

"I saw Antonio's dick. Not impressed."

"Maybe I'll show you mine. Open wide."

"I'll fucking bite it before I suck it."

I snap my teeth at him.

"Feisty. Now I get why Niko likes you. Definitely not for your skinny ass. He likes it rough and kinky."

"Been watching him to get off?"

How the hell does he know that? Niko said it's been ages since he's been with someone.

"He and his brothers enjoy certain clubs. They offer a fuck ton more than just strippers."

"Sex clubs."

I try not to sound shocked.

"Yes. Their tastes all lean toward being doms. Has he spanked you yet? Did it make you come? Did he chain you to his bed and make you beg?"

No, but I would. If it weren't this skeezy guy saying this raunchy-ass shit, it would be hot thinking about Niko doing just that. I know next to nothing about doms and subs, and I don't think I'm a sub. But Niko could do just about anything, and I think I would ask for more. Sex isn't our problem. We're great at that. It's everything that happens when his cock isn't in me that's the problem.

"The only one who's going to beg is you. And he still won't let you live. Niko is not the type of man you take something from and get forgiven. If you hurt me, it'll only be worse."

"He has to find me first."

"Are you five? This isn't hide-and-seek."

It goes dark as we enter the Lincoln Tunnel. Why the hell are we going to New Jersey? Do they have their own warehouse there? Is that where they're taking me? Oh, fuck! Are they taking me to the Newark airport? Am I headed to Russia?

My heart is racing, and I'm trying not to panic. While my mind is racing in one direction, it's waiting for this guy to strike in the dark. I won't be able to fight him off. He's way bigger than me, and I can't see a damn thing because of the tinted windows. Why does this tunnel have to be so long?

We burst back into sunlight, and I blink several times. I'm not ready for my hands to be yanked behind my back. I almost slide off the seat, but I feel handcuffs snap around my wrists.

"What's your name?"

"Wouldn't you like to know?"

"Fine." *Asshole.*

I hear duct tape ripping, so I twist to see. That only gives him easier access to my face. He slaps it across my lips and catches some of my hair. It makes my eyes water, but I refuse to cry. I notice that we're not headed south, but north. Not to the Newark airport. We're on the interstate, and I recognize the George Washington Bridge coming up.

We return to Manhattan, and now I'm completely confused. I watch the street names as we head northeast. We're headed to the Bronx? This is like the least direct route. Does he think Niko won't follow? I've heard a motorcycle revving, even though I can't see it. Is it Niko or someone else? Part of me prays it isn't him. He's alone. He's going to die before he can rescue me.

I expect us to pull up to some deserted building, probably covered in graffiti or something. Instead, it's a typical house sitting on a bit of a hill. The garage is at street level, and the house is above. It's two-stories. There's nothing remarkable about it. The car pulls into the garage, and I hear the engine turn off, then the garage door closes. I hear it thud as it hits the ground. Only then does a backdoor open. A hand reaches in and grabs my upper arm and practically yanks me from the vehicle. I stumble as I try to get my feet under me.

I'm going to die, or I'm going to Russia. I've seen where we are, and I've seen faces. I'm tied up and in a secondary location. The odds look like death. Why couldn't I just listen to Niko? If this were a movie, I'd be looking at the dumb blonde on the screen and saying she's getting what she deserves. Except, this is real life, and I'm the dumb blonde.

"She's not as pretty as I expected."

I look toward the door into the house and find a guy with dark hair and nearly black eyes looking at me. His hands are on his hips, and his button-down strains over his muscles. He has a wicked scar down the side of his neck and under his collar.

"Yeah, well, she takes a good photo."

"She needs fattening up if they're going to buy her. She's too thin even for Russian men used to half-starved whores."

"Fffrrr."

They can't understand my fuck you. They just laugh. More like fuck me. The driver is still holding my arm, and the guy who kidnapped me grabs the other. They pull me toward the door. I could go limp or drag my feet, but being awkward is more likely to get the shit beaten out of me than keep them from getting me in the house. I need to bide my time. Watch and listen. And pray to everything under the sun that Niko finds me.

"Did you turn off her phone?"

The guy at the door steps out of the way as he asks the two guys dragging me.

"Fuck. No."

"Car—"

Mr. Scar Neck is pissed at Prince Not-So-Charming. Mr. Doesn't Talk reaches into my purse that's now stuck to me since they cuffed my hands behind my back. He pulls out my phone. He forces my thumb onto the screen to unlock it. I don't know what he's looking at, but the location services are still off from when Niko and Anton came to my parents' house. Anton turned them off while I was outside with my dad. The guy drops it on the ground, but the case protects it. That is until he slams his foot on it and crushes it.

"When's our uncle getting here?"

"My brother went to get him."

They're talking as though I don't know they're Mancinellis. I heard Maksim and Aleksei talking the other day, and Niko's already mentioned the guy. Salvatore is the New York don. I don't know their names, but they seem like little boys trying to impress the don to prove they're ready for the grown ups' table. But they're little boys with big toys. There's a veritable arsenal laying on the dining room table. There are knives, guns, and I don't know what else. But they look like they're ready for a war.

I push my cheek against my shoulder until the tape comes loose. I spit and keep pushing my shoulder against my mouth until I can speak.

"You have all that because you know what's going to happen when you face the Kutsenkos. If you need that much to defend yourselves, you're already fucked."

"Shut up, *puttana*."

"*Idi na hui zasranets*." Go fuck yourself, shitass.

"What did you just say?"

Prince Not-So-Charming sounds like a whiny-ass little bitch. I just shrug one shoulder and laugh.

"Google translate it."

"Bitch."

"So you keep saying. I'll be sure Niko knows you've been extra shitty to me."

"You're never seeing lover boy again."

Finally, Mr. Doesn't Talk says something. I look at him at shake my head.

"I guaran-fucking-tee you, you will not come out on top. Maybe you don't have your own women and that's why you don't get it. He told me he'd burn everything to the ground before he loses me. You've just poked a Russian bear. Three little Italian wolves are no match. I hope you didn't drink much today, because I guarantee you're going to piss yourself before the day is over."

"Shut the fuck up."

Once again, I'm not prepared for the fist coming at me. This time, everything goes black.

Chapter Sixteen

Niko

There have been moments etched in my brain because of trauma. Seeing Carmine Mancinelli push Stasia into a car with a knife at her ribs is among the worst.

"Maks, Carmine took her. Gabriele was driving. I couldn't get to her. We're headed into the tunnel."

I'm on my brother's bike, talking into the helmet's Bluetooth. I'm following the town car into the Lincoln tunnel. I have the license plate memorized.

"They're going to Jersey?"

"My guess is to confuse Stasia and lose me. I think they're going to head north and come back into New York via the George Washington Bridge. But why back into Manhattan?"

"The Bronx. My guess that's where they're really headed. Luca owns some real estate close to Little Italy. I bet they're taking her to one of those. If Salvatore didn't sanction this, they won't take her directly to him. That gives us some time, Niko."

"No, it doesn't. They aren't working for him, so they'll do whatever the fuck they want. I need all of you, Maks."

"I know. I'm texting our cousins now. Aleks and Bogdan are here and suiting up. I'm half dressed."

That means they're putting on all their bulletproof gear. Vlad was KGB and connected to the Podolskaya. He trained us to be paramilitary. We have the gear, the weapons, and the skills. The Italians only have two out of the three, and only the ones you can buy. Our skills were beaten and carved into my family.

"Call Mama. Let her know we may be gone for a while. When we get Stasia, I want to take her to Mama's. I don't want any of this near the twins. Mama needs to stay with Laura."

"I'm already working on it. Christina is on her way here."

"Did Stasia find the tracker I put in her purse?"

"No. I'll pull it up. Hold on."

It's not that I thought she would bolt. Again. I was afraid someone might take her. That's why I slipped a tracker into her purse the morning I dropped her off at Maks and Laura's. I thought about how pissed she would be if she found it, and it tempted me not to do it. Now I'm glad I did. They've either turned off, disabled, or broken her phone. And I know her location services are off. I stressed that several times.

"Niko, it looks like they just got on the bridge."

"I know. I can still see them. But wherever they take her, I can't pull up outside and wait for you. I've got to stay back, even if it kills me."

"We're going to get her, Niko."

"I know, but it doesn't mean the wait is any easier."

"I know that better than most. We're coming, little brother."

"Thanks, old man."

He calls us all little brother, and we all call him old man.

We have since we were kids. It's just our thing. But it's more reassuring than anything, save for a hug from my mom. I hang up with Maks and focus on following the town car. They have to hear the bike. Out of all our vehicles, it's the only one that announces we're coming. Once we cross the bridge back into Manhattan, I stay a few cars back. It gives me a chance to see each turn and follow them. As we cross into the Bronx, I slow down and fall back a few more car lengths. I watch them pull into a driveway, then into a garage. The door closes before anyone gets out.

I turn around and park the bike three blocks from the house and wait for my brothers. It feels like it takes a lifetime for them to arrive. When they do, it's in two bulletproof SUVs. Our vehicles have tires that will still roll, even after being shot. The windows are bulletproof, and the doors and underside are all armored. They're veritable tanks.

"We tracked them to three blocks down."

Sergei has a laptop in his hand as he gets out of the second row. Aleks tosses me gear. I open the back doors of one SUV and strip. I don black utility pants, a black long-sleeve pullover, and a bulletproof vest. I've never dressed so fast in my life.

"I know. I saw them pull into a garage."

"Niko, here."

Misha, Sergei's younger brother, hands me a pair of heat-seeking binoculars.

"They're going to have people on the lookout. It would be better if we wait until dark."

"The fuck we are, Bogdan. That's seven hours from now. Way too much can happen in that time."

"They won't hurt her."

This is the second time in one day that I want to strike one of my brothers. They see it because Maks and Aleks step between Bogdan and me.

"We're only assuming what they plan to do to her. We don't know for sure. Maks, you need to call Salvatore. I want to talk to him."

Maks nods and pulls out his phone. Salvatore, along with the heads of the other syndicates, is on speed dial.

"Maksim, what do you want?"

I speak instead of my brother.

"Always a pleasure, Salvatore. Do you know where Luca, Carmine, and Gabriele are right now?"

There's a pause.

"What did you do to them?"

"It's more like what are they doing to my woman."

"What?"

"Salvatore, your nephews think their balls have dropped. They took my girlfriend. They put a tracker on her car. They went to her parents' home in Maryland, and Luca stood in front of it to take a picture. Carmine grabbed her off a bus less than an hour ago. You have a mutiny on your hands."

"How do you know I didn't order this?"

That gets a snort from all of us.

"If Sylvia goes missing, don't assume Maks ordered it."

"Stay the fuck away from my wife."

"If she went missing, you know Maks didn't order it. That's my point. Women and children are off-limits."

"You said girlfriend. It's wives and children."

"Maria isn't a child anymore and not anyone's wife. I bet your niece would sell for as much as whatever Luca asks for my girlfriend."

"Stay the fuck—"

"For fuck's sake, Salvatore. No one is taking your fucking women. I just want mine back. Get your fucking nephews under control. Consider this a fucking courtesy because all eight of us are here. They won't survive if I don't see her walk out of that house in the next three minutes."

I hang up. Now we wait. But we don't stay where we are. I jump into the first SUV as everyone gets back into them. We pull up even with the house. Those of us on the house's side roll down our windows. Those on the far side get out and position themselves next to the hood and rear bumper.

"No one moves until she's with us."

I know my family won't, but I feel like I have to say it. I put the heat seeking binoculars to my eyes. They show there's five people inside. Carmine, Gabriel, Luca, someone else, and my *malyshka* on a chair. Is it another one of Salvatore's nephews or some goon Luca dragged into this?

We watch as the front door opens wide enough for Stasia to pass through. She steps onto the stoop before being shoved forward. She can't brace herself and pitches toward the stairs. I'm out of the car and running toward her, my rifle trained on the front door, waiting for someone to shoot me. I get to her as she rolls to the ground. I look up and see a gun pointing at me. I fire, and it disappears as the guy holding it falls backward. The door slams shut.

"Stasia?"

I sling the rifle over by back and scoop her into my arms. She's bleeding, and her arm isn't hanging right.

"Daddy. You came."

"Always, *malyshka*."

"It hurts."

"I know. I'm going to get you to our doctor."

Once I'm in the SUV with Stasia in my lap, the others open fire. They shoot out the windows on the first and second floor. No one cares if we hit anyone or not. The point is to leave a message. If they were smart, they all ran for the basement.

Misha and Pasha are always our drivers for missions like this. Both vehicles' tires squeal as we peel out.

"Here."

Aleks hands me a stack of gauze squares. I press them against the cut on Stasia's head. I watched it hit the edge of a step. She whimpers, but her eyes remain closed.

"*Malyshka,* I know it hurts. I'm sorry, but I have to put pressure on it. Head wounds bleed a lot."

"Everywhere hurts, D—Niko."

Bogdan looks back at me from the front passenger seat and cocks an eyebrow. I glower at him. He nods, and I see understanding. Interesting. I did not know that about him and his wife. Aleks and Pasha are oblivious, or at least pretend to be.

"I know. We're going to go to my mom's house. Our doctor's name is Boris. He's going to meet us there and take care of you. He's taken care of all of us, my dad, and my uncles."

She tries to shake her head.

"Rest."

"No, Niko. This is a trip to the hospital. Something is seriously not right. I can't feel my legs."

I look down at her before I look at Aleks and Bogdan. Aleks presses on his earpiece and talks quietly in Russian. I can't hear who answers him.

"*Malyshka,* I need Aleks to hold you for a few minutes."

"No!"

She tries to sit up but screams in pain.

"Stasia, I cannot take you into the hospital dressed like this. I need Aleks to hold you. My clothes are in the back. I have to put them back on."

She looks up at me before she looks at Aleks. I follow her gaze and notice Aleks appears much more sympathetic than I have ever seen him before.

"I'll be as gentle as I can, Anastasia. I don't want to die today."

He winks at her as he opens his arms. It's awkward, and I'm terrified to move her if she has a spinal injury. But none of us can go into the hospital in tactical gear. As is, they'll drop us off and leave. The moment Aleks has her, I climb into the third row and reach into the trunk to grab my clothes. I change as fast as I can.

I crawl back over the seat, careful not to jostle Stasia. Aleks hands her back to me, but he leans forward to keep the pressure on her head wound. We're headed to the Queens location of the best hospital in New York. It's in Flushing, but it's the closest one to my mom's house and Maks and Laura's. I would take her into Manhattan, but that's a thirty-minute drive. The Bronx to Flushing is less than twenty. That's assuming there aren't any major traffic delays.

All of us have complicated relationships with God. We're all lapsed Russian Orthodox. We all were altar boys before we moved to America and for the first year we were here. It's hard to believe even the most merciful God can forgive our sins. But it doesn't stop me from praying right now. I recite every prayer I ever memorized in Russian. I repeat them in English. I add my own intercessory prayers in between. None of it is about me. I don't ask God to heal her for my sake or for her to live, so I can be with her. I just want her to be well. After all this, I doubt she'll ever let me see her again.

"Niko, will you stay with me?"

Her voice sounds so tiny. She needs someone until her parents can get here. I won't abandon her, but I'm prepared for the inevitable.

"Of course, *malyshka*."

"I don't just mean while I'm in the hospital. I mean, for good. I'm so sorry for what I said and how I've behaved. It wasn't just my life I risked. I saw all of your family. You all came for me. Your mom and both sisters-in-law and the twins could have lost you all because of me."

"Shh, no more, Stasia. Just rest."

"No. Not until I have your answer. I made such a colossal mistake, even before I left the house today. I was going to talk to you, but I got a text from my mom. At least, I thought it was her. They hacked my phone. I was going to tell them I want to stay with you. I needed to see them one more time in case..."

"I'm not going anywhere if you're not by my side."

I kiss the uninjured side of her forehead. How did Maks and Bogdan cope so well while their wives were in danger? I'm barely holding it together. Aleks's free hand rests on my shoulder, and he squeezes.

"I'm sorry about earlier."

I look at my older brother, guilt for yet another mistake gnaws at me. He shakes his head before responding.

"We were pressuring you too much."

Her voice trembles as she speaks.

"What happened earlier, Niko? When you were talking outside with your brothers."

I glance down at Stasia. Her eyes are closed.

"Nothing."

"You promised not to keep secrets if you don't have to. Is this really something I can't know?"

I will not keep secrets or tell lies if I don't have to.

"We were talking about the message we got. They frustrated me, and I was ready to leave in a huff. Aleks grabbed my arm, and I nearly swung at him."

"What happened with Bogdan? I could see outside."

Stasia tries to turn her head toward the front seat, but winces.

"I almost hit him, too."

"Niko, maybe it's a mistake to ask you to stay. You can't fight with your brothers over me. No."

Bogdan looks back at us again.

"Anastasia, if my brother didn't care about you, he wouldn't have been frustrated. There's something about our family. When we meet the right person, we know from the start. Niko let you into our lives because he wants you to stay. We thought he was going to ignore what we know about how our family loves. We shouldn't have pressured him when he thought he was doing what's best for you."

I look at Bogdan as he talks, and our eyes meet. I swallow and nod. He spoke the truth. From what we know about our parents, they fell in love as children. My aunts and uncles fell in love within days of meeting each other. Sergei and Anton have been together since we were teens. Maks and Laura got married within two months. Bogdan and Christina only took longer because of her injuries from a car accident. They were ready to marry within two months, too.

"Niko, lean forward. I need to whisper something."

I lean over Stasia's mouth. Her breath tickles my ear.

"If something is wrong with my legs, and I can't be a real partner to you, then you have to move on."

"You can always be a real partner."

I know what she means, and I won't even entertain the idea.

"Niko, sex has—"

"I swear to you, Stasia, if you finish that sentence, the moment the doctor tells me you're well enough, I will turn you over my knee and paint your ass red."

I'm whispering, but I think Aleks, Bogdan, and Pasha hear me. I'm certain they don't hear Stasia when she responds.

"Promise?"

"Don't doubt it for a moment, *printsessa* I already have a

bone to pick with you about leaving the house today. But that can wait."

Her eyes flutter open for a moment, then a pained expression mars her face before her entire body goes lax. I lean over her again, but I don't feel her breath. I put my fingers to her throat and can barely feel something that might be a pulse.

"Pasha, hurry. She's not breathing. Aleks help."

Together we lay her on the seat while we kneel between the seats. I breathe for her, and Aleks does chest compressions the entire way to the hospital. When we pull into the ER driveway, Pasha hops out and opens the door on my side. Bogdan goes in to get help. The time to worry about people seeing how we're dressed is over. Nurses, or whoever they are, rush outside with a stretcher. Bogdan and Pasha get back into the car. Aleks helps me pass her out of the backseat. They put an oxygen mask over her nose and mouth while a woman steps onto a crossbar on the stretcher and takes over chest compressions. I know when my brothers and cousin leave, but I don't look back. I run into the ER with Stasia.

"She lost her balance as she stepped off the steps in front of our house. I was still inside. She screamed, and I saw her fall down them. There were six. She said she can't feel her legs. She stopped breathing about three minutes ago. We've been doing CPR the entire time."

I know the lasting effects Stasia faces from not breathing on her own for three minutes. But I don't want to think about them. I don't want to think about anything but the vacation I intend to take her on once she's better. Her birthday is still next week. We might not travel that soon, but I'm taking her away from all of this, at least for a little while.

"Sir, who are you?"

A woman approaches from my right. I don't look at her. I'm

still beside the stretcher. But they're about to take her through secured doors. I have her hand in mine.

"Her husband."

I know what I feel. It's Stasia's hand squeezing mine. Her eyes flutter open, and the nurse stops the compressions. It's only for a moment, but I can breathe again.

"I need you to fill out some paperwork."

I'm left standing at the doors, watching them as they swing closed. My *malyshka's* on the other side, and I have to trust that they're going to heal her. I take a deep breath before I look at the woman. She hands me a clipboard, and I realize I won't know half the information on the forms. I said I was her husband because her parents are likely still in Virginia. Someone needs to be able to decide on Stasia's behalf. It's not because I know I want her as my wife. It's not because I intend to spend the rest of my life with her. Bullshit. It's exactly because of that.

I take a seat and stare at the papers. I must have been sitting here for at least a half an hour, and the papers are still blank. The woman keeps hovering, but she says nothing. My guess is I'm not the first distraught person to sit in the waiting room.

"Niko?"

"Mama?"

I look over as my mother sits next to me. She wraps her arms around me, and I sag against her. It's what I did the night Yuri and my uncle came to tell us my father would never walk through our door again.

"Shh, *pchelka.*"

Little bee. It's what my mom called all of us when we were little. That one word takes the weight of the world off my shoulders. I'm twenty-eight, and I need my mom. I feel my eyes watering, and I don't hide it from my mom. I look up at her, and she wipes the tears from beneath my eyes.

"One of Luca's men pushed her down the steps outside the house where they kept her."

"I know, *pchelka*. Maks told me. I came before he even got back to the house. Once everyone is clean and dressed, they'll come. Laura wants to, but she knows she can't bring the babies in here. She's thinking about you, though."

"I know. It's better if they don't come somewhere full of germs."

We sit together for an hour before my family arrives. It's like the fucking cavalry rolls in. We avoid hospitals like the plague. Partly because the injuries we get usually require a call to the police. And because we draw way too much attention. Sergei and Misha are blond and blue-eyed, like my mom. They look a lot like her. Enough that people often she thinks she's their mom, not mine and my brothers'. Anton and Pasha have our dark hair, but they have dark eyes. My brothers and I are such a blend of our parents' genes that we look like our cousins on both sides of the family. We're all unusually tall, and our physical training has made us all broad-shouldered and muscular. We look like an NFL first string, but none of us is anything but bone and muscle.

"Have you heard anything?"

Maks takes a seat on the other side of me.

"No. You should be home with Laura."

"She practically slammed the door in my face. She was insistent I come. This is where I belong, little brother."

"Thanks, old man."

Maks wraps his arm around my shoulder and gives me a tight squeeze. I stand up when Aleks and Bogdan join us. I embrace all of them before they hug our mom. My cousins come over and greet my mom with hugs of their own. Maks and Aleks have their arms around me, and I face Bogdan.

"I know how you feel, big brother. We're here as long as you want us."

For a year, Bogdan outranked me. He used to call me that to taunt me. He did it in front of a girl I liked, and I didn't speak to him for nearly a month. The first day it was because I was genuinely pissed. After that, it was to torment him. Since then, he's only said it as an endearment.

"I don't know how you did it, Bogdan. I feel like I'm going to crawl out of my skin. If I didn't need to be here, at least in the same building as Stasia, I would have destroyed anything Salvatore has ever valued. I would have taken from him the way they took from me. I wouldn't kill them. Oh, no. I'd leave Luca, Gabriele, and Carmine broken beyond repair, but alive."

"I talked to him, Niko. He said he's going to handle his nephews."

"What, Maks? Send them on vacation to Palermo until he thinks I'll forget."

"No. He's really pissed. I have never heard his tone like that before. I guess Carmine, Gabriele, and Luca were with him when I called back."

"He can suck a dick for all I care right now."

"Salv—"

"What the fuck is that son of a motherfucking bitch doing here?"

I cut off Maks as I see the Devil walk in the door. I push Bogdan out of the way and storm over to Salvatore.

"Get the fuck out. I don't give a fuck if your granny is dying in this hospital. Get out before you wind up in the motherfucking morgue."

I don't yell. I don't need everyone in the ER to know what's going on. But I'm six inches taller than Salvatore on his best day. He's almost my size build-wise, but I'm nearly ten years younger and in way better shape.

"Nikolai, you and I need to talk."

"The fuck we do. Leave."

"No. I need to talk to your whole family. What Luca started is bigger than I can fix. Where are your sisters-in-law and the babies? I see your mom."

"Why?"

"Niko, I'm serious. If they're not here, you need to send all your men wherever they are."

He walks past me, toward my family. Everyone has a gun and a knife, but no one reaches for their pistols. Everyone slides a hand into at least one pocket. Salvatore raises his hands.

"Galina, it's nice to see you."

My mother responds with a nod. The ice she's shooting from her eyes makes Salvatore freeze for a moment. She raised four sons who now run New York's bratva and are among the wealthiest men in the world. He'd do well not to underestimate my mom.

"Maksim, Niko won't say whether Laura and the twins are here, and he won't say if Christina is either. Wherever they are, you need to increase your guards. You need to get Alina, Svetlana, Radomir, and Grigori there, too. Vlad's brothers are on their way."

We've encircled Salvatore, and he knew what we were doing. He has his back to men willing to stab him in it. He looks at my mother.

"Galina, I love my wife and believe she's one of the most beautiful women I've ever seen. But everyone knows you're *the most* beautiful any of us have ever seen. You don't look any older than the day you arrived in America. You're in danger as much as Anastasia is. They are coming for you, too."

Vladislav Lushak, psychopath that he was, was one of six sons. Four of them have already died. But the two left are just as psychotic as he was. He looked at our mom one too many times. He tried to force his way into her house seven years ago. He didn't know all four of us were over. He tried to take her. Maks killed him before the rest of us even knew he was in the house. We were in the backyard, ready to have dinner. Maks was already being trained to replace Vlad one day. Everyone swore their loyalty to Maks the next morning. He's been *pakhan* ever since he was twenty-three.

"What did Luca do, Salvatore?"

Maks stands in front of him. He's standing where no one else but us can see. He puts his hands on his hips, flashing the guns holstered beneath his arms.

"He thought it would impress me and the others if he scored a huge payday. He started putting out feelers to the bratva in Chicago to find out what Anastasia would go for if he sold her to the Podolskaya. He was going to ransom her to you, Maksim. We all know what lengths you'll go to save a young woman from being trafficked. But Luca—I don't know how he could be so fucking naïve—didn't seriously consider that anyone he talked to in Chicago would contact people in Moscow. He never spoke to anyone in the Podolskaya, but they found out. They know you're all involved, and they know that Anastasia's the daughter of someone who was bratva. They don't know any specifics about her father, but they know what the star tattoo means."

"Did Antonio target her?"

"No. That crazy bastard wanted her for himself. He thought it would put him in my good graces if he could get her to me. I refused. You know I don't put women and children into this. It's when I refused that Luca got this great idea of his."

"When do they get here?"

I'm snarling. I'm more enraged than I have ever been in my life. I don't have to tap into any hidden well of violence to want to tear him apart. I would do it right now if I didn't know my family would stop me.

"I don't know. It's not like they fly commercial. I just know from Luca that they're coming. He got a call between when you got Anastasia back and when I beat the shit out of him."

"You beat up your own nephew?"

I don't believe him. He reaches for his pocket, and everyone takes a step forward. It's like the fucking hokey pokey.

"Just getting my phone. I knew you wouldn't believe me." He pulls it out and unlocks it. "See."

He holds up a picture of his fist plowing into Luca's jaw. The guy looks like shit. Salvatore swipes left and pulls up a video. He turns the audio low before he plays it. It's Salvatore's voice we hear.

"Last I checked, I'm alive and still the don. You acted against my wishes and thought it would impress me. You're lucky you are my heir, or you would be dead." Salvatore's fist lands in Luca's sternum. "You think you're ready to take my place, and the first job you pull on your own, you fucking pick the best way to get us all annihilated. Did you learn nothing from the Irish? They went after the Kutsenkos' women, and now look at them. Both leaders dead within weeks of each other. Half their leadership is dead after the bratva gunned them down on their own land. They took Laura and tried to kill Christina. You really thought you could do something so fucked up and get away with it. That they would hesitate to retaliate. You stupid motherfucking bitch ass cunt."

Salvatore's elbow flies into Luca's face, and the guy's body sags forward in the chair he's strapped to. Salvatore walks over to Carmine and his goon friend Gabriele. He picks up a pipe and swings it toward Carmine, but he doesn't hit him.

"A little birdie told me something very interesting, Carmine. It seems you've been holding out on us. You're a manipulative little fuck. Apparently, you're the one who planted the idea that Luca should organize this little adventure in stupidity. I found out that you're behind a lot of shit, aren't you? I've been waiting for you to step up for years, and all this time you've been playing me. You get your brothers and cousins to do the dirty work while you spend our money and accept being my little bitch because it keeps your hands clean."

Salvatore slams the pipe into Carmine's knee cap. The man doesn't flinch. He could be one of us for how little he shows any reaction. Salvatore's fist lands against Carmine's nose. I can see Salvatore's expression clearly in the video. He's annoyed that Carmine doesn't react, nor does he pass out. He moves on to Gabriele.

"Nobody likes snitches."

Salvatore's watching Carmine even though he's standing in front of Gabriele. Carmine and Gabriele have been best friends since they were kids. Gabriele's usually the muscle who comes with Carmine. He's quiet except for when he cracks his knuckles. He thinks he's a fucking Hollywood mobster.

"It was time for you to know, *zio*."

Salvatore steps closer to Carmine after the younger man calls him "uncle."

"Time to know what?"

"I'm not the dumb shit you've always believed. Just the opposite. I know Gabriele told you everything. I sent him to. If I've done all of this while everyone thought I was some buffoon. Imagine what you could do with me whispering in your ear instead of Luca."

"You want to oust Luca as my heir?"

"No. I don't need to be don. But I've proven I'm not the little boy everyone kicked. I'm way worse than anyone realized because no one knew I was the one who planted every seed that's grown into a mighty oak over the past ten years. You all think you've come up with so many genius ideas. But think back. How many came from conversations had with me?"

"So you're a sociopath."

"Aren't we all? We extort, bribe, and kill anyone who doesn't do what we want."

I'm watching this in utter disbelief. I've told my brothers for years that I think Carmine is smarter than anyone has given him credit for. This proves it. He's either going to get promoted or end up dead. Salvatore looks like he's trying to decide.

"You planted this idea in Luca's head, and now we will have the Russian bratva encircling us. And when they fight each other, who's going to be in the middle, shithead? You're not a mastermind. You're a fucking sack of shit who's going to get us all killed."

"Nope. The Podolskaya only want three people, and they've already paid half a million to get them. Anastasia, her father, and Galina."

"No women or children, Carmine. It's all that separates us from the animals."

"Wives. And neither woman is one."

"Galina is the Kutsenkos' fucking mother. Maksim fucking gutted Vlad for looking sideways at her. Anastasia is Niko's woman. Married or not. You dumb fuck. When do they get here?"

"I don't know. I'm not their fucking travel agent. If they're getting involved after Luca's inability to be subtle when he asks questions, then we should get paid to facilitate their trip. We're bounty hunters."

Salvatore backhands Carmine before the video ends. He looks at me as he drops his phone into his pocket. I see actual regret in his eyes. I've never seen it before, but I can recognize it.

"What's going to happen to them?"

"That's my problem, Niko."

"Not good enough. Deal with them, and I won't. Leave them to get away with this, and I will burn it all to the ground."

"Apparently, that's your favorite phrase. Anastasia told them you said that before Carmine got her in the car."

"I meant it then, and I mean it now. I give you fair warning, Salvatore. If Anastasia doesn't fully recover from this, there is nowhere your family will be safe."

He takes a step toward me, and the circle tightens.

"You think you can threaten me and that I'll back down."

"Yes. Dare me, Salvatore. No one outside of eight men knows what any of us are truly capable of. You think you know how Vlad corrupted us. But you can't imagine all that he taught us that we're yet to do. You will eat my shit and drink my piss before I peel the skin from your body. I will slice you thinner than deli ham until there is nothing left of you. Until your body simply can't handle the pain. It will be the slowest torture you've ever seen, far worse than anything you've ever done. Test me, Salvatore."

Something flashes in his eyes, and I know he believes me. There are degrees of torture that my brothers and cousins swore we would never do, even though Vlad trained us for it. I'm ready to break that vow if Stasia doesn't heal.

"I will not kill them, but I will make them suffer. That's the best I can tell you, Niko. They broke our family oath, and I take that seriously. I know people call me old-fashioned and old school, but I do not accept targeting women. If I did, it makes the women in my family targets. I will not allow that."

"Mr. Kutsenko?"

Chapter Seventeen

Stasia

I don't remember most of the ride to the hospital. I thought I was dead, but I'm awake, so I guess not. One moment, Niko was dressed again in regular clothes and holding me. Then my chest hurt, and everything else went numb. I remember nothing after that. I don't remember passing out. I don't remember getting out of the SUV or entering the hospital. I could hear Niko's voice at one point, but I couldn't seem to draw in a breath. Now air is coming into my nose and mouth. I keep telling my hand to reach for Niko, but it won't cooperate.

I can hear Niko's voice again. It's like I'm underwater. But I know it's him. I struggle to understand what's happening. I know I'm in the hospital, but why? I try to flex my fingers. I can. I try to move my toes. I can't.

"I'm her husband."

I feel Niko's hand in mine as my eyes open. It's only for a moment, but I squeeze his hand as hard as I can. The weight that kept pressing on my chest stops. I realize someone was giving me CPR. I must have stopped breathing. I want to hold his hand longer, but everything goes black again.

I'm awake again. There's a dull pain all over my body. I hear beeping and look up. It's the heart monitor. Two bags are hanging on the IV stand. I wonder if one of them is the magic medicine that's taken away most of the pain. I flex my fingers and my toes, happy that they move on their own. My eyes close again.

"Mrs. Kutsenko?"

I love the sound of that. Can I get him to repeat it like six thousand more times? Twelve days ago, I knew nothing about the Kutsenkos. Eleven days ago, I started a new job. Then Niko protected me a week later from my ex-boyfriend, and I had sex for the first time. Is it that mind blowing for everyone? Today, he protected me from some mafiosos who kidnapped me.

"Mrs. Kutsenko?"

Yes, say it again. Five days ago, I was with my parents and agreeing with my dad to trust Niko. An hour later, we weren't talking. It was one day in bed together, then three days of barely speaking or seeing him. Then I royally fucked everything up by running away...on foot.

"Mrs. Kutsenko, if you can hear me, can you nod your head? You've been asking for your husband."

"I can hear you. Sorry. It took a bit for my brain to clear. Everything's foggy."

"That's normal. I'm Dr. Nguyen, your surgeon. You were pretty banged up when you came in here. Your husband said you tripped and fell down your front steps."

Niko can't exactly tell anyone that an Italian mobster

pushed me down the steps before my—boyfriend's?—family shot up the house they kept me in.

"Yes. I wasn't paying attention and turned back to tell him something while he was in the house. I lost my balance and fell."

The doctor looks at me for a long time, and I wonder if my story doesn't match Niko's. I doubt he would have said anything more complicated, since he had to know someone would ask me.

"Are you sure, Mrs. Kutsenko?"

"Yes. Very."

"There's a very nasty bruise on your back that didn't happen today."

"I've had a bad week, Doctor. We have an entryway table. I was carrying in groceries, and my flip-flop snapped. I fell to my side and landed against it."

I have had a flip-flop break, and I have fallen because of it.

"Mrs. Kutsenko, if you're being—"

"Doctor, I'm going to stop you right now. My husband would never hurt me. Just the opposite. He's a little too cautious about anything happening to me. Clearly, I'm accident prone. And if it were someone else who did it, well—my husband is just the right amount of protective."

"All right. If you change your mind—"

"I will not. I know his size and mine makes it look like he could snap me in half. But my husband would never hurt me. And if he did, he has three brothers, four cousins, two uncles, two aunts, two sisters-in-law, and his mother who would never forgive him. When can I see him?"

I'm growing anxious the more the doctor presses. I get it. I completely understand how it looks, especially with the older bruise. I don't know if the doctor recognizes Niko's—supposedly our—last name, or if he's seen Niko's size, but I know why he's asking. I don't like it. I'm insulted on Niko's behalf, and I'm getting angry.

"I'll fetch him in a moment. I want to go over a few things. You have a couple bruised ribs, a jarred shoulder, and two discs we had to replace in your lower back. You're going to need to spend the night here. If you can tolerate solid food and complete some exercises, we should release you tomorrow. It's going to be a few weeks before you feel more like your usual self."

I press my lips together, and I can feel myself blushing.

"Doctor, we're still newlyweds. Um, when can we have sex again?"

The doctor nods, and I think my first question being when I can be intimate with Niko must allay some of his doubts. I think he hears the eagerness in my voice.

"When you are ready. Some positions may not feel comfortable. If that's the case, then avoid them."

"So in a few weeks, a few months?"

"A couple weeks most likely, Mrs. Kutsenko. I'll get your husband."

I watch the doctor leave, and I'm impatient for Niko to come back here. I'm surrounded by sliding curtains, so I must still be in recovery. I wonder how long I've been here. It feels like it's taking forever, but I know the doctor has to go to the waiting room, and he's probably explaining things to Niko.

Waves of regret crash over me as the minutes tick by. I caused this. I did this to myself by ignoring Niko's protocols. He did it to keep me safe, and I basically gave him the middle finger. I didn't ask for the *Cosa Nostra* or the Podolskaya to take an interest in me. But I knew the risk. That's why I lied and ditched the guards. That makes me doubly selfish and stupid. I'm lucky to be fucking alive. But what's way, way, way worse is the danger Niko and his family faced to rescue me. I could have avoided it all. I feel so shitty.

What is Niko going to say when he sees me? I want to tell him I'm all in. What if he's the one who says he wants out? I don't know that I can do this without him.

Chapter Eighteen

Niko

Six of us turn toward a man in scrubs coming through the door. I push past Salvatore, no longer caring what happens to any of the Mancinellis. At least, not until I know about Stasia. My mom comes to stand beside me and takes my hand.

"I'm Dr. Nguyen. Mrs. Kutsenko suffered two badly bruised ribs. The fall jarred her shoulder but didn't dislocate it like we suspected. However, two discs slipped in her lumbar spine and caused them to compress her spine. That's why she couldn't feel her legs. There was no damage to the spinal cord. We replaced both discs. That's what took so long."

I feel my mom's shock when the doctor addresses Stasia as my wife, but she says nothing. She won't until the doctor is gone.

"When can I see her?"

"She's still in recovery, but she's insistent that she sees you. She woke up calling for you. I'll take you back."

I speak to my mom in Russian.

"Telling them we're married was the only way I could make sure they would let me know what's happening. Her parents aren't here to decide for her."

My mom only nods and stands on her toes to kiss my cheek. I wrap my arms around her and once again feel calm.

"Go see her, *pchelka*."

I follow the doctor until he takes me to a sectioned off area with a curtain drawn. He pulls it back and steps aside. There's my *malyshka*. She's groggy, and there are machines all around her. She has an IV, and electrodes on her chest. I see the wires leading to them. The calf compression machine is whirring as it fills up with air, then releases the pressure.

"Niko?"

"Yes, *moye sokrovishche*."

"What does that mean? It's not a phrase I know. I think I need to learn more Russian, or I'm never going to know what's going on."

She speaks as though we have a future together.

"It means my treasure."

"Is that what I am, Niko? Even after all this."

"Always."

I step close enough to stroke her head and kiss her forehead. There are stitches that close the gash that bled so badly. I take her hand and notice how fine her bones are. They never felt fragile before this. We watch as the doctor steps out and closes the curtain. My lips meet hers, and fireworks go off. This is not the kiss someone who just came out of surgery should have. But neither of us wants to stop.

"*Papochka*, the doctor said that I can probably return to regular activity in two weeks. But he said no vigorous exercise or contact sports for six to eight weeks, and that assumes I'm healing well. You know what that means."

"You think our sex counts as a contact sport?"

My lips twitch, and she shrugs her uninjured shoulder.

"Do you mind waiting that long?"

The smile drops from my face as I lean closer.

"Our sex is the best anyone could ever have. But that is not the only reason I'm drawn to you, Stasia. You're intelligent, brave, way too reckless, kind, good with children, funny, and a shit ton more. You may be gorgeous and have a body that makes me eager to sin, but there is far more to you than being a good lay. I want to have sex with you because it brings us closer, makes us one. It's not just to get off. But I don't have to have sex to still want you as my partner, *moye sokrovishche*. Besides, your *solyanka* is better than my mom's. I'm keeping you for that alone."

"You only had a spoonful."

"That's all it took."

When our eyes meet, she knows I mean more than cabbage and potato soup. I kiss her forehead again.

"I was teasing about the contact sports and all those weeks, but it is good to know that you want me for more than just that. I worried you didn't feel the same as me."

"Stasia, how do you feel about me?"

"In some ways, confused, and in other ways, certain. I'm confused how I feel so strongly about you after only a few days. But I'm certain that I lied in the car to hurt you because I was confused. I've wanted to be with you—I've wanted *you*—since the moment we met. You were so good with your nephew. Then the way you protected me. It should have freaked me the fuck out that you followed me and that you beat the shit out of a guy in front of me. But everything felt right with you. I don't even know why I got so upset in the car. You were only offering what I already knew had to happen."

"Because that day was too much."

She nods.

"I regretted it the moment I said it. But I kept reasoning with myself that it was for the best. It hurt so fucking much to sit across from you at your dining room table, and you barely talked to me. Then you came into my room and barely looked at me. Seeing you in those boxer briefs. I nearly mauled you. But then, after I found you playing the piano, you shut your bedroom door in my face. I thought you couldn't stand me. You avoided me all together yesterday, and what you said this morning..."

"I said it because my brothers annoyed me, not because I meant it. It hurt that we were so intimate, and yet, you still didn't know if you wanted my affection."

"I realized that while I was with *them*."

The doctor said nothing about Stasia being assaulted. I assume he would have, since he thinks I'm her husband. Part of me desperately wants to know what happened during that time, but part of me wants to run away rather than hear the truth. But I have to know.

"Stasia, can you tell me what happened from when you got on the bus until I got to you?"

"Yes. I—"

"Mrs. Kutsenko, we're going to take you to your room. Your parents are here."

The nurse interrupts us and shoots me a look I don't understand. She unplugs Stasia's IV and monitor before unlocking the gurney. She pushes Stasia out of her secluded area, and that's when I realize how the nurse addressed Stasia. I look down, and Stasia is looking up at me. She holds out her hand, her brow furrowed. I take it and walk beside her. We get to her room, and I wait until she's settled in bed, and we're alone.

"*Malyshka,* I told them I'm your husband, but your parents

must have corrected her. Without them here, no one could decide for you. I—"

"I like that idea."

"You do?"

You could knock me over with a feather.

"Yes. Maybe we could wait until I'm not in a hospital gown to decide, but I think Anastasia Kutsenkova has a nice sound to it."

"You know, it could just be Kutsenko."

"I like my way better. It has a ring to it."

I'm holding her left hand, and I run my thumb over her ring finger. We both look at it. I bring her hand to my lips and kiss it as the door opens. Her parents rush in. I try to let go, but she wraps her fingers around mine and holds on like she thinks I'll float away.

"Peanut."

Her dad comes around to my side. He kisses her cheek as I step away. It's too awkward for me to hold on, but she looks back for me. Yuri sees her and shifts, so I can reach her. Allison's face looks like she's just drunk sour milk. She's glowering at me.

"Stop, Mom. Who knows what would have happened to me if Niko didn't save me? It's my fault this happened. I thought you sent a message for me to meet you at the U.N. I wanted to tell you I want to stay with Niko. I knew he wouldn't be pleased if I went alone, and I knew you wouldn't be pleased to see him. I lied to the guards and said Niko and Maksim gave me permission to go for a walk. Two guards came with me, but I ditched them at the subway."

"You still wouldn't be in this mess if—"

"Yes, I would. I know what's going on. When I transferred to the bus, a guy sat next to me. He tried chatting, but I wasn't interested. He held a knife to me when I stood to get off. Niko fought two guys to get to me, but Carmine shoved me in the car. Niko, I heard your motorcycle. I knew you were following until the last few blocks. I knew you would come."

"Always, *moye sokrovishche*."

"She's a treasure way too valuable for you."

"Mom!"

"Stasia—"

"Her name is Ana."

This isn't getting us anywhere. I've had time with her alone, even if it isn't nearly enough. I lean forward and kiss her cheek. I'd rather kiss her lips, but we already infuriated her mother enough. I let go of her hand, but she tries to grasp mine.

"Spend some time with your parents, Ana."

"Do not call me that, Nikolai."

She glares at me.

"I'll be back soon."

"No. You're deciding for me again, and that's what made us argue the last time. Mom, you made decisions that might have been fine when I was a child, but they are not fine now that I'm an adult. I refuse to have you three fighting, and I won't lie here while you refuse to consider what I want. Either you all listen to me, or you leave. Niko, stay."

"All right, but I'm going to step outside to call my mom. Everyone is downstairs waiting to know how you're doing."

"Everyone?"

"My brothers, cousins, and mom. My sisters-in-law and the babies are at Maks and Laura's. My mom got here first. The rest came a little later."

She nods, and I know she understands that means after they weren't dressed like they'd stepped off a battlefield. I step into the hallway and dial my mom's number.

"Mama, she's going to be all right. She's awake and feisty. Her parents are up here."

"That's wonderful news. Do you want us to stay or go?"

"You can go. Everyone needs to get to Maks's."

"Svetlana, Alina, Grigori, and Radomir are already there. Hold on...Misha and Pasha are staying. The rest of us will go to Maks and Laura's. They're coming up."

"All right. Thank you, Mama."

"I love you, *pchelka*."

"I love you, Mama."

I slip back inside, and the conversation stops. I look at Yuri, who appears frustrated. Allison is still glowering, but her face is red. And Stasia is crying. I cross the room, and Stasia reaches for me with the arm that isn't in a sling. I try to take her hand, but she grabs my shirt and pulls. I'm careful not to put any of my weight on her chest or arm as I lean forward.

"What's wrong, Stasia?"

She shakes her head as she clings to me. I lean to whisper in her ear.

"I can't help if I don't know what's wrong, *malyshka*. You're scaring me."

My heart is racing. What the fuck happened in the two minutes I stepped outside?

"Tell him."

Stasia snaps at her mom, who refuses to look at me. I turn my head to see Yuri, who is now glaring at his wife.

"Leave my daughter alone, and I won't turn you over to the feds."

I stand and look at the woman and remind myself over and over that she's trying to protect her daughter.

"An anonymous tip won't get you very far. We've been through that, and we're still here. You'd have to testify. You won't. You never will. Because if you did, you'd be putting your husband on death row or shipped back to Moscow. You are too far in to turn me over without ruining your family. Do not pit me against you, Mrs. Antonov. The only one who loses is Stasia. I will never ask her to choose, but we both know who she would. Is that what you want?"

I'm banking on being right. The way she's still clutching my shirt, as though I might walk away, or someone might take me away, makes me confident that I am.

"She would never pick—"

"Yes, I would, Mom. I know you don't get it. I don't have the words to explain it. But I have never been more miserable than I was the past three days. I told you, I was going to the U.N. to tell you I was staying with Niko. Even if we aren't a couple, I still feel safest with him."

"Then this is about convenience."

"No. I thought love at first sight is ridiculous. I thought people who wanted to romanticize their relationships or brag made it up. I tried listening to my head that I shouldn't be with Niko. Look at where I ended up."

"It's infatuation."

"Allison, you don't know Niko's family, but I do."

Yuri finally speaks up. Is that it, though? He looks at me and puts his hand on my shoulder.

"I don't know about his two married brothers, but I know how his father and uncles were about their wives. Everyone called it 'Kutsenko *chary*.' I don't know if it was just charm or sorcery. Either translation probably works. Neither Svetlana nor Radomir were Kutsenkos, but it seemed to rub off on them. It did on me. Allison, I wanted to marry you within an hour of meeting you."

"You did?"

"I didn't exaggerate that day, and I don't now. I didn't say it because I thought it would scare you away. When you meet your soulmate, you know. It was that way for Kirill and Galina as kids, and Grigori and Alina as teens. It seemed contagious because it happened with Radomir and Svetlana, and us. The joke began because women used to follow Grigori and Kirill like they were rock stars, but they never cared. Once other people knew about the men and their wives, it became more of a thing about kismet. You know what I would do—what I have done—to protect you, Allison. Niko will do the same."

Allison and Yuri look at each other for a long time before Allison looks down at Stasia.

"I'm scared for you. I know what your father did, and I don't want that life for you."

"I know, Mom. But even if Niko weren't in the picture, I'd still be sucked into this. I was the day I met Antonio. I didn't know not to tell him about Papa's tattoo or not to mention Papa being in the army. Things would be way worse without Niko, Mom. It's not convenience. It's about being able to breathe when I'm with him. I'm as comfortable with him as I am with myself."

Allison looks up at me. Her shoulders slump as she nods.

"You keep trying to make peace with us and between Ana and me. I keep making it worse. I think you understand how I feel, and I appreciate that. This is not easy. This is history repeating itself and exactly what Yuri and I wanted to avoid. But we made some huge mistakes, even if our intentions were good. It's easier to lash out at you than admit we're largely to blame. If I'm being honest, I've known since the other day that Ana's safest with you. That hurt. I didn't want to let go."

"You don't have to let go, Mrs. Antonov. I'm not taking her from you."

She nods, and I think she finally believes me. I reach out my free hand, which is my left, so it's awkward. But we shake, and this time, she doesn't look at it like a snake ready to bite. I shift my attention back to Stasia.

"I need to know what happened after you got in that car."

Stasia inhales deeply and nods as she exhales.

"It's not good, Niko."

Chapter Nineteen

Stasia

To say this has been a shit day seems like a moronic understatement. Niko stepped out for like two minutes, and my mom immediately threatened to report him and his family to the FBI and a slew of other federal organizations. I stared at her for a minute before I burst into tears. My dad tried to convince me she's just scared. She tried to convince me to break up with Niko. And all I wanted was for Niko to hurry and get back inside the room.

Listening to my dad describe Niko's family made me feel a lot better. Whatever it is—magic, sorcery, charm—it describes us. And apparently, it describes my parents too. They've always said it didn't take them long to fall in love. They neglected to mention the five years they were mostly apart. I have a ton of questions about that.

Now they're waiting for me to tell them what happened while I was with the *Cosa Nostra*. I spot someone at the door and lean to look.

"It's Misha and Pasha. Everyone went back to Laura and Maks's, but they're staying until I tell them to go home."

Niko and my mom just made nice, but his stare is challenging again. It tore me in half when he talked about me choosing him over my parents. He was right. I would. But I hated anyone had to say it. She nods, and I realize my body just relaxed. I didn't realize how tense I was.

"I told Niko about how I ditched the guards that I lied to so I could go for a walk. I told him about getting on the bus and having a guy sit next to me. It turned out to be Carmine Mancinelli, one of don's nephews. Niko fought off two guys blocking him from getting to me. But Carmine shoved me in the car at knifepoint. I could hear Niko's motorcycle behind us until just before the house they took me in."

Niko strokes back hair from my forehead. It's so soothing. He is so incredibly gentle with me when I need it. I'm eager to heal enough to do more. I almost forgot my birthday is next week. I know what I want for my present. His dick in a bow.

"When they got me inside, I peeled the duct tape from my mouth by nudging it with my shoulder. Carmine put handcuffs on me while we were in the car, and Gabriele crushed my phone, so you couldn't track me."

"I was already outside."

"I thought so, but I didn't tell them that. Luca seemed like he was in charge, but something about Carmine gave me the heebie jeebies more than Luca or Gabriele. It was like a silent menace. Luca barely looked at Gabriele, but he was wary of Carmine, even though he gave the orders. There was a slew of weapons on a table. It looked like they were kitting out an army or ready for a shootout."

"They had to know we would come."

"I'm sure they did. I was definitely the lure. They said as much. But—" I close my eyes. I don't want to talk about the rest. "—their original plans changed from ransoming me to you. They assumed they wouldn't have to hand me over to you. There are men coming from Russia soon. They're the brothers of that man you told me about, Papa. The one who—" I look at Niko.

"Vladislav Lushak."

Niko says the name with no emotion. It's like he's retreated into his robotic appearance rather than let any of us in and see how he truly feels. I can only imagine.

"Him. Luca said that they were going to finish what Katerina started. Niko, who is Katerina?"

I watch him swallow. He doesn't look like he wants to answer, but he's promised me more than once that he won't lie if he doesn't have to. I think he's deciding if this is one of those times when he can tell me the truth.

"Katerina was a woman I dated just after I graduated from college and joined the Elite Group. She moved to New York from Chicago. She said she was from a bratva family there, and it checked out. We'd been dating about three months when men started following her. I had a security detail on her, so we knew the moment it happened. We increased it, and she was next to never alone. Then she started getting calls and texts threatening her. She told us it was an ex-boyfriend back in Chicago and the reason she left. The threats were to sex traffic her to Russia. I thought I was falling in love with her, so I proposed. We all knew that women and children are off limits, so that's why I offered. She took advantage of it."

Niko exhales deeply as our gazes meet. I know he doesn't enjoy telling any of this. And I know he feels badly that I'm hearing about a woman he thought he would love and planned to marry.

"None of it was real. Not the threats. Not being from Chicago. Not how she felt about me. She was Podolskaya, or rather one of their women. She was Vlad's niece. All of her paperwork in the American system was fake. The Podolskaya were paying off the *pakhan* in Chicago to substantiate the lies. The plan was for Katerina to ingratiate herself into my life and my family's. She would have been an Elite Group member's wife. They thought she would gain information she could share with the bratva in Chicago and in Moscow."

"What happened, Niko?"

He can no longer meet my gaze. I can't tell what he's thinking or what he's feeling. He's shut me out. He may as well be invisible for all that I can tell that he's present in the moment. I squeeze his hand. When he finally looks at me, it's a stranger looking back. There's none of the warmth I'm used to. There's none of the humor or kindness, frustration or desire. It's just blank.

"She put a gun to my head and tried to force me to open a safe in a former Elite Group member's house. I heard her take the safety off. She was prepared to kill me if I didn't do what she wanted. She underestimated how much stronger and faster I was than her. It's the only time in my life—she's not a threat to my family anymore."

He killed her. He went against the cardinal rule of no women and children. He feels guilty. Now, I see it. This must have been six years ago. He's carried this with him for that long.

"Would she have hurt your family?"

"Absolutely. My mom was there. Katerina tricked me. When I got to where she was, she had my mom blindfolded, gagged, and tied to the chair. She took the blindfold off just before she put the gun to my head. My mom saw everything."

I nod. What is there to say?

"Is that why the Podolskaya is coming, Niko?"

I look back at my dad and shake my head. Niko shrugs.

"No, Papa. Luca figured out that you must have been

important to them. There's someone in Chicago he talked to about me. I don't think he actually talked to anyone in Moscow. I think he's banking on everything falling into place. He planned to lure you in, Papa, making you think you could save me. I don't think including you was part of the original plan, but someone must have told him that the Podolskaya would want you, too."

I don't want to tell Niko the next part. He might let no one see his reaction, but he's going to be pissed. Like really, really pissed.

"He held a gun to my head and wanted to record me telling you lies about me being all right. He planned to sell Papa and me to the Podolskaya. He was going to use those recordings to bribe you into paying a ransom, but I would already be in Russia by then, and Papa would already be dead. He knew you would pay, Niko. He knew because everyone knows your family does not tolerate sex trafficking, and he knew we were involved. Someone saw us leaving my place together. When Antonio didn't come back, they sent someone to watch me."

"Salvatore was here earlier."

Niko's voice is devoid of emotion, just like his face.

"He was? I heard Luca talking to him. I recognized the name when he called the person on the other end *zio*. I didn't understand what they said because it was all in Italian. He'd barely hung up when you arrived. Whatever Salvatore said made him willing to release me. I don't think any of them would have if Luca hadn't talked to his uncle."

"Yeah. Apparently, they thought they could make a deal behind Salvatore's back, *moye sokrovishche*. Salvatore didn't even remotely sanction any of this. They're also coming for my mom. As best as Salvatore knows, the Podolskaya don't know who you or your dad are specifically. They just know that he has the eight-point tattoo and was Podolskaya. I'm sure they've guessed. Luca may have appeared to be in charge, but it was Carmine who was really pulling the strings. According to a video I saw, they've already paid Luca and Carmine half a million dollars for both of you and my mom."

"What's Salvatore going to do?"

My dad's face is as blank as Niko's. I hadn't noticed until now. It's fucking eerie. I look at my mom. She's stoic, but I can still tell what she's feeling. My dad and Niko are in another realm from any training my mom must have received.

"He wouldn't say. It's up to him, as far as he's concerned. I disagree. If anyone steps off a plane from Moscow, they won't be getting back on. And I will make sure Luca and Carmine realize just how wrong they were to think they could come near my girlfriend."

"I have old scores to settle, Niko. I go too."

"Papa!"

"Yuri!"

My mom and I speak at the same time.

"It ends now, Allison. If it doesn't, then Ana is never safe. Vlad's brothers are the reason any of us were in Chechnya. They're the ones who told the Elite Group to send us. They wanted us gone, so they could get to Galina. Even with four kids, they still watched her. The boys were old enough for them to figure she was done having kids. If she wasn't pregnant, then she was fair game again. They no longer cared that she wasn't as slim as she'd been thirteen years earlier. That she'd had four kids would have made her even more desirable to some buyers."

My dad looks at Niko.

"Vlad's older brothers tried to snatch Galina just before they sent us to Chechnya. Kirill made it clear that anyone who came near your mother would suffer the most brutal fate. It's the only time he rivaled Vlad when it came to violence and torture. Vlad saw it all because Grigori, Radomir, and I made sure he did. I still have nightmares about that night. Do you remember how Vlad was missing his little finger on his left hand?"

I doubt Niko has forgotten a damn thing about that monster. Niko nods.

"Your father did that. Slowly. I'm certain that's why it took nearly ten years before Vlad actually approached Galina. Your father left a lasting impression. Grigori and Radomir no longer had any control when they arrived in America. No one knew Vlad was already here. No one knew where he went. When your family got here, Vlad had all the power. If they'd done more to keep all of you out, what Kirill did to his brothers is what they would have done to all of you and made your mother, aunts, and uncles watch. Vlad didn't make empty threats, and he had the men to ensure it happened. Since I was there that night, they held me partially to blame. It wasn't by accident that I ended up in that minefield. Vlad's younger brothers arranged it all the way from Moscow."

"But you stayed after the war ended, Papa."

"They owned me. Or at least they thought they did. They didn't know I was feeding information to the Americans."

I lean my head back and close my eyes. This is all so fucking complicated. All these names that I didn't know a week ago. All the lies and secrets that I never guessed. The betrayal and deceit. No wonder my mom wants me nowhere near all of this. But it was inevitable. Even if I never met Antonio, there was always the possibility that somehow, someone would find us.

"So somewhere between what Luca told me and what Salvatore told you lays the truth."

I open my eyes and look at Niko. He nods. I close my eyes again. This is just as overwhelming as it was in my parents' living room. Except this time, I'm in pain. I reach for the button the nurse gave me and press. It's supposed to trigger more pain meds through my IV. How long does it take for me to feel it?

"Stasia?"

Niko's looking at my hand, which is beneath his. He must have felt me hit the button.

"I'm all right, Niko. Just a little uncomfortable."

I'm a fuck ton more than just a little. I'm also exhausted. Anesthesia doesn't exactly give you restful sleep. I'd prefer being cuddled up against Niko like I was for only one morning.

"Stasia, you need to rest."

"Don't go, Niko."

The last thing I want is for him to leave. The last time he stepped out of the room, my mom laid into me, and I burst into tears. I don't think that'll happen again, but I don't want him to leave. Besides, we have a lot to talk about still.

"Peanut, we're going to let you rest."

"Where are you staying?"

Niko looks between my parents, who look at each other. They must have rushed up here and not thought that far ahead.

"I'll have a car come to pick you up, and you can stay at my brother and sister-in-law's house. Maks and Laura have plenty of space, and they will be happy to have you stay. You can come and go whenever you want. A driver will be at your disposal."

"We don't know—"

"Yuri, you were my father's friend. My mother is there and so are my aunts and uncles. Please consider staying with them. We want you there, and it's convenient."

My parents look at each other again before they both nod. Niko steps away from the bed and pulls out his phone. We can hear him, but he's given my parents space to say goodbye.

"How did you know what happened? How'd you know to come up here?"

"Maksim called."

My mom sounds as exhausted as I feel.

"We'll be here in the morning, sweetheart."

"Thanks Papa. The doctor said that if I can complete all the exercises, then they will discharge me tomorrow. Niko can let you know if it's worth coming here or waiting until we get to Maks and Laura's. I know he won't take me to my place or his."

"All right. I love you."

"I love you, too, Mom. I love you, Papa."

"I love you, sweetheart."

Niko returns to my bedside and smiles at my parents.

"Maks and Laura are happy to have you stay with them. Be prepared. There are a lot of people there. My three brothers, two sisters-in-law, two uncles, two aunts, four cousins, and my mom. Plus, two infants."

"And a partridge in a pear tree."

I grin, and my parents chuckle. Niko shrugs. I think he loves having a large family and being with them. I wonder what it would be like to live surrounded by so many loved ones. My parents leave, and Niko pulls a chair closer to my bed.

"Niko, what happens next? I mean, with us?"

"What do you want, Stasia? I won't push you."

"I was serious earlier. I like the sound of Anastasia Kutsenkova. Do you?"

I'm nervous that he's changed his mind.

"I like it better than anything else I've ever heard—other than when you moan because I'm making you come."

"Daddy!"

I hiss the word, but I'm smiling.

"Stasia, we are likely never going to be a typical couple. I know it's been a couple weeks, but I feel like every day has aged me ten years. I know you might not be ready to say I do, and I get that. But I want us to be together. If that's in separate homes or living together as a dating couple, then I'm happy with either choice."

"It sounds so odd for you to say it's only been a couple weeks. I know that too, but you're right, it feels like years instead of days. Do you believe in soulmates?"

"Yes. My parents were undoubtedly soulmates. My dad's been dead for seventeen years, and I know my mom misses him as much today as she did when he died. I don't know that she would have made it if she didn't have four sons to raise. I know I wasn't sure how I was going to survive losing you."

"I'm sorry, Niko. I truly am. I regret so much of what I've done the past few days. I caused all of this."

"Don't do that, Stasia. Did you make some poor choices? Yes. But you didn't know any better. Not really. This is all new to you, and you've had it all dumped on you. I've seen my brothers and their wives. If I didn't believe in soulmates based on my parents, then I would because of them. I see in us what I saw in my parents and what I see with my brothers. I want that with you."

"I want it too. I don't know Bogdan and Christina, but I know I want what Maksim and Laura have. And I only want that with you."

"Let me take you away next week for your birthday."

"Is that wise? With everything that's going on?"

"Yes. I want to treat you to something nice, but I also want you away from New York until we know what's happening. I'd already planned to take you somewhere, but I hadn't picked a place. I decided the day you told me your birthday was in three weeks."

"That was the night you stayed at my place. I said it when we were in the kitchen."

"I know. *Malyshka*, I knew before I kissed you that I wanted you by my side for good. I knew the moment we shook hands. I didn't believe in love at first sight back then, but now..."

Niko shrugs. He looks anxious and unguarded. He's letting me see that. He's being vulnerable in front of me, and I know how precious this is.

"Niko, drop the bed rail and lie next to me."

"I don't want to hurt you."

"Please."

He's careful as he lowers the rail on my good side. He arranges the tubes and wires, so he doesn't press on anything. He's barely on the edge, and he looks so nervous.

"Daddy, I won't break. I have a bionic spine, and I only bruised myself otherwise."

"Don't joke, or you will go over my lap the moment we leave here."

"Promise?"

"Yes, *malyshka*."

"Why did the chicken cross the road?"

"I warned you about making jokes, and that's a horrible one."

He snares my lips in a kiss that has been brewing for days. Finally. I give myself over to it, and things feel right in the world again. We rest our foreheads together as I run my fingers through his hair.

"Where do you want to go, Stasia? Anywhere in the world. My brothers and I own a jet. We have homes around the world, or I can arrange for the best resorts or hotels."

"Of course, you can."

I grin. How easy it is to forget that a billionaire is lying on a hospital bed next to me.

"Can we go somewhere in the Mediterranean? Or is that a little too close to you know where?"

"Russia? No, it's not too close. Do you want to sail or stay in one place? Do you want to visit more than one country?"

"I'd like to go to Greece."

"Yacht or hotel?"

"Mmm."

"Both it is."

"I didn't say that, Niko."

"I know. I decided for us, *malyshka*."

"Because you're in charge?"

"Because I want to spoil you."

"Thank you, Niko."

I can't stifle the yawn that escapes. I try to cover my mouth with my hand, but I can't reach between Niko being next to me and my other arm in a sling.

"Stasia, you need to sleep. I'll stay with you. That loveseat converts—"

"If I move over, I can make more room."

"I'm way too big to share, Stasia. I'm already crowding you."

"Niko, please don't go. Not even three feet away."

I feel tears welling in my eyes.

"Shh, baby girl. I'm not going anywhere. Are you scared I'm going to leave while you're asleep?"

"No... Yes... I don't know. I just want to be next to you. Everything goes to shit when I'm not. I know your cousins are outside the door, and I know there's plenty of hospital security, but honestly, I'm scared when you're not next to me."

"Do you think Luca or Carmine will come here?"

"Or whoever's coming from Russia. Or the Irish. Or the Cartel. I don't know what to think about all of this. The drugs in this IV definitely help, but I'm still sore all over. It's impossible to get comfortable, but the best I've felt since waking up is when you're next to me."

"I'll do whatever you need, *moye sokrovishche*."

"I like that as much as *malyshka*. But I want something I can call you. How about *sakharok?*"

"Piece of sugar?"

I grin.

"You can be awfully sweet when you want to be."

"I'll be whatever you want, Stasia."

"*Sakharok* it is! Now, shh, *papochka*. I'm tired, and I'm sure you must be too. You look wrecked."

"Thanks."

He doesn't exactly sound appreciative. I kiss his cheek as I settle against him. He's careful as he eases his arm behind my neck. I roll onto my good side as best I can. He adjusts the sheet and blanket around me.

"Sleep, *malyshka*. I'll be here when you wake up."

I'm drifting off as I hear him whisper.

"I love you, Stasia."

I'm certain he thinks I'm asleep.

"I love you too, Niko."

He kisses my head, and I wish everything could be as blissful as it is now. I doubt it will be.

Chapter Twenty

Niko

The last few days have aged me. I brought Stasia home from the hospital this afternoon. We're in the guest room Laura offered, and I can tell Stasia is still exhausted. She passed her exercises with flying colors despite being in pain. I think she desperately wanted out of the hospital because she didn't feel safe there. It breaks my heart to know that.

"*Sakharok*, will you help me in the shower? I know I'm allowed to move my shoulder now, but it hurts if I raise my arm too high."

"I'd love nothing more, *meelaya*."

If I'm her sugar, then she's my darling. I don't think there's a damn bit of me that's sugary, but she enjoys calling me that. That could be the only word she utters again until I die, and I would gladly hear it every time.

"Can you check the dressing, please?"

"I'll put a little more tape on it, then I'll put fresh gauze and everything on once we're done. Can you stand long enough? Do I need to order a shower seat? Do you—"

"Niko, I'm all right. Stop whittling. I want help as much for my hair as to see you naked. Stop wasting time."

"Cheeky, *malyshka*."

I guide her into the bathroom and help her undress.

"When do I get that spanking you said I earned?"

I can't imagine doing anything remotely like that when I can see the bruising marring her entire body. It's not like the one from the entryway table, which was bad enough. There are bruises across her back and on her belly. Her legs are the only part that didn't suffer. I can only shake my head.

"Come on, *moye sokrovishche*. We'll both feel better once we're clean."

I turn on the shower and wait for it to warm up while I strip. Once I'm sure the water is comfortable, I step in first and hold her hand. I don't trust the slippery tiles. Maybe I should get one of those rubber suction cup mats. She steps toward me, and I think she needs my support. I wrap my arm around her, high enough to not be anywhere near her incision. She wraps her hand around my cock, which is, of course, already hard. Thinking about Stasia makes it come to life. Being in the same room as her makes me want to adjust my pants. Seeing her naked is making me leak. And now she's touching me.

"Stasia—"

"Niko, let me. Please. I just want to touch you. Your body is exquisite, and I enjoy knowing I can pleasure you."

"You do a shit ton more than just pleasure me."

"Maybe we can start there for now."

"I'm nervous."

She laughs, turning her head against her good arm. When she looks up, I can tell she's fighting her laughter. She sucks her lips between her teeth, but there's mirth in her eyes.

"I mean about hurting you."

"I know, but it still sounded funny coming from you."

"I love you, Stasia. I'll always be nervous about your wellbeing."

I will. I am so much larger than her. I fear not being gentle enough with her. I fear rushing her when she still needs rest. I fear her doing too much too soon.

"Daddy, will you kiss me, please?"

"Yes, *malyshka*."

It comes out a reverent whisper. I cup her jaw with my free hand, my fingers tunneling into her blonde hair. She's stroking me, and I rock my hips each time her hand slides up my cock. I want to be inside her, but it's way too soon. I don't even like her standing in the shower. I can't possibly have sex with her yet. But, fuck, her hand feels amazing. She's varying the speed, pressure, and giving her wrist a twist. I'm going to come embarrassingly fast.

"Stasia, slow down. Unless you're tired and need—"

"Daddy, shh. I'm enjoying myself. Try to enjoy yourself, too."

"I'm enjoying myself so much that I'm about to come."

She squeezes and increases her speed. That's all it takes. My head tilts back under the water as I come against her belly and mine. The hand that held her face slips between us. She widens her legs enough for me to slip my hand between us.

"You will tell me the minute anything hurts. Do you understand me, baby girl?"

"The only thing that hurts, Daddy, is my pussy. And that's because it's empty and aching for you. I'd prefer your cock, but I know you won't give me that yet."

I'm slow as I slide my fingers into her. I still have my arm wrapped around the middle of her back to support her, but she leans forward to rest against my chest. She strokes my arm, shoulder, and over my chest. Fuck, now she's kissing up my neck and nipping at my earlobe.

"Stop tempting me, *malyshka*. You're adding to your spankings."

"I know. The goal is a hundred."

I snare her mouth in a kiss that has her digging her fingers into me. Her nails press into my skin, and I love it. I love the tinge of pain. She's not the only one who likes to receive it, and I know I'm not the only one who likes to give it.

"Daddy, I'm close. May I come?"

"Yes, baby girl."

"Hmmf."

"What does that mean?"

"I thought you would tell me no. I thought you might edge me for a bit. Niko, I'm injured, but I'm not broken. I don't want everything to change between us with our sex life. I enjoy the delayed gratification and submitting to you. Please don't take that away."

"Whatever you want, *meelaya*."

I slow my fingers, working inside her cunt longer between thrusts. My thumb moves in lazy circles on her clit.

"I feel you're close, *printsessa*. If you come, I'll be very disappointed in you."

"I'll try, *papochka*. I don't want to disappoint you anymore."

That's like a bucket of cold water. I lean back so we can look at each other.

"Stasia, you don't disappoint me. I don't love the choices you've made, but I understand them. I've made a mess of introducing you to this life. I've left you floundering."

"You gave me the space I thought I wanted. You didn't disappoint me, Niko. If you were a disappointment, I wouldn't love you the way I do."

"I can say the same for you."

She nods and rests her head against me again. I go back to finger fucking her. I'm hard as a fucking rock again. How the fuck does that happen? I'm not nineteen anymore, but she does this to me. I can't get enough.

"*Malyshka*, come."

She exhales in relief, and I feel her cunt tighten around my fingers. Fuck, she's so goddamn tight. I press kisses to the uninjured side of her forehead, her cheek, and her lips. She wraps her good arm around my waist.

"Let me wash your hair."

She turns around. I lather shampoo into my hands and work my fingers into the nearly waist-length blonde hair. I didn't realize it was this long since she often wears it in a ponytail or messy bun. I massage her scalp, and her upper back rests against my chest. We're careful not to have anything rub against her incision. Once I'm through with her hair, I squeeze body wash onto a poof and run it over her body as she rinses the suds from her hair. She watches me as I wash myself. Once we're dry, I'm careful as I peel away the dressing over her surgical site. It looks way better than I expected. There's a type of clear film over the incision, kind of like a glue. She has dissolvable stitches. I put a fresh covering over it before we walk into the bedroom.

"Daddy?"

"Yes, *malyshka*."

She looks hesitant to ask for what she wants. She shakes her head and looks toward the closet where her clothes hang. Someone went to her place and gathered most of her belongings. Only the furniture, linens, and kitchenware remain.

"Stasia, you can tell me what you want."

"It's stupid and embarrassing."

I cup her face with both hands this time and tilt her head back.

"We're partners, remember? If there's something you want or need, I don't want you to ever feel like you can't tell me."

She looks skeptical. When she tries to nod, I release her face.

"I want to sit on your dick."

She blurts it and turns fire engine red. The color fills her face and down her neck. I try not to laugh before I walk backwards to the bed, her hand in mine, as I draw her with me. I sit and am cautious as I put my hands on her waist. I lift her, and she wraps her legs around my hips as she slides down my cock.

Her sigh sounds like it comes from her soul. She wraps her arm around my back and sags against me. Her entire body goes lax. If I didn't know better, I would think she'd fallen asleep.

"Is this what you need, *malyshka*? To be close to *papochka*?"

She nods. I stroke her wet hair as my other hand rests on her ass. Neither one of us tries to make it into sex. We're just joined and at peace. Never would I imagine being inside her and not trying to make her come, not getting myself off. But this might be the best thing I've ever done.

"If you get bored, tell me, and I'll get off."

"Stasia, this is about the most sublime thing I've ever experienced. It ties with making you come for the first time."

"Really?"

"You knew what we needed. Being one. This is a kind of intimacy I never thought about. I enjoy discovering and sharing these things with you. I want you to stay where you are as long as I can keep my dick hard."

She does something that squeezes my cock, but she doesn't move.

"Fuck, Stasia. You're going to make me come, and then it'll be over."

"Nope. I'll do Kegels and never let go. Your dick is mine now."

"It's always been yours, *meelaya*. You said you wanted to be a monogamous couple. I want that and to be a married couple. When you're ready, I'll ask."

"Does that mean today?"

We both laugh, but we both know that there's seriousness to that question.

"If that's what you want. And you can be Mrs. Kutsenkova, even if Kutsenko works for a man or woman."

She leans back and nods.

"You don't think it's too soon, *malyshka*?"

"It probably would be if we were any other couple. It hasn't even been ninety days like on that TV show. Hell, it hasn't even been a month. We don't have to have the wedding today, but I want you to know that I wasn't loopy on the drugs when I told you I want to be Mrs. Kutsenko for real. I want people to use my first name because they don't want to confuse me with the other wives, just like you want to use your first name, so people don't confuse you with your brothers. I want to turn around when I hear Mrs. Kutsenko and know that person might be talking to me. I want to be the one you come home to. I want to be the one you can trust and turn to when it's us against the world. I want you to want to come home because you know I'm waiting there for you. I want you."

It's the opposite of the last time we had a similar conversation. She's saying what I've desperately needed to hear. I knew she didn't mean it when she told me she didn't want me. And I know she means it even more when she says that she does.

"Even though I want to stay like we are forever, and I can't think of a more perfect way to be one with you, I'm not asking the day after you get out of the hospital. I want it to be special and not tinged with the memory of violence and fear."

"All right. But I'm not patient, Niko. If you don't ask soon, I'll get a ring and ask you."

I wouldn't put it past her.

"Fair, *malyshka*. You look tired. I know you didn't sleep with nurses coming and going every two hours."

I tighten my grip, prepared to lift her off me, but she does another Kegel. Her movement and mine press her clit against my pubic bone. Her hand squeezes my shoulder. I flex my hips while holding her in place. I do not want her moving and hurting herself. My movement is enough to make us both come. We sit together until my body no longer cooperates.

As we crawl into bed, I kiss my sort-of fiancée's shoulder. I've already thought about our trip. I'm going to ask her properly in Greece. And God help any motherfucker who thinks to mess this trip up.

Chapter Twenty-One

Stasia

It's been two weeks since I left the hospital. We've just landed in Greece, and I can't wait to see what Niko planned. I wasn't up to such a long flight, even in a private jet, before this. Niko's family has joked about building a compound, so everyone can live close together. But we know it would only draw unwanted attention. In the meantime, everyone in their family, plus my parents and me, have been staying at Maks and Laura's. They bought such a large house because they wanted to have room for family to stay. I don't think they expected everyone to practically move in. But plenty of people to help with the babies have allowed Maks and Laura to sleep.

"Close your eyes, *malyshka*."

"Daddy, I already know we're here."

I keep my voice low. I don't mind people hearing Niko call me baby girl, but it's uncomfortable for people to hear me call him Daddy. I'm worried they'll judge. Niko's hinted that Maks and Bogdan probably have similar relationships, but I can't do it. I've never heard Laura or Christina call their husbands that, either.

"That doesn't mean there isn't a surprise for you."

"You mean beyond the amazing private jet your family owns?"

"That wasn't a surprise. I told you how we were flying."

"But you didn't mention that it may as well be gold-plated for how nice it is."

"Close your eyes."

I sigh as my shoulders drop. I relent and close them. He slips a blindfold over my eyes and helps me out of my seat. I can hear other people moving around. Sergei, Misha, Anton, and Pasha came with us. Not exactly a romantic addition to our getaway, but I'm glad they're with us. I feel better for it.

"Niko!"

"Any excuse to have you in my arms is a good one. I don't want you to trip."

I know he'd carry me down the steep steps even if he hadn't covered my eyes. I rest my head against him as he steps onto the ground. There's a hot breeze that blows my hair back from my face. Niko steps onto something that shifts beneath us. We must be on some type of boat. He sits with me on his lap. Saltwater sprays onto us as the small craft takes off. I turn my head as though I might see something, but it's dark beneath the sleep mask.

"I have no idea what to expect, Niko."

"Good."

"Can you give me a hint?"

"I can, but I won't."

When the boat stops, Niko stands and steps up. He carries me a little way before he eases me onto my feet. He turns me toward the direction we came from.

"Are you ready, *meelaya*?"

"Yes."

He lifts the mask from my face, and I look out at the Mediterranean. The sky is the purest blue I've ever seen, with puffy white clouds scattered like someone tossed them toward the heavens. The water shimmers and is clear enough for me to see at least fifty feet down. Where we stand is a patio that ends in the water. There's no guard rail or retaining wall. An infinity pool to our right shows our reflection. Anyone in it would feel like they could swim right into the sea.

"Daddy."

It comes out on a breath. No one is around us.

"Do you like it so far?"

"Yes. It's breathtaking."

"I agree."

I look back over my shoulder to find Niko looking at me, not the view. I turn in his arms and wrap mine around his neck. My shoulder's still sore, but I can move it. My ribs are mostly healed, too.

"Do you want me to show you around?"

"Is this your house?"

"It is now."

"Now?"

"I bought it for us, Stasia."

"Us?"

He nods. We stopped by his penthouse to pick up Sammy, who Aleks promised to look after while we're gone. We went to my apartment, and I agreed to put everything in storage. I don't want to know what Niko said to my landlord, but he agreed to break my lease. Niko asked me to live with him last week, and I agreed. I know this vacation will be a test of sorts, but I'm confident we're compatible, not just in love but in living arrangements. We're talking about buying a house in Queens. Bogdan and Christina live around the corner from Laura and Maks, who are ten minutes from Galina. I didn't know he'd already bought a house for us.

He takes my hand and walks me around. The place is large for Mykonos. I can't believe I'm staying somewhere so famous and exotic. It reminds me that Niko and his family have a kind of wealth I don't know that I can ever grasp. He's going by the photos he saw online, but he gives me the grand tour.

"What do you want to do first, Stasia?"

I waggle my eyebrows at him.

"If we get in the water, will your cousins give us enough space for you to fuck me?"

Niko's face goes red as he looks over my shoulder. I squeeze my eyes closed. Fuck me.

"We'll give you plenty of space. None of us wants to see Niko fumbling around."

"*Zatknis' mudak.*"

Niko mutters, "shut up, asshole" as Pasha walks by. My ears are on fire.

"Did that answer your question, *moye sokrovishche?*"

I nod. I practically sprint into the master bedroom. Someone's magically made our luggage appear in here. Niko threatened to unpack everything and leave it behind when he saw I had more than bikinis, sunblock, and my toothbrush in the bag. He bought me a couple of bathing suits I could only wear in Europe. I'm not even certain I have the balls to wear them in public. They might be for a private viewing in here.

"How about this one?"

Or maybe not so private viewing in the sea.

"Niko, you really want people to see me in that?"

"I'm not worried about my cousins, and no one else is here right now. A staff will come for meals and to tidy up, but they won't linger."

"Where are your cousins going to be?"

Niko shrugs.

"Somewhere out of sight but close enough if we need them."

There's something about the way he says that. I cant my head and furrow my brow.

"Niko?"

"Hmm."

"What aren't you telling me?"

"Nothing. They will be here if we need them, which I don't think we will. But they'll be discreet. They know it's a romantic getaway for us. They know how important this is to me that you have a good time. And they want you to enjoy yourself after everything that's happened in the past month."

"All right."

I change into the suit Niko bought me—or rather the tied together dental floss—and insist upon wearing a cover up until we're at the water's edge. I turn in a full circle, shading my eyes. There isn't a direction to look where the view isn't spectacular. I squint to see a couple on a beach just beyond the wall that surrounds the non-waterfront portion of this villa. Two men. One with blond hair, and one with dark. Sitting side by side, resting back on their hands, their arms overlapping.

Holy shit.

"Niko, is that...?"

Niko stills before he grabs my arms and spins me around. He's never been this kind of rough with me. His blue eyes are spearing me into place. I shake my head, and his eyes narrow.

"Niko, I will not tell anyone. I'm happy for them. I didn't know, but I've thought more than once that if they were gay, they would make the perfect couple. So much about them being in sync makes sense now. Their secret is safe. I know why."

He eases his hold on me, and I see the relief. He lets me see it.

"Niko, I'm half Russian, but I was raised here. I don't believe in the old-world ways. I like your chivalry and your charm, but I will not police anyone's love life."

"But you understand why no one outside the family can know?"

"Yes. I swear, Niko. They've been nothing but kind and welcoming to me. Hurting them is the same as hurting you, and I never want to do that again."

"Thank you, *malyshka*."

I cup his cheek and press a soft kiss to his lips.

"If we marry, your family becomes my family. There's nothing more important than them."

"If?"

There's a note of uncertainty, and I see a flash of worry.

"Daddy, when. Is that better?"

"Come here, *printsessa*. Take off your cover up. I have something for you."

His voice is much lighter, and there's mischief in his eyes.

"Is it a belated birthday gift?"

"Maybe."

"Is it your dick in a bow?"

My question surprises him. He stops short, then laughs. Like really laughs. A belly laugh. I've never heard it before. He picks me up, and I wrap my legs around him as he wades into the water.

"Is that what you've been wishing for, *malyshka*?"

"Maybe."

"I've got my dick, but I'll have to look for a bow later."

"Can I have that present now?"

I squeeze my thighs to rise and fall against his cock. Fucking board shorts and bikini bottoms. I notice there's a bench built into the rock where the ground drops off. Niko pushes down his shorts before sitting. He pulls my g string aside, and I slide onto him. It's like coming home after a long day at work. I feel comfortable enough to talk about some heavy shit.

"I know we just arrived, but we've been avoiding talking about what's going on. I haven't asked you questions because I didn't want to know while we were at home. It was too real and too nearby. What's happening?"

"As of right now, nothing. Luca, Carmine, and Gabriele disappeared. I'm certain Salvatore left them alive. He can't lose two nephews and a cousin of some sort. Luca's his heir. He won't want to train a new one. He has two young daughters, so they aren't an option. Patriarchal, I know. But that's how it is. None of us has heard a whisper about Vlad's brothers. We've put out feelers to the family we still have in Moscow. After how badly things went with Katerina and how Vlad died, we've had a truce of sorts with the Podolskaya. They've stayed away from our family still in Russia."

"But they could still plan to come to New York."

"Yes. Sergei hacked into *Cosa Nostra's* accounting system. He got into Luca's, Carmine's, and Gabriele's offshore accounts. None of them have received half a million dollars. No one we tracked has any unaccounted-for business transactions. Carmine may have been bluffing with Salvatore. Especially since there's still no evidence that any of them spoke to someone in the Podolskaya."

"Could this all blow over?"

He's hesitant to answer.

"Niko?"

I shift, and he groans.

"Fuck, baby girl. You make it impossible to think straight. I love it when we're like this, but if you move again, I'm going to fuck you. It's been hours since the last time I was inside you."

"Like four. We did it in the cabin on the plane."

"That's a long fucking time when you make me so horny."

"You old goat."

His hands grip my hips as he lifts me up and down to ride his cock. I can barely remember my name, let alone what I just asked. I gladly move along with him. When he sets a pace he likes, he pulls my hands behind my back and clasps my wrists in one of his hands. The other fists my hair. He yanks back until he can kiss my throat.

"Your pussy is heaven on Earth."

"I think the same about your cock."

"Even without a bow?"

I giggle.

"I want to hear you laugh every day for the rest of our lives, Stasia."

Our lips meet, and it's the same fireworks show that always goes off. I missed my pill for a couple days, but I got my period last week. I've taken it religiously since, so we've abandoned condoms. I never believed there could be that big a difference. But fuck. Riding him bareback is incredible. He lets go of my hair to pull my bikini top triangles apart and down. He alternates tits. I have no concept of time as we fuck.

"*Papochka*, please, may I come?"

"Yes, *malyshka*. I'm so close too."

Our lips meet again, and I can feel him pulse inside me as I contract around him. Will it always be like this with us? At some point, the urgency to be together will wear off, and so will some of the novelty. But will the need to become one always remain? I pray it does. I will do my damnedest to make sure it does.

"Stasia, I love you."

"I love you, Niko."

We're spent and holding one another. In moments like this, the contrast between our roughness and our softness with each other is stark. It suits us perfectly.

"Every time we do that, I feel closer to you, Stasia. I don't know where I end, and you begin. You're part of me. That's why I haven't backed off on your guard detail. We have had no threats, or even hints of them, but losing you would be the same as losing myself."

"I know you make my safety a priority, and I will never take it for granted again. The idea of being separated from you again is so overwhelming, it makes my chest hurt. Tell me what's going to happen as best you can. Worst-case and best-case scenario."

"Best-case is we return home, get married, and start a family when we're ready. We live blissfully, and your parents come to visit as often as they want. Or they could move to New York."

"You don't mean in with us, do you?"

"You look and sound horrified, *printsessa*. And no, definitely not with us. I plan to have my way with you anywhere and everywhere anytime we want. We cannot do that with your parents living there."

"Phew. Good. But what's the real best-case, more immediate possibility?"

"The Lushaks don't come. We find out that everything those shitbags said was exaggeration and posturing. Even if it isn't, the Lushaks realize how foolish approaching us in America would be."

"Worst-case?"

Niko looks out to sea as he gazes past my shoulder. He presses me against his chest, and it almost feels like he's saying goodbye.

"Niko, take that off the table. You dying is not even remotely part of a worst-case scenario."

"Stasia, you know it is. I don't plan to die before I'm eighty, but it's possible. Can you live with that? It's part of being a bratva wife."

"I don't want to, but I'll have to. I won't give you up."

He sighs.

"They come to America, and they try to get you, your dad, and my mom. They succeed, and it forces my family and me to go back to Moscow. Misha and Pasha were there last year for a funeral. But other than them, no one has been back in a decade. None of us wants to go. The funeral was for a guy they'd known since preschool. He'd been an informant for us and died for it. They lost a close friend and felt responsible for his death, even if indirectly."

"If I end up in Russia, I'm never seeing you again, am I? You following me would be about retribution, not recovery."

Niko presses me back so we can look at each other.

"It will always be about getting you back. I told you, I will burn everything to the ground before I let anyone take you from me." He closes his eyes. "You know there is a side of me I never want you to see. It's the one I keep hidden from the world, and particularly from you. But it's way darker than anyone other than my brothers and cousins know. We all have it within us, and we've sworn to never let it loose. But I will not hold back if the Podolskaya takes one more person I love. My dad wouldn't be dead if they hadn't forced him to fight in Chechnya. If any of them come near you, I will let the real monster out. The one Vlad trained us to be. It's the only way they will understand."

He opens his eyes, and he allows me in. I see how conflicted his soul is, how resolved he is to protect me, and how much he fears my reaction to what he's said.

"Nikolai, you are the bravest man I have ever met. I don't care what any other wife or girlfriend says. You love with your whole heart, even when you refuse to show any emotion. I know you do. I see it with your family, and I feel it. You are not a monster, even if you have to act like one sometimes. It doesn't define who you are outside the warehouse or away from these people. I know you'd be protecting me, but you'd be protecting your family, too. Whatever you have to do, do it. Do not *ever* fear my reaction to you protecting the people we love. I will *always* stand by you."

"You don't know—"

"And I pray I never have to. But there is a ferocity in all of us when it comes to those we love. It drives us to do what we'd otherwise think is unspeakable, unfathomable, to keep them safe. I may not have your skills, but do not doubt for a moment that there is nothing I wouldn't do for you."

Niko tries to shake his head, but I hold it firm.

"Listen to me, Niko. I need you to understand this. I am not exaggerating. Maybe I'm warning you. But I mean every word I've said. A month ago, I couldn't imagine the extremes I realize I'm willing to go to. I couldn't imagine my dark side being so consuming and violent. But you are not alone in your devotion. Your feelings for me are not stronger than my feelings for you. Your commitment to me is not stronger than mine is to you. They are the same. You are my soulmate. Without my mate, what is left for my soul?"

Niko stares at me and blinks. I can see he's holding back, and it's a struggle. It's the only chink in his emotional armor I've ever seen. He's trying to keep his feelings from me, but he can't. I don't want him to.

"Niko, I love you."

He nods and swallows, still unable to speak. I place my hand over his heart, and he does the same to me. We've exchanged passionate kisses and tender kisses. But this one—this one is something else entirely. This is elemental. One day, I hope we speak aloud our wedding vows. I will mean every pledge I make, and I know Niko will mean his. But this kiss? This surpasses anything we could ever put into words.

"I love you, Stasia."

We sit together until the sun sets. We watch it slip beneath the horizon before we go inside to dress for dinner.

We've been here for four days, and it feels like it's been a heartbeat. He's taken me swimming, had a dive instructor teach me to scuba, taken me parasailing and on a catamaran. But that's all been in the afternoon. I sleep late most mornings, as the excursions exhaust me, so I usually take a nap before dinner. The constant sex is enough to make me need more sleep. If we're not asleep or away from the villa, Niko's usually buried in me somehow.

I've just woken up from one of those naps, and Niko leads me to the terrace. I can't believe the exquisite meal set out before us. Niko pulls out my chair for me and a man appears with a bottle of wine. He could be a ghost for all I know. He comes and goes throughout the meal and is completely unobtrusive. Food and wine magically seem to appear in front of me. When we finish, Niko smiles.

"Are you ready for the first of your surprises, *malyshka*?"

Niko's tone and his expression tell me what kind of surprise it will be, even if I don't know the specifics. I eagerly nod. He helps me from my seat and leads us to our bedroom. I glance around. The chef and waiter, along with Niko's cousins, are nowhere to be seen. Niko closes the door behind us. I move to go farther into the room, but he yanks me back and spins me against the door.

"I'm going to do dirty, dirty things to you tonight, baby girl. You're going to need to sleep the morning away after I'm done. Do you submit to me, Stasia?"

"Always."

Goosebumps prickle my arms, and my nipples harden. I know it'll be delayed gratification tonight, but I want to hurry and get to it. Niko's breath tickles my ear, making me shiver as he kisses behind it.

"Every part of you is mine, *malyshka*. I'm going to fuck all of you tonight. Then I'm going to make love to you."

I know the difference, and I'm eager for both. I discovered what making love was the day after we returned from Baltimore, and I nearly threw it all away. Since then, we've had all kinds of sex. Rough, gentle, kinky, vanilla. But we both know which one our partner needs. It surpasses a physical connection.

Niko releases me and walks to a chair beside the window. He moves it to the center of the room and sits.

"Strip for me, *malyshka*."

I felt awkward as fuck the first time I did this for him. I didn't feel sexy. I felt gangly. But he enjoyed it. I watched him struggle not to touch me, how the bulge in his pants grew uncomfortable enough to make him arrange himself more than once. I saw the lust in his eyes. Any doubt I had vanished as I saw how much he wanted me. The power I felt for the first time. No man has ever made me feel so desirable.

I reach behind me to unzip my dress as I walk forward. I let one strap fall down my shoulder before I let the other one drop. I inch it down my chest with each step, but I stop just beyond his reach. I turn my back to him as I let the dress fall forward. I hear his grunt of annoyance. I reach back and unfasten my bra, tossing it back at him as I watch over my shoulder. The dress drops to the floor, and I widen my feet since I haven't bothered with panties in days. I bend forward until one hand touches the floor while the other strokes along the back of my thigh. Then I spread my ass to him.

I'm not prepared for him to grasp my hips, pull back, and impale me with his cock. The silent bastard. I still haven't learned to sense him the way he does me. He thrusts into me over and over, one hand pressing between my shoulder blades.

"Tease me and keep me from enjoying all of you, and I punish you, *malyshka*."

I feel the moment he comes. He stills except to rock his hips.

"Your pussy is mine, and my cum in it says so. When you feel it slide down your thighs, you'll remember it's not yours anymore."

"Yes, Daddy."

Fuck. I love when he talks like that. I know he's always protective and just the right amount of possessive, outside of sex. But when he talks to me like that, I'll do just about anything for him.

"Go stand by the foot of the bed."

"Yes, Daddy."

I feel his cum with the first step. I want to squeeze my thighs to keep it inside me. I'm still taking my pill religiously, so I'm not worried.

"Put your arms up and spread your legs. Make an X."

It's a four-poster bed, but I'm not tall enough to grasp either side of the king size bed. Niko places a bag on it that I haven't seen before. He pulls four sets of cuffs. He attaches them to the posts, then my right wrist and ankle first before repeating his process on the left. He goes back to his bag of goodies and pulls out my vibrator. The big one that's almost comparable to him.

He comes to stand behind me, trailing his fingers along my spine from top to bottom. I can't help my shiver. He twists and presses the plug I've been wearing since we dressed for dinner. I don't know how I made it through the meal, sitting with it in. I got hornier with each course, and Niko knew. He kept grinning and insisting I not cross my legs. He took mercy on me between the salads and main course and moved his chair beside mine. He fingered me until I came. He barely finished before the waiter came out with our fish. He's driving me crazy again.

"You can come whenever you need to, *malyshka*."

I've learned what that means. He's not being generous. Oh, no. It means death by orgasm. He's going to make me come over and over until I can't remember my name, I can barely stand up, I can't talk, and my clit is overly sensitive. But it also usually means he'll go down on me and make it all feel better before fucking me. He turns it on and holds it up for me to see it vibrate. He slides it into me, and there's no resistance between my wetness and his cum. My legs tense, and I wish I could cross them. I'm fighting not to come, but it's a losing battle. I close my eyes as the orgasm crashes over me.

I barely catch myself from screaming as the riding crop lands across my ass. Fuck, that stings. Niko rubs out the burn. Then he lands it across my ass again. The sound of it whizzing through the air, then my moan as he rubs my ass, becomes a steady cadence against the buzz of my vibrator. I'm sweating as I take one slap after another. He gives me a break when I rest my head against my arm. I wipe my forehead against my bicep and straighten.

"More, please, Daddy."

I feel him hesitate. He's already given me ten swats. I wiggle my hips. He grabs each ass cheek and squeezes.

"Daddy."

I can only describe the sound as a croak.

"Who decides?"

"You, Daddy."

"What happens to baby girls who think they know best?"

"They don't get to come."

It's all part of the game we play. He listens to me when I ask for more and gives it to me. But it's always in some way other than what I ask for. This time he pulls the vibrator from me and pulls my hips back as he kneels behind me. His tongue slides inside me, and my legs tremble again. When he gets to my sensitive clit, he's gentle. He sucks, and it's more soothing than anything else. It brings me back from the edge. He rubs my ass again, this time taking the burn away. He lets me come once before he straightens. He walks around the side of the bed and watches me speculatively. When he decides whatever he's going to do next, he unfastens me.

"Go sit in the chair, *moye sokrovishche*."

I follow his instructions and watch when he pulls some type of contraption out of the bag. He walks to the end of the bed and climbs onto it, then stands. He has a strap of some sort that he flings over the exposed rafter above the end of the bed. He catches the end that goes over the wood beam. I notice a carabiner, but he steps down and blocks my view.

"Come here, *malyshka*."

My eyes widen as I see what he's set up. Holy fuck. I mentioned one time I was curious about sex swings. Now there's one hanging in the bedroom of our villa. He guides me to recline into the straps, and I trust him that it will support me.

"Grab onto the hanging straps. Good. Rest back on the swing while I lift your legs."

I do as he tells me, trusting him implicitly. He brings my feet to his chest before he fists his cock and guides it to my pussy. His hands go to my waist, and he thrusts.

"Aah."

I don't scream, but neither am I quiet. He lets the swing help move me as his thrusts push me away, and the swing slides me back onto his cock. My legs are long enough to rest my calves on his shoulders, letting him in deeper. Our eyes meet, and everything else in the world ceases to exist.

"Do you like this, *moye sokrovishche?*"

"So much, *papochka*. You're so deep. I—It's never been quite like this."

"I know, baby. That's why I got it."

His hips keep slamming into me, setting a punishing pace. Nothing has ever felt like this. Our sex is always amazing, and he's taught me things I never imagined. But this position is new. It might be my favorite.

"Are you close, Stasia?"

"Yes. May I come?"

"Yes. I want to watch you as I fuck you."

He looks down to watch his cock slide in and out. I use the straps to help me pull up, since I want to see too. The change in position sets me off. My back arches as my hips drop. Fuck me. He's going faster and harder. How has he not come yet?

"You have the most perfect little cunt. Come on me, Stasia."

"I am, Daddy."

My abs quivers as my arms shake. I'm clinging to the straps until I'm spent. Niko helps me off and takes my place. He reclines, and I climb on and straddle him. He pushes off and lets the swing move. We press our bodies together and enjoy the moment of intimacy. But we can't ignore our need to move, to both come. I pull my legs up until I can slide them into loops I find. It gives me leverage to ride Niko. The swing moves back and forth as I move up and down.

"Fuck, Stasia. I'm putting one of these in every room of every home we ever have."

"Promise?"

"Yes, *moye sokrovishche*."

"Do I feel good, Niko?"

"Yes. Stasia, I'm too close. What do you need me to do? I can't last much longer. Fuck."

I shake my head as I ride him faster. As I feel it starting, I arch my back and press my tits together. He accepts the offer and sits up further. The moment he sucks my tit, I come. I clench as hard as I can around his dick.

"I'm coming, Daddy."

"I know. Me, too."

I see the sweat beading on his brow and his concentration as he keeps me coming. Yes, sex is a big part of our relationship. Would plenty of people say it's most of our relationship? Probably. I love getting Niko off, and I sure as shit like it when he gets me off. But it's been more since the beginning. I can't put it into words.

"Baby girl, it's like I feel your soul touching mine when we're together."

I guess Niko can. That's how I feel.

"You know I love it when I make you come, and it's obvious how much I like it when I come. But if someone asked me what I liked best about our sex life, I would say it's the feeling of being one."

I shrug, embarrassed by what I said. He cups my cheeks and kisses me.

"That's not insignificant, Stasia. It's how I feel. I worry sometimes that you feel like that because you haven't had the experience to compare."

"I don't need it, Niko. I've heard my friends talk about sex. None have ever described it the way I feel with you. Not even Gracie, who's engaged. This connection doesn't happen for everyone, even if they're in love."

Niko stands up, and I wrap myself around him. He carries me to the bed, and we pull the covers around us once we're on it. He brushes the hair back from my cheek.

"I love you, Stasia. You're the part of me that's been missing."

I grin.

"You complete me."

He chuckles and presses a kiss to my lips before I shift to rest my head beneath his chin. Just before we fall asleep, Niko promises me more surprises. I pray the only ones I get are the ones he plans.

Chapter Twenty-Two

Niko

We've been on Mykonos for ten days. Jet lag and Stasia's need to rest kept us close to the villa for the first few days. We've slept late, which I never do. We've had picnics on the beach just beyond the villa. We've walked into town and visited the shops. We've eaten most of our meals on the terrace. And we've made love anywhere out of my cousins' sight. Stasia's been patient when we get to stores, and we wait outside while one or two of my cousins sweep the area. She hasn't minded having shadows other than our own. I'm proud of how she's adjusting, and she's far more thoughtful about my cousins' comfort than I am.

"Niko, let them eat. It's practically noon. I'll be out in a moment."

"No. No one eats before you do."

"Then you shouldn't let me sleep so long. It's not right to hold everyone's breakfast hostage because you kept me up too late. Sergei! Anton! Tell your brothers to have breakfast. Niko, stay away from them. I'm warning you."

I wander into the bedroom and kick the door closed. Stasia's standing by the closet and jumps. She's still not used to how quietly I can move. I always know where she is, even when I can't see her. She hasn't mastered that skill with me yet. I wrap my arm around her waist and press my cock against her ass.

"Warning me about what, *malyshka*? Do you make the rules?"

"No, *papochka*. But you're being unkind to your family."

"It is not their vacation. If they want to come to Greece on their own time, they can."

"That doesn't mean starve them! Besides, they're big men. They need sustenance if they're to have the strength to guard us."

"Us?"

I know she's teasing me. She shrugs and tries not to smile.

"I think a baby girl who disobeys her *papochka* gets a hot ass to sit on."

"Niko—"

She sees my expression.

"*Papochka*, we can't keep them waiting."

"They're not. They sat down the moment you told them to."

"So everything is fine."

"The only fine thing in this room is your perfect ass, which I intend to warm."

I pick her up and carry her around the waist until we get to the bed. I sit and flip her onto my lap. She's wearing a sundress and no panties. That was the one thing I refused to let her pack. I pull the material up to her waist and take a moment to enjoy the view. I'm concerned that she's lost weight since her surgery, but I have said nothing. I know she's noticed. Once in a while, she'll make comments about her body that make me wonder what people have said to her over the years. I think it's the sexiest thing I've ever seen, but I worry about her right now. Hell, I worry about her all the time.

"Five spanks on each side for being disobedient and disagreeable. Hold my ankle if you think you can't keep your hands out of the way. What's your safe word?"

"Capt'n Crunch."

"And what happens if you need to use it, and you don't?"

"You'll edge me all night."

"Do not let me truly hurt you."

"Niko, time out."

I let her get up, and she sits next to me.

"You need to stop worrying that every time I breathe, I'm going to get hurt, or that any time you touch me, you're going to hurt me. You're going to give yourself an ulcer, and frankly, I don't want to hear it. I know our roles, and I genuinely submit, but I'm not actually a child. I have some common sense, despite what I've shown. I know our rules, and I've agreed to them. I've followed them every time. What happened to me was my fault. It wasn't your lack of controlling the situation. It wasn't your lack of care. It was me, Niko. And only I can do better. Stop punishing yourself."

"I—"

"You are about to see if I can flip a man twice my size and twice my weight over my lap. Argue with me, and I shall spank you."

"God, I love you."

She's right. I'm like a broken record. But her feistiness will keep us in bed all day. I pull her in for a kiss and try to lie us down. She resists.

"I have a spanking waiting for me, then breakfast. I'm starving."

I settle her back over my lap and swat her ass five times on each side, like I said I would. She settles her dress in place after she stands. She kisses me and steps around me.

"Oh, no. You're not leaving me like this. My cousins aren't going to see me with a hard-on for my girlfriend."

"I know for a fact, it wouldn't be the first time."

She tries to bolt for the door, but once again, I snag her around the waist. I steer her into the bathroom and slam the door shut. There's no way we can have sex in the bedroom without my cousins figuring it out. There's a slight chance that they might have a moment of doubt if we're in here. I lift her onto the counter and toss up her dress again. She holds the material out of the way as I unfasten my pants. I give her my thumb to lick and suck as I thrust into her. Her right leg rests on my shoulder as I surge into her over and over.

"Daddy, harder. I will not break."

I catch myself before I share my worry. The look she shoots me dares me to say what I'm thinking. Instead, I redouble my efforts to fuck her the way she wants.

"Daddy, I need to come."

"So?"

I cock an eyebrow, challenging her. I rub her clit, and I watch her eyes practically roll back in her head before she closes them.

"Daddy, please, may I come?"

"No. Because I'm too close. We know what happens when I let you come, and I'm this close. I'm not done with you yet."

"I thought this would be a quickie."

"Who decides, *malyshka*?"

"You do, Daddy."

It is going to be a quickie because there is no way I can hold out, but she doesn't need to know that. I thrust into her four more times before I growl at her.

"Come."

I wrap my hand around her throat and press against her artery. She looks at me and tries to sigh. She likes breath play. We've experimented a few more times. Any time I've had an inkling of doubt that she trusts me, I remember how she gives over control to me when we're having sex, and especially times like this.

The moment I feel her cunt spasm, I feel my cum entering her. I release her throat and watch a euphoric glow spread over her face. We hold each other as we catch our breath.

"You know, if we filmed a porn, we could make a million dollars."

She winks at me as she slips off the counter.

"And I would gouge out the eyes of any guy who watched it."

"Hmm. I would do the same to any girl. Maybe not a porn."

"I don't share, *malyshka*."

"I know." She winks. "Neither do I."

This time when she bolts for the door, I let her until I realize what she's running toward.

"*Meelaya!*"

"Too slow, *sakharok*."

I watch her snag the last two chocolate-filled croissants. My cousins are watching us and laughing. I roll my eyes as I approach Stasia. She shakes her head.

"Nope. Not sharing. You shouldn't have been mean to your cousins."

"You sound like my mom, except she would make me share."

A speculative look enters Stasia's eyes before she laughs. She shakes her head again and moves out of my reach.

"You're really going to hide behind Anton and Sergei to protect your pastry."

"Yup. You guys would defend my chocolate croissant, wouldn't you?"

"To the death."

"Shut up, Anton."

"Grouchy. Someone didn't get enough sleep."

"Shut up, Sergei."

I'm laughing too. I love seeing Stasia so comfortable with my family and how welcoming they are to her. I look at Misha and Pasha and wonder if their turn will come before Aleks's. They're the only three left.

"Bring your pastries with you."

I brought our bag with towels, sunblock, and a few other essentials out with me from the bedroom. I hold out my hand, which Stasia takes without hesitation. She follows me out to where the tender stopped when we arrived. It's there again, but a hundred yards away is a private speedboat.

"I wonder who that belongs to."

Stasia points and looks at me. I grin.

"You?"

"At least for today. If you like it, then it can be ours."

She closes her eyes for a moment and shakes her head.

"Boys and their toys."

I lean over and whisper in her ear.

"I know a baby girl who likes her toys, too."

She's adorable when she blushes. I do it on purpose sometimes just to see it. I help her onto the smaller boat before helping her onto the speed boat. It's large enough that my cousins can spread out. We sit under the sunshade, but we still have enough room between us and the captain to feel like we have some privacy.

"It's about a two-hour sail to Santorini. We're going to spend the day there."

"That sounds terrific. This has been such an amazing vacation, Niko. Thank you."

Wait until our honeymoon. I don't know what we're doing yet, but I've set the bar high. I pull out the sunblock and a hat I remembered to pack at the last minute. Stasia's so fair, I've worried that she would burn. But I've kept that to myself since she applies sunblock and wears her hat without fail. I never took myself for a worry wort or a nervous nelly, but I am around Stasia. She truly is a treasure. She's precious to me. Seven months ago, when Bogdan and Christina got engaged, I remember watching Bogdan's proposal. Never could I have imagined seven months later, I would be ready to propose to anyone. I was certain I would never be ready ten months ago when I saw Maks propose to Laura. I never considered finding someone who is the other half of me. I would have laughed if anyone told me I would know within days of meeting the right woman that she is who I want to spend my life with.

"Niko, do you want to have children?"

"Before I met you, no. I was steadfastly against it. We all figured Maks would have to, even though he didn't want to before meeting Laura. The rest of us didn't want to bring another generation of Kutsenkos into the bratva. Now? I'm torn. I want a family with you, Stasia. I think about it often, but I think about what happens when they aren't babies or kids anymore. No one can ever make them have the childhood I did. But there would be expectations for them. I fear daughters more than sons, even though sons would be expected to serve as I do."

"Why do you fear daughters?"

"Because we've seen the old rule that women and children are off limits is no longer followed by other syndicates. Salvatore might, but his nephews don't. Enrique might, but his nephew Juan made life difficult for Laura when she rejected him. Donovan went after Laura, and Declan did even worse to Christina. Only the bratva has stayed true to their oath. I would *never* permit an arranged marriage for any of our children, and absolutely not for a daughter. Maks wouldn't dream of suggesting it, especially now that he has Mila. But there are older members who would push for it."

"Does that mean you don't want children?"

I lace my fingers with hers. I'm glad she asked this question today. It's something I've wanted to talk about.

"I want a family with you, Stasia, in whatever form that comes. If it's one, ten, or none, I'll be happy and proud."

"Do you want one soon?"

"That depends on what you want, *meelaya*. There's plenty of time to decide whether you want to go to law school or do something else. Kids can wait until after you've established your career, if that's what you prefer."

I see her considering what I've offered. Stasia will give up so much of her life to make one with me. I want to support her in whatever dreams or aspirations she has, and I will fight tooth and nail to make them happen.

"Your mom is a pharmacist, right?"

I nod.

"Laura went to law school, and Christina went to grad school."

"Yes."

I can't tell what she's thinking, but something is bothering her. I squeeze her hand, and she looks up at me.

"You have very accomplished women in your family. What about your aunts?"

"Aunt Svetlana is an art teacher, and Aunt Alina is a nurse."

"They all work outside the home. Was that because they had to?"

"For my mom, yes. Once my dad was gone, there was no choice. She trained to be a pharmacist while Russia was still part of the Soviet Union. She had to do a lot to prove she was qualified when we moved here. My aunts worked because it helped the family, but they also love what they do. Why do you look so worried?"

"I—"

She won't look at me until I nudge her chin.

"*Malyshka*, you can tell me anything. What do you wish to do? If you don't know yet, that's fine. You're twenty-three. You have plenty of time to figure it out."

"I think I know what I want, but—"

"Stasia, are you worried I would disapprove? Your career is not mine to decide. I'll support you no matter what."

"I want to be a stay-at-home mom."

She looks at her lap, and she looks completely defeated. I don't understand why.

"That sounds like the hardest and most rewarding career I can think of."

"It's not because you're rich, and I'm lazy."

I lift Stasia onto my lap.

"I know it isn't, and I never would have thought that. Are you scared I would? That other people in my family would?"

"All the women in your family have careers outside the home, and probably half have advanced degrees. I've already seen that being bratva is a family business of its own. Laura and Christina have positions within Kutsenko Partners. They contribute."

"Stasia, what any of my brothers' or cousins' wives end up doing is their business within their home with their husband. I only care about what you want. If being a stay-at-home mom is what you want, what would fulfil and make you happy, then that's as important as any other career the women in my family have. It's no secret that my brothers and I are rich. There are very few people in this world who have as much as we do. Anyone could accuse who we marry of marrying us for money. I do not believe you would do that. That's not who you are. If you were, you could find a billionaire who comes with a much easier life."

"You don't think it's too old-fashioned?"

"Of course not."

"And if I change my mind after we have kids?"

"Then we both better drive cars that can fit car seats."

She smiles, and it's like the sun just came out from behind rain clouds. She leans against me as we watch the world go by. We sit in content silence most of the way, pointing out things periodically.

"Niko, look."

Stasia points to Santorini's famous blue roofs. She stands as we come to the dock. I look around and spy what I expected. Stasia hasn't noticed. I struggle not to rush her like a kid at Christmas. Misha and Pasha step onto the dock ahead of us. I disembark and help Stasia off the boat before Sergei and Anton follow us. Stasia is tall, but with five of us around her, it limits her view. We make our way to a beachside restaurant, and we're almost to our table before Stasia squeezes my hand.

"Niko?"

"Yeah?"

"Why's our family here?"

"I invited them."

"Why?"

"Because I thought it would be nice to have them here today."

"Niko, even Laura and the twins are here. Why did they fly

halfway around the world to meet us while we're on a romantic getaway?"

I can't tell if she's stymied or annoyed.

"You'll see, *malyshka*."

I lead her to the enormous table where my family and her parents await us. I guide her to a particular chair and pull it out. I pull out mine as I hand her a menu. She opens it, and her brow furrows. I doubt for a moment if she can read Cyrillic. I thought she could.

Osobyy ulov dnya, moya malyshka. The special catch of the day is my baby girl.

"Niko?"

She finally looks at me. Her eyes widen as both hands cover her mouth. I pull her left hand away and place it over my heart as I look up at her from bended knee.

"*Vyydesh' za menya zamuzh?*" Will you marry me?

She nods vigorously.

"I need to hear it."

"*Da.*" Yes.

The sweetest word I've ever heard. I pull out the ring box that's been pressing against my leg since we got on the speedboat. I flip the lid open, and she glances at it for only a moment. She's more intent upon looking at me. I lift her hand from my chest and slide on the ring. She hasn't looked at it yet. Instead, she leans forward and cups my face. She leans to whisper in my ear.

"Yes, Daddy."

If my niece and nephew were older, their parents would cover their eyes. It's not a kiss we should exchange in front of either of our parents, but I don't care. She said yes. I stand and lift her out of her seat.

"I love you, Stasia."

"I love you, Niko."

"Do you like it?"

"Huh? Oh. I haven't really looked."

I let go of her, and she looks down at her left hand.

"Holy moly. Niko!"

"Do you like it?"

I think she does, but I didn't think I would have to ask twice.

"This is the most beautiful ring I've ever seen."

My mom helped me pick it out. It's a four-carat oval diamond set in platinum with two carats of marquise cut diamonds on either side of the center stone. I worried it would be too large and ostentatious on her fine-boned hand, but it looks exquisite. As much time as I spent searching and deciding, after our conversation earlier, I'm not surprised that she's more intent upon looking at me than her ring. She's not with me for my money. I don't doubt she'll cherish the ring and appreciate its value. But she's saying yes to me, not what I bought her.

"The twins would say welcome to the family, Auntie Anastasia, if they could stay awake long enough."

I look at Laura, who is beaming at Stasia. When she looks at me, her expression clearly says I told you so.

"Congratulations, sweetheart."

"Thanks, Papa."

I spoke to Yuri last week about my wish to marry Stasia, and he gave his consent immediately. We both knew I didn't need it, and Stasia would decide regardless. But the tradition excited me. Having my father's best friend be part of our family is bittersweet. It makes me miss my dad while giving me a piece of him back. Allison has walked around the table to hug Stasia. She opens her arm to include me in the embrace.

"I'm sorry, Niko. You are welcome in our family. There's no one better for—Stasia—than you."

"Thank you, Mrs. Antonov."

"Allison."

"Mom, it's still Ana to you and everyone else. I only like Niko to call me Stasia. I hope that's okay."

Allison looks relieved. She nods and kisses her daughter's cheek, then mine, before going back to her seat. My mom is next. She still gives the best hugs. Stasia's are entirely different, so there's no comparison. But no one else has ever made me feel like my mom does. Loved, protected, good enough, appreciated. It's just a mom thing, I suppose.

"*My gordimsya vami.*" We're proud of you.

I know she doesn't mean she and the other members of our family sitting with us. I kiss her cheek.

"Thanks, Mama. That means everything to me."

"*Pchelka,* I'm so happy for you."

She offers Stasia a hug and kiss too before we all sit for the meal. The hours go by in a whirl as we chatter, laugh, drink, and celebrate. It reminds me of family gatherings when my dad was still alive. I look at my mom, and it's as though I can see my dad sitting next to her. Stasia squeezes my hand, and I look at her.

"Your mom's right. I'm certain he's proud of you."

We share a last kiss before it's time for my family to go to their hotel and for me to take *moye sokrovishche* back to the villa for our private celebration.

Chapter Twenty-Three

Stasia

I can't believe this entire day. I never would have guessed our families would be waiting for us. When I fantasized about a man proposing to me, I never envisioned anyone being with us. But having everyone there was perfect. Laura and Christina told me how their husband's proposed, and I realized Niko and I were part of a family tradition. It was important to him to have the people we love share this moment. It made it doubly special for me.

"Sergei, organize the shifts after everyone sweeps the grounds."

Niko and I are waiting on the small boat that ferried us from the speedboat back to the villa. His cousins climb off and fan out. Five minutes later, Sergei gives us a thumbs up. Niko helps me onto the terrace and spins me for a kiss. It's a promise of what's to come, but I can't help smiling throughout it. I don't think I've stopped smiling since he proposed.

"Stasia, I'm going to check with the guys that everything is ready for our departure tomorrow. I'll be in, in a minute."

"I know you will."

I wink as I turn toward our room. I kick off my sandals and carry them as I cross the villa. As I approach our room, I notice the curtain billowing away from the window. Niko and the others insisted that we not open them, and not just because we have AC. They said it made the place unsecured. I turn on my heel and run. I hear someone behind me. I try to go faster, but the floors are slick under my bare feet. An arm goes around my waist, and I fight to get free. I throw my head back and hear a nose crack. A hand wraps around my throat and squeezes mercilessly.

"If you kill her, there's nothing to sell."

A voice comes from behind the man who grabbed me. He eases his hold, but he has to wrestle to get my arms pinned to my sides. I throw my head back again, but this time he's prepared. I kick my heels against his shins and snap my teeth at his hand as he tries to cover my mouth. I'm making no progress as the guy drags me back toward the bedroom. I try to go limp and make my dead weight harder to maneuver, but I weigh far too little to make a difference. I drag my feet, then try to spin around. I get one of my arms free as I twist. My thumb goes to his eye, and I press as hard as I can.

"*Shlyuha.*" Whore.

Podolskaya. Or men they sent. Where're Niko and his cousins?

"*Eedee v zhopu.*" Kiss my ass.

"*Ya trakhnu tebya v zadnitsu.*" I'll fuck you in the ass.

He's not moving as fast as he argues with me, so I keep talking.

"*Krutee peedalee paka nye dale.*" The literal meaning fits here. Pedal away while still not beaten up. But I mean fuck off.

Despite slowing him down, he hauls me into the bedroom and pushes me toward someone. I catch myself and turn around. A man with matching scars running from his ears to his chin grins.

"Someone will enjoy breaking you."

"You have to get out alive."

"Kutsenko! Come get your whore!"

The man staring at me yells. *No, no, no!*

I hear feet running toward us as the man I'm standing in front of and the man who grabbed me point guns toward the door.

"Niko, no!"

Neither man is ready for me to rush the door and slam it shut. A bullet lands in the wood next to my head. I don't know if they fired it at me, as a warning to Niko, or at Niko as I slammed the door shut. I flick the lock.

"Stasia!"

"Niko, they'll kill you."

"We will, Kutsenko."

The one who grabbed me speaks as he fists a handful of my hair and tries to pull me back. Except he didn't restrain my arms. I turn, practically ripping the hair from my head, and drive the heel of my hand under his chin as my fist plows into his nose. It's enough for him to let go of my hair, but it pisses him off even more. He lunges at me and slams me into the door.

The door has an old-fashioned lock, so I pull the key from it. The room is long, but it's not too wide. Holding the key like a knife, I shove it into the guy's neck then shove him as hard as I can with my other arm. My shoulder screams in pain, but it allows me past my attacker. I hurl the key out of the window and into the sea.

The moment I know Niko can't get into the room for them to execute him, I cease resisting. I already know they're going to take me. My shoulder and head throb, and my ribs don't feel as healed as they had. Rather than hurt myself further or deplete all of my energy, I give in. Niko will come for me. But he can only do that if he's alive.

"I love you, Niko!"

"Stasia!"

"I love you!"

"Stasia! I love you! Stasia!"

"Say goodbye."

A man steps away from the bathroom. I hadn't noticed him. I'm looking at a psychopath. His eyes. There's something in them—or maybe it's what they're devoid of—that makes me know this is a Lushak.

"You're Vlad's younger brother, aren't you?"

"How'd you guess?"

I keep my thoughts to myself.

"Smart, *malyshka*. That's what he calls you, isn't it? Keep your opinion to yourself. No one wants to hear them."

It sounds like such a perversion—sacrilege—for him to call me that. It only makes me more determined. Not only am I getting back to Niko, they will pay.

I feel my arms yanked behind me and zip ties bind my wrists. A cloth with something sweet smelling comes toward my face. They're going to knock me out. But all the while, I don't break our locked gazes. I see something flash in Vlad's brother's eyes. An emotion. It's uncertainty. Someone didn't train this man as well as Vlad trained Niko. He didn't mean for me to see it because now I see anger. Niko only allows me, or anyone else, to see what he wants. He lets me in. This man didn't mean to. As long as there's uncertainty, there's doubt. This motherfucker just met his match. I will burn everything to the ground before I give in.

The cloth covers my face, but I can still breath. It's not

smothering me like I expected. I feel my legs buckle underneath me. My eyes drift closed. I feel someone pick me up, and I think I'm passed through the window. The cloth is still against my face. Where are Sergei and the others? Are they dead? I thought this would knock me out immediately. Why am I...

Where am I?

The last thing I remember is a cloth coming toward my face. What next? I wrack my memory. I thought they were going to suffocate me, but I could still take four or five breaths before everything went black. Every breath made me inhale that sickly scent. Chloroform?

Wherever I am is pitch black. I stay still, straining to hear anything. Am I alone?

There's nothing there. There's no sound. There's no air current that I can feel. It's like a vacuum. Like they have sucked everything out of this space but me. They stretched my arms over my head and off to my right. I wiggle my fingers and find they can move. I move my arm and hear the first sound. It's metal shifting, then banging against something. I'm chained standing up. I remember taking my shoes off in the villa. I'm still wearing my dress. That's a plus. I take a step to my right and hit something. It feels like corrugated metal. A shipping container. Am I in one? Are they shipping me to Russia? To the Middle East? Where the fuck do women go who are sex trafficked?

I test the chain and find there's enough slack for me to lean against the wall. It takes a lot of the strain off my shoulder, but the chain isn't long enough for me to sit. They want me uncomfortable. It's to fatigue me and wear down my spirit. They want to break me physically and mentally. They took me to break me emotionally. Selling me isn't the only thing they want. They want Niko to know they're going to destroy me.

Stupid, stupid motherfuckers. His brothers may be a couple hours away by boat, but it must be like a fifteen-minute flight on their jet. Even if something happened to their cousins, Maks, Aleks, and Bogdan will come. My dad and his uncles are with them. That's six men at least, and eleven most likely. How many came from Russia?

I wasn't supposed to know, but Niko and his cousins traveled with a cache of weapons and ammunition. I stumbled in on them checking everything. Niko thought I was in the kitchen, but I came to offer them sandwiches the second afternoon we were at the villa. I stood and stared for a minute before I nodded, then asked what kind of cheese they wanted.

Niko followed me back to the kitchen, afraid it scared me speechless. It shocked him when I said I appreciated being well prepared and that I want him to teach me to shoot.

"You're awake."

A door's yanked open, and a spotlight floods the container. It was night when they took me. It still must be if these bright streetlights are still on. How did they know? I looked up and saw no light of any kind to indicate a camera. Infrared? Niko told me they had heat-seeking binoculars when they came to get me in the Bronx.

"Where am I?"

"Still in Greece."

That doesn't mean Mykonos. I squint into the light and try to see any landmark. There are buildings nearby, so we're not out to sea. I don't feel any kind of movement beneath me.

"Am I going to Russia?"

"Depends on who buys you."

"Do you have my dad and Galina?"

"That's not your concern."

Great. That either means they do, and they want me to suffer knowing that. Or it means they failed and are too pissed to admit it. Either way, that makes nothing feel better. If they have them, will they keep us separated? Probably. As much as misery loves company, the agony of not knowing is far worse.

"What's your name?"

"Gleb."

Heir of God. His parents filled his head with bullshit from the start.

"I'm starving. I'm already scrawny. I can't afford to lose any more weight."

The man approaches, leaving the door open. It gives me a better view of what's beyond the container. It looks like a warehouse, but I can't see the water. Does that mean it's on one of the other three sides? Is this one that could be loaded onto a train like a boxcar? Are there trains that run to Greece's neighbors? Is it Eurail? So many fucking questions. He pinches my right nipple through my sundress. I don't flinch, but it hurts like hell. And not in the way I like with Niko. He twists, trying to get a reaction from me. It's practically agony now, but I won't betray any emotion. I keep telling myself to think how Niko would handle this.

"High tolerance for pain. I can think of several men who would pay a fortune for you, even if you have the body of a ten-year-old boy."

Well, that feeds into every insecurity I've had. But I don't care. I will not let it affect me. Niko's attracted to me, and that's all I care about. Though the idea of being sold is beyond terrifying. The abuse that awaits is nearly enough to paralyze me mentally. I can't let it.

"Then you should feed me."

"You'll last a little longer. You had a big dinner last night."

They were watching us. Or someone was, and they

informed Gleb and the other two. Now that the light isn't casting a shadow on him, I can see he's the one who grabbed me in the hallway. I think I broke his nose. He has gauze shoved up each nostril.

"You'll do well, *malyshka*."

I fucking hate hearing him call me that. It only makes me more resolved to survive, so Niko can find me. I will not let Gleb or any other man ruin that endearment for me. It's Niko's.

The sound of my stomach rumbling echoes in the metal container. It feels like hours since Gleb came to taunt me. I thought about keeping track of how many times I counted to sixty, but even my attention can't be held that long. And it became more demoralizing than informative. It rained, and I'm as good as being in a tin can. The water hitting the metal was deafening. It's probably too much of an inconvenience for them to bring me food. The only upside is that I haven't had to pee. I'm not looking forward to dealing with that.

"How's our little prisoner?"

It's Gleb again. It's still dark outside, so maybe it hasn't been as long as I imagined. I can't see him beyond a shadow moving toward me. I take steadying breaths when I want to tremble with fright.

"Your stomach is louder than a fucking elephant."

They could hear that. There is a camera with a microphone in here somewhere. At the very least, they have some type of listening device around here. Good to know. I would start screaming just to punish whoever is listening, but I don't need to go hoarse.

"Then you should feed me."

"What are you willing to do for food?"

Not murder you the moment I can. I remain silent. I won't beg, and I won't argue.

In the dark, I don't realize how close he is until a hand wraps around my throat. A thumb tries to press into my mouth. Gross. I don't know where that's been.

"Suck."

I consider resisting but have a different idea. I part my teeth enough for it to slide past. I suck on it twice before I clamp my teeth down. I clench my jaw with every ounce of strength I can dredge up after being chained to a wall for hours. This man tries pulling free. He squeezes my throat tighter, but the support of his hand under my chin actually makes it easier to bite harder. I can taste his blood on my tongue. It makes me want to wretch, but I don't let go. There's a popping sound as he tries to pull his thumb back again.

"*Shlyuha!*" Whore!

He can call me that all fucking day. The palm of his free hand lands across my cheek. My head snaps to the side, tugging his thumb with it. He howls. His fist lands in my belly, making me sag as far forward as the chain will allow. It only drags his thumb down. He howls again. I'd turned my head just before I ensnared Gleb's thumb, so it's caught between my molars.

Can I bite through the bone?

The second door at the end of the container flies open and two men charge in. I straighten and shake my head as wildly as I can, Gleb's thumb still in my mouth. One man yanks my hair, snapping my neck back while another squeezes my jaw. I swing my head sideways, as though I want to bring my ear to my shoulder. I nail the guy holding my jaw in the nose. I feel blood splatter my neck. He pinches my nose closed. My lips are open, so I breathe through my teeth. I haven't eased the pressure despite how my jaw cramps. It's actually making it easier to hold it shut.

The man with my hair brandishes a knife against my throat. Maybe they will kill me. But if the plan is to sell me or ransom me, not only won't they kill me, they won't mar me too badly. The blade nicks my skin, but it doesn't press any deeper.

"Let the bitch go. She's going to fucking bite through the bone."

Gleb speaks in Russian, and every word sounds like a challenge. He hasn't made a sound between his last howl of pain and his command. Maybe Gleb learned some of the same things as Vlad. But clearly not as well. I know I'm causing him pain. I don't relish it, but it's satisfying. The knife moves away from my throat, my hair's free, and my nose is no longer pinched. But I still haven't let go. His blood is pooling in my mouth, and I can barely keep from swallowing or vomiting. I'm going to have to release him and spit or accept that I'm going to swallow someone else's blood.

"*Upyr.*"

I think Gleb means the literal translation. Not asshole or moron. He means vampire. Maybe I am.

I hear a key in a lock, and suddenly the chain goes slack, then slides from my wrists.. My arms are mostly asleep and burn. I struggle to control them. I clasp my hands together into one fist. The moment my arms are free, I swing them to my right. The man who held my nose stumbles backwards. The man who held the knife is the one who released me. He's still a couple steps behind me. I let go of Gleb's thumb and spit the mouthful of blood at him. I run. I don't look back. I don't check if anyone is following me. I bolt.

It's an easy drop from the container to the ground. I gather my dress above my knees and run like I'm going for the gold at the Olympics. I hear shouts behind me, but I'm outpacing them. I ran hurdles in high school. It's been several years since I've attempted them, so I'm testing my luck. I make it over a barrel laid on its side. I make it over several crates. I don't know where I'm running to, but it's away from those three.

"Papa!"

I scream as loudly as I can.

"Galina!"

Even if I can't get to them, if they're here, they know I'm alive. Maybe Niko is close and can hear me.

I spy a gate, and I swerve to run toward it. There's a barrier, one that's like an arm that goes up and down. I can't go over it, so I'm going to have to go under. I'm so fucking close. I still hear feet behind me, and mine hurt. But I don't slow down. That is until a guard steps in front of me, and I ram my chest into the barrel of a rifle. I wait for it to fire.

I'm still breathing. I'm not dead. He didn't shoot me.

"*Ty russkiy?*" Are you Russian?

"*Ti?*"

Greek. I recognize the word "what" from a couple of YouTube videos I watched to learn a few phrases before coming here. I only know how to ask things like where's the bathroom, where's the restaurant. I didn't learn the word help.

I try to move aside, but he won't let me. He must see the men getting closer.

Fuck me. They have probably paid him off. He's not going to let me go. I'm not fucking Rambo or G.I. Jane. I don't know what the fuck to do with the rifle in front of me. I wish my dad had taught me to use the one he has. Another missed opportunity.

"Anastasia!"

"Papa! Papa!"

I'd know that voice even once I'm dead. I can't turn my head away from the Greek guard because I don't trust him not to shoot me. Then again, if he's going to, it won't matter which way I face.

"Anastasia, if you wish your father to live another night, step back."

The command is in Russian. I recognize the voice as the one from the attacker with the scars. I look over my shoulder and see a man standing behind my father. He has a pistol to my dad's head. Two more men stand in front and slightly to the side. They're pointing rifles at my dad. I put my hands up and take a step back from the Greek guard. So fucking close. But close is only good in horseshoes and hand grenades. What I wouldn't give to have one.

"Ana, no!"

My dad doesn't want me to give up, to move away from the gate. But what can I do? I'm not getting past. Trying will get us both killed. I turn slowly. As I get a clearer view of my father at gunpoint, something shatters in me. A rage unlike anything I have ever imagined I could possess pulses through me. Is this how Niko gets when he's at the warehouse? It's like everything comes into crystal-clear focus. I look at each face, emblazoning them in my memory. I look at what each man is wearing, what weapons I can see. Some have bulletproof vests on, and some don't. I'm sure they're like the Kutsenkos and carry knives in their pockets.

I approach slowly, my hands still raised. No one turns toward me. They're going to keep using my dad as a hostage to control me. When I get close enough to see my dad's face under an overhead spotlight, I can see they've beaten him badly. They broke his nose, and his eyes are nearly swollen shut. They're already black and blue. That rage threatens to erupt, but I force it back down to a simmer.

"Where's Galina?"

"Wouldn't—"

We're sticking to Russian, I guess.

"They didn't get her, Ana."

My dad blurts out while another man tries to taunt me. Thank God.

"How'd you get my dad?"

"We told him we had you. It was come with us or watch us kill you on a phone screen."

I walk a few steps closer until I can see the slits that are my dad's eyes. The eyelids are puffy, but I can see the blue beneath. No one is looking at him right now. They don't see his expression. It makes my blood run cold. If he directed it at me, I would shit myself. They've discounted him as too injured. Maybe none of them are fathers. Maybe they don't care about their children. But I know, as long as my dad breathes, he hasn't given up on me. He's biding his time, and I'm going to have to do the same.

Scarface grabs me and yanks my arms behind my back. Pain shoots through my healing shoulder, but I don't react. I see my father's eyebrows go up. I can tell he's surprised that I don't react. Odd time to wonder if that makes him proud of me. I wait for zip ties, but nothing happens. More fool are they. The soulless looking man approaches me.

"You nearly bit my brother's thumb off. I think we'll get you a muzzle."

I know this man is Vlad's younger brother, and so is Gleb. Who's the man with the scars?

"Which brother are you?"

"Yaroslav."

I look at my dad again. They aren't nearly done torturing him. Taking him was about punishing him. Taking me and trying to get Galina is about superiority over the Kutsenkos. They have me, but they won't kill me. It would be a waste. But they will kill my father. I need time for Niko and his family to get here. What the fuck am I going to do?

"I think you're going to entertain us."

Chapter Twenty-Four

Niko

I now understand how Maks felt when Laura was taken. The consuming, burning rage. The need to get my woman back, and the need for retribution. Only one of those can wait. Maks, Aleks, and Bogdan, along with my uncles, met my cousins and me with the jet at the private airstrip on Mykonos. We were wheels up three minutes after they landed. Uncle Grigori and Uncle Radomir are basically retired from the bratva. They support my brothers and me as the Elite Group, and they lend their muscle when needed. This is one of those times.

"Does this remind you of when you were younger?"

Uncle Radomir walks past me as he asks.

Before Vlad believed we were ready to go out with the men, he would force us to help them get ready.

"You haven't been part of an operation like this since I was a teen. But it's obvious how deeply engrained your KGB and bratva training was. It's been nearly fifteen years, but you move like men who just walked off the battlefield."

I look toward Sergei, who's already suited up, and sitting at a table with his laptop.

"Sergei, are you picking up on Yuri's tracker?"

"Yeah. They're headed northeast. They're definitely flying since it's farther to the mainland from Santorini than from Mykonos. My guess is toward the Port of Piraeus. It's one of the busiest on the Med. There are bound to be ships they can smuggle them onto."

"Bogdan, I know how much that necklace means to you and Christina. Thank you for giving it to Yuri."

"No worries. I'm getting it back."

My younger brother might sound nonchalant, but as he straps his pistol to his right thigh, there is nothing jovial about his expression. He wants his wife's necklace back—it has some sentimental and private meaning—but he'll do anything to get my fiancée and my future father-in-law back. It's been nearly two hours since the Podolskaya took Stasia. Time has never moved slower.

"The tracker on Stasia's bracelet still isn't pinging. I still doubt they have two planes, so if they're flying from Santorini to the port, then they're taking a boat from Mykonos. They'll get Yuri to the port before Stasia. I'm sure they want him there to make her cooperate."

Sergei's been working nonstop, hacking everything he can think of to find Stasia.

"We'll get them back, Niko."

Anton's got a concussion, but he insisted on coming. We've all fought with worse. Sergei has a cut across his shoulder Anton had to stitch. They both trained as paramedics in college. They're who fix us when it's not quite bad enough for our doctor.

"Misha?"

"I'm coming. Fuck, Sergei. What the hell did you do when you were putting those stitches in?"

"Stop whining, little brother."

Misha walks across the cabin from the lavatory before he claps his hand on Sergei's shoulder and squeezes.

"Thanks for taking care of me, big brother."

They glare at each other, but it lightens the mood, even if only for a minute.

"Anton's right, Niko. You'll have her and be demanding privacy before you know it."

Pasha keeps his voice down as he comes to stand next to me. Of all my cousins, we're the closest. We're a lot alike, and we used to spend the most time together when we were kids and not with our own brothers.

"At least they didn't touch your pretty face, Pasha."

Aleks grins as he tosses Pasha a magazine of bullets. Everyone always says Pasha's the handsomest of all of us. Women melt when he looks at them. He doesn't do commitment, so he barely notices now that he's not a teenager.

"You're sure you're up to this?"

I look at Maks, and I see his genuine concern. He's not patronizing me. He's truly worried. I took the worst beating. Anton's concussion came from a pipe to the back of his head. Mine came from a wall and fists.

"Yes. I can't not go, Maks. You know that. Even if it wasn't about Stasia, they stabbed and ran with Sergei and Misha. It's how they got into my bedroom so fast. Pasha was outside when it all started. He shot the man who came after him and shot the two who got me."

"From how your face looks, I'm surprised you broke an arm and snapped a kneecap.

"That was before one of them rammed me headfirst into a wall."

According to Anton, I have a mild concussion too. The one whose kneecap I busted slashed me across the thigh, but it wasn't deep. Anton stitched it. I broke my right little finger, landing a punch when I fell off balance. But my heart hasn't stopped racing since I found Sergei and Anton. They understand why I didn't stop the moment I spotted them. I ran to my bedroom.

"I get it, but I don't want to lose my little brother."

"And I don't want to lose my big brother, either. Keep up, old man."

"Yuri's tracker is still pinging, but do you think he's alive?"

I look at Bogdan as he asks. None of us knows for sure. The moment I called Maks to get him and the others to come, Aleks got our uncles and Yuri to join them. Yuri demanded a tracker. He knew all of us wear them. Christina offered hers as the most inconspicuous for a man. It's part of a male lion pedant she always wears, so Bogdan had the tracker added after he gave it to her.

"I think so. They want to punish him, so it will not be quick. He knew that when he stepped out of the hotel first. That's why he went first. They would have shot anyone else. They wanted him."

I nod as Uncle Grigori slings a rifle over his shoulder and reassures us. According to Uncle Radomir, who followed Yuri out a minute later, he saw four men rush Yuri and shove him into the back of an SUV. My brothers and uncles boarded the jet and came to Mykonos ten minutes later. The women and the twins all have two guards assigned to each of them, so there're sixteen men guarding them.

"Your mom is safe too, Niko."

Uncle Radomir hands me the camouflage face paint. We're

all worried about the women in our family, but everyone knows Vlad's brothers and their men targeted my mom, too. Uncle Radomir heard one of them yell they needed to get her. He shot the man in the head. The rest drove away with Yuri, probably to the airfield.

"They had a small head start, but we'll still get to the port before they can get Anastasia there."

I nod as Aleks tries to reassure me. I know it will take them longer to sail from Mykonos to the Port of Piraeus than it will take us to fly. But my family still had to get here from Santorini, which delayed me leaving Mykonos. What was my choice? I need Maks, Aleks, Bogdan, Uncle Grigori, and Uncle Radomir too much not to wait. I just need my *malyshka* to hold on. I'm ready to burn everything to the ground if I have to. That seems to be my new mantra.

"They aren't fucking here."

I run my hand through my hair. We arrived at the harbor two hours ago. We've opened every container on the docks. We've boarded the boats anchored in port. We've bribed and beaten anyone who didn't answer the first time we asked. They are not at the Port of Piraeus.

"Yuri's tracker had him landing and coming here. It's still here, Niko."

"Then why haven't we found it, Sergei? Why haven't we found either of them?"

What the fuck do we do now? Stasia's tracker still isn't working. We can't find Yuri or his tracker, even though the signal is pinging here. I turn to talk to Sergei.

"Is it possible for them to hack Yuri's tracker and redirect the signal?"

"No. None of our trackers are like that on purpose."

"Then why can't you find them, Sergei?"

Bogdan steps in front of me.

"He's doing the best he can. You know that. Back off and let him work."

"Back off?"

"Yes. Niko, we get it. I get it. But bellowing at him won't help his concentration or make his computer work faster. This isn't you. We do not lose our shit. We do not forget our mission. We need you the way you are when we're at work. I told Maks the same thing when we went after Laura. You told me the same thing when we dealt with Declan after Christina's accident."

Bogdan cups the back of my head and draws my forehead to his. I exhale, and he draws me into his embrace. Fuck, loving someone and fearing losing them this much is its own type of torture. How did my mom and aunts endure this for years when my dad and uncles went to war?

"I got it."

I turn to Sergei.

"You won't like it, Niko. It's in the water just off that dock."

"Did they drop it there? Or do you think Yuri is dead?"

"I don't know. We need to get someone in the water to find out."

I look at Pasha. He's the best free diver of all of us. He dove competitively in school, and he goes to the Caribbean to dive and scuba when he can. He's already stripping. The best he's done is thirty feet, so I hope the water's not deeper than that.

"Be right back."

I watch him ready his breathing before he goes in. It's dark, but some of us have headlamps along with our NVG. Anton gave Pasha his. We see the light flick on as Pasha descends. I know it's only a matter of seconds, but it feels like forever before the light changes direction, and I see Pasha kicking toward the surface.

"Only this was down there."

It's the necklace. Bogdan snatches it from Pasha, and we can all see his relief, even though it means we're no closer to finding Yuri or Stasia.

"Thank you."

I speak quietly to Bogdan.

"I won't lie and say it doesn't mean a great deal to me and to Christina. But it's jewelry. I can replace it. We'll find them, Niko."

"I've got something!"

I swing around to Sergei, who's using his touchscreen to enlarge something.

"She's on foot and running, Niko. It looks like she's headed toward the gate at a train yard near here."

I watch the dot moving, then it halts.

"What happened?"

As I ask, the dot moves slowly back in the direction it came from. Why's she going backward? Did they get her?

"We know where she is, Niko. We can be there in twenty minutes."

I nod as we head back to the SUVs Maks somehow arranged. I didn't even think to ask. I get into the front passenger seat next to Misha. Normally, Pasha would drive the other car, but I know he's got to get dressed. I saw him climb into the back as I passed the rear vehicle. He won't make us wait.

I look out the window as we drive along dark streets. It's nearly morning, and Stasia's been away from my side for five hours. I'm trying not to fidget or tell Misha how to drive.

"I lost the signal, Niko. I think whatever they're keeping her in is blocking it. She hasn't left the train yard."

I nod. I close my eyes and think about holding Stasia again. I want to smell her perfume. She always smells of jasmine and crisp apple. I want to kiss her from head to toe, worship every part of her. I want to hear her call me Daddy again. I just want her in my arms. It's the only time the world feels right.

How much more of this can she take? My sisters-in-law suffered similar dangers to be with my brothers. But is Stasia really willing to accept this?

"We're a quarter mile away. We stop here."

I look at Misha and try to understand what he's telling me. I nod and get out of the SUV in a trance. I put my earpiece in and pull down my NVGs. Things snap back to reality as I look toward the fence I can see in the distance. Somewhere on the other side is my *malyshka*.

I inch forward with Maks at my side. He'll let me lead this one, but as *pakhan*, he will never put anyone in front of him. He will be our shield, not the other way around. I admire him more than I realized. He sacrificed so much when we were growing up to protect us. He endured the worst of Vlad's mental and emotional torture, while, as the youngest, Bogdan got the worst of the physical. I glance back at my brothers, cousins, and uncles. None of us asked for this life. None of us have ever wanted it. But since we're all stuck in it, I'm glad that I'm bound with my family.

I aim my rifle toward the guard at the gate. Stasia got to there. Did he keep her from getting out?

We creep closer until I'm able to slam the butt of my rifle into the guy's head. He collapses like a rag doll. Once we're through the gate, we fan out in our pairs. Bogdan and Aleks, Radomir and Misha, Grigori and Pasha, Sergei and Anton, and Maks and me. We move systematically, checking any open containers. We keep radio silence, using hand and arm signals to communicate.

"Vlad trained you well."

It's a voice speaking Russian over an intercom. I look at my uncles, and I can see the hate radiating from their faces. They must know this voice.

"But he didn't train you well enough to protect your woman, Niko."

I ignore the jab. We're still inching through the yard.

"She was feisty while I fucked her. But I tamed her."

He's goading me. I won't lose my focus.

"She practically swallowed my cock. Made me come faster than I expected. You trained her well. Your little virgin whore."

How did he know she was a virgin? Did Antonio tell Luca, who told whoever it was in Chicago, who then told this fucker?

"My one regret is not being the one to break her in. She took me in the ass like a pro, Niko. She's ready for sale now that I know she has all the skills she needs."

Stay focused. Ignore what he's saying.

"You shouldn't talk about my daughter like that."

There's a gunshot and nothing else.

Chapter Twenty-Five

Stasia

I'm tossed back into a container, but it wasn't the one I escaped from. My dad's with me, and no one chains us to a wall. But I hear the doors being bolted, and I'm once again in the pitch black.

"Papa?"

I whisper, convinced this container has a camera and microphone, too. My dad slides closer to me and puts his arm around my shoulder. He whispers in my ear.

"Maks and the others flew to Mykonos. I wore Christina's lion necklace that has a tracker on it, but they took it from me. They must have guessed. Niko is on his way, sweetheart."

"I don't know if my tracker is working inside these containers."

"I don't either. I think they used this one and whichever one you were in specifically. One guy mentioned activating something before they put me in here. I heard when you arrived."

"How'd they get you, Papa?"

"I went out first. We knew there had to be men waiting for us. They thought they had to convince me, but I went willingly because I had the tracker on. Radomir took out one of them, though."

"Papa, you—"

"Of course, I did. You're my peanut. I'll do anything. And I know Niko will too. What happened at the villa?"

"They were waiting for us. I don't know about Niko's cousins."

"They're all alive."

"Thank God. One of them grabbed me and pulled me into the bedroom. Niko came running, but I knew they would shoot him. I got free and slammed the door shut and locked it. I tossed the key into the sea. They were going to take me, regardless. I didn't want Niko dead in the process. They put something over my mouth that knocked me out. I woke up a while ago in a container. Gleb came to talk to me. Then he left and came back a little bit later. I nearly bit his thumb off. The others came when he screamed."

"I heard that. I knew it wasn't you screaming."

"I fought to get free again and ran. I made it to the gate."

"I know. They pulled me out of here and dragged me. I saw you running, my little gazelle."

"It was fine until the guard stopped me."

We lapse into silence as we listen. We're huddled together. It's colder in this container than it was in mine. I can feel air moving in here. I move onto my hands and knees.

"Ana?"

"There's air coming in from somewhere."

"They'll know you're moving around."

"I know."

I crawl until I find a gap in the metal. I slide my fingers into it, careful not to cut them or get them stuck. I pull up, and it gives way a little. The jagged edge cuts into my hand, but I can still make the hole bigger. It's still dark out, but the lights allow me to see when I put my eye to the hole I've made. I can see feet.

There are six sets of boots in a circle. Three must belong to the men I met, and three must be the ones who took my dad. There are eleven on our side, including Niko. I just have to be patient. I try to hear, but their voices don't carry. When two sets walk toward me, I scramble back to my dad. Was no one watching the surveillance or is someone coming here because I alerted them to what I did?

The bolts keeping the doors locked move, then one opens. The two men climb in and pull my dad out with them. I try to hold on to him, but one slams me against the wall, and I hit my head. I see stars.

"Papa!"

"I love you, sweetheart."

"Papa! I love you."

I'm tired of saying that to the men in my life as though it's goodbye. I shake off the dizziness and crawl back to the opening I made. I fight with the metal, but I'm able to expand the hole. It feels like it takes forever, but I make a space wide enough for me to slip through. I don't know anyone short of a child who could get through. I picture for a moment Niko trying and getting wedged in there. I creep along the side of the container, but I freeze when I hear someone being punched. I peek around the corner and see Scarface beating my dad.

That rage fires inside me again. Watching a man attack my dad is pushing me past reason and the limits a sane person would have. I know I don't know how to use any of the rifles the men carry. But if they're anything like Niko's family, they have more weapons somewhere. The arsenal Luca had spread on the table in the Bronx house had knives, pistols, rifles, and I don't even know what some things were.

When I look around, I spy a building with a light on inside. Other than the guard at the gate, there doesn't seem to be anyone else around. I don't want to let my dad out of my sight, but I have to. If that building holds any weapons I can steal, then I will. Seeing how my dad takes this beating and how fast he pulled the rifle out of our hall closet makes me confident that he could handle any weapon I find.

I slip along the containers and watch the entrance to the building. Is this where the other three men went? I inhale and sprint across the fifty feet between the last container and the door. I hurry inside, then freeze. No one yelled an alert, so I don't think anyone saw me. I think about where I saw the light coming from in this building and head toward it.

"You don't belong in here."

I spin around. It's Yaroslav.

"Did you think I would give up trying to get free?"

"You would if you knew what was good for you."

He lunges toward me and catches my left wrist as I flee. He pulls me back against him and tackles me to the ground. I land hard with him on top of me. He pulls at my dress, revealing my breasts. My thumbs go to his eyes, and he howls with pain. He slaps me, and I bite my tongue. He fumbles with my dress, trying to pull it up, but he's trapped it between us. His thigh pushes between my legs and up toward my pussy. This is not happening.

He's so intent on trying to suck my tit and pull up my dress that he doesn't realize I'm not fighting him harder. I'm searching for a weapon. Success. I find his gun. I don't know how it works. I'm as likely to kill myself as I am him, but I'll take the chance. I pull it from the holster at his back, and he freezes. He reaches back, but I already have my finger on the trigger. My thumb is already on something kinda like a latch. I pull it back and twist my wrist. I pull the trigger.

The gun must have a silencer because it doesn't make the sound I expected. I'm still blinking, and I feel no more pain than a moment ago. I don't think it hit me.

Yaroslav's weight shifts as he pushes up onto an elbow. His hand goes around my throat and squeezes harder than I'm prepared for. He just keeps increasing the pressure until I see stars. I try to make my brain work, but it's getting fuzzy. I try to push him off and realize I'm still holding the gun. I pray it has more than one bullet. He pushed up on his left arm, which allows me to pull my left arm between us. I put the gun to his cheek and pull the trigger again.

I scream as blood and other stuff splatter me. I know what it is, but I don't want to think about it. I'm covered in it, and it's a struggle to push him off me. I scramble to my feet, slipping in the blood pooling around his body. I hold on to the gun and run toward the light as I tug my dress up over my breasts. Someone's going to find him and know I did it. They're still beating my dad. That only leaves me as the culprit.

"Ana!"

I look back and see my dad limping toward me. I turn and run back in the direction I came from.

"What happened?"

"He knocked me down and tried—I shot him twice."

It's the first time I really look. I see a wound near his right shoulder blade, then I see most of his face is missing. I look up at my dad, who's watching me. He nods and takes the gun from me. I take his free hand, and we hurry toward the room with the light.

"Papa, how did you get away?"

"They left me with three young men. They were about your age, born long after the Soviet Union fell. They thought age gave them the advantage. Clearly, no one trained them the way the KGB trained me or the way they taught my generation of bratva. Shame on Yaroslav and Gleb."

"Are they dead?"

"Yes."

I don't ask more. It's better if I don't know. The room we run to is open. There's a man in it gathering weapons. I signal for my dad to step back. I whisper in his ear.

"Who is that? I never heard his name. I think of him as Scarface."

"Nikita Zakharov. He's linked to the Balashiknskaya gangs. The other bratva didn't convince them to get involved in Moscow when I lived there. They didn't want the government's attention if they were linked to bratva violence. I know nothing about them now, but I recognize him. He's about ten years younger than me. I gave him those scars."

No wonder they want retribution. I nod as my father tries to draw me away. My wet foot skids on the tile floor and makes a noise. Nikita turns to us with a gun raised. My dad pushes me out of the way and covers me with his body as I hear a bullet shatter glass.

"Papa!"

He doesn't answer.

"Papa!"

"I'm alive."

"Are you hurt?"

"Looks like he is."

I look up to find Nikita laughing at us. My dad shifts and pushes something under me. It's a knife. What the fuck am I supposed to do with this against a gun?

Nikita drags my dad off me and punches him in the sternum. He lands another punch to his cheekbone, and there's a horrible crunch. I look for the gun I gave my father, but it skidded down the hallway.

"Papa!"

I push myself up and find the knife my dad gave me. Where the hell did he have this hiding? It's practically a machete or something. Nikita puts his gun to my dad's temple.

"Urrr-rah."

I growl as I bring the sword-knife thing down on his arm. I swung it over my head with both hands. It slices through half of his forearm and leaves it dangling. The gun falls to the ground, but so does my dad. Nikita drops to his knees to reach for it. I kick it away, and a need for vengeance screams in my head.

"Ana, no."

I hear my dad, but I can't make sense of what he said. I have hold of Nikita's hair and yank it like my attackers did to me way too many times. I place the knife to his throat and am about to slice him when I have a different idea.

"Get away, Papa."

"Ana, don't do this."

I move the knife to the top of Nikita's forehead. It's at his hairline.

"Papa, go."

"Vlad trained you well."

Where the hell did that voice come from? It's over a loudspeaker. Who's it talking to?

"But he didn't train you well enough to protect your woman, Niko."

Niko's here? I look down at Nikita, and my need is only stronger. I hear the voice still talking over the intercom, but I don't know what it's saying anymore. I feel my dad pull at my arm, but all it does it pull the blade back toward me. It starts to cut, and Nikita howls.

"Papa, that's Gleb."

My concentration breaks long enough to recognize the voice.

"I know. Ana, don't."

"Papa, go before he does something to Niko. I won't forgive you if you don't."

Nikita's trying to fight me, and every move he makes pushes the blade deeper along his scalp. Nikita's screams fill the air, so I can't hear Gleb well. It comes in bits and pieces.

"She—ready—sale—know—she—has—skills—needs."

I hear my dad over the speaker and down the hallway.

"You shouldn't talk about my daughter like that."

There's a single gunshot. Was that my dad? Did he shoot or get shot?

"You're going to pay for everything you did to my dad."

"Did you know Yaroslav is the one who sent your dad into that minefield? I was there that day. I was a teenager. I watched Kirill's body explode into bits that rained down like chunks of pork."

"*Poshol na khuy.*" Fuck you.

I drag the blade back toward me as Nikita screams. This pales compared to the pain he and the others caused the people I love. It doesn't feel like nearly enough vengeance for what they took from the Kutsenkos. But it's the best I can do. I draw the blade across his throat when I'm done with his head.

"Stasia! Stasia!"

"Niko?"

I look back over my shoulder and recognize him. My mind is fuzzy, as sanity competes with the need for more violence.

"Stasia!"

I let go of Nikita and climb to my feet and turn around.

"Stasia!"

It's sheer terror I hear in Niko's voice.

"Niko, I'm fine."

Is that my voice? It doesn't quite sound right.

"Stasia, let go."

I look down and realize Niko is trying to pry my hands open to take the knife. I look past him at his family as they stare at me. I look down again, but this time at myself. I see everything I'm covered in. I flinch as reality slams into me. It's so forceful I stagger back a step. Niko grabs me and pulls me against him.

"Niko, my dad?"

"I'm here, sweetheart. It's over."

"Is it really, Niko?"

I whisper because suddenly it's all too much.

"Yes, *malyshka*. We're going home."

I nod. When I try to look back over my shoulder, Niko doesn't let me. I push away from him. I look at what's left of Nikita's head. I don't feel a moment's remorse. I don't know that I ever will.

"He was there that day. He saw it happen. He made a joke about it. He shouldn't have done that. If he'd kept it to himself, he might have been alive for you to kill, Niko."

"Stasia, don't look anymore. Come with me."

I nod, but I don't turn away. I burned the image into my brain. I did this. I was capable of this. I believed I was, and I warned Niko I was. But to see what I've done—I'm numb. Niko scoops me into his arms as Aleks and Pasha move to help my dad. We head back out of the building the way we all came in.

"Wait. Put me down, Niko."

"Stasia—"

"Put me down."

I punctuate each word with emphasis. I look down at Yaroslav. I did this too. What have I become? Is this who I am now? Or will I go back to who I was?

"It was his fault. He ordered you into that field, Papa. He got what he deserved."

"I know, sweetheart. Let Niko take you outside."

"All right, Papa."

Niko lifts me again, and I curl against his chest. My mind is settling. There's no ringing in my ears. My pulse isn't pounding against my temples. Rage isn't making my lungs feel too small and my heart too big. Papa told me it was kill or be killed when he explained his life before America. I understand now. Yaroslav—his death happened the way it did because the gun was all I could reach. Nikita—his death was to punish, but I don't even remember deciding on what I did.

"Can we go straight home?"

"We will, Stasia But we have to get our families."

"There's not enough room on one plane for everyone."

"I know, *printsessa*. They came in our jet and another one that they rented."

"Okay."

I close my eyes and sag against Niko.

"Can I have a shower?"

"Whatever you want, *meelaya*."

"Are you—can you—"

"What, Stasia?"

"Can you live with what I did, Nikolai?"

Chapter Twenty-Six

Niko

Never could I have imagined the sight that just greeted me.

Stasia is in my arms, her eyes closed, but her voice is clear. Her question breaks my heart. All of this does. That I left her so vulnerable. That she resorted to such violence. That she has to live with this for the rest of her life. It will change her. It can't not.

"Yes, *malyshka*. I can."

"I never thought I would make good on my warning that I'll do anything to protect you. I guess it also meant anything to avenge you."

"Shh. Rest, Stasia. We'll talk about it after you're clean and you rest."

"I can't let my mom see me like this. She'll never understand."

"I know. She's still on Santorini. We're on the mainland.

We'll find somewhere to get you cleaned up. I brought you spare clothes."

I don't think she realizes how her sundress is barely covering her breasts. I can't ask what happened yet. And I know that whoever did that to her is dead, so there's no one for me to kill to avenge her. My tiny *sokrovishche*, my tiny treasure, against two men who were double her size. It makes my chest hurt picturing it.

I carry her outside and look around. Where can we take her to clean off? Misha has the back doors of the SUV open. I put her down, and she reaches for me.

"I'm going to clean your face, Stasia. Is that okay?"

"Of course. You don't have to talk to me as though I'm a child or I'm slow."

"I'm sorry."

"I'm sorry. I shouldn't have snapped at you. I'm a bit out of sorts right now."

A bit? Fucking understatement of a lifetime.

"Maks, can you get the wipes we use to get the camo paint off, please?"

Maks tosses me a tube of wet wipes made to cut through the layers of paint we're all wearing on our faces. She hasn't commented on it, and I don't know if she's noticed.

"You look like something out of a Vietnam movie, Niko. You do realize that the dark colors only make all of your eyes stand out more. Only Anton, Pasha, and Grigori don't have eyes that look like they glow in the dark. Theirs are so dark, they look hollow. That's all I could see running toward me at first. Fucking freaky. Maybe it works to your advantage."

If she thinks our blue and brown eyes are freaky, then I can't let her see herself. The red contrasting with her blue eyes is something out of a slaughter movie. Fucking Carrie-looking shit.

"Close your eyes, Stasia."

I wipe her face as gently as I can while still getting the—gunk—off. I don't want her to see what's coming off. It's even turning my stomach, and I've seen this before. When I've gotten everything off as best I can from her face and neck, I work on her hands.

"Is she all right?"

I look at Aleks, who's looking as anxious as he did on the way to the hospital. I shrug. I truly don't know. Seeing her holding the bloody knife and the top of Nikita Zarkhov's head—that will haunt me for forever. It will replace plenty of other nightmares. I didn't know what to think when I ran past Yaroslav. The fucker looks—looked—just like Vlad. Way too many emotions rushed forward. But when she asked me to put her down, and she looked at him, I realized where the missing part of his skull and brain went. I do not have a weak stomach, but I struggled not to vomit.

"I'm fine, Aleks. Filthy and traumatized, but overall, fine."

She still has her eyes closed as she speaks. I'm scrubbing her hands and trying to get most of the blood off. There isn't much more I can do without hot water and soap.

"Niko, I need to speak to my daughter for a moment."

Stasia's eyes flutter open. She looks like she wants to ask me to stay, but she nods. I step away to give father and daughter some privacy. I step around the open back door and double over. I rest my hands on my thighs as I try to breathe. I did this to her.

"Sweetheart, we have to talk before we go anywhere."

"I don't want to, Papa. I'm tired. I just want to be with Niko."

I shouldn't listen, but I can't catch my breath enough to move. I'm fighting the need to scream or cry. My chest still aches as though there's a vise around it.

"Then just listen."

"Fine, Papa."

"What you did today will stay with you always. You reached inside and found the monster that lurks in many of us that only comes out when we reach a point of no return with our desperation or a need to protect. What you felt today is what Niko and his brothers and cousins keep hidden, what they don't let come out. But they all know it. They've all been forced to feel it. If you need to talk to Niko, do not hide from him. Do not pretend like everything is all right if it's not, and it won't be. I'm your dad, and I understand as well as Niko does. It's inside me and has been forced out, too. But I'm not your partner, your soulmate. He isn't your other half just when things are good. He understands in a way that nearly no other man can. Do not feel like your burden is too heavy to share with him. He's the best person to turn to. Do you understand, sweetheart?"

"Yes, Papa. Do you think what I let out today will stay with me? Or do you think it'll go dormant again?"

"I don't think you'll ever face a situation like you did today. You killed to protect yourself. But you also did it because you absorbed Niko's pain when you learned what those men did. I saw it. I couldn't have convinced you to stop, even if I hadn't gone after Gleb."

My eyes are closed as I listen to Yuri. Someone approaches me. I think Sergei or Anton from the brief whiff of cologne. But whoever it is leaves me alone. I'm glad. I shouldn't eavesdrop, but I think Yuri knows I can hear.

"Papa, are you disappointed in me?"

"Never, peanut. I'm heartbroken that we pulled you into all of this. I'm heartbroken that they put you in a position of needing to defend yourself or escape capture. I'm heartbroken that this brought out a part of you I prayed you would never discover existed. But I'm proud of your strength to survive. I'm proud of your devotion to your fiancé and his family. I'm proud of you. Period."

"Do you think I disappointed Niko? His life was so much easier and better before I came into it."

I'm ready to rush around the backdoor and correct her, but Yuri speaks again.

"Do not let him hear you ask that ever again, Ana. That man loves you with his whole heart. He's devoted to you because he loves who you are. He is not disappointed in you. He will regret for the rest of his life that we put you in this situation, just like I will. But you survived. That's what matters most to him. He wants to spend his life with you. His life is better now that you are in it. Believe him when he tells you that."

"That's how I feel about him. But—"

"Don't you think he feels the same way, too?"

"He shouldn't."

"And neither should you, Ana. This life is complicated in any and every way. It's why your mom and I tried to keep you away from it. But this is as much a part of our fate as finding our soulmates was."

"Thanks, Papa."

I glance over my shoulder and can see through the back side window. Stasia's leaning against her dad, and his arm is around her shoulders. He rests his cheek against the top of her head. I feel like an intruder watching them.

"Can Niko come back now, Papa? I'm sure he's worrying."

"Sure, sweetheart."

"Niko?"

I take a steadying breath before I answer.

"Yeah, I'm coming, Stasia."

When I step around the door, Yuri smiles at me. Looking at

Uncle Grigori is like looking at my father. It's fucking painful as shit sometimes and can make me feel better than nearly anything else sometimes. But the way Yuri's looking at me makes me feel like I have a dad again. He lets go of Stasia and stands. She opens her eyes and watches as Yuri pulls me into his embrace. I squeeze my eyes shut. I take a shuddering breath as I wrap my arms around him.

"*Radnoy*." Family.

That one word from Yuri, one that my dad used to say to my brothers and me every night before we went to bed, is everything. I nod against his shoulder as I choke back my tears.

"I will never be Kirill. I'm not your papa. But I am here when you need one."

"Thank you, Yuri."

I can barely get the words out. I take another deep inhale before I feel composed enough to step back. Stasia is watching us.

"Papa?"

"I'm just making sure Niko knows he's our family now. We are one."

"Thank you, *batya*."

I surprise myself at how easily the old-fashioned word for dad came out. Yuri rests his hand on my shoulder.

"*Umnista*."

That one word has a wealth of meaning to me. It's most closely translated as clever. But I know Yuri means "that's my boy."

I look at Stasia, who's watching us. She opens her arms to me, and I pull her into mine. Yuri leaves us as we finally kiss. The ache in my chest loosens. My ears stop ringing. And my mind and spirit are at peace. This isn't the end of what happened today, but I'm with my *malyshka*, and she's where she wants to be. With me.

"We have to go soon, Niko. We can't linger anymore."

I nod to Maks and know he's right.

"Can you get me a blanket and a hat?"

He returns with what I asked for. It's my cap that he found. He must have gone to my go-bag. The blanket must have come from the common gear bag. I wrap it around Stasia and put the hat on her head.

"We're going to go, Stasia. Maks will have figured out where. You can get cleaned up there. I brought you jeans and a shirt."

She nods and gets off the back of the SUV. She climbs into the second row. She sits between Bogdan and me. Anton and Sergei are in the third row. Misha and Yuri are in the front. Pasha's driving the other vehicle with our uncles, Maks, and Aleks. Stasia sags against me, and her eyes drift closed. She barely notices when we stop. It's a motel close to the airfield. It looks decent from the outside. It also looks like the type of place people don't ask questions. I watch Maks go inside, and he comes back out in a few minutes. He hands me the key through my open window.

"Come on, *moye sokrovishche*."

"Hmm?"

"We're going to get cleaned up, then we're going to meet our family."

She wakes up for that. She walks with the blanket wrapped around her, her head down, and the cap pulled low until we get into the motel room. I have my go-bag with her spare clothes and my regular ones. I grabbed hers while my cousins packed our weapons. I wanted her to have something of her own. I hope it will make her more comfortable. She follows me into the bathroom and lets me undress her before I strip. I see more new bruises, but they aren't as bad as I feared.

Once the water is warm, we step inside. She wraps her

arms around my waist as I drape mine over her back. She rests against me, and I think she might have fallen asleep. I watch the water turn red as it runs down her hair and over her body.

"*Malyshka?*"

"I'm not asleep, *papochka*. But I feel like I could sleep for a week. I'm listening to your heart. It's comforting. Did you hear what my dad said earlier?"

I hesitate.

"Yes."

"Good. Niko, I know what I did. I know the gravity of it. I'm not in shock and unable to process everything. I can, and I have. But I'm still going to have questions, and I need your help to deal with what I've done. Mmm. Not what I've done, but why I don't feel guilty about it. I feel like I should, but I don't. Does not having any remorse make me a sociopath or psychopath? Does it make me like *him?*"

She doesn't have to say Vlad's name for me to know who she's talking about.

"No. At least not in our world. I admit, I never imagined you could or would do what you did to Nikita. But I understand the emotion that drove you. I felt it too as I waited to get to you. I was prepared for it. You weren't. Our way of life creates a different standard of morals and ethics than the typical person. I won't reject you or villainize you for doing something I already know I'm capable of. I will do everything I can to make sure you never have to again."

"I know."

"I think you should talk to Laura about this. She can handle the details if you want to share them. She didn't do it the way you did, but she defended herself and Sergei. And Sebastian."

"Can't forget that lovebug dog. Can we get one like him?"

"Yes. Christina already has her eye on a litter. Laura struggled with not feeling guilty about what she did to protect Sergei, Maks and her friends who were in Maks's penthouse, and Bastian. She may understand even better than I can."

"Okay. Will you help me wash my hair? I don't want to touch it."

I'm gentle as I wash her hair and massage her scalp. I run the bar of soap over her until the water runs clean. Then I scrub myself, getting the last of the paint off my face and neck. I know everyone is waiting, but I don't care right now.

"Stasia?"

"I need you too, Niko."

Our mouths collide as our tongues duel. I know we will share pleasure, but that's not what this is about. As I lift her, and she wraps her legs around me, our gazes meet. I slide her down my cock, and we're one again. Indivisible.

"I love you, Stasia."

"I love you."

I press her back against the wall, but neither of us moves for a few minutes. We just hold each other as we see our love reflected in each other's eyes.

"Niko, can we get married soon?"

"Like in a month or two?"

"Like a day or two?"

"You're as bad as Maks."

I laugh, but she frowns.

"He did a shit job when he tried to propose to Laura the first time. And it included announcing they were getting married in two days—which he eventually pushed to three. Issues with the Irish made it urgent, but everyone knows he wouldn't have been patient even if there weren't any threats. Once he decided to propose, nothing was going to stop him from making Laura his wife before the end of the week."

"I am as bad as Maks. I feel the same way. Even if this

hadn't happened, I would still want to get married sooner rather than later."

"Whatever you want, *malyshka*, Daddy will give it to you."

"Will Daddy give me an orgasm right now?"

She's trying for humor, and I appreciate it. If that's what she needs, then I laugh along with her.

"Only because there are people waiting on us. Otherwise, I would make you wait."

She tightens her core around my dick, and I'm ready to shoot my load.

"*Malyshka.*"

"Yes, *papochka?*"

She offers an innocent expression, but I see the weariness, stress, and fear in her eyes. I press her head against my shoulder as I thrust into her.

"Let me take care of you, *malyshka.*"

"I need you, *papochka.*"

Our kiss is one of our tender ones. This isn't about fucking. This isn't about getting off. This is making love. I can wait to rejoin the rest of the world. I just pray the rest of the world can wait for us.

Chapter Twenty-Seven

Stasia

My mom is struggling to look me in the eye. I can't tell if it's guilt, suspicion, disgust. I don't know. I know my dad will never tell her the gory details of what I did, but we've already told her I had to kill two men to escape. We're on the plane back to New York, and I'm exhausted. But every time I close my eyes, I see what I did. Every time I open them, I see my mom watching me.

"I'm going to talk to my mom."

Niko has been my shadow since he found me, and I need it. I need his silent strength and reassurance. He hasn't asked me for any details, and I'm not ready to tell them. But after talking to my dad, it's good to know that I can turn to Niko. He's not looking at me like my mom is. I don't want to leave the security of his embrace as we sit beside each other on a sofa in the jet's main cabin. However, I need to.

"Mom?"

"Will you sit with me?"

"Of course. Are you all right?"

"I am now that you're safe."

I lean into her embrace, knowing she needs this as much as I do. Maybe more. She hugged me for five minutes when we reached Santorini. It was smothering, but she's my mom. I can't conceive how she must have felt because I'm not a mom yet. I've never seen her look so haggard as she did when I stepped off the plane.

"Do you have questions?"

"Plenty, but I don't think I want the answers."

I realize I've become Niko and my dad. There are secrets I will now always keep from my mom, questions I'll refuse to answer.

"Ask me what you want, and I'll see if I can answer them."

"Did they—hurt you more than I can see?"

"No. They kept me chained up in a container until I got free of it. Then they put me back into one with Papa. I escaped that one after they took Papa. I had to fight off a man who knocked me down. But nothing like that happened."

"Are you staying with Niko?"

And there it is. She knows the answer.

"You know I am."

"Good."

"What?"

That wasn't what I expected.

"Your dad's been right all along. It's hard to let you go, especially into a world we've spent twenty-three years trying to keep you away from. But no one will love you more or protect you better than him. I'm jealous that you'll turn to him now, but I understand. I'll get over that. I regret some of our choices as your parents, but not others. It gave you as normal a childhood and college experience as we could. But I know now that we should have told you before you left home. It was naïve to think the bubble would last forever."

"Mom, Niko isn't taking me from you. We're adding him to our family."

"Rationally, I know that. But it's not so easy to convince my emotions. You're my one and only. It's not like chickens. I can't just hatch some more if something happens to you."

My mom tightens her hold, and I find I appreciate it more than I did at first. I lean my head against her shoulder, and she strokes my forehead and hair like she did when I was little. I close my eyes, and I finally don't see my newly etched memories.

"Mom, I don't want you to feel guilty. I know it's easy for me to say, but you are not responsible for what happened. Even if I'd told no one about Papa's tattoos, I still would have met Niko. Even if I'd told no one about Papa's tattoos, they still held a grudge."

"Ana's right, Allison."

My dad comes to sit on my other side, and my parents make a sandwich with me in the center.

"Allison, they've been watching us for two decades. They told me things that they could have only known through surveillance. Someone in Chicago reaching out to them only spurred them into action. They didn't want Ana sold to another bratva. Gleb and Yaroslav described Ana's tenth birthday party at the laser tag place. They described her high school graduation. They gave me our address and hers. The only things they couldn't tell me were what happened inside buildings. They saw snippets of our life."

"Why didn't they do something sooner if they've known about us all along?"

My mom sits up, her brow furrowed.

"Because other than one call to Radomir and Grigori

every year on the anniversary of Kirill's death, I've never breathed another word to a bratva member. We live somewhere with a Russian community but not the mafia. You no longer work in Russian intelligence. They put me on the back burner. We weren't a threat. But Ana became an opportunity."

I look at my dad, and I can see Niko behind him. He's watching us, and I know almost everyone can hear us. I think it's just as well. Three senior members of the Podolskaya are dead. That won't just blow over. Understanding why this happened will be important as Niko and his family plan what comes next.

"But how?"

"Polina Semenov."

My mom jerks away and stands. Her distress is clear. My heart aches for her as tears stream down her cheeks.

"My best friend."

"Yes, Allison. They sent her just like I was to America, and just like you were to Russia. I had no idea. She's from—or at least she said she was from—Sochi. I had no reason to doubt her."

My dad enfolds my mom in his arms, and I move back to sit by Niko. My mom needs the comfort only my dad can offer.

"*Malyshka*, I'm sorry that woman betrayed your mom."

"I suppose that's always a risk."

"It is."

I look at Niko, and I think he's remembering Katerina. I lift his arm to wrap around my shoulders as I lean against him.

"I know you have a doctor who stitches you up and everything. Do you have a therapist?"

Niko looks down at me. He shakes his head, then stops.

"She's not officially one for us, but there's a wife who is. Her husband works directly under Sergei. I've known him the entire time I've been here. I went to school with both of them. I think she would be a good person to talk to."

"Can I trust her?"

"Yes."

"Would you come with me?"

"Because you don't trust her?"

"Yes. You heard what happened to my mom. I have nothing to hide from you about what they did. You were with me when I learned about my family. But I'm not so quick to trust anymore."

"I'll do whatever you need, *malyshka*."

"Thanks, Daddy."

Niko lifts me into his lap and covers us with a blanket. This is where I belong. I made peace with my mom. My dad is safe. Everyone came back with no significant injuries. And Niko is holding me. I feel myself drifting off, and when I wake, I know there were no nightmares.

"Niko, why is he here?"

I heard raised voices and Sammy swearing. That bird has been a saving grace over the past week. He's made me laugh countless times, and I'm now comfortable enough to take him out of his cage to let him sit on my shoulder.

I was upstairs with Laura and the twins. Bogdan and Christina went back to their place for the first time last night. So did Galina. Niko, my parents, and I are still staying with Maks and Laura. Neither Niko nor I are in a hurry to go back to his penthouse. A few bad memories usually aren't enough to make people move, but we want to start fresh together. We put an offer on a house two streets over from Laura and Maks. It's cash, so the owners accepted immediately.

"He wants to see you."

"No. I do not want to see him."

"You don't have to. Go back upstairs."

"Ms. Antonov!"

I grit my teeth and inhale.

"Mr. Mancinelli."

Niko steps in front of me to shield me, and Salvatore appears insulted. Niko just crosses his arms. If this weren't such an awkward situation, and Niko's brothers weren't behind Salvatore, I would have a far different reaction to Niko's bulging muscle straining beneath his t-shirt.

"Ms. Antonov, I offer my sincerest apologies. I know that does nothing to make things right. But it's rare that I offer them."

"What happened to your nephews?"

I deserve to know this. Salvatore looks at Niko and raises an eyebrow. Niko shakes his head.

"What am I missing, Niko?"

"Salvatore showed us a video of how he dealt with his nephews while I was waiting for you to come out of surgery."

The only part of me that has had any prolonged pain is my lower back. I felt none of it when I was held captive. It came back when I woke up during our landing. I could barely move. Niko had to carry me off the plane and insisted that we see Boris, their doctor. The man is the size of a mountain with bushy eyebrows but is shockingly gentle. And apparently, only patient with women. He took x-rays. Everything checked out, but I'm still sore.

"Are they dead?"

"No, Ms. Antonov."

"They should be."

"I know your fiancé and his family agree. But they are still my family."

"Can I sell them to the Russians?"

Salvatore stares at me for a moment, trying to gauge how serious I am. I don't blink.

"They wouldn't take them."

"What are you doing to ensure they never come after me? I'm sure they blame me for whatever beating you gave them."

Salvatore inhales.

"Ms. Antonov, I can't tell you that. I wish I could, but just like your family has secrets, so does mine."

My family. He already sees me as a Kutsenko. Good.

"Salvatore—"

"Just one more thing, Niko. You've already heard this, but I wish Ms. Antonov to hear it too. It's what I told Maks after what happened to Laura, what I assumed my nephews knew. An attack against the bratva women cannot stand. If I do nothing, it makes the *Cosa Nostra* women vulnerable. I have a duty to them, just as Maks has a duty to your women. I will allow no one to believe silence is consent. This resolves nothing that stands between the bratva men and the *Cosa Nostra* men, but I pledge my people will protect and defend the women and children of other syndicates."

Is he suddenly a cop? A superhero? Protect and defend. I look at Maks, Aleks, and Bogdan to gauge their reactions, but I shouldn't have wasted the breath. I can't tell anything.

"Niko, can I believe Mr. Mancinelli?"

"About this, yes. Anything else, never."

I step around Niko, who reaches for me, but I move aside. I walk until I'm looking Salvatore in the eye. My height has its advantages.

"Mr. Mancinelli, I choose to believe you. I choose to forgive you, but I have not yet forgiven your nephews. I may not. But I will never forget the role your family played in this. I can't say that my fiancé and my in-laws will ever feel as I do, but no one in your family is worth the wasted emotions from me. I know now what I'm capable of. If you break your pledge, it's not the men in this family you should fear. Come near any of our women or our children, and I promise you'll beg my family to make me stop."

"The women in this family are not to be crossed. But you, Ms. Antonov, are enough to make the Devil piss himself. I shall keep that in mind. Again, I offer my apologies."

Salvatore dips his chin to me before looking at Niko and his brothers. He walks silently to the door. I watch through the glass as he gets in his car. It goes through the gate and pops the trunk. One of Maks's guards drops the weapons they must have confiscated into it and slams it shut. Then the car is gone.

"Stasia?"

I look toward Niko and reach out my hand. When he takes it, I turn toward his brothers.

"I am not interested in repeating what happened. It will take me time to come to terms with what I did and the person I discovered I can be. But I did not lie to Salvatore. You've welcomed me into your home and your family. You've made me feel a part of it since the beginning. I'm an only child, so my parents have been my world most of my life. I'm not used to having so many people around me, but I love it. I do not doubt that being part of this family is what will heal me. Thank you."

I can barely get the last two words out as my throat tightens. Each brother steps forward, starting with Maks. Their hugs reassure me I am welcome, and I am safe. The kiss on the cheek is sweet and to taunt Niko. I wrap my arms around Niko's waist and rest my head on his shoulder. I'm home. Not because it's Maks and Laura's house. I'm home because Niko is my other half. His brothers disappear, leaving us alone.

"Do you believe him, Niko?"

"Yes. I was there when Laura was taken. I heard him

pledge his support to Maks for the reasons he gave today. I don't know what he did with Luca, Carmine, and Gabriele. But it was something severe. They made him a liar and embarrassed him. He can't and won't forget that. He hasn't remained the don this long without people fearing him with good reason. I want my pound of flesh and to exact my revenge, but I'm satisfied that Salvatore is handling it."

"Then I can be satisfied, too."

"How're you feeling today?"

"Better. Talking to Annika everyday helps. My back doesn't hurt nearly as much as it did."

"Your parents head home tomorrow."

"I know. I'll miss them."

"I know you will, *printsessa*. I was thinking about a distraction for you."

"A distraction?"

"Yes. I have a surprise for you. Somewhere I want to take you."

My eyebrows shoot up.

"Here in the city, *malyshka*. Tomorrow night."

"Will you tell me where?"

"That's not how surprises work."

"How will I know what to wear?"

"That won't be a concern."

His smile is wicked, and I get a sense of what he might mean. I slide my hands up his chest and around his neck. We've been discreet while staying in Maks and Laura's home so filled with family. But this kiss is one I hope no one stumbles upon. He walks me backwards until we get to the half-bath. Once we're inside, he locks the door.

"Can you be quiet, *malyshka*?"

I nod.

He lifts me onto the counter and pushes up my skirt. I've

abandoned wearing underwear since they either don't stay on or get ripped. He leans to whisper in my ear.

"I'm going to do everything I can to make you scream. Let's see how quiet you are."

"Niko, your family. My parents."

"Try hard, *moye sokrovishche*."

"Can I try your hard dick?"

"You have a dirty mind."

"That's not a no."

Niko pauses and looks at the counter, then the wall behind me. We haven't had sex on anything but the soft mattress in our guest bedroom, not even in the shower. It's been so we don't jar my lower back anywhere else.

"Tell me if I'm hurting you, Stasia. Te—"

"I know, Daddy. I haven't forgotten your rules or what a twitch you get into."

"Twitch? You'll feel me fucking twitch."

I pull at Niko's belt and unfasten his pants as he unbuttons the shirt I'm wearing. I feel him unclasp my bra, so I let it and the shirt drop from my arms. His mouth goes to my tits immediately. He feasts on them, and the sensation flows from my nipples to my pussy. His fingers dig into my hips, the hold controlling whether I can move on my own—which I can't. My hands brace me behind my back as he thrusts into me.

"You're mine, Stasia."

"I am."

"All mine. Mine to love. Mine to please."

"That's what I want."

"Is that all you want?"

"No. I want to come."

"Not yet. I haven't heard you scream."

"Daddy."

"That wasn't a scream."

"You know I can't."

"Too bad. If you come, I'll turn you around, spank you, and fuck you from behind."

He knows I don't mind doggy style, but it's not as satisfying. But I want that spanking. He hasn't given me one since Mykonos.

Chapter Twenty-Eight

Niko

I'm by no means out of shape, but my *malyshka* is insatiable. I wouldn't have it any other way, but she might be the death of me. I swallow her scream as she comes on the bathroom counter. I pull out and lift her off it. I press her to lean over the sink as I fist my cock. I stroke it as I land five sharp slaps to her little round ass. She watches me, and I can tell she doesn't approve of my stroking myself. I grin before stepping behind her. I lift her left leg and rest it on the edge of the counter.

"You have such a perfect little pussy, baby girl."

"It's all yours, Daddy."

It is. And I claim it again. Tumultuous doesn't even describe how this relationship started. We've faced more challenges than most couples do in a lifetime. But we've weathered these storms together. Without these challenges, I wouldn't blame someone for saying our relationship is just about sex. But no matter how amazing sex is, I don't know that anyone would endure what we have just for a good lay.

"Daddy, please."

I hear the need for me, and I love it.

"Come, *malyshka*."

I'm certain she hears it echoed in my voice. I thrust into her one last time before I wrap my arms around her waist and kiss along her shoulder and up her neck. We both tense as our orgasms hit us. I rest my forehead against her shoulder as she watches us in the mirror.

Her hands cover mine, and I think about what she told me she wished to do for her career. I'm not sure I'm ready to share her yet. I look at Maks and Laura and consider how quickly she got pregnant. I know they wouldn't give up being parents for anything in the world, and I want to be a dad one day now that I've met Stasia. But I'd like more time with just her.

"What're you thinking about, Niko?"

"About us. Our future."

"Oh?"

"Now that we're together, I want kids. But I selfishly want your entire attention for a while before we have them."

"I'm okay with that. Niko, I'd really like to travel more before we have any. I understand now why my parents couldn't take me a lot of places. But there is so much I want to see."

"Where would you like to start?"

She shrugs.

"Where would you recommend?"

"I'm fond of the Caribbean, but I also like several parts of Canada. Banff is gorgeous. Can you ski?"

"Yes. That's one of the few things we did. We used to go skiing in Pennsylvania if it was a quick getaway. Otherwise, we went to New England. I can ski and snowboard. I've always wanted to try the old-fashioned snowshoes. You know, the ones that look like giant tennis rackets strapped to your feet."

"Was it your mom or your dad who enjoyed it more?"

"Are you kidding? My dad would be happy to never see snow again in his life. It was my California-raised mom who thought it was terrific to go to 'the' snow."

She's adorable as she makes the air quotes and rolls her eyes playfully. If she enjoys skiing, then I'll take her wherever she wants to go. New England, Canada, the Alps. I hate the snow, and I hate remembering being so cold on my way to school as a kid in Moscow that the inside of my nose would freeze. Maks used to threaten to snap it off. But I can suck it up for her.

We've put our clothes to rights, so I peek out of the bathroom and see no one. I open the door all the way, and we make our escape. We pass Pasha, who shakes his head in mild disgust. I glower at him, but Stasia giggles. It's the sweetest sound after fearing I might not hear it again. We cuddle together in one of the family rooms—there are three in this house.

"*Moye sokrovishche*, I told you I have a surprise for you tomorrow night. What else do you want? Do you want to go back to work for Laura? Find another job? Plan a wedding?"

"Work for Laura if she'll still have me. And plan a wedding. Maybe we don't have to get married right this minute. But sooner rather than later."

"Pick a date. We'll make it work. It can be here in the city or a destination wedding. A big one or a small one. Whatever you want."

"Thanks, Niko. I'll think about it."

"Niko!"

"Yeah, we're in the family room, Bogdan."

I hear shoes running across the tile floor. I look back and see my baby brother. He has a gash to his right temple, and his left fist is bandaged.

"Stay here, Stasia. Do not get up."

She looks at me, but I'm already running toward Bogdan. I steer him toward the kitchen.

"Stasia, go upstairs."

"Ni—"

"Please. Now."

I hear her taking the stairs in a hurry.

"What happened?"

"The Italians hit Ivy. At least, we think it's them."

"What the fuck? Fucking Salvatore."

"I know. I'd just gotten there when it happened. We aren't even open yet. It's like what happened at Pussycats. Stuff broken and graffiti on the walls. We can't open tonight."

"Didn't you have three VIP parties?"

"Yeah. That's close to ten grand in sales down the shitter."

"Do Aleks and Maks know?"

"Yeah. They're headed to the warehouse."

"Did you get anyone?"

"Misha and Anton have five headed there. I'm not so sure it was Salvatore, though."

"Luca and Carmine?"

"Maybe. None of the men have said a word, so we're guessing they're Italian, but we aren't sure."

"Do they have the flag tattoo?"

"No. But they aren't Irish or Cartel. And definitely not Triad."

My brow furrows as I consider what Bogdan said. I get the first aid kit Laura keeps near the sink. I take care of the cut on his forehead while he washes his hands. I use skin glue to close the cut before Bogdan gets ice for his hand.

"Does Sergei have any ideas?"

"No. Anton called him and asked him to get the security footage from the last few days. They knew their way around."

"Why'd you come here?"

"To let you know you don't have to come. I knew if I called, you'd insist."

"Of course, I'm coming."

"Niko—"

"Niko?"

I look toward Stasia, who's standing in the doorway. She's ashen as she holds up her phone.

"You need to go."

I glance at Bogdan before walking over to her.

"I told you to go upstairs. What happened?"

I look at her phone. A text came in from a blocked number. It's in Cyrillic. I didn't even know Stasia's new phone was set for that. I never thought about it.

We're not through yet.

"Podolskaya?"

"I don't know, *meelaya*. Maybe. Or it could be Luca and Carmine. It wouldn't be impossible for them to translate the message into Cyrillic and send it."

"You need to go, Niko. I'm safe here with Laura and the guards. My dad's here too."

"I know I can't stay. I want to, but I need this to end."

"I understand. Be careful."

"I love you."

She offers me a kiss before she points to the front door.

"I love you, Niko."

Bogdan follows me out, and a driver is already waiting for us. I look back as Stasia stands by the front door. I hear Laura's voice, and Stasia turns back to answer my sister-in-law. She glances at me and waves before she shuts the door.

Can't we have one fucking day? It started out great, and it's already gone to shit.

"You're Russian but not Muscovites. American?"

All five of our guests are naked and hanging from meat hooks. We recognize all their tattoos, and all of them are American quality too. My fist slams into the sternum of the one we figure is the leader. His tattoos say bratva, but his clothes said American. Even the way he carries himself and looks around makes me think he's Russian, but not from Russia. He doesn't look at me. I speak to him in our native tongue, hoping to hear him speak. It'll tell me where he's from faster than if he names a place.

Bogdan has the pliers and clicks them open and close. He catches the leader's nose between the tool's pincers and squeezes. The man grits his teeth and tries to breathe through the pain. His discomfort is plain to see. Definitely not Moscow Podolskaya.

"Oskolki."

Aleks steps around the last one to my right. He spins the guy and points to a brand. Chicago. Progress.

"Which one of you talked to Luca?"

No one answers. I adopt a bored expression and shake my head. I cross my arms and smile at Bogdan. There's no humor on his face. He moves to the next man, except he puts the pliers around his balls and squeezes hard.

"*Peez-duî atsyuda.*" Get the fuck off.

"Answer my brother."

Bogdan squeezes hard enough that the guy will probably never get another hard on in his life. He keeps the pressure steady as the guy breaks into a sweat and trembles. I listen to my brothers and cousins laugh. They come to stand behind Bogdan and me, their laughter heckling Bogdan's target.

I pull out my knife and lunge at the first man. I bring my blade to where his ear meets his head and press.

"I will cut all the way through. If I don't hear what I want, then you won't hear at all."

"Promise me a quick death, and I'll tell you."

I look down the end of the line to the youngest man. He must be about Stasia's age, maybe younger. This might be his first real mission beyond street hustles. It's going to be his last.

"Tell me what you know, and I'll decide whether it's worth a quick death."

Of course, it isn't. He's willing to betray his brethren to escape torture. There is no reward for that.

"Luca Mancinelli has his eye on some Chicago *Cosa Nostra* chick. The girl's dad is high up and said Luca had to prove himself. It was the girl's dad who suggested hitting you hard. Luca said he'd blow something up or take out some of your men. It was the girl's dad who told him to take one of your women. It was a shitty coincidence for your woman that she'd been dating one of Luca's guys. It was Carmine who pointed out that they knew there was a Russian girl with a bratva father. Then she started dating one of you. She was already the target, but she became valuable with that little piece of info."

"So Luca contacted you to ask how much she would be worth in Moscow?"

Maks steps forward. I can't ask all the questions, or it'll be too obvious that Stasia is mine. Right now, they don't need to know that. It'll keep them wondering.

"Yeah."

"And?"

Aleks slaps the kid as he asks. I suddenly feel way older than twenty-eight when I look at this guy who's probably twenty-one.

"I made the call."

"Bullshit."

Sergei leans forward into the guy's face. He doesn't blink. He's always been able to stare the longest. It's fucking unnerving if you aren't used to it. He used to fall asleep with his eyes open as a kid. Fucking cree-py.

"I did."

"Bullshit."

Sergei still hasn't blinked.

"Fine. I was there, though."

"And?"

It's Pasha's turn. He takes the pliers from Bogdan, who finally lets go of the other guy's balls. But I'm pretty sure he castrated the motherfucker. His balls look rather—deflated. Pasha puts the pliers to Chatty Kathy's nipple and twists. The kid screams.

"Whiny little bitch. Why'd you bring him?"

I look at the leader while I point over my shoulder to Pasha's victim. I watch a spark of anger enter this guy's eyes.

"Oh-ho-ho. Get this. The gossiper is the leader's little brother."

Now I see surprise from the leader.

"How'd—"

The younger man catches himself, but it's too late. I got confirmation from both of them.

"What's your name, Chatty Kathy?"

He watches me, debating whether it's worth confessing. Looks like he takes the easier road. At least, he thinks it is.

"Milo."

"What's your brother's name?"

"Roman."

I turn toward the leader.

"Your baby brother sold you all out, Roman. And you let

him. Did you really think letting Milo talk would actually make his death easier? Now, you've just made it fun."

I drive my fist into the leader's face. I land the first punch against his cheekbone and the next under his chin. His head snaps back before he shakes it off. Pasha squeezes the pliers on the other guy until he breaks through the skin. He pulls away, taking flesh with him.

"Enough."

It's the first time this man's spoken. He's the oldest, maybe a little older than Maks. Early to mid-thirties is my guess.

"What's your name?"

Maks asks, but we all want to know.

"Vasily."

"Have something to say, Vasily?"

Maks takes the lead again.

"Yes. All five of us are going to die before we leave here. You aren't the only ones who still have family in Russia. You're not the only ones who try to protect them, give them what they can't get for themselves. The Podolskaya found our families in a village an hour outside Moscow. It was do this for them, or watch them stream our families' executions. We believe in leaving women and children alone, but not at the expense of our own families. You know how they are."

We do. That's why we left Moscow. I want to look at my brothers and cousins, but I can't. It would give away too much. They would know that I understand and even feel a little sympathetic.

"What now? Does Luca get the girl?"

I'm genuinely curious. I wouldn't mind learning her name too. It could come in handy. I move to stand in front of one of the two men who still hasn't spoken. I grab a handful of his hair and yank backwards as I step to his side.

"I don't know."

"I think you do."

"Semyon and Taras know nothing. Our *pakhan* made them come."

I turn to Vasily. Aleks holds a knife to the man's belly.

"Can you answer my question?"

"Not for certain. I think the don set him up, though. She's been dating some guy since she was in high school."

"Sucks for Luca."

Pasha makes the comment, and we all laugh. I hope he gets fucked over.

"Why are you here? Why hit our nightclub?"

Maks steps in front of Roman. They've all figured out who he is. Roman's not feeling so ballsy now that they've watched us and figured out Maks is our leader.

"*Pakhan*, the Podolskaya didn't get what they wanted, and they're smart enough not to step foot in the U.S. That meant finding someone here to do it for them. Like Vasily said, they know where our families are."

"Why our nightclub?"

"They've failed twice to get the woman. Once here and once in Europe. Now, they're after your businesses."

"And your *pakhan* thought pissing me off was the better option."

Roman doesn't answer. No one needs to. Maks will make a call later to let the Oskolki know what a shitshow this turned into. He'll remind them they get nothing in or out of the U.S. from Europe or the Caribbean without us. Sure, they can get some drugs brought north through Mexico, but it's nowhere near as secure or the quality of the product we provide.

"Is there anything else you wish to tell us without being tortured?"

Misha asks as he smacks a metal pipe against his palm. No

one speaks up, so he goes down the line, swinging the pipe into each set of left ribs. Milo is the one who speaks up.

"You know our *pakhan* is old enough to be all of our grandfathers. He's the last of us to have true bratva ties to the motherland. When we don't come back, he'll be done. None of our Elite Group agreed with this mission. They knew it was suicide to come up against you. The ties between the Oskolki and the Podolskaya are done. Our Elite Group knows staying on the Ivankov bratva's good side is way more important than remaining allied with the Podolskaya."

"You want me to believe you're not a threat anymore?"

Maks locks eyes with Roman. I can see the man's trying to keep his balls from shriveling under Maks's stare.

"Yeah. We have our own problems. We don't need to add New York to our list."

"When you don't return, won't there be problems with us, then?"

Roman shakes his head while Milo speaks.

"No, *pakhan*. Like I said, the Elite didn't agree with this. We all knew we couldn't refuse, but we all knew the chance of us surviving was next to none. Even if we'd gotten away with the break-in today, we were supposed to do more. You would have found us. Out-of-town Russians showing up in bratva neighborhoods? The hope was we could fuck up enough shit before being caught."

Maks turns to all of us.

"Anything else you want to know?"

We either shake our heads or stay quiet. Misha and Pasha pull out their guns while the rest of us go into the office. They'll put bullets between each set of eyes, then toss them into acid. Maks and I strip to take the first showers. We both want to get back to his house. He wants to see Laura and his children. I want to see Stasia and spend a little more time with her parents before they leave.

"What do you make of the thing with Luca and the girl?"

I talk as I turn on the water. I lean out of the shower to speak to my brothers, Anton, and Sergei. I lather the shampoo and scrub all traces from my hair. Then I run the surgical soap over me. Aleks looks up as he peels off his socks.

"I think he got fucked over. But I don't know if she was a girl he was into, or if he was into the access he thought he would get."

"I agree, Aleks."

I barely hear Bogdan as I stick my head under the water to rinse the last of the suds off me. I turn off the shower and grab my towel. I step out, and Bogdan takes my place. Aleks takes Maks's as I wrap the towel around my waist.

"What do we do with that info? Tuck it away for a rainy day?"

Sergei shakes his head as Anton asks. Sergei is the head of our intelligence gathering, so what he explains reassures me.

"No. Let me see what I can find. That isn't nearly enough yet. None of Luca's, Carmine's, or Gabriele's accounts show unexpected deposits. I don't think they got paid for anything, despite what Carmine said. I want to see if any expenses show up in Chicago. We haven't seen or heard about them since we got back. Salvatore said he would take care of it. I think he sent those fuckers to Chicago."

I button my shirt as I share my thoughts next.

"Probably. And I was hoping to beat the shit out of them. It's going to be awhile. My guess is they'll barely be breathing by the time they get back. Luca failed the don's test. Salvatore will have sent Carmine as the failed mastermind and Gabriele as—I don't even know. Because he doesn't like Gabriele."

Maks stands next to me as we dress. He turns to me as he slides his wedding ring back on.

"I know you want your pound of flesh, Niko. But things are done with the Podolskaya, and the Oskolki owe us. For now, we may have to be satisfied with that. Now that those houses aren't on fire, we can plan for how to deal with the Italians."

"I want the satisfaction of my fist hitting their faces. But I can wait. A strategy is better than an impulse."

It was something Vlad drilled into us. The psycho was right. Not striking back right away will leave the Italians to stew in their own juices, wondering how and when we will. If is not the question.

"Thanks for letting us sleepover, old man."

"Let's go home, little brother."

Chapter Twenty-Nine

Stasia

I worry about my parents returning to Maryland. No, there's not bratva there, but there are people tied to them. If my mom's best friend betrayed her, who else would do the same?

"Mom, Papa, can I talk to you before you go?"

I stand in the doorway to my parents' guestroom. They went home to Pikesville for a few days while Niko and I were in Greece, but he'd already told them his plans. They went long enough to grab clothes and a few other essentials they hadn't brought their first time up here.

"Sure, sweetheart."

"I talked to Niko last night. Turns out he'd already talked to Maks. We want you to move up here. We want you to be closer to us."

I don't want them to move in, just close. My parents look at each other before they look back at me. I know what they're going to say.

"Papa, you cannot stay there. It doesn't matter who Mom works for. We know that now. Please see it's safer if you're closer to us."

"I left this life behind, Ana."

"It didn't leave you. Twenty years they've been watching our family. They were probably watching Mom and me while you were still in Moscow. I don't enjoy thinking about you being unprotected now."

"We can't just quit our jobs and leave our home, Ana."

"I know, Mom. I didn't mean for you to do that. But you can look for jobs and homes up here. Once you find something, you can put the house on the market. I know it might take a few months, but I really don't feel comfortable with you being down there anymore."

"Stasia's right."

I turn to find Niko standing behind me. He kisses my cheek as he puts his hand on my waist.

"No one here expects you to return to this life. But we can offer you protection that you won't have in Pikesville. Sergei is digging to see if anyone else is watching you. You know how it works. Someone else is. There's always a backup in case a person is compromised. You don't know who the secondary is. What we learned today lets us know the Podolskaya won't come after the Ivankov, but that doesn't mean they've settled the score with you, Yuri."

I look up at Niko, who is now beside me. I want to know what he learned. Will he tell me?

"Can we come in?"

Niko waits until my mom nods before walking with me to the loveseat near the window. My parents sit on the bed. Niko holds my hand and rests it on this thigh.

"Long story short, Luca was put up to doing something against us by the Chicago don. They got in touch with the

Oskolki. Their *pakhan* still has connections in Russia, and the Podolskaya threatened the families of the men who broke into our nightclub today. Since the Podolskaya failed twice and won't come to the U.S., they thought the Chicago bratva could go against us. Maks is talking to the *pakhan* now, but I'm confident they won't be trouble again. The Moscow bratvas will keep their distance like they have for nearly twenty years. We're safe. But a lone couple in a Russian community? Who knows who Polina talked to over the years or how many contacts she has? We would all feel much better if you lived closer. We can provide security, but you aren't bratva. No oaths, no duties, no contact with anyone outside our family."

My parents look at each other again. I wonder if Niko and I will get to where we can read each other that well. I feel like we're halfway there already.

"We'll see what we can do about work, then decide."

"Mom, couldn't you try to get a position with the U.N. for real?"

"We'll see. There's a Department of State field office here. Maybe I can get a transfer. But you know that a condition of my employment was that we no longer had contact with the bratva. The State Department and the U.N. are likely impossible options unless I'm reporting to them about your family, Niko. I won't consider that."

"Dad?"

"Yeah. I can probably work remotely for my company since it's IT. I'll have to see. But I can get a job just about anywhere."

"So you'll consider it? Allison, Yuri, we really want you closer because you're family. It's not just about security."

"Niko's right. We'd like to travel for a while, and I enjoyed working for Laura, as briefly as it was. But we want a family in the next few years. I didn't grow up with one around. Niko's is huge. I want you both to be part of it, too."

"We're not saying no, Ana. Your papa and I will make some inquiries and talk to a real estate agent. We'll see what happens, then go from there."

"I can live with that."

Niko and Maks missed dinner, so they go to the kitchen to eat. My parents head to bed since they're getting on the road early. I'm half asleep by the time Niko climbs into bed next to me.

"Do you think they'll move up here, *sakharok?*"

"You calling me a piece of sugar still makes me laugh. But yes, I think they will come up here. I hope so."

"Thank you for talking to them with me."

"They're my family too, now. Having your dad around is a little like having my dad back. Uncle Grigori and Uncle Radomir have been amazing surrogates, but knowing I'm going to have a father-in-law feels different. It helps that he and my dad were close friends. I wasn't sure how I would feel when I realized who your dad was. Then seeing him in person—it was a lot. But I want them here. Your mom too. I always understood how she felt, so I couldn't blame her."

I cup his cheek in the dark and press a kiss to his lips. I draw him over me as I roll onto my back. It's the middle of the night before we fall asleep.

"Niko! This is incredible."

I'm certain my mouth is hanging open as I walk around our suite at The Mark in Midtown Manhattan. After my parents left this morning, we had a picnic in Central Park and walked around a few museums. We had dinner at a Michelin star restaurant, a horse-drawn carriage ride—the privately arranged sort, not some hack off the street kind—and now Niko's brought me up here. He said he had a surprise to distract me once my parents left. But I never imagined it was this luxurious.

As I cross the living room and enter the bedroom, I spy a massage table. I look back at Niko, whose expression is purely predatory. He looks like he's The Big Bad Wolf, and I'm Little Red Riding Hood. I'm thinking of something he can gobble up. I glance into the bathroom and find our toiletries already unpacked, and our clothes for tomorrow hanging in the walk-through closet.

"Strip, *malyshka*."

Fuck. That tone. If I still wore panties, they'd be soaked.

"Can you do my zipper, *papochka*?"

I can reach, and he knows it. But I think we'll both enjoy it more if he helps. Usually, we get dressed together, but tonight, I'd insisted that we dress separately. I thought the room the concierge showed me before dinner was our suite for the night. I don't even know where Niko went to get dressed. Maybe in here? As he slides the zipper down my back, I know he's seeing a peek of what I'm wearing beneath. I had to ask Laura to convince Maks not to have anyone open the box when it came from the lingerie store, and to not tell Niko that I received a package. I think the delivery woman had a heart attack when she arrived with it. She bolted back to the cab that waited for her. The security can be a little overwhelming.

"What are you wearing, *malyshka*?"

I push the dress down my hips and let it pool at my feet before I turn to face him. It's insanely expensive, so I feel horrible that it's on the floor. But I don't want to ruin the effect.

"Do you like it, Daddy?"

He wraps his hand around my throat and pulls me toward him. His kiss is rough and possessive. I think that's a yes.

"You are about to make me toss out all my plans for tonight.

I planned to wait a little while before I mauled you. But you look—fuck, Stasia. You're gorgeous."

The bustier is the same shade of blue as his eyes. The garter belt and garter are slightly darker. They're all lace, so they hide nothing from his sight. I turn around and bend forward, giving him a view of the sapphire-colored rhinestone plug I've been wearing since before dinner.

I know the spanking is coming, but I'm still not ready for the force. His hand on my hip keeps me steady as two more swats land across my ass. He twists the plug as he eases it in and out.

"*Malyshka*, you are the very best kind of temptation. To know I'm going to spend the night buried inside you is enough to make me leak."

"Are you?"

"Find out."

I turn back to him and slide his suit coat off. He pulls his tie loose, and we drop his clothes onto the bench at the foot of the bed. I unfasten his belt and his pants while he toes off his shoes. He pulls the belt from his trousers before sliding them off. When he bends to take off his socks, I snag my dress from the floor and lay it across the bench. I couldn't concentrate until my three-thousand-dollar dress wasn't in a heap. I reach for his boxer briefs and hook my fingers on the waistband, but I wait. When he nods, I pull them down. I watch his cock spring free. I still have the same reaction every time I see it.

Holy fucking shit. Knowing I get that buried inside me all night is enough to make my pussy a fucking slip and slide.

I'm still in my three-inch heels, and I know he loves seeing me in the lingerie and stilettos. The bench at the end of the bed has the upholstered high scroll arms. He guides me to lean over one.

"What's your safe word, Stasia?"

"Capt'n Crunch, *papochka*."

"Good, *malyshka*."

I reach forward and use my hands to brace myself before the first swipe of the belt lands on my ass. This is pure play. He's light with each swat. They're not hard enough to leave any marks. He's told me he will never use a belt for any type of punishment and only the lightest pressure for pleasure.

"Spread your legs wider, *malyshka*."

Gladly. I follow Niko's instructions and immediately, three fingers plunge into me.

"Daddy!"

"Do you want me to stop?"

"No. Please, Daddy, more."

"And if I don't think you should get more yet?"

"Then your baby girl might expire right in front of you."

"So dramatic."

But he increases the speed as he finger fucks me. He knows when I'm close, so he pulls away. Two more swats from the belt make my pussy pulse. I force myself not to stomp my feet between the slight sting in my ass and the ache in my cunt.

"Stand up, *moye sokrovische*."

I follow his instructions and let him turn me to face him. He kisses my cheek and trails his lips along my neck as he drops the belt behind me on the bench. He unfastens the bustier as he works his way down my cleavage. The lingerie makes me look more endowed than I am, but his groan as he sucks on my tits tells me plenty. He likes them just as they are.

"Stroke me, Stasia."

I barely hear his whispered request. But I hear the hunger in his voice. I love knowing that I do that to him. I fist his cock as he alternates tits and rubs my clit. We're both getting too close. He pulls away and kisses his way down my belly, over my left hip bone, then over my right. He stands and unfastens my garter belt as I slip off my heels. He rolls the garters and thigh highs down my legs and places everything on the bench before he lifts me off my feet. I wrap my legs around him, expecting him to enter me, but he doesn't. He snatches his tie from the bed and one of my garters.

He carries me to the massage table and eases me down onto my belly. The tie is soon my blindfold, and the garter restrains my wrists.

"You are everything to me, *malyshka*. I think you're beyond beautiful, and I crave your body every minute of every day. But I love you because you're intelligent, resilient, brave, independent, and caring. Those are just five of the hundreds of qualities that draw me to you like you're my North Star. You've been through hell and back with me, and you're still here. I love you."

He kisses between my shoulder blades as he walks to the end of the massage bed.

"Niko?"

"Yes, *printsessa*."

"Can I tell you why I love you?"

"I'd like to hear it."

"Can I sit up and look at you while I do it? You got to see me while you explained."

He helps me up and slides the blindfold off.

"You are all the things you said about me. Despite the life that's been given to you, despite what you have to do and the person you have to be, you are loving and gentle. You're optimistic and easygoing. You make me laugh as much as you give me strength. You let me be who I am while being just the right amount of possessive and protective. You make me feel precious, like I really am a treasure. I love you, *papochka*."

I move to roll back onto my belly, but he fists my hair. His kiss is hungry and forceful. It's almost too much. There's a desperation there that I'm not used to. I shake the garter from my wrists and open my legs that hang over the side. He steps between them, and I wrap my arms around his back. I welcome his tongue as it sweeps my mouth. I suck on it, and his hand tugs harder on my hair. He loves it when I do that, and I love it when he's rough.

"Do you really mean all that, Stasia? Do you really love me like that?"

"Of course. You know that, Niko."

The way he swallows then rests his forehead against mine, I wonder if my suave and confident fiancé might not be as secure as I assumed. I cup his face.

"Look at me, Niko."

I'm the one with the commanding voice now.

"I love you. You are not a perfect man, nor am I a perfect woman. But you are the perfect partner for me. Never doubt that. My dad told me more than once that you will love me with your whole heart, that you will do anything for me. You need to know I feel the same way. I love you with everything I am. When we have kids, I won't love you any less for letting them into my heart. We will make them together, and they will be an extension of my love for you. Maybe it is the 'Kutsenko *chary.*' I think you're rather charming. Or maybe it is some type of spell you've cast over me. But whatever it is, you're my soulmate."

"*Rodstvennyye dushi.*"

He whispers the Russian term for soulmates before he lifts me off the table and carries me to the bed. I hold on as he climbs onto the bed. Our kiss is slow as he eases into me. Gone is the roughness from a moment ago. It's replaced with tenderness. This isn't about fucking. This is making love in the truest sense. We join our souls as one, just like our bodies. He rolls us until he's on his back. He watches me ride him before I pull on his shoulders. He sits up, and we wrap our arms around each other. There is nothing between us in this position. It's intimate and erotic. We move together, neither in a hurry. It's the longest we've ever lasted, but neither of us wants to break the trance.

"*Ya lyublyu tebya.*"

We whisper, "I love you" together. My hand over his heart, and his hand over mine. He may call me his treasure, but I treasure the life we're building. Together. Forever and always.

Epilogue

Niko

"Calm down, little brother. You're jitterier than I was on my wedding day."

"So much for you being the easygoing one, big brother."

I'm standing with my brothers. Maks and Bogdan are grinning and goading me. Aleks is watching and trying not to laugh. I'm trying not to pace. The Russian Orthodox priest doesn't look amused by any of us.

"Ahem."

I look over at Aleks, who nudges his chin and looks over my shoulder. I spin around, and everything else disappears. The only thing I see is my *malyshka* walking toward me. I don't notice her gown or her veil. I barely see that Yuri is walking her toward me. I forget about the blue sky, the rugged mountains, or the crystalline water behind me. Banff is one of the most beautiful places I've ever been. And I couldn't give a shit as I wait for Stasia to reach me.

I clasp my hands to keep from grabbing her away from Yuri when he stops to kiss her cheek. I force myself not to yank her next to me. Instead, I pretend to be far calmer than I am as she places her hands on top of mine. Laura, Christina, and her friends Beth and Gracie stand beside her. My three brothers stand beside me. Our families watch as we exchange our vows in an outside ceremony.

I barely notice as Laura quietly interprets the service for Stasia's friends and Christina. Since the men in my family and Yuri are all lapsed Orthodox, Stasia suggested the service take place outside. She wanted a religious one, and I liked the idea too. But all of our transgressions seem too many and too severe to marry inside a church. It feels sacrilegious. We found a Russian Orthodox priest willing to conduct the ceremony beside the lake, and I'm glad we chose this.

"The servant of God, Nikolai Kutsenko, is married to the servant of God Anastasia Antonov in the name of the Father and of the Son and of the Holy Spirit."

I listen to the priest as he recites the ancient vows my parents must have shared. When it's time, Bogdan hands me the rings.

"Through a ring the authority was given to Joseph in Egypt; through a ring Daniel was glorified in the land of Babylon; through a ring the true identity of Thamar was discovered; through a ring our heavenly Father showed mercy on the prodigal son; for He said, Put a ring on his finger."

We exchange our rings during the Service of Betrothal. During any other wedding ceremony, this would pretty much be it. But I've loved watching the Service of Crowning since I was a kid. I never imagined I would take part in it or the Ceremonial Walk that comes after the Gospel reading. I'm pleased we can do all of this, even though we're outside. I wasn't sure that we could. It feels like a full Orthodox wedding. I didn't think it would matter as much as it does.

"Hello, Mrs. Kutsenko."

I whisper to Stasia as the service ends.

"Hello, Husband."

I love the sound of that. Our family beams at us, and I know I have the widest smile I've ever worn.

"I love you, *malyshka*."

"I love you, *papochka*."

The wedding party is discreet and gives us space to share another kiss. This one isn't the polite one we shared in front of the priest. This is our celebratory kiss that we've officially bound our lives together.

"Let's celebrate with our family, and then we shall have our private celebration."

"Daddy?"

"Yes, baby girl."

"I'm not wearing any panties."

I grin. I'm not surprised. But somehow, today seems like a day she should have.

"What should I do about that, *malyshka*?"

"Oh, definitely a spanking."

"If you think so. Let us eat and drink and have our cake. Then I shall have my dessert."

"Promise?"

"Absolutely, *moye sokrovishche*."

I always keep my word.

Don't miss the next installment

Preorder and have it ready when you wake on Nov 1st.

She can pretend not to notice…

They say I'm the best looking in my family. I couldn't care less.

But her…She takes my breath away.

Not everyone sees her the way I do. That's fine by me because she's mine.

I pity those who think they can come between us.

I won't stop until she's at my side. Mine to touch. Mine to love. Mine to push to her limits then bring her back.

She's my everything. She's my soulmate.

The Bratva Beauty is an interconnecting, standalone Dark Mafia Romance with a HEA and no cliffhanger. It contains extra-steamy scenes that will make your toes curl and your granny blush. This is book four in *The Ivankov Brotherhood,* a six-book series that'll keep you warm at night.

Preorder now for Nov 1st..

Thank you for reading The Bratva Treasure

Sabine Barclay, a nom de plume also writing Historical Romance as Celeste Barclay, lives near the Southern California coast with her husband and sons. Growing up in the Midwest, Celeste enjoyed spending as much time in and on the water as she could. Now she lives near the beach. She's an avid swimmer, a hopeful future surfer, and a former rower. She loves writing romances that will make your toes curl and your granny blush.

Subscribe to Sabine's bimonthly newsletter to receive exclusive insider perks.
www.sabinebarclay.com/joinnewsletter

Join the fun and get exclusive insider giveaways, sneak peeks, and new release announcements in
Sabine Barclay's Facebook Dubious Dames Group

Do you also enjoy steamy Historical Romance? Discover Sabine's books written as Celeste Barclay.

The Ivankov Brotherhood

Bratva Darling

BOOK ONE SNEAK PEEK

LAURA

As I sit across from the four Kutsenko brothers, I press my lips together to keep from drooling. No four men should be so strikingly handsome. Not all from the same family, anyway. I fight a valiant battle against letting my gaze drift toward the eldest, Maksim, whose ice-blue eyes bore into me. After years of negotiating billion-dollar investment contracts while facing countless ruthless businessmen, I've learned to keep my expression studiously blank. But it's a true struggle today. Instead, I focus my attention on the squirrelly lawyer sitting across the conference table. While he's disingenuous with each comment, he's a good negotiator. But I'm better. How cliché am I?

While I feel Maksim watching me, I focus on Dmitry Yakovitch as he continues to argue the merits of the venture capitalist company I represent, RK Capital Group, merging with Kutsenko Partners. What he means is the merits of Kutsenko Partners acquiring RK Capital Group, then stripping it and making it another money-laundering shell corporation. While most people in New York have little awareness of the Russian mafia, I do. The Kutsenko brothers' names appear on no titles or deeds anywhere in New York City, but it wasn't difficult to determine which shell companies likely belong to them. Their assumption that I'm unfamiliar with them is proving beneficial to me as they continue to whisper amongst themselves in Russian. I think they may even believe they're convincing me that they don't speak much English.

The senior partners of RK Capital Group know who I'm negotiating with, though they may not know I'm aware of these Russians' more nefarious operations. They've given me the go-ahead to agree to a merger with an eventual acquisition, but only for the right price. A price to the tune of twenty billion dollars. Considering an investment firm like Goldman Sachs is worth nearly one-hundred-and-twenty billion dollars, my clients' asking price appears reasonable.

"Mr. Yakovitch, I shall stop you now." I raise my left hand, pen caught between my index and middle fingers. When I have his attention, I lean back in my chair and casually twirl the pen over my index finger and thumb. "Fifty billion is my clients' asking price. You know that. Your clients know that. RK doesn't oppose the merger. What they oppose is the insulting offer you've made. It's nearly noon, and I'm hungry, Mr. Yakovitch. I have a delicious ham sandwich waiting for me. I even have three chocolate chip cookies waiting for me. If we aren't going to make any progress, I shall let you go, so I can move onto my eagerly anticipated lunch."

I cant my head just enough for me to appear as though my gaze rests solely on the opposing attorney's face, but I can see each Kutsenko brothers' reaction. My face battles yet again against showing my emotions as I fight not to smirk. Their muted but surprised expressions confirm what I already know.

"Please tell your clients to make a reasonable counteroffer, or I will conclude this meeting and enjoy my ham sandwich and cookies."

Dmitry glares at me before turning to Maksim and his three brothers. In rapid Russian, he doesn't interpret my suggestion. Oh no. There's no need for that. I can't catch every word because his voice is too low. But I catch something along the lines of "The bitch refuses to budge. What now? A fucking ham sandwich. More like a stick up her ass."

Maksim swivels his chair to look at his brothers. In Russian, he says, "Fifty billion is ridiculous. She's not so stupid or naïve not to know that. My guess is they'll settle for twenty billion. We offer fifteen."

"That's barely better than what we already offered," Aleksei, the second-oldest brother, argues. "She'll be eating the fucking sandwich and dipping her cookies in milk before we walk out the door. We need the buildings."

"We offer twenty, Maks," Bogdan, the youngest, insists.

As I watch the brothers discuss, their voices barely lowered, I pull my lunch sack from the black leather satchel by my feet and set it beside my laptop. It's a ridiculously pink floral bag with an embroidered monogram, the L and D overlapping. It's an empty prop, but they don't know that. I watch as five sets of eyes narrow. I offer a smile that would appear innocent in any setting other than this meeting. It's patronizing, and I know it.

Bratva Sweetheat

Bratva Treasure

Bratva Beauty (Coming 11.1.22)

Bratva Angel (Coming 12.13.22)

Bratva Jewel (Coming 1.24.23)

Printed in the USA
CPSIA information can be obtained
at www.ICGtesting.com
LVHW042226220923
758581LV00003BA/28